BAY AVENUE I:

The Inheritance

by Jill Hicks

This book is a work of fiction. Names, characters, businesses, organizations, places, events, and incidents either are the product of the author's imagination or are used fictitiously. Any resemblance to actual persons, living or dead, or events is entirely coincidental.

Cover photograph and design by Bill Hicks

2nd Edition: 5/25/16
3rd Edition: 6/6/18

Originally published in 2012 as "Will Power"

This book is dedicated to
Jamie & Jessie

PROLOGUE

There are many great stories where the end is just the beginning. Ours is such a story. How could we have known what awaited us beyond the tragedy of death? That day would be the catalyst for all of our future joys and sorrows.

CHAPTER ONE

GINNY

The five of us were standing together in Memorial Park Cemetery, located in the seashore town of Lewes (Loo-iss), Delaware. Lewes is a quaint, historic town situated at the mouth of the Delaware Bay. Its cozy streets are lined with a mix of charming Colonial and Victorian homes, little boutique shops, and fabulous restaurants. It is inhabited by a substantial number of year round residents, yet manages to make room for the population explosion that occurs every year between Memorial Day and Labor Day. Its oceanfront and bayside beaches attract many summer tourists.

Like most small beach towns, the local residents know the best restaurants, bars, pizza joints, ice cream parlors, and fishing holes. The Lewes police strictly enforce the twenty-five mile per hour speed limit through town and everyone knows to stop for pedestrians in the crosswalks.

Fortunately, the sidewalks roll up early every night, including weekends. By nine o'clock, a hush falls over our small town.

This is Lewes.

On this particular September day, the summer season was in our rear view mirrors, and it was quickly fading away like a setting sun over water. The pace around town was beginning to slow down and the traffic on Route 1 was less congested. You could actually make it through two consecutive traffic lights without having to stop. Lewes was becoming "Slower Lower Delaware" once again.

Sadly, this day's scene would become all too familiar to our family. As the rest of the world was living out a normal autumn day, we were at the site of a six-foot hole in the

ground with a casket suspended above it. The grim
weather complemented the occasion and the heavy
overcast skies completed the day's sentiment by making it
downright cold, damp, and dreary.

Derek, the oldest of the three brothers, was rather tall
and he was standing straight up, the same way his dad liked
his Manhattans. He was appropriately dressed wearing a
long black overcoat. His gloved hands were down and
overlapped in front of his body. His black pants were
perfectly hemmed to the top of his polished black shoes. He
wore a dark pair of Ray-Ban aviators. His chin was up. His
facial expression was frozen stiff like a celebrated figure in
a wax museum, of which there were none in Lewes. In his
stance, his feet were slightly apart. Occasionally, he rocked
back and forth on his heels. If the President of the United
States were there, one would have understandably
mistaken Derek as a member of the Secret Service. I kept
waiting for him to lift his lapel and whisper orders into a
hidden microphone, directing his team to keep their eyes
on me. I always felt as though Derek had his eyes on me,
watching my every move. Typical Derek, he liked having
everyone and everything under his control.

Derek's wife, Susan—thank God for Susan—was like a
welcomed cool breeze on a stifling hot day. At 5'10" she
was nearly as tall as Derek. Even on a gray day like that
one, her short silky blond hair reflected the invisible sun's
radiance. She was thin, but not model-anorexic thin. Her
smiles could melt an iceberg, saving the Titanic, and she
could always find a silver lining beneath the darkest storm
cloud. I often thought of Derek and Susan as a mismatched
couple. Along with his stubborn streak, Derek was narrow-
minded. She, on the other hand, was open to the
world. Susan and I had become fast friends in those early
days.

Dylan, the middle one of the three brothers, was the
quiet one. I think most people would describe him as
thoughtful, respectful, and kind. He was often the mediator
of the other two. It came naturally to him. That day, Dylan
was wearing his trademark pair of jeans, a comfy sweater,

and his leather bomber jacket. His hair had a natural wave and body that most would kill for, the kind you want to run your fingers through, if given permission. And, one could not help being drawn to Dylan's inescapable sexy bedroom eyes. I thought, *"Surely, he's a heartbreaker."*

After the pastor left the cemetery, allowing us privacy to say our good-byes, Dylan nervously kicked at the grass beneath his feet.

"Do you think Dad would have wanted it this way?" he asked. "Maybe we should've had him cremated and then thrown his ashes to the wind, or bury them in the sand, or scatter them over the bay. Do you think he's OK with this?"

I wasn't sure if Dylan really wanted to engage us, or if he was just thinking aloud.

"It's just that he loved the water so much," Dylan continued. "Perhaps a burial at sea would have been more appropriate. Then again, he is next to Mom, now."

That was our Dylan, always second-guessing himself. He was the overly cautious one. He was seeking Derek's confirmation that everything was done just as their father would have wanted. When Derek didn't respond, Derek's wife, Susan, slipped her arm under Dylan's to let him know that someone was still listening.

Then there was Dan, the youngest of the three and the love of my life. At 6' 2", he was the tallest. He had thick dark locks of hair that curled at the ends, accentuating his alluring facial features. His crystal blue eyes were matched only by a summer sky following a violent storm. His jaw was strong as if chiseled from stone. His lips were as soft and warm as a lightly toasted marshmallow and as luscious as a perfectly ripe peach. His lips he had promised to me.

In essence, all three men were very sexy, strong and magnetic. However, on that day they were vulnerable, and seemingly scattered.

Dan would have been wearing his coat except he had hung it over my shoulders to make sure I was staying warm. Holding my hand, I could feel him shiver from time to time as a cold front moved over us.

Dan and his older brothers quietly shared a few memories, putting off the inevitable. With the future beckoning and the past calling out, Dan felt the desire to stay and the need to go. He didn't want to leave his father behind, and he didn't want to move ahead without him.

It all seemed so surreal, magnified by Derek's stoicism, Dylan's pain expressed through his questioning, and Dan's rare state of apprehension. They would miss their dad terribly, each in his own way.

I was so glad that Susan was there with us. She was the safety net when it came to the family's occasional imbalance. Susan finally broke the emotional stalemate by suggesting we go back to their father's house. She and I had prepared a light lunch and had dropped it off prior to leaving for the cemetery. With the western skies turning darker, we began the small recession to our cars.

We arrived back on Bay Avenue just as the heavens opened up. All three cars merged into the small area allotted for parking between the road and the house. Susan and I each threw open our passenger doors and ran toward the back door of the tiny beach cottage. (We considered the "back of the house" the side that faced Bay Avenue and the "front of the house" the side that faced the Delaware Bay. We knew it was backward, but it was the way we liked it.) With the rain coming down in buckets, water was spraying in every direction under our feet. We screamed and carried on like schoolgirls. Once up the steps and at the backdoor, our laughter escalated toward hysteria as we realized our dilemma—neither of us had a key. Nice and dry in his Ford Explorer, Derek was in no hurry to save us. He was annoyed that his wife had been so silly, especially on such a grave day. She was, after all, the one who had decided to bolt without him. Dylan, alone in his Dodge Ram truck, was still sorting through his questions. Obviously, he had not left all of his doubts at the cemetery. Dan, on the other hand, enjoyed every minute of our panic. He finally emerged from his Jeep Wrangler and came to the rescue.

"Seems you ladies have a problem," Dan observed as he slipped his key into the lock and pushed open the door. He stepped aside and waved us in. For the three of us, the comical dilemma helped to ease the solemnity of the day.

Water puddled on the old wood floor inside the kitchen as Susan and I shook out our wet clothes and hair. She looked none-the-worse in her drenched state. I, on the other hand, with my curly amber-red hair, looked like the burning bush of Moses that someone had unsuccessfully tried to extinguish.

Dylan materialized at the door next. With Dan stationed at the door and three of us now safely inside, Derek finally exited his Ford Explorer and came in to join us. Stomping up to and through the back door, he marched right past us. Our folly was immediately halted by the scowl on his face, freezing us in our saturated shapes. It became clear with his snorts of disapproval that he had assumed the paternal role, and what he said would go. Without stopping his march, he sternly asked us to clean up the water on the floor. He removed his coat, tossed it over a kitchen chair where it proceeded to drain more water onto the floor. He then paraded into the bathroom, shutting the door behind him. With hands over our mouths, Susan and I doubled over and tried not to laugh. I'm not even sure why it struck us as that funny. His reaction was rather sad. Susan, in between muted snickers, assured us that Derek would eventually calm down.

All of us stayed at the house that night. It continued to rain as several late night storms rumbled through the area. The following day, the boys had an 11:00 appointment at the offices of Sable & Sable for the reading of the Last Will and Testament of David Grant Carter.

The law firm employed by their father was known around town for eating their young. The boys were not sure what to expect, but it didn't take long for them to find out.

DAN

The offices of Sable & Sable were located above the retail shops overlooking the canal on Pilottown Road. The décor and ambiance of this attorney's office did not fit the stereotype. It was contemporary in style. No dark paneled walls. No heavy ornate cherry desk. No high-back leather chairs. No oriental rugs. No large portraits of the old geezers who had founded the firm.

She, on the other hand, seemed to fit the mold. Dylan immediately got the cold shoulder when he had mistaken her—his father's attorney—as the receptionist for the firm. As she pushed him aside and walked past, you could feel the ice crystals snapping in her wake. It was impossible for us to picture our Dad in that office and working with that particular attorney.

Facing the canal, her spacious office featured high ceilings and a wall of tall custom windows. Her desk was a long, glass top table. It was angled to allow her a full view of the water. From her seat, she could watch the boats rocking in their slips. She could see the diners on the deck of The Lighthouse Restaurant raising their glasses and forks as the wait staff moved around them. Her view was right out of a Donald Voorhees watercolor.

She introduced herself as Ms. Courtney Sable. Emphasis on the "Mzzzzzz," whatever that means. Looking her straight in the eye, while sizing her up, Derek shook her hand and positioned himself as the one in charge. Introducing Dylan and me, Derek believed that he had everything under control. He soon found out differently.

Contrary to her hard exterior, Mzzzzzz Courtney Sable's hand was rather soft and seemingly fragile. She was mysterious in some ways and bluntly direct in others. Within minutes, she had completely unarmed us, though Derek would never admit to it.

As she glided around her see-through table and into her chair, Dylan's eyes followed her. Her smooth gait had hopelessly mesmerized him. She took her seat, crossed her endless long legs, and adjusted the hem of her skirt as if it were all a seductive dance. She motioned toward the contemporary, ergonomically correct chairs in front of her desk and we sat down as directed. She remarked how cute it was that all of our names began with the letter D. Then, solemnly, she expressed her condolences, apologizing for having to meet David's sons under such somber circumstances. David Carter, he was our dad.

She paused and then cleared her throat.

She looked right at Dylan. Her imposing stare created the illusion that she was three inches from his face. She pointed an index finger to her eye.

"Eyes up here," she seemed to be saying.

Oh great, she actually caught him gawking.

His cheeks flushed, and he was reduced to an adolescent schoolboy. We knew then that there were icebergs in the water. We were becoming painfully aware that one was ripping through our three-compartment hull that very minute. Our ship was listing heavily.

Wasn't this meeting supposed to be amicable? We were there for the reading of our father's Last Will and Testament, for God's sake. Derek or Dylan must have provoked her. I've heard that sharks do not attack unless provoked. She barely knows us . . . or does she?

With the formalities over and having everyone's attention, Ms. Sable opened our father's file, which was neatly arranged on her desk.

"Your father was a wise man, but I guess you already know that. He arranged everything so that the distribution of his estate would be rather simple. However, as you are all well aware, he liked to do things his own way. As long as I've known him, he never followed the norm for normalcy's sake. So, with that said, Dan, he named you, his youngest son, as Executor."

Huh . . . ?   What . . . ?

Derek's head whipped around with a "why you?" look on his face. His body language settled somewhere between hurt and angry. It seemed he had been knocked down from his presumed favorite son status. His coup of the paternal role had been placed in jeopardy. I had a feeling Mzzzz. Sable was going to begin picking us off one at a time. I braced myself.

"There must be some mistake," Derek challenged.

Dylan said nothing. *Smart move.*

I must admit, I was not expecting the assignment, nor was I prepared for it. Obviously, none of us was prepared for that pronouncement. Being the first born, we all assumed Derek would be given that responsibility. It was his birthright, wasn't it?

"Are you sure?" my voice cracked, thinking it was all a big mistake.

The three of us were sitting straight up by then, ergonomically correct, of course. However, Derek slid his butt to the edge of his seat and leaned in her direction, positioning his body ahead of us, and two feet away from the document in her hand. He wanted proof, and despite his lowered legal status, he wanted it first, and he wanted it before she went any further.

"Your father made it very clear that he wanted his youngest son, Daniel, to handle his estate. It's spelled out right here," she said, pointing to a specific location in the document.

She handed the papers to Derek, pausing only for a second or two. Then, when she was ready, she continued, always maintaining control of the meeting.

"Notice the signature and date at the bottom of the last page."

With all of us pressed in, she reached across and flipped all of the pages, exposing the last. She gave our eyes just enough time to focus on the scribble. Sure enough, there it was, the signature of David Carter. We should know. We had studied it and forged it many times. The date was fresh, only two weeks old.

Two weeks? He made a revision two weeks ago?

Then, she snatched the document back and handed a copy of the "Last Will and Testament of David Grant Carter" to me. Keeping Derek in the corner of my eye, I reluctantly received it. It was then that I had wished Susan and Ginny were with us. Then again, maybe it was best that they had not witnessed that side of our brotherhood. We had yet to get into the meat of the document, the stuff that created family feuds, and already the meeting had turned awkward, to say the least.

"This copy is for you, Daniel, and I will maintain the original here in my office."

My dad loved to surprise us. He had surely succeeded this time, and his young attorney had lived up to the reputation of her law firm. She ate red meat, swam with the sharks, devoured her children, and anything else in her way. I had a feeling there was more in her arsenal. She seemed to be having way too much fun. Was it possible that this was Dad's last big joke played on us?

She finally addressed the inheritance.

"Your father had two life insurance policies, each valued at $250,000. Derek was named sole beneficiary of one, and Dylan was named sole beneficiary of the other. Daniel, you are not named on either policy."

She paused and looked up from the paperwork.

My heart sank. The only way I could rationalize my exclusion was that I was the youngest. Maybe he just never got around to it.

But his latest revision was made two weeks ago?

I tried not to look disappointed. *"It's just money,"* I told myself. My dad meant more to me than all the money in the world.

"What about Dan? Are you sure there aren't three policies there? Are you sure that our father didn't name Dan as a co-beneficiary?" It was just like Dylan, the middle brother, to always look out for everyone else.

"No, he didn't. In fact, he was very clear about it."

"I guess you're screwed, little brother," Derek chuckled in jest. I'm sure he meant it as a joke, but it was hurtful.

Dylan shot Derek a look of daggers.

The attorney continued. Looking directly at Derek, she said that I, Daniel Scott Carter, the youngest son of David Grant Carter, was to receive sole possession of the beach house on 408 Bay Avenue, in Lewes, Delaware.

What . . . ?

She paused to let it sink in.

Concealing it inside, I was ecstatic. However, I felt immediately pummeled by a wave of guilt. It was a weird sensation. I loved that beach house, but I never expected to inherit the whole thing. I was so excited that I wanted to jump out of the chair and do a chest bump, but with whom? Certainly not with Derek or Dylan. They looked too shell-shocked. On one hand I wanted to celebrate, and on the other, I was anxious and concerned.

What was Dad thinking?

I looked over at Derek and Dylan. Their eyes were glazed over. I could have imagined it, but I thought their chins were on the floor. I could hear their wheels spinning. I knew them all too well.

DEREK:
When did all this happen?
    Oh, that's right, two weeks ago.
Where was I?
    Clearly, not in Dad's favor.
Who's responsible for this?
    It had to be Dan. He's the one that made out in all of this.
    I knew there was a reason he visited Dad every chance he got, and he's been dragging his girlfriend along, and she's been all nicey-nice to him.
    This sucks.
    They took advantage of Dad and manipulated him. They had planned this all along, and I never saw it coming.
    How did I miss it?

Dylan's thoughts were always a little more convoluted and more difficult to read. They were usually self-deprecating, too. He stared straight ahead to the wall behind Ms. Sable. It was adorned with all of her degrees, licenses, and various other acknowledgements of her success and high esteem.

DYLAN:
I don't understand.
Dad never showed favoritism before. At least, I don't think he did.
I did everything he had asked me to do.
I never asked for much.
Did I do something to upset him?

I was afraid to speak. I didn't want to throw more trouble into the already murky water, which was now threatening to become toxic. What was done was done. My emotions were in a free fall. Was it a dream? I didn't want to wake up and find it gone. Yet, it felt like the beach house had just become a wall between my brothers and me.

Did I really feel bad for them? Of course, I did. Dad cut them out of the one thing he considered priceless. It was awful and admittedly, shamefully, awesome all at the same time.

I wanted to call Ginny and give her the unbelievable news, but I didn't want Derek and Dylan to think any less of me, and less of us. I knew they were hurt. I would've been devastated, too. I would've been angry—angry with my brother, and angry with Dad—as if losing him wasn't already enough for us to deal with.

GINNY

My understanding was that the estate consisted of two life insurance policies and the family beach house. Derek and Dylan were named as beneficiaries of the two life insurance policies, each valued at $250,000. Dan received the beach house and a small amount of cash remaining in his dad's checking and savings accounts. Dan was also named executor of his father's Last Will and Testament.

From what Dan shared with me, Derek and Dylan took the news about the beach house pretty hard. He said the attorney—which he emphasized was a young woman— expressed her condolences and then got right down to business. He said when they got into the distribution of the estate the office got very quiet. He said the tension in the room felt like a vise grip tightening around his skull. He described Derek as a caged lion, pacing and becoming more and more agitated, hungry for somebody's head.

When they had arrived back at the beach house, they looked as if each of them was in their own world. They were unusually quiet, and that never happened when the three of them were together. While eating sandwiches they had brought back for lunch, they briefly mentioned the contents of the Will and shared a few forced niceties. After they teased Dylan about his obvious attraction to their father's attorney, they started to cheer up a bit. They serenaded him with Heart's, "Barracuda." Dylan denied all of it. Susan turned to me with an inquisitive look on her face and shrugged her shoulders as if to say, *"What gives?"*

Dan announced that he was drained and was going upstairs. He motioned a plea for me to follow. I wasn't sure where it was leading. We had had afternoons when we would sneak away and lock the door behind us. However, I didn't get the impression that this was what he had in mind. I followed, nonetheless hopeful.

As it turned out, Dan just needed alone time, and on that day, his alone time included me. It was a sign that we were indeed becoming more than just a boyfriend/girlfriend "see-how-this-goes" couple. He was "letting me in" more and more. Quietly bursting at the seams, he told me what had really happened at the offices of Sable & Sable. Yet, as he spoke, there was apprehension written all over his face and weighing him down. I understood everything . . . and nothing.

When Dan shared all of the details that he could recall, his concern, mixed with slight sentiments of celebration, hovered in the room. I, too, was somewhat elated and yet, apprehensive. I wasn't sure how it would affect Dan and his brothers. I wasn't sure how all of this would affect us. How would it affect the sisterhood that had been growing between Susan and me?

Dan talked himself out and soon fell asleep. He looked peaceful then, unlike two hours before when they had arrived back at the house. As I watched over him, I stroked his hair and wondered what he might be dreaming of.

Dan was an architect. He dreamt big. He had a gift for grand design and every minute detail. I remember how he would proudly show me his latest work.

* * *

The beach house was an old cottage that had been in the Carter family for three generations. It was built in the 1930's, and in the last two decades, only the bare minimum had been done to maintain it and keep it inhabitable. Despite its condition, it had served the generations well as a summer vacation home. When serious squabbles regarding its upkeep and use began to escalate and tear at the fabric of the family, they regrettably decided that it was time to sell. Being a sentimental guy and loving beach life, Dan's father got the money together and bought-out the other family shareholders. He immediately sold the homestead in Unionville, Pennsylvania, and made Lewes his permanent residence.

It was a beautiful location that overlooked the Delaware Bay. Facing north to the water, the outside deck was protected from the heat of the day. One could watch the sun rise and set over the water without moving their deck chair.

The house was a small two-story cottage with three bedrooms and one and a half baths. I guess you could say two full baths if you included the outside shower, although Dan corrected me, saying it didn't work that way. The first floor was divided into two open spaces. The kitchen side faced Bay Avenue, and we called that the back of the house. The dining/living area faced the Delaware Bay, which we referred to as the front of the house. Dan said it boasted 2,100 square feet of spacious living. Later, I learned that he was being sarcastic.

The rickety splinter-possessed wraparound deck was indeed one of the house's best features. Speaking from experience, Dan said that running across the planks in bare feet guaranteed you a trip to the crammed downstairs half bath with his mother, a needle, and a pair of tweezers. He said his mother preferred using the downstairs half bath for the gruesome procedure because of its bright ceiling light. Dan suspected that because it was an interior room under the stairs, it also allowed his mother to close the door and muffle the boys' over-dramatic screams. If heard, he was sure the neighbors would have called the local authorities.

I wished I had met their mother. Dan's stories and descriptions of her made her sound like someone I needed in my life. She died of breast cancer when Dan was only twelve years old. Scarred young by the slow, agonizing death of his mother, his heart was now laid open and raw, again, by the sudden loss of his father. The family's future became even more fragile and uncertain with the reading of Mr. Carter's Last Will and Testament and all of its implications.

* * *

Dan loved the time he had spent at the beach house with his dad. After we had become a couple, Dan took me along for weekend visits and vacations. He and his dad would sit out on the deck, share a beer, and dream aloud. They spoke of leveling the old cottage and building a fine beach house worthy of its picturesque location. They scribbled ideas and sketched drawings on napkins, scrap paper, or whatever else they could find. Houses and lots all around them were being bought up, torn down, and rebuilt into massive and much sought after vacation homes and investment properties. Over the decades, the Carter beach house had become dwarfed by its new and improved neighbors.

When at the beach, Dan loved to cook, especially with his dad. They both had a flair for taking ordinary ingredients and turning them into extraordinary delights. They would fraternize in the kitchen or over the grill. Alcohol was involved most times. . . . No, scratch that . . . every time. I was allowed to partake in the liquid refreshments; however, I was not permitted to interfere with their creative culinary experiments. They claimed they enjoyed surprising me, and true to form, they always succeeded. With each visit, I would leave a few pounds heavier than when I had arrived. To continue their exploits, their self-described dream beach house would need to be outfitted with a commercial kitchen, among many other luxury amenities.

I cherished Mr. Carter's love and acceptance of me. You see; I became pregnant before Dan and I were married. In fact, we had not yet broached the nuptial subject before conception had apparently taken place. Our first visit to Lewes in my pregnant and unmarried state, we had decided to keep it a secret from his dad and especially his older brothers. We needed time to get used to the idea ourselves. Dan mentioned that Derek and Susan had been trying to have children for years. Unfortunately, they had been unsuccessful, and we didn't want to be insensitive to their circumstance by preempting their hopes and dreams.

That particular evening, his dad made a lavish meal starting with oysters on the half shell—Dan's favorite. Carrying a tray with a circular arrangement of a dozen raw oysters, he joined Dan and me on the deck. I began to gag at the site of the slimy not-sure-they-were-dead-or-alive jello-y mass of mucus. I could feel whatever was in my stomach from lunch trying to hock its way back up. The sight of the gray limp blobs created small convulsions in the pit of my gut. When Dan picked up the first oyster and loudly slurped its contents into his mouth, I ran for the bathroom. I didn't make it in time, and his father witnessed the unfortunate outcome. Behind me, it left a great impression on the living room rug. Thank God, Dan came to my rescue and made quick work of the mess he, in many respects, created. Upon making my return to the deck, still a little green, the oysters were gone, and the two of them allowed me time to recover.

"Nothing a little salt air can't cure," his dad remarked with a somewhat devious grin. I had witnessed that identical smirk on Dan's face many times before.

The sun began its descent into the water, and a chill started to roll in. When putting the finishing touches on dinner, Dan's father invited us inside. Dan motioned for me to sit next to him and pulled out my chair. He sat down and slid his chair over against mine. Whispering, he assured me that everything would be OK. He leaned in to seal his promise with a kiss. The still vivid vision of his slurped oyster played with my already overactive senses. Repulsed, I pushed him away. Being persistent in his attentiveness toward me, he patted my still tight little belly. Lowering his head and continuing in a whisper he said, "I see this little one is going to give us a run for the money!"

He lifted his head and kissed my hand. Looking into my eyes with his beautiful blues, he soothingly murmured, "I love you so much."

The world and every nasty oyster in it departed at that moment. I nuzzled into his shoulder and found rest and recuperation there. It was more therapeutic than all the oceans covering the earth. Dan would always be my safe harbor.

The aroma coming from the kitchen was heavy, and probably would have been delectable if not for my delicate condition. I could hear something sizzling in a fry pan. His dad shouted out that everything was just about ready. Dan asked if he could help, but his dad insisted that we stay seated and allow him to entertain. Mr. Carter first brought out a bowl of green salad, followed by steamed broccoli and mashed potatoes. So far, I was in good shape. I could feel my stomach starting to settle. Somewhat recovered, I reached for my napkin and placed it in my lap. As I raised my water glass to my lips, his dad entered and announced the main course: pan-fried soft shell crabs. Dan's joy filled the air. He was like a kid at Christmas.

"*I can do this*," I tentatively reassured myself. "*They probably taste like chicken and have the texture of onion rings. How bad can that be?*"

Taking hold of my hand, Dan asked his dad if he could say the blessing. Following the "Amen," his dad lifted his wine glass. Sensing a toast coming on, Dan lifted his, and I followed suit. His dad proclaimed, "Here's to Ginny!" The two of them raised their glasses higher and then savored their first sip while I furtively set my wine glass down on the table. With the prayer and toast well executed, his dad began passing the dishes. A serving of mashed potatoes, several florets of broccoli, and the smallest crab on the platter now occupied my plate. I looked at the crab that was blindly staring back at me. Maneuvering it with my fork, I turned the crab in the opposite direction, facing it away. Much better.

So far, so good.

Knowing his dad would jump up and leave the table to fill any request I would make, I thought of asking for something from the kitchen. Then, when he left the room, I could slide the amaurotic crustacean onto Dan's plate. It was a good plan, and it would have worked, except when I was ready to carry it out, I looked over at Dan's dad. He was sucking the rest of a crab leg into his mouth like an errant spaghetti noodle. Under normal circumstances, I would have found it extremely funny. Fortunately, that time I made it to the bathroom in time. Dan ran after me. Shutting him out and in between retches, I begged him to go back to the table with his dad.

Ten or more minutes later, I opened the bathroom door, exhausted, and hoping they had not missed me. When I looked up, all I could hear were the quiet waves of an almost still bay. The men were silent, too. Their sympathetic eyes were on me. The jig was up.

"Is there something you two need to tell me?" his father asked.

I immediately burst into tears. Dan came over and stood behind me. He wrapped his arms around my waist and proudly announced, "Dad, you're going to be a grandfather!"

You would have thought that Mr. Carter had just learned that he had won the lottery. His eyes grew wide, his jaw dropped, and then his mouth broke into a huge smile. How he got from his chair to us so quickly, I would never know. It sure was good to feel his excitement as he held us in his embrace. That was when it finally dawned on me that our baby would be a blessing after all.

The mashed potatoes and broccoli were excellent, especially the mashed potatoes. It was one of the best evening meals the three of us had ever shared together.

The next morning, I awoke upstairs alone in bed, alone in a room that faced the bay, alone with the rising sun peeking through the blinds, alone with my thoughts, and alone with the serene steady rhythm of the waves. I placed my hands on my belly and smiled knowing that, in reality, I would never be alone again.

Oh, my God! My parents! They don't know. And we've already told Dan's dad. My mother will be beside herself.

My mind was racing and my heart was trying to catch up. My mother was going to go ballistic, screaming that my life had taken an irreparable turn for the worst. Honestly though, the real truth was that she would be angry and upset because I had ruined *her* life, not mine. How would she explain it to her friends at the country club? And, worse yet, what if her friends found out before she did? We had to head it off.

* * *

I was my parents' only child. They doted over me and still do, in their own uniquely different ways. My father's attention was a blessing; my mother's was a curse. My father's love was transparent and sincere. It resided in his eyes, his words, and in the ways he cared for me. Regarding my mother, I had to build a fortress to protect myself from her attacks, and it had required more fortification in recent years. When I was young, I received her rage as something I must have earned and therefore deserved. As I grew older, I began to question if everything was entirely my fault. I had tried many various ways to please her and draw out her motherly instincts, if she possessed any. Her reactions were always so unpredictable. At home, I never felt good enough; however, in public, she raved about her "one and only." In conversation, she would find ways to insert that her daughter was a summa cum laude Yale University graduate.

"Ginny," she would boast, "is going to be a pediatric surgeon like her father. She's been accepted at Yale University and The University of Pennsylvania for her doctorate work. While U of P is a fine school, I think she should stay closer to home."

With my mother, I knew I had to stay in her social good graces and continue to support her bragging rights. Alternately, I was my dad's unconditional treasure.

Going away to school would be good for me, just as meeting Dan was good for me. Getting pregnant? Perhaps my life as I knew it was over, and that was not necessarily bad.

* * *

Dressed and moving downstairs, I walked up to the breakfast table where Dan and his dad were immersed in a conversation regarding a morning news story.

I interrupted them. "Good morning, Mr. Carter. Dinner last night was absolutely wonderful. And, thanks again for being so understanding. Your acceptance means so much to me."

"What's not to accept? You're going to make us both the happiest men in the world!" he exclaimed, waving his finger between Dan and himself.

"Hmmm . . ." I'm sure I was blushing. "Would you mind if I borrowed your son for a moment?"

"My dear, you'll learn very soon that you never really own your children. And, please, call me Dad. Now, scoot you two."

There it was; Mr. Carter, uh . . . Dad . . . could not have been happier, and I could not have been more scared. Dan was completely oblivious to the gravity of our situation. He scooped up his coffee mug and followed me out to the deck. What I would have given for a cup of strong black coffee that morning.

Stepping through the doors and out onto the deck, I inhaled the salt air and released a long sigh. I felt the tension start to leave my shoulders. I hoped my anxiety would take a ride out on the next wave. I faced Dan. Taking another deep breath, he cut me short.

"What's so important that you couldn't sit down with my dad for breakfast? He really thinks you're cute, you know—barf and all!"

"Dan, this is serious. We told your dad about the baby before telling my parents. My mother is going to be devastated and disappointed on so many levels, especially if she hears it from someone else first."

"Ginny, relax. Who on earth is she going to hear it from? My dad can keep a secret. Besides, the only people he talks to are his breakfast buddies at the Blue Plate Diner. This will be a tough one for him to keep, but he'll understand the situation."

"And how am I going to tell my parents? What am I going to say? Mother, Dad, you are about to become grandparents. Sorry we didn't have 'that little talk' first, Mother. It sure would have been helpful. Oh, and you remember Dan Carter, right?"

Studying my face, Dan remained silent.

"I think we need to call them tonight," I strongly suggested.

"Ginny, are you sure this is something you want to tell them over the phone? We should tell them in person, together. I want to be there when you tell them. I want them to know how much I love you and that I will do everything possible to take care of you and our baby."

He pulled me in and very softly kissed the top of my head. Lifting my chin, he kissed my lips, holding them against his for a sweet second or two. Pulling back, his voice was soft and without worry, "Good morning, beautiful. You do look radiant!"

Wow, people really say that.

It was rather nice to hear, and I was glad he had said it first. After awhile, I knew I would cringe when someone described me as "radiant." I had heard horror stories of women and their radiant raging hormones.

"So, when and how are we going to break the news to my parents?" I asked.

Still holding on to me with his arms locked around my waist, he calmly spoke as if the answer was obvious.

"We'll drive up to Darien one weekend and give them the good news. In the meantime, I will plead with my dad not to tell a single soul, not even my brothers. We'll let him know he can be 'in-on-it' as long as he doesn't spill the beans to anyone."

"OK, Mr. Everything's-Going-To-Be-All-Right, perhaps you should do all the talking when we get to Darien."

Realizing he had just committed himself, Dan lifted his head, closed his eyes, and chuckled.

Without another word, he let me know he would do whatever it took. His body against mine helped me leave reality behind, if only for a moment. For the next two minutes, perhaps longer, we stood on the deck and we . . . well . . . quite frankly . . . made-out like two irresponsible teenagers. And, why not? We were pregnant and barely twenty-two. We had nothing to lose and everything to gain.

In Lewes, we had made many great memories during our visits with Dan's dad. If only the weekend with my parents had gone as well, who knows what could have been?

* * *

(Back to the present.)

Dan eventually woke up. The morning at the attorney's office had worn him out. Moaning and stretching, he kicked the covers off and sat up as if he were trying to make sure it was not a dream. He was searching. No, it was real. I was real. He was real. His father's death was real. The baby growing in my belly was real. He looked at me, took my hand in his, and silently assimilated all of it.

With the wind gracefully causing the curtains to dance

to the sound of children playing somewhere on the beach below, nothing needed to be said. Trying not to be too obvious about where we were headed, we slowly removed what little we had on. Pulling me in closer, Dan kissed and held me. His body was warm and firm. We made love as he sought assurance that all would be right. That if all else failed, having lost his father and feeling as if he were losing his brothers, he needed to know that he would not lose me. Moving over him and holding his hands down over his head, I took the lead. Rendering him defenseless, I whispered that I would always be there. I told him my love ran deep, and he was now written on my heart forever. I could feel him confidently and slowly receiving my promises. As the tide changed, Dan let go . . . and let go again. When he opened his eyes, I saw his faith in our future and his sorrow as he let go of his past. We stayed there, between the two, until I could no longer feel the muscles in my legs. I rolled off, pulled his head to my breasts, and gently stroked his hair as he softly sobbed.

"I will always be here for you, Dan. I will always love you."

Still wrapped around him, he finally let go of the day.

SUSAN

While the guys were at the offices of Sable & Sable for the reading of the Mr. Carter's Last Will and Testament, Ginny and I went to the Food Lion. We picked up a few snacks for the afternoon and steaks for dinner. Nothing extensive, we would all be leaving in the morning.

Sometime after noon, the guys returned from their meeting. My husband, Derek, said that they would have been back sooner except Dylan and Dan wanted to stop by Capriotti's Sandwich Shop out on Savannah Road. While their order was being made, they went across the street to Roadster's Liquor Store for obvious reasons.

Reunited back at the Carter beach house, we all sat out on the deck for lunch. The boys filled us in on the attorney, her office, and the contents of their father's Will. They teased Dylan about his new barracuda girlfriend. They tried to reason their dad's motives, but for the most part, they felt as if they had just buried a man who was withholding secrets, a man they had not known as well as they had thought.

After sandwiches, chips, and beer, Dan said he was exhausted. He and Ginny excused themselves and headed inside. Dylan wanted to take one last walk on the beach. My husband, Derek, said he had some things to think about alone, so I joined Dylan on the beach. We walked nearly a mile before turning around at the Lewes Yacht Club. Dylan was quiet most of the time. We stopped once to watch a black lab repeatedly retrieve a tennis ball. His master threw it out into the water a bit farther each time. When the dog finally tired, he shook his body, head to toe, and lay down in the sand as if to say, "Game over." Dylan said if he lived at the beach, he would definitely have a dog.

Sometimes, I think Dylan should get a dog. Then again, a dog has needs, so maybe not. Then again, maybe Dylan needs to be needed.

I've heard that babies can change lives, but if you're thinking about having a baby, you should get a puppy, first. But I'm ready to be a mom, and Derek wants desperately to be a father, I think. I'd rather have a baby first and watch someone else's puppy.

Yes, Dylan should get a puppy.

We had a late dinner that night. After everything was cleared, cleaned, and the trash was taken to the curb, everyone slowly began turning in for the night.

After midnight, the house had quieted, and I could not fall asleep. I was plagued with incessant tossing and turning, so I decided to tiptoe downstairs and get some fresh air. As I descended the steps, I was captivated by the full moon smiling over the water. Its reflection created a silver runner from the dark horizon to the shoreline. It crawled across the floor of the living area and in the wake of its glow every piece of furniture cast a long shadow. Its lunar pull beckoned me out to the deck, so I headed in that direction. Suddenly distracted by a light left on in the kitchen, I saw someone moving about. Allowing my eyes time to adjust, I peered around the corner.

Wearing only a T-shirt and pajama bottoms, her red hair tied up in a messy bun on top of her head, Ginny was busy rummaging around with a plate in her hand.

I jumped out at her. She screamed and threw marshmallows into the air. Graham crackers and pieces of Hershey's chocolate went flying everywhere. She laid one hand over her chest, and with the other she braced herself against the counter as she tried to catch her breath.

"You scared the living shit out of me!"

"Gotcha! What are you doing?"

"Making S'mores in the microwave. I'd offer you some, but half of them are on the floor, now."

In retaliation, she grabbed the bag of marshmallows and began pelting me with them. I picked one up and popped it into my mouth.

"Five second rule!"

"Wait! Stop! We need them!" Ginny shouted with her hands up.

Calling a quick truce, we made another plate full of S'mores, two mugs of hot chocolate, and took it all outside.

Out on the deck, we pulled two Adirondack chairs together. With a nip in the air, I went back inside and gathered up two blankets to curl up in. We slid back into the chairs and toasted our hot chocolates.

"Here's to sneaking out past midnight!"

"To sneaking out, indeed!"

I stretched out my legs and propped my feet up on the rail. Ginny, shorter than I and unable to reach the rail, curled her feet beneath her body.

We both sighed and enjoyed the waves, the stars, the carpet of glitter cast by the full moon over the water, and the songs of night creatures. A chill ran through me and shook my mug.

"Whoops!"

I had somehow managed to avoid spilling its hot contents into my lap.

"This was quite the day, wasn't it?" I said, not sure whether I was making a statement or asking a question.

"Sure was. I'm so sorry everyone is leaving tomorrow. I'm really going to miss all of you," Ginny responded.

"Do you guys know what you're going to do?" I was curious to know.

"About?"

"About the beach house."

"Oh. Dan really hasn't had time to digest it all. The house needs so much work. I suppose he should consider the option of moving down here to take care of it. Since graduation, he hasn't had much luck finding work back in Connecticut, anyway. I'm not sure, though. I guess he'll figure it out. For now, we'll both go back to New Haven."

"If he does decide to move, would you move down here with him?"

"I would love to." Ginny turned and smiled. Her eyes were filled with the possibility.

"If you do, can I come visit you?"

"You'd better! Every single weekend and vacations too!" she happily demanded. "Honestly, Dan is so excited about the house. He loves this place, but he doesn't know whether to be happy or feel guilty. He's having a rough time reading Derek and Dylan. He's afraid they might be upset. It has been an awkward day in that respect."

"I think they'll work it out. Maybe this was all part of a plan. Not that we would ever want their dad to leave us, but you know how they say that God always has a way of making things work for the best?"

"I suppose so. Maybe Dan will be more excited about this once it all settles. He and his dad used to talk all the time about how they would rebuild this place if they had the money. They used to scratch things out on paper or anything else they could find. It's a shame we didn't save some of those doodles. Some of their ideas were quite extravagant." Ginny shook her head and chuckled as she reflected back. "His dad would encourage Dan to dream big. And Susan," she continued, "sometimes I felt like his dad knew us better than we knew ourselves. Sometimes, I felt like he knew me better than my own parents."

I knew exactly how Ginny felt.

"Actually, the timing, sadly, was good for us." I picked up where Ginny had left off. "Derek and I have been trying for three years now to have children. Infertility treatment is so expensive and not covered by insurance, so Derek won't even talk about it. Now, with the inheritance, maybe he will at least consider other options. Maybe Mr. Carter did know us better than we know ourselves."

A pause . . .

"Ginny," I said, waiting to make sure I had her full attention, "maybe you and Dan will get married, and then we can be pregnant together. We can shop for baby furniture, baby clothes, strollers, car seats, diaper bags, and all the toys guaranteed to transform our babies into little geniuses." I was obviously excited about the idea, and I think I went on for a while. "And we could be mothers and aunts together, and Dylan will be the best uncle ever!"

I heard no response from Ginny, but I could sense that something was wrong. She wasn't sharing my excitement. Instead, she was quiet and distant. She was staring out across the water.

"Ginny, are you OK? Did I say something wrong?"

She slowly turned toward me. With tears in her eyes, she looked straight into mine.

"Susan, I'm so sorry, but I am pregnant . . . now."

I didn't know what to say. She was obviously upset and I couldn't find the right words.

"Does Dan know? You aren't going to . . . ?"

"Of course, Dan knows, and we would never consider any option other than to have this . . . I mean . . . our baby. We promised not to tell anyone, but you are the closest person I have to a real sister. We did tell Mr. Carter. Actually, after I barfed two times during one of his elaborate dinners, he guessed it."

I started laughing, and then she did as well. Ginny explained how she had christened the living room rug during her first episode.

"Poor Dan, he cleaned it up. He tried his best to keep it from his dad. Meanwhile, I was in the bathroom revisiting lunch."

"Oh, you poor thing."

"His dad figured it out. It certainly didn't take a genius to do so."

"Do the boys know?"

"Oh, no! And you have to promise not to tell them. You're not supposed to know, either. But Susan, I need someone to talk to. I need a best girlfriend, and you're it."

We hugged, laughed, and cried.

She had dreams, and I had not lost hope.

I was happy for Ginny. I really was, but how fair was it? Derek and I got married so we could begin a family. Then, nothing happened. I was so frustrated.

Damn it, Ginny is going to have a baby!

"Ginny, I will always be here for you. Always. I would be lying if I said I wasn't envious. In fact, I'm very jealous that you're going to have a baby. But it's going to be the greatest thing ever! When are you due?"

"March."

I did the math in my head.

"Oh, my gosh, didn't you guys spend a lot of time down here in June and July, after graduation?"

She smiled with her face down, and without saying a word, she acknowledged the possibility.

"To sneaking out!" I proposed.

"To sneaking out, indeed!"

Once again, we made a toast with our hot chocolates, which were less than lukewarm by then. It didn't matter. We knew our friendship could celebrate anything and survive everything, and survive we would.

DAN

Everyone was gone.

Dylan left shortly after breakfast. He had arrived two days before with one duffle bag and an emptied travel mug. That day, he quietly repacked, refilled his travel mug with coffee, and was on his way back home.

Derek and Susan hovered a little while longer. Derek took a morning jog out to Cape Henlopen State Park and back, while Susan slept in. When Derek returned, he jumped into a long hot shower. I could hear Susan beginning to stir. After dressing, they both came downstairs with their bags packed, ready to go. Susan sat at the table with Ginny. The girls talked quietly, promising they would call and see each other soon. Derek poured his coffee and then walked about the house. I am sure that in his mind it would be the last time the beach house felt like Dad's house, a summer get-a-way for the family. His boyhood memories were fading fast, and he was trying to hold on. I wasn't quite sure how to assure him that things would be no different, because I didn't know how to reassure myself.

My brothers were leaving . . . and Dad . . . he was gone forever.

After their Explorer turned off Bay Avenue and was out of sight, Ginny and I breathed a collective sigh of relief. We had held our breaths for the last twenty-four hours. We stared at each other and then looked around the house. We weren't quite sure what to do next.

In the silence, I could hear my Dad moving about the kitchen, or whistling as he weeded the sparse gardens along Bay Avenue, chatting with other elderly neighbors who had stopped to say hello. Walking past the sliding doors, I saw two Adirondack chairs pulled together on the deck. I could envision Dad sitting in one of them as he read his morning paper.

Dylan had stayed in Dad's room the past two nights. Later, as we moved from room to room, stripping the sheets off the beds, Ginny observed that Dylan's pillow felt damp. It was then that we knew how he had spent his nights. My eyes watered at the thought. I had to walk away.

Ginny was the best thing that had ever happened to me. She knew when to give me space and when to move in and cover me. She gave me space that morning. By noon, she had most of our things packed and staged to go. I found her on the deck, seated in the very chair where I had envisioned my dad. Her eyes were closed. Her angelic face was tilted slightly back and lifted toward the sun. Her unruly amber hair was gently moving with the bay breeze. Her hands were lying across her stomach, a beautiful place that would soon change and stretch as her body nurtured and carried our baby. She was so beautiful. I could not have been more in love. I wanted to wake her and tell her so. I wanted her to know that a day would not pass without her in it. I wanted to tell her how I could survive anything as long as I knew she was with me. Knowing that she would soon give me the best gift ever, I felt a sense of adoration I never knew existed. I wanted to scoop her up in my arms and never let a moment of disappointment or harm ever come near her, but I knew it was best to let her rest.

As she napped, I contemplated loading everything into the Jeep for our trip back to Connecticut. Then, I decided against it. I couldn't do it. I couldn't leave, and I didn't want her to leave me there. I needed to stay. I needed Ginny to stay with me.

My head was telling me to go back to our apartment in

New Haven. We had renewed our lease back in May, and we had rent and bills to pay. I would look for work and Ginny would continue on to medical school. That was our plan. However, other than that, there were no other obligations waiting for us. We had friends there, but truth be known, my brothers were the closest people to me. Dad and I had a special bond, but who could ever fill that gaping wound? Probably, no one. I could feel my emotions taking over.

I have to get ahold of myself. I have to stop the lump in my throat from rising up.

And then, I wept. I pulled myself back upstairs, curled up onto my father's unmade bed, and wept. My mouth wanted to cry out, but like a bad dream the sound was so deep that it couldn't be heard, not in this world. My teeth clenched in between silent sobs. It went on for some time. Eventually, I gave out. My heart could no longer feel its pain. My body no longer had the energy to fight. I was spent and numb. I was tired. I wondered how Derek and Dylan were doing, especially Dylan, because once he arrived home in Unionville, he would be alone.

DYLAN

Losing Dad so quickly was such a shock. One minute he was alive and probably enjoying a summer sunrise as he read his paper. The next minute, he was gone.

Learning of my inheritance was another jolt. I never imagined. I certainly didn't expect it. I wasn't quite sure how to handle it. Two hundred and fifty thousand dollars is a lot of money. However, I would have traded it all to have my dad back, as long as his return would not include his having to suffer when death would finally come again.

We're all going to die at some point in time. If there was

one good thing about Dad's death, it was that he didn't suffer.

After the business of Dad's Will was taken care of, I could no longer stay at the beach house. I just had to get out of there. I felt so alone in that house. Derek had Susan, and Dan had Ginny, and for that matter, Susan and Ginny had each other. Don't get me wrong; they're all great people. I was glad Susan had walked with me on the beach to the Yacht Club. If she had not been there, I probably would have broken down, altogether. And though there were just a hand full of people and a dog on the beach, I didn't want anyone to see me in that broken state. I was afraid that if I started, I would not be able to stop. It was like looking into a well and not being able to see the bottom. If I jumped in, how long would it take to hit rock bottom? I was scared of how deep my pain might actually be. So, I needed to get home to find out. I needed to be home . . . and alone. I certainly didn't want to cry in front of Susan, either. And that dog on the beach, I felt just like that dog, waiting for someone to throw something for me to retrieve. The chase would have, at the very least, given me a sense of purpose, something to consume my anxiety. I needed someone to pat me on my head and tell me that I was a good boy and that everything was going to be OK. I wanted someone to hold my head in both their hands and rough me up a bit. With Dad gone and my brothers' pre-occupation, I felt like I had nowhere to turn, other than to return home to an empty house.

* * *

We had spent our summers in Lewes, but we grew up in Unionville, Pennsylvania. It is a small village located about forty miles southwest of Philadelphia. When I say small, I am not exaggerating, like some do. It has one 4-way stop sign at an intersection bordered by several of its original structures dating back to the early 1700s. The village is situated just north of Kennett Square, Pennsylvania, the mushroom capital of the world. No kidding. Kennett

Square produces more mushrooms than any other place on earth. If you like mushroom soup or mushroom anything, the restaurants around Kennett Square are the place to go.

Just north of Unionville is some of the most beautiful horse country in the world. Most of it belongs to the King Ranch. Yes, we are the best in horses and mushrooms. If you get up early on a fall morning and drive north on Route 82, you can see the horses and the Cheshire hounds gathering for the start of the hunt. It's a beautiful sight. Another equine event is the Willowdale Steeple Chase on the Dixon Stroud Farm located at the intersection of Routes 82 and 926. Once Dad, Derek, Dylan, and I attended as spectators. It was Mother's Day, a day that was hard for us, but we felt close to her there. Mom loved the horses and the races are really quite incredible. The property is groomed and the jumps are elaborate. When the horses run, it awakens all of one's senses: the sight of their muscles rippling with nostrils flared, the smell of their sweat. You can feel the ground shake like a small earthquake as they near your position. It"s the sound that appeals to me the most. The hoofs rumble across the landscape like thunder as they make contact with the earth. You can hear them as they nick a rail, sometimes followed by the sound its vibration through the air and the twang as it bounces off the ground. You can hear the heavy breathing of the horses as they round the turns. In the surrounding fields filled with trailers, other horses whinny and snort as if to cheer on their comrades. As the horses and their riders pass by, the crowds call out. Because it's held in an open field, it's not like loud raucous stadium noise. You can hear each individual person shouting for his or her favorite.

On that particular day, we walked through the antique car display where I had the opportunity to sit in the driver's seat of a 1959 Chevy Corvette. We didn't have a camera with us, so this beautiful woman, who wore no ring on her finger, took my picture. She said she would send the picture to me, so I gave her my address and cell number, hoping it was a ploy and I would hear from her soon after. I never saw the picture, and I never saw or heard from her again. Just my luck with women running its usual course.

However, the area is probably best known for the world-renowned Longwood Gardens. A fellow Quaker named George Pierce purchased the property from William Penn. Over time, the Pierce family amassed a large number of various trees. They then opened their estate to the public. It is said to be one of the first public arboretums in the country. However, they later sold it to Pierre S. du Pont who, in his effort to save the trees from becoming lumber, made it what it is today. It boasts beautiful trees, gardens, a conservatory, and fountains. I lived within three miles of Longwood. I grew up playing in the fountains on hot summer days and hiding from my brothers in the children's garden. When I was in high school and after the gardens closed at night, my buddies and I would sneak in. Sometimes we would take our girlfriends with us. We were almost caught, once. That's when I learned that my girlfriend at the time could outrun me. I never saw her again. It was just another example of my luck in love running its usual course, again, quite literally.

After graduating from Penn State University with a degree in Business, I moved back home with my dad. I didn't find a full-time job right away, so I filled my days with another one of my favorite pastimes—woodworking. I built chairs, tables, rockers, and rocking horses. After running out of room in my dad's basement, I began to earnestly sell the items that I had in inventory, first on eBay and then on my own website. My girlfriend, at the time, helped me build the site. After the website was up and running, things just kind of fizzled out between us. I remember her once saying that I was just using her, which I didn't quite get. Even though I didn't feel like we had quite the right chemistry for a lifetime together, I was always respectful and honest with her. I took her to nice places, and we seemed to enjoy each other's company. I was always there for her ups and downs. I guess things had run their course, but I didn't believe that I had deliberately used her. Anyway, I started receiving requests to build custom entertainment centers and other cabinetry. After my reputation was established and the business took off, I bought my own place. Good thing, because a year later my dad sold his house and moved to Lewes.

Not only did I need the room to expand, I realized that living with my dad was not the way to impress the ladies. Fortunately, I found this great fixer-upper on the outskirts of the village. In my new home, my neighbor to the east was the Unionville Elementary School. My neighbor to the west was a graveyard. It was easy to see that neither would cause me any trouble. My house was built in the early 1800's. The original part was a brick center hall colonial. The interior featured random width pine floors that were in need of refinishing. All the doors, window frames, and mantels were natural unadulterated oak. Speaking of mantels, the house had four fireplaces. They were located in the kitchen, living room, dining room, and master bedroom. The kitchen was outfitted with oak cabinetry and standard appliances, nothing fancy. It still had the original cast iron wood stove used for cooking and baking. The stove added a lot of character to the place. Every once in a while on a cold snowy day, I would light it up. Decades after the house was first built, a library and den were added on to the back of the house. Unfortunately for the seller, and fortunately for me, the later addition was termite infested, which allowed me room to negotiate a much better price. Speaking of negotiating, two other items were noted: the electric service in the original part of the house was not up to code, and the roofs on both buildings leaked in several areas.

Yes, there were two buildings on the property. The second was a really cool barn. It had no heat or air conditioning, but that was something I could deal with later. With its concrete floor, double doors, and drive-up ramp, it was perfect for my shop.

That was my home. It was a work in progress. It was all I had and all I needed.

GINNY

I can't say where the day went. In the morning, everyone said their goodbyes and headed north. I packed our things and then napped. I found myself easily tiring in those days. By late afternoon, Dan had decided to stay a while longer, and hunger was setting in. I didn't have any cravings, as yet, but I noticed my appetite was becoming more voracious with each passing day. Dan suggested we get out of the house and go out for an early dinner. We settled on going to Irish Eyes. Located on the Lewes-Rehoboth Canal, it was close by, no more than a half-mile away. Hopefully, we would score a table on the outside deck. Feeling like I had done nothing that afternoon, I suggested we walk. At least then I would feel like I had earned the right to satisfy my hunger pangs.

I visited the bathroom before we left. That would become a ritual during my pregnancy. I washed my hands, splashed water on my face, tied my hair back, and I was ready to go. We crossed Cedar Street and walked up East Market Street to Angler's Road. I was several inches shorter than Dan, but able to keep up with him. I was sure that would not last much longer. I wondered what it would feel like when my walk became a waddle. I prayed that that would never happen. I wondered how I would carry. I wondered how much weight I would gain. I wondered if I would be able to recover my figure. I wondered if my hair would fall out. My brain wandered a lot, then. My brain could have been falling out.

DAN

With the summer season all but over, we had our choice of tables on the deck. The outside bar was crowded with local residents. Laughing and sharing stories about the vacationers, the fish they had caught, and the ones that got away, they were all talking above their own noise. As I sat and enjoyed the view and my lovely company, I thought I recognized a voice heard over the din at the bar. I turned in my seat to scan the patrons. Following the direction of the voice, my eyes fell upon someone from my past.

Not sure I wanted to revisit that time in my life, I returned to the menu in front of me. I no longer heard the voice at the bar. It had relocated itself and was standing between Ginny and me. A hand was on my shoulder and the other was extended.

"I thought that was you. Long time no see," he said.

I slid my chair back and stood up, now taller than him, and I shook his hand.

"Hey! Dex, how have you been?"

"I'm doing well. I'm so sorry to hear about your dad. He was a great guy. I'll really miss him."

"Yeah, it's been a rough week. Uh, Dex, this is Ginny. Ginny, Dex."

"Nice to meet you, Ginny."

The burn scars on his right arm caught her eye.

"Dex, my brothers, and I used to hang out down here when we were younger," I explained to Ginny.

"Yeah, we go back a ways," Dex chimed in.

"So, are you visiting?" I asked him.

"No, I live here now."

"You do? Where?"

Dex pointed over toward the dock.

"Right there, on the Right Tackle."

He was pointing toward a fishing boat that was gently rocking in her slip at the end of the dock. She was a good forty-plus feet long with a wide berth. Her high tuna tower left no doubt that Dex was into some serious fishing.

"Are you crewing her for the summer?"

"Nope, she's mine. I couldn't afford property down here, so I bought a boat."

"You always were a rebel."

"Yeah, some things never change. Do any fishing lately?" he asked.

"No, not for several years now."

"Well then, you'll have to come out with me sometime. With the cooler weather coming, things should start picking up here real soon."

"That sounds great!" I said, feigning excitement. I was not really sure I wanted to be out to sea on a boat with Dex. As I tried to politely end our little visit, the waitress stopped by to take our drink order.

"Well, enjoy your dinner. You know where to find me. Ginny, it was nice meeting you," Dex said before disappearing back to the bar and back to his rowdy friends.

Yep, some things never change.

After the waitress took our order, I took a deep breath and relaxed.

"Who is he?" Ginny asked.

"He's a guy we used to hang out with. He's a year or two older than Derek. Back in the day, the two of them were real troublemakers. They used to drop firecrackers in the trash barrels on the beach, run behind the dunes, and watch the trash blow up. They had started a few small fires in the process. One night, they sneaked out and dragged boats that were laid up on the dunes down to the water and set them adrift. They would say they were going to Rehoboth and then drive to Ocean City, Maryland. Lord knows what they were doing half the time."

I leaned a little closer to Ginny so no one else could hear.

"One night he burnt down a boathouse, or so they

say. He claimed he didn't do it. Derek said he wasn't with Dex when it happened, yet swore Dex had started the fire. They could never prove anything, but Dex ended up taking the fall. He was later acquitted, thanks to the same law firm that handled my Dad's Will. Dex and Derek had a big falling out over it. We really didn't see Dex much after that."

Ginny stared at Dex and then looked back to me.

"What a shame. Was anyone hurt in the fire?"

"No. However, a beautiful mahogany Chris Craft Runabout was burnt to a crisp. That was the real crime. After getting away from it all, I can't imagine why he would want to come back and live here now."

GINNY

Without jobs and my mind totally disconnected from medical school, other than our lease, we had nothing left to hold us in Connecticut. We decided to break the lease and give our ninety days notice. My parents were disappointed with our decision. While angry about our so-called "predicament," my mother was convinced that if I kept the baby, I would need her help. Nothing could have been further from the truth. She suggested that I come and stay with her in Darien. I don't believe she had faith in our relationship. She didn't have faith in Dan's commitment to our "*little predicament*" either. She was convinced that after the baby arrived, Dan would become an absentee father and eventually leave us. "You two won't last six months after that baby is born," she sneered with brutal contempt. My mother's presence was like a poison to me. Dan, bless his patient and forgiving heart, had the ability to let things roll off his back.

We had made our decision. In November, we would vacate the apartment and move to Lewes. After contacting his brothers and asking for their help, we made all of the necessary arrangements to move our belongings the day before Thanksgiving. Then, we would all stay and share Thanksgiving dinner at the beach house. We had not told Derek or Dylan about the baby, yet. I thought telling them while we were all gathered around the table for the Carter Family Thanksgiving Dinner would be a nice touch.

Early Wednesday morning, Derek, Susan, and Dylan met us in New Haven. The guys loaded up the U-Haul truck while Susan and I packed up the kitchen and other small miscellaneous items. After everything was packed, Susan and I began the cleaning process. Not knowing about my *little predicament*, Dylan asked me to help him move a table down to the truck. Susan jumped in, saving me from making up some lame excuse for not wanting to lift heavy objects.

Dan and I didn't own all that much and our apartment was small, so it was not long before we were packed up, cleaned up, and ready to leave. Good-bye, Yale. Good-bye, New Haven. Good-bye, Connecticut. Good-bye, everything I had known up until then.

It was a long drive to Lewes. Dan drove the U-Haul truck, Dylan was behind him in his Dodge Ram loaded with several pieces of furniture, and Susan followed in their Ford Explorer carrying all of our electronics. I drove my CR-V, which left Derek to drive Dan's Jeep. We had to make several stops along the New Jersey Turnpike. During our first stop at the Thomas Edison Rest Area, just on the other side of New York, we discussed whether we should cross the Delaware Memorial Bridge or drive the length of New Jersey's Garden State Parkway and take the Cape May-Lewes Ferry to the Delaware beaches. The expense of taking all five vehicles on a ferry adventure over water kept that conversation very short. So, we drove the length of the New Jersey Turnpike, crossed the Delaware Memorial Bridge, picked up I-95 on the other side, and then on to Route 1 South, giving us a direct path to the Lewes cut-off. Five hours behind us, and with one more under our wheels through Delaware, we finally landed in Lewes.

Leaving the covered furniture in the trucks until the

next morning, we carried our suitcases in for the night. We figured that on Thanksgiving Day, while the turkey was in the oven, we would tackle co-mingling everything we had brought from Connecticut with Mr. Carter's furniture that he had left behind.

For dinner, we ordered Pizza from Grotto's and cold beers were in the refrigerator. Susan and I drank water. Dylan said we were wimps. Derek looked puzzled.

Later that evening, we took turns using the bathrooms as we prepared for bed. I remember that I had left my overnight bag downstairs, so I crept down the steps, picked up my bag, and started back up. Suddenly, I felt a sharp pain causing me to wince. Once it subsided, I took two more steps, and then the pain shot through me much deeper and more severe. Trying desperately not to alarm anyone, I managed to squelch my cry. To resume my climb up the stairs I held my breath and clenched my teeth. I had to make it back to our room. At the top of the stairs, the pain barreled through me once more. Radiating throughout my abdomen and legs, it lowered me to the ground. I had one hand on the rail and held my stomach with the other. Blood now covered my legs and was puddling on the floor beneath my feet. I felt myself losing consciousness.

The last thing I remembered was Susan coming out of the bathroom and screaming my name.

I woke up in Beebe Hospital. I didn't know how I got there. However, as soon as I saw Dan's face, I knew how I was leaving.

CHAPTER TWO

GINNY

Two weeks before our move, Dan had secured a job with Delmarva Architects, a firm with offices in Lewes. He was concerned about missing work and afraid to leave me home alone, so Susan volunteered to stay with me for at least the first week. She and I watched morning TV shows like Good Morning America, Ellen DeGeneres, Rachel Ray, and The View. I looked forward to my cup of black coffee each morning and hated the reason why I was now able to indulge in it. In the afternoon, we would play cards and work on jigsaw puzzles together. We avoided movies, soap operas, and any dramatic series, realizing that most would contain content that could cause me to reflect on my loss. So we elected to watch cooking shows instead. We would make a list of ingredients needed for our favorite recipe of the day and then take a quick trip to the Food Lion. It was so much fun to cook with Susan. We looked forward to surprising Dan when he got home. He thought he and his dad ruled the kitchen? Forget that! Susan and I had taken charge.

Susan was the one person who understood me. She helped me learn to co-exist with the emptiness that had tried to consume me. She was my life-saving champion.

SUSAN

It was good to get Ginny back to the beach house. I stayed with her through her first week home. Denying the brokenness of her heart, Ginny tried to maintain a sense of normalcy the best that she could. I tried not to crowd her. I suspected that in private she would let her guard down and take time to grieve on her own. A couple of times I caught her just standing in the middle of what she said would have been the baby's room. I stepped away and gave her space during those times.

She had just barely begun to show, so most people didn't know. She shared with me that she did want to have children one day, but for now that little girl had stolen her heart, and yet, she never had the chance to sing her a lullaby. She never felt what it was like to look into her baby's eyes as she nursed her. She never had to change her diaper. She never saw her smile, or heard her cry. She wondered how the room would have smelled and sounded if her little girl, Lily, had been there.

We talked a lot about God in those seven days, especially when she shared her hurt or felt angry.

When she tried to think ahead, when she tried to comprehend her life without her baby, she also expressed that she didn't know where it left her relationship with Dan. She loved him dearly. Yet, she felt that she had failed him: first by becoming pregnant, and second by losing their baby. To her parents' great disappointment, she had passed on medical school, too.

She spent a lot of time asking, "What if?" What if she had left her overnight bag downstairs? What if she had not made the trip to and from Connecticut that day? What if she had stayed in Lewes to prepare Thanksgiving dinner? What if she had gone to live with her mother? What if God terminated the pregnancy because she would have been a lousy mother? What if God terminated the pregnancy because Dan was not supposed to spend the rest of his life with her? What if, eventually, Dan was supposed to marry someone else? Of course, I had no answers for any of it. All I could do was listen.

Lily was buried next to her Pop-pop and Grandmom Carter. When she was laid to rest in her tiny box, Dan and Ginny went alone to the cemetery to say goodbye. A small marker would be placed there in several weeks. Every day thereafter, Ginny and I visited the cemetery to place flowers and leave unspoken prayers.

On Sunday, Derek came to pick me up and take me back home to Valley Forge, Pennsylvania. He surprised us by bringing flowers for Ginny and a book, "Safe in the Arms of God, truth from heaven about the death of a child," by John MacArthur. It was as if he had heard all of Ginny's questions and knew of at least one place to help her find some answers. I was greatly touched by his thoughtfulness. That was the man I had married.

Derek and Dan spent some time together on the beach tossing a football in the cold salt air. I watched as they stood below the dune and chatted. Derek patted Dan on the back before they made their way back inside. I promised Ginny that I would call her everyday, which I did. I knew I would be lonely without her, and she without me.

Back home in Valley Forge, I was left with my own isolation. That week was not a time to share with Ginny how desperately Derek and I had wanted children. I could not share with her how Derek was still not willing to pursue other options. There, in Valley Forge, young couples with their children surrounded me. They were in a state of perpetual motion, taking their kids to school, soccer games, birthday parties, and to visit their grandparents.

When Ginny and I were together, we were happy. Apart, I was sadly alone.

DAN

The days after Susan left, I made every effort to be home for Ginny when I could. I left for work later in the morning and came home earlier each day. On the weekends, I slept in with her. When we did finally crawl out of bed, I would make a big breakfast for us. I took her shopping during the day and out to dinner in the evening. After several weeks of this, she said it was time to stop smothering her, that she would be OK. She assured me that she was not going to kill herself, and promised that she would kill me if I didn't stop.

To compensate for my extra time at home, I set up a drafting table in one of the spare bedrooms, the one that Dad had used as an office. Filled with his spirit, I had hoped that that room would give me the inspiration I needed. I didn't know if it worked that way; however, because I believed it could, it actually seemed to make a difference. I always had several projects going at a time. At Delmarva Architects, I was part of a team designing an addition for the "Children's Beach House." It was a place built by the du Ponts for children with special needs and their families. During one of our visits, I was drawn to a group playing outside. They were happy, healthy, and smiling. I couldn't help but think of our own daughter. Perhaps God took her because something was wrong? People who don't know what else to say, or feel compelled to heal you, use that rationale freely as if they had the magic words to make everything better.

What makes them think it's that easy, or that they would know God's will?

The truth is God knew we would have raised Lily and loved her no matter what. We would have given our lives for her. Ginny would have been an amazing mother. It was the very reason she hurt so deeply. It was the same reason I loved Ginny so much. It was the very thing that makes her who she is. I knew I would ride it out with her, forever, if she would let me. But, deep down, I needed to know God meant us no harm, and I told him so.

Early in December, Ginny suggested that we decorate for Christmas. Thinking it might help, she was ready to try and cheer up the place. We strung white lights around the deck rail. We purchased a small six-foot blue spruce and placed it in the living room in the corner by a window overlooking the water. We owned some decorations that we had moved with us from the apartment in New Haven; however, Ginny wanted to go with more of a beach theme using natural ornaments.

Sometimes, the very reasons I loved Ginny so much also meant a lot of extra work! We collected some shells and pieces of driftwood from the beach, which took some doing because it was freezing out there. The frigid bay breeze cut right through every layer and stung our faces. It was hard to imagine a time when we sat in the sand with barely a stitch on. I suggested we use seaweed or dune grass as tinsel to throw over the boughs. That didn't fly with Ginny. So, we went to the Christmas Shop in Rehoboth and purchased some ornaments that looked like sandcastles, fish, or seagulls. Everything had to be indigenous. That meant no colorful tropical fish. No Nemos. We also picked up several strings of blue lights. I protested, stating that blue lights had nothing to do with Christmas. She said she had an idea, and if I didn't like it, we could take them down and return them. Otherwise, I needed to trust her. I suggested we string Dolle's saltwater taffy and petrified boardwalk fries. That was when she realized I was just trying to get a rise out of her. She scolded me, followed by a jab to my bicep. I was so happy to see her returning to her feisty self. We stopped at the Shell Shop on Route 1 and purchased a dozen ornamental starfish.

Back home, (I was still getting used to calling the beach house "home.") she entwined the strings of white and blue

lights together. I helped her wrap them around the
tree. Then we added the other ornaments we had found or
purchased. We placed a large starfish on the top. I thought
we were done, but she sent me down to the beach with an
empty bucket. She said not to come back until it was filled
with sand. When I returned, she poured the sand all
around the bottom of the tree, directly onto the floor, mind
you. I wasn't sure how we would clean it up after
Christmas, but it didn't much matter. She was returning to
the "anything goes" Ginny I once knew and loved. I realized
then how much I had missed her.

After dinner, we turned off the lights, except for the blue
and white lights on the tree inside and the white lights
wrapped around the deck rail outside. We sat down on the
sofa with two glasses of wine and enjoyed the peace and
quiet.

The house was drafty, and the old heat pump blew
lukewarm air. On that cold December night, I wrapped a
blanket around us as we cuddled together. We wondered
what everyone else in the family was going to do for
Christmas Eve and Christmas Day. We debated whether or
not we should invite them down to spend it with us. I
thought we should take a drive to Connecticut and visit
with her parents. Ginny was dead set against it. She
decided that when she was ready they could come and visit
us. In the end, with a bottle of wine polished off, we
decided to invite everyone down to spend Christmas in
Lewes at the Carter beach house.

With all the talk about family, we had allowed our
conversation to drift toward wondering aloud what
Christmas would have been like seven months pregnant or
the following year when Lily would have been nine or ten
months old. An OK sadness fell over us. We were still
learning how to navigate those moments together.

"Ginny, you know we can try again, someday."

"You'd really want to do that . . . with me? What if I can't
get pregnant? What if I miscarry, again?"

"Then I would want to be there with you, again. If we
have children, that would be great. If we don't, that would

be OK, too."

"Dan, what exactly are you saying?"

I lifted her chin and turned her beautiful blues to mine.

"Ginny, I'm saying I want to spend the rest of my life with you. I want you to marry me. Will you marry me, someday? Someday, soon?"

She didn't say anything, at first. A tear started to drift aimlessly down her cheek. Then, more tears followed. I could feel her body shaking in my arms and under the blanket.

"Oh, Dan, I was so afraid. I'm still afraid. I'm afraid to look at a future without you. I love you more than you will ever know. I need you more than you will ever know. And after all we have been through, you would still want to marry me?"

"After all we have been through, I could never be with anyone, except you. I want to spend the rest of my life with you: good times and bad. I want to be with you . . . forever."

Ginny and I had not made love since before that awful day in November. I wanted to. Lord knows I had wanted to. It took every ounce of willpower not to make advances, and after that day, Ginny had never initiated anything. I think she was living with guilt and felt it undeserving to allow herself pleasure of any kind, especially anything that intimate and satisfying. But there we were, tied together by arms and legs under our blanket in the soft glow of blue and white lights. We whispered words of love and desires for one another as our lips brushed and kissed. She let out a long sigh, indicating her final surrender. I picked her up and carried her upstairs to bed.

We made passionate love that night. Eyes open, I moved very gently over her. I wanted to make sure I was not rushing or hurting her, that every move I made would do nothing less than show her how much I would always care deeply for her. Erotically pressing in to me, I watched as she slowly came. I could no longer hold back.

There we stayed, connected in a place without time. We slept and made love again. We woke in the morning and made love gently and quietly, once more. We hugged, kissed, and stayed close throughout the day. We had missed each other so much.

That afternoon, I went back to the Christmas Shop and bought four more strings of blue lights. I wrapped them around the white ones on the deck rail. Our life together was beginning to reassemble itself.

GINNY

We began to make our wedding plans. Undeterred by her lack of love for Dan, I knew my mother would want to make a fuss and put on a big show for her friends and my father's colleagues. I knew she would want the event to take place in Connecticut, in her church, and with her pastor. She would want a monumental and hugely expensive reception at the Wee Burn Country Club. Dan and I would be coerced into posing for thousands of staged photographs, many of them with her, as if we were going to be splashed on the cover of People magazine. I would have to do all of those silly dances, and it all meant that I would have to spend enormous amounts of time with my mother on the phone or on trips to Darien to make it all happen. It would be her day, not mine. I knew Dan would be respectful and honor my mother's wishes; however, I had no desire to be a part of her circus.

I shared all of my concerns with Dan. After I ended my rant, he weighed in.

"It will be your day. How would you like to do this if there were no obstacles?"

"I would want it to be you and me, your brothers, and Susan. And . . . I so wish your dad was still here. I think he would have wanted to host the ceremony on the beach in front of the beach house. What do you think?"

"Can we wait until the weather is warmer to grant his

presumed wishes?"

"Definitely."

"And, your parents?"

I knew we would have to address it. They *were* my parents, after all. My dad was tons of fun. Absent my mother, he and Dan probably would have hit it off.

"Well, my Dad would be crushed if he didn't get to walk his only daughter."

"I think it would be a huge mistake not to invite them."

"OK, but they'll have to stay at the Rodney Hotel. They certainly can't stay here."

After thinking it through, I planted my feet firmly in the ground. My mother could be present, but it would not be her wedding extravaganza.

"After a brief ceremony, we'll go out to dinner for a small family celebration," I insisted. "Nothing big."

"We'll need a pastor, a date, time, and a place," Dan said, as one who likes to work with a well-thought-out plan.

"Whoa, Cowboy! Do we need to decide all of that now?" I asked.

"No, but we should, soon, so everyone has time to make their plans and request vacation time. And I have to plan our honeymoon, etc., etc." He winked. "That sort of stuff."

We set the date for early May. Susan was thrilled when I told her the news. I was not ready to tell my mother. I wanted to enjoy the holidays without any complications— just for a little while longer.

DEREK

The phone seemed to ring exceptionally loud that night. Susan answered the call and within seconds she was squealing and jumping for joy.

"Congratulations! When's the big day? I just knew it! I can't wait to tell Derek!"

At first, I thought she was talking to someone in the neighborhood or from church. But then, she handed the phone to me and said Dan wanted to talk.

Great. I hope he makes it quick, because I'm tired and I don't want to talk about the house or hear that Ginny's knocked up again.

"Hey, Dan, how are you doing?"
"We're doing great. We've got some news."
"OK, shoot."
"Ginny and I are getting married!"

Before responding, I paused to collect my thoughts.

"Am I on speaker phone, Dan?"
"No."

Silence . . .

I was making my way into my office so I could shut the doors behind me. Susan didn't need to hear what I was about to say.

"ARE YOU FUCKING NUTS?"
"Derek, I'm not kidding, we're getting married."
"I heard you the first time. What the hell are you thinking? Is she pregnant, again?"

Silence . . .

I knew I had ruined his little party, but he was such a baby sometimes. Every now and then, someone needed to shake some sense into Dan. He had just graduated. Why the rush? Why was he running headlong into marriage? Ginny must have been behind it. I was willing to bet that it was the house that she really wanted. I knew she liked Dan and all, but she loved that house.

"No, Derek, she's not pregnant, and it wouldn't make a difference if she were."

"Listen, Dan. You dodged a bullet the first time. Why don't you give yourself some space and time? What's the big rush?"

"What do you mean, 'I dodged a bullet?' I was devastated. We both were. We both wanted Lily. And her name is Lily, Derek. She has a name—Lily. She wasn't a bullet. Don't ever make that reference again. Do you hear me? Don't ever say that again, and especially not around Ginny."

I could picture Dan on the other end of the line with his fist tightened and jaw clenched. I had seen his rampant loyalty before. One time a kid posted a picture on-line of Dylan getting a swirly in the boys' locker room. When Dan found out, he punched the guy's lights out. Dan did all the swinging. Afterward, I told the poor bastard if he said one word about it, he would deal with me next. Dan was a crazy man that day. No one messed with Dylan after that. Come to think of it, no one messed with me, either.

"Dan, you've been through a lot: Dad, the house, starting a new job . . . and . . . uh, Lily."

Silence . . .

"Dan, listen, I'm only thinking of you. You're my . . ."

Dan cut me off. "Derek, it's not just me anymore. Lily was a part of me, and Ginny is a part of me, too. I don't ever want to be without her. I know I'm supposed to say that I appreciate your concern, but honestly, I don't."

Silence . . . and more silence . . .

"Dan, are you still there?"
"Yeah."
"I don't know what to say. Someone needs to tell you. But, if you go through with this, you know I will be there for you. Right?"
"I know, and I hope that one day you will care for Ginny the way I care for Susan."
"You know I will. You're my brother."

Silence . . .

"And, Dan . . ."
"Yeah . . . ?"
"I'm really sorry about Lily. I really am."
"Thanks, Derek."

We said our cold goodbyes.

Less than a minute later, Ginny called back.

Oh great, here we go, again.

But, as it turned out, Dan was supposed to invite us to Lewes for Christmas. Susan was so psyched about all of it, but I really didn't want to go back there ever again. I just could not get used to the idea of Dan and his soon-to-be-bride having sole possession of it all.

DYLAN

A week or two before Christmas, Dan called to tell me that he and Ginny were planning to get married in May. It was about time. Dan assured me that Ginny was not pregnant again. I don't know why he felt compelled to tell me that. I was just plain happy for both of them—baby or no baby. They'd been through so much together. Honestly, I don't know what more life could have thrown at them that they had not already conquered. It was safe to say that they could survive anything.

As for me, I would gain another sister. Susan is a rock, and Ginny could be uproariously funny. We Carter boys had better watch out. I could only imagine that once Ginny got her feet back under her, those two would be a force to be reckoned with! Plus, I knew it would put pressure on me to find someone that fit the family mold. Derek and Dan had definitely struck it rich in the better half department.

Dan asked me to come down in early spring to help him make repairs to the deck. The ceremony would be held on the beach, but he wanted to have a very small family reception on a newly repaired deck. He spoke of candles and white tablecloths, the whole nine yards. He was thinking of hiring a caterer and a string quartet, as well. He said, and I was not allowed to speak a word of it to Ginny, that he wanted to surprise her with a reception at the house. That was our Dan, a hopeless romantic. He said I could bring a guest. I told him I would see what I could do about that in my spare time.

In the meantime, they invited me down for Christmas. Honestly, I had not even thought about Christmas. Well, that's not exactly true. I had thought about it somewhat. In my entire life I had never spent a Christmas away from my dad. I had been going to Lewes for Christmas every year since Dad had moved there. So, I thought it best not to think about it at all. I wasn't sure about spending it in Lewes, either. Somehow, I was afraid that being in Lewes and surrounded by the other four, and the talk of wedding plans, would make me feel even lonelier. But, I would rather that than be in Unionville and undeniably alone.

GINNY

Everything was happening so fast. We were going to host the Carter Family Christmas right here in Lewes. I wanted to make sure it was special so that, hopefully, it would be the first of many more to come.

With the holiday season upon us, Lewes was tastefully adorned with pine garland, sprays, and wreaths. Almost every home had candles in its windows. I loved how most displayed their Christmas trees in a front window so we could appreciate them from the street. As we passed by each house I imagined the warmth of the families that might live inside and thought, *"This is what makes a house a home."* Collectively, the area seemed magical. Coming down Savannah Road, as we approached the canal, we could see the drawbridge outlined in white lights and planters filled with Christmas greens. Crossing over the drawbridge, I pointed out that even Dex had his boat decorated with white lights strung up and down the tuna tower. A nearby sailboat had a star at the top of its mast.

Making a left at the Dairy Queen, we started down Bay Avenue. Many of the homes beyond the canal and on the bay side were summer rentals, so they were dark and empty. However, ours was radiating tranquility. The blue and white lights around the deck rail facing the bay were not visible from the parking area, yet they cast a beautiful blue glow on the sand surrounding the house, as if the water itself had risen and was beautifully illuminated. We also had white lights scattered in a dense pattern on the ground by the back kitchen door that gave the appearance

of blanketed snow in the dark of night. One little tree by
the back stairs was decorated in colored lights. Parked in
the drive and sitting in the passenger seat of Dan's Jeep, the
reality of marrying him and raising a family in Lewes began
to sink in. I could hear our children giggling and running up
the steps. I could envision Dan chasing after them. I was
feeling like the luckiest girl in the world, which conflicted
with the way I would always feel about losing Lily. It was
hard to grasp how our future happiness could ever co-exist
with so much sorrow from our very recent past.

We had seen Dex a couple of times since our first
meeting: once again at Irish Eyes and another time at the
Food Lion Supermarket. He suggested that Dan wait until
spring for their fishing trip, noting that it was "cold as a
bitch" out there. He said he had hung up his fishing gear for
the winter and took a construction job to make ends
meet. Dan asked Dex if he was going out to the West Coast
to be with his family for Christmas. Dex shook his head and
said he wouldn't be able to make the trip. Well, you could
see where that conversation was headed. The next thing I
knew, Dan was asking, "Why don't you come spend
Christmas with us?"

I wasn't quite sure how I felt about having a stranger—
an acquitted pyromaniac—in our home. Dan knew him
well enough, I supposed. Setting one extra plate at the table
would not be all that bad, or so I thought. Later, Dan said
he wasn't sure of the "frenemy" status between Derek and
Dex. He wasn't thinking about it when he had extended the
invitation. We guessed we would know where they stood
soon enough.

DAN

With Christmas and its onslaught a week away, Ginny and I got into a discussion about religion, which was a good thing. I think every couple should have that talk before they get married.

"Do you believe in God?" Ginny popped the question one night as we were lying in bed.

"Sure. Do you?"

"I'm not sure, anymore. I think I do. Lately, I've been so conflicted. Losing Lily . . . I just don't understand why we deserved that."

"We didn't, Ginny. We didn't do anything to deserve or cause what happened. God didn't act out to intentionally hurt Lily, or us.

"How can you be so sure?" She asked timidly.

"Well, I guess that's why they call it faith."

Hearing her sniffle as she tried to prevent the wound from reopening, I pulled her a little closer. I knew enough to know that I was not the cure to her pain. I could only stay by and watch after her.

"Ginny, bad things happen. It's a broken world. It's not our fault, and God didn't lash out at you, Lily, or me."

"It just hurts so much, and I'm so damn mad. I'm so angry with God, if there is a God. Then, I think if he really exists, it's probably not good to be angry with him. But I don't know who else to be angry with, so I start blaming myself."

"Ginny, it's OK to be angry with God."

"Are you sure? I mean, really angry."

"Of course, who else is there to yell at when bad things happen? When things are out of your control, your anger with him, in a backhanded sort of way, acknowledges that he is God. That's got to be better than denying his existence altogether."

"Did you do that? Did you yell at God?"

"Yes, and I think it was OK. When we lost Lily, I was furious, but I don't think God was upset with me for taking it out on him. I think he just kind of listened and let me yell until I wore myself out."

"Did you find any answers?"

"Yes and no. There may be things we'll never know, but God is still God. He's still in control. However, some find that frightening, fearing he could allow it to happen all over again. But frankly, when things go that terribly wrong, I need to know that there is a God. I need to believe that there is someone out there that is bigger than me and has a grand plan to make all things right one day."

"I just wished he would have stopped it," she whimpered.

"I know, baby. I wish he would have, too. And that's exactly why I'm so angry with him, too."

Ginny exhaled, like she had been holding something back for a long time. She was afraid that if she even thought about being upset with God, she would surely be sentenced to something far worse.

What could possibly be worse than to live it all over again? And, that's always a possibility.

"Ginny," I whispered, "I know Lily is all right, and we'll be all right, too."

"How do you know that?"

"I would tell you, but you'll think I'm crazy."

"Dan, if I'm going to marry you, I have a right to know just how crazy you are."

"Well, sometimes it seems like God speaks to me."

"He does? I've never heard him speak."

"Well, it's not like I hear his voice, like I hear yours. He speaks to me in ... in ways ... in lights and illuminations ... like stars, sunsets, lightning, and fireflies. It actually started before we lost Lily, perhaps to help me recognize his signs in the days that would follow."

Ginny didn't say anything. I feared that she surely

believed I was some sort of religious freak. So, I figured I should cut my losses and not elaborate. Or, I could try to explain myself.

"It was Thanksgiving Day. We had just lost Lily, and you were in the hospital. I had nothing to be thankful for. I was alone and angry in a house that was full of people. Susan was trying her best to put something together for dinner. It was too late to do anything about the turkey, but she somehow managed. Dylan and Derek were watching football. There was a U-Haul truck parked out back that was partially unloaded, and inside there were boxes everywhere that needed to be unpacked. I knew I was going to explode, and I couldn't do it there in front of everyone. So, I went for a run. I was running as fast as I could up Bay Avenue. I believed if I ran hard and fast long enough, I might be able to outrun all that had happened to us. When I got to the inlet, no one was there. Everybody was probably home eating turkey and stuffing, where you and I should have been. We could have been thankful that we were going to have a little girl. But we weren't. I was hurt and furious, and because I couldn't help you or escape it all, I raged, and there was no one better to rage at than God.

"Now, don't let this next part scare you, but I crawled out onto the rocks. I dared God to take me out, right then and there. And when he didn't, I started picking up those rocks and throwing them at the water as forcefully as I could. In fact, I wanted to throw myself right onto those rocks. I wanted to feel pain. I wanted physical pain. I needed pain that I inflicted upon myself. Pain that I controlled. Not this stuff that wells up inside until it feels like it will blow open your guts. Anyway, I eventually exhausted myself. I just sat there. For how long, I don't know. The sun was about to set, and the water became smooth as glass. It was moving like long strands of silk ribbons. It was silver, like polished platinum, and as the sun dropped below the horizon, the sky turned pink and lavender and so did the water. It was so calm, so serene, and it made me think of a beautiful girl named Lily. I couldn't throw another rock. It was as though God took it out of my hands and put it down. That's when I knew he didn't leave me. That's when I knew Lily was all right. That's when I knew we were going to be all right, too."

I could feel Ginny relaxing in my arms. She turned toward me.

"Dan, I'm so sorry. I didn't know you were hurting that much."

She snuggled in a little closer.

"Do you really believe all that?" she asked.

"Yes."

Ginny whispered, "That's beautiful, Dan. I wish I could hear him like that."

Soon, she drifted off to sleep.

Ginny's parents called the next morning while she was in the shower. I took the call. They asked if we had made plans for Christmas. Her mother was hoping we would come to Connecticut to spend the holiday with them. I thanked her for her gracious invitation; however, we had planned on spending Christmas in Lewes and we would love it if they could come down and spend a few days with us.

Later, Ginny's exact words were, "Are you out of your friggin' mind?"

It seems I get asked that a lot, lately.

I tried to explain that we could not ignore them and pretend that they didn't exist. They would be the only grandparents our children would ever know.

"Now there's a reason not to have children," she fired back.

"Ginny, babe, I would give anything to have my mother and father here, especially if and when that day comes. I think you're being a little selfish."

"Selfish? I'm being selfish? You don't know selfish until

you've spent a day with my mother."

I thought back to the first time I had met her parents. Actually, up until then, it was the only time I had spent with them. We had traveled up to Connecticut to tell them that they were going to be grandparents. It was a disaster. Dr. Huff greeted us at the front door of their ginormous eight-bedroom house in Darien. It was located just off Hollow Tree Ridge Road, bordering the Wee Burn Country Club. I had to take Ginny's word that the house had eight bedrooms. I never got the tour. In fact, we were there for less than an hour.

* * *

Passing through New York and entering Connecticut, it had become a colorful drive. The New England foliage was just beginning to turn. The smell of fallen leaves, hot apple cider, and football were in the air. Having been on the road for six hours, we were getting a bit punchy. We turned up the music and sang loudly through Greenwich and Stamford.

The Huff's driveway was more like a private road than a driveway. As we drove past the trees that lined the smooth lane of macadam, the view opened up to a magnificent home. I remember thinking it was bigger than any home I had ever seen, and we had some grand homes in Unionville, Pennsylvania.

I would like to think that I am not one who is easily intimidated. However, I was overcome with a sense of inadequacy. How was I going to provide for someone who grew up in this kind of affluence? I felt like I should park my beat up Jeep around back.

Sometimes, I think Ginny could read my mind. As I approached the front circle, she said, "Park it right here, soldier."

Trying to take it all in, I got out and looked up, then to the left, and then to the right. As if I were blind, Ginny took my hand and led me up the steps to the palatial portico. When her dad opened the wide, double doors to us, you would have thought that he had been standing there all day, just waiting for our arrival. The extravagance of it all made me feel like a pauper, one who had clearly lost his way.

Dr. Huff was about my height, maybe an inch shorter. His hair was brown and thinning. He had bright blue eyes and a gentle smile, two of Ginny's best features. He looked very comfortable in his oversized sweater, khaki pants, and deck shoes. He gave Ginny a long embrace and told her how much he had missed her. Then he shook my hand, acknowledging that I must be Dan, the man Ginny had been raving about. It dawned on me, then, that we probably should have made an effort to visit with her parents long before that day. Why, after two years, had I never met her parents?

Through the front doors and into a large foyer, we removed our coats. The ceiling of the foyer was two stories high. The grand area was lit by natural sun during the day and not one, but two huge crystal chandeliers, one behind the other, during the night. With large custom palladium windows across the front, the chandeliers were the centerpieces inside and outside the house. It appeared there was another entrance hall beyond the foyer. That was where we saw her mother descending a wide floating spiral staircase. Immediately, I recognized where Ginny had gotten her beautiful auburn hair. Her mother literally glided down the steps as if she were making a grand entrance at a royal ball. Mrs. Huff was all smiles. When she approached us, I noticed she had emerald eyes and the whitest teeth I had ever seen. She obviously took very good care of herself. She gave Ginny a royal hug and a kiss on the cheek, leaving airspace between the two of them. When she held out her hand to me, I didn't know if I was supposed to kiss it, genuflect, or just shake it in the usual customary fashion. I chose the latter as Ginny's father introduced us. So there it was, I had finally met Victoria and Dr. Stanford Huff. He said I should call him Stan.

Stan escorted us into the living room. Located to the right, beyond the second entrance hall, it was a long room with another high ceiling. It was filled with antique furniture and two large oriental rugs that divided the open space into two halves. On one end, two sofas and several chairs were centered in front of a fireplace. The warm fire added a soft glow to the august atmosphere. It crackled like music on a frigid winter's day. The other end of the room was home to a Steinway concert grand piano. With its polished lid slightly opened, it was begging for someone to sit and play.

Ginny and I sat next to each other on one of the sofas. Once I settled in, I noticed that Victoria had not taken her seat, as yet. Highly annoyed, she glared at me as if I had offended her. I stood immediately and waited until she sat down first. Later, Ginny told me that her mother was playing me.

Her father offered us a drink. Ginny said water would be fine, and I agreed to have the same. Stan asked if we would mind if he made himself an afternoon aperitif, as he put it. With our completely frivolous blessing, he walked toward the paneled wall opposite the fireplace. He picked up a remote, and I kid you not; the wall revolved, revealing a fully stocked bar. I gave a stupefied gasp at the sight of it, and I think I swore lightly under my breath. Ginny grabbed my knee, warning me to keep it together.

Once her father had his drink in his hand and a glass of wine poured for his wife, they got comfortable and the conversation began with a few pleasantries. Then, at Mrs. Huff's request, I shared where I grew up and how we ended up in Lewes. Oddly enough, Stan knew of Unionville. He had a friend who was on the board of the New Bolton Veterinary Center that was located several miles from my home and down a beautiful stretch of country road. Of course, I had never heard of the guy before. He obviously traveled in loftier circles than my family. Mrs. Huff asked how we met, which I was sure Ginny had already told her several hundred times. When we finally ran out of conversation, and the only sound in the room was the crackling of the fire, Ginny apparently thought it was time to break the news.

"Mom . . . Dad . . . we have something to tell you."

Now there's a sentence that will get the attention of every parent.

Ginny paused. We had rehearsed it a million times, but now that we were going live, all of our rehearsal time was for naught. We had forgotten our lines.

I jumped in and took the lead.

"Doctor and Mrs. Huff, I want you to know that I love Ginny very much. I plan on working very hard, and I will take good care of your beautiful daughter." I could feel Ginny rolling her eyes.

"What are you trying to tell us?" Dr. Huff asked, looking rather confused. I could see Mrs. Huff's defenses going up. Looking back, I realize my preface sounded more like a proposal was forthcoming than the news we were about to deliver.

Ginny jumped back in. "What he's trying to tell you . . . is that . . . we're going to have . . . a baby. . . . I'm pregnant."

With a frown on one side of his mouth and a smile curling up on the other, Dr. Huff was unreadable, much like the Mona Lisa. It was impossible to discern his immediate reaction.

Victoria? That was a whole different story. A purple-red began crawling up her neck and into her face. I thought she was going to have a seizure; when finally, she stood up and blew a gasket.

"VIRGINIA-LOUISE-HUFF, HOW. COULD. YOU! How could you do this to us?"

"And YOU," she roared, pointing her finger at me, "You leave this house, immediately! GET OUT OF MY HOUSE!"

I stood up. "I'm so, so sorry." I turned to leave. I looked back at Ginny, "I'm so sorry, Ginny."

That was the first and only time I had ever apologized about it. I was not sure what had just happened other than I had obviously screwed up. I started heading for the door. Hearing a scuffle, I looked back. Dr. Huff had his arms wrapped around his wife. Not as a sympathetic embrace, but rather in a straitjacket hold so she could not hurt Ginny, or herself. Then a sense of duty to Ginny and our baby came over me and I couldn't leave as I had been commanded to do. If Ginny was in harm's way or was going to be verbally battered by this, I had to stay with her and protect her. I was the one who should receive the consequences, not Ginny. I quickly returned to her side. Victoria was screaming and kicking, telling Stan to let her go. Ginny was crying and begging her mother to stop and try to understand. The situation was escalating rapidly, especially with my reappearance.

"I understand perfectly well. You are NOT having this baby. How could you walk in here and think this is all right?" The beautiful woman who had descended the staircase just a short time ago was now spewing venom and obscenities. At first, I placed my hands on Ginny's shoulders to let her know I was there, but when the spewing of toxins showed no sign of stopping, I moved my body between her and her mother to absorb the impact should she escape her husband's grip.

While valiantly wrestling with his thrashing wife, Ginny's father spoke cautiously to both of us.

"I think you'd better go."

And so, we left. As we got back into the Jeep, we could still hear her mother screaming inside. Her strong, ugly words were bouncing off the walls with angry resonance. Soon, but not soon enough for Ginny, we were back on I-95, headed south.

It's noisy riding in a soft-top Jeep. You can hear the road under your tires and the wind rushing past your vehicle and every other vehicle within view and then some. Until you get used to it, it feels like everyone else on the road is right on top of your bumper. However, our silence could be heard above all of that. As we drove through the Bronx, the hulks of burned out cars left on the side of the highway caught my attention. Broken down for whatever reason, their owners, for their own safety, had abandoned them on the shoulder. Like shadows in the night, marauders moved in to strip and destroy what was left. The roadside drama playing out depicted the way I was feeling. Who was I? I had always been welcomed in the homes of my friends. I was "that nice young Carter boy." I was the one with the good manners. I was the one with whom mothers wanted their sons to hang out and their daughters to marry.

What happened back there?

It was getting dark as we crossed the George Washington Bridge. I turned up the heat to combat the chill that was invading the Jeep's drafty interior. Across the river, illuminated skyscrapers formed the New York City skyline. The realization of the long ride ahead of us was setting in. We had planned on spending the weekend in Connecticut. We didn't make it past the living room.

"Ginny, are you all right, sweetheart?"

"No." She began sobbing. "I was thrown out of my own house."

"You weren't thrown out of your house."

"Well, I sure couldn't stay."

"Ginny, I was the one that was thrown out. You were *advised* to leave. There's a clear difference."

"OK, ok but only a slight one. Still, she expected me to throw away our baby, Dan. She wanted me to abort her grandchild. I can never go back there. Never."

"Give her time, Ginny. She was obviously in shock and upset. It was her immediate reaction to something she had never anticipated. With time, she may get used to the idea. And once the baby arrives, she'll come around."

"Part of me hopes she doesn't come around."

"She's going to become a grandmother, of course she'll come around."

Silence . . .

"Well, to make matters worse, I have to pee so bad I can't stand it."

She was chuckling in between her sobs. I had noticed that she had become a bundle of emotions as her pregnancy wore on. I chalked it up to her raging hormones. It was almost endearing, in many respects.

We pulled into the first New Jersey Turnpike rest area. I hated those rest areas. They always smelled like New York City subways, even in the food court. How do people actually eat there? I waited inside for Ginny. I knew she had to be starving. While she was in line for the ladies' room, I did a little research. When she finally emerged, she looked exhausted, but a little less frazzled. She leaned into me.

"Ginny, there's a Hilton in Woodbridge. I'm going to call and make a reservation. We'll be there within the hour. We can order room service."

"Just like in the movies?"

"Just like in the movies."

"Candles and all?"

"Candles and all, if you really want them."

She gave the idea a very tired, compliant nod. We started across the parking lot for the Jeep. I glanced over at her. Her face was drawn and there was no spark in her eyes. It was as if the whole family ordeal had stolen her spirit and locked it away in an eight-bedroom castle dungeon we had left behind. I was tempted to pick her up and carry her to the Jeep. *Oh, what the hell.* I scooped her up. With her arms around my neck, she buried her face into my shoulder. An older woman coming toward us asked if Ginny was OK.

I answered, "Pregnant and exhausted."

The woman sighed, "You are a wonderful husband, and you're going to be a great father."

From her lips to God's ears, I could only pray she was right.

* * *

I knew Ginny was right. Her parents would definitely have an impact on our Christmas. But I was certain I had done the right thing.

"Dan, are you listening to me?"

"Huh . . . ? Yeah."

"Dan, I haven't told them that we're planning to get married. I didn't think there was a rush to tell them. The coward in me said this time I should just call them and get it over with. Or, maybe I should send them a letter or a telegram. Then my mother would have something to rip up, instead of me."

"Ginny, they're your parents. If nothing else, I think your dad would want to be a part of it."

"And you think I should tell them face-to-face? Over Christmas dinner?"

"When, Ginny? If not then, when? We're getting married in six months, and we have no plans to go back and see them. Every time I suggest it, you never want to talk about it."

"Do you want to go back there, again?"

"Ginny, you have to tell them. We needed to invite them for Christmas for so many reasons. You can't just keep running away from them. Think of your father, he'd be heartbroken."

She started to soften with thoughts of her dad.

"I do miss him."

"Ginny, I don't think we can delay this. It will only make matters worse."

"Dan, how many times do you have to run into a brick wall to realize it hurts and it's not a safe thing to do? Spending time with my mother is insanity."

"What about your dad? Who's really getting hurt here?"

"It's my family, Dan."

"It's going to be mine, too."

"You should have asked first."

"You're right, I should have asked first. So, what do you

say?"

"What can I say? You've already invited them. You want a family? They're all yours."

I had tried to take Ginny shopping for a ring numerous times. She would always avoid it saying we didn't have the money or that it was not an immediate necessity. I knew it would be the perfect Christmas gift. She couldn't refuse it then! I needed to talk to Susan and take matters into my own hands.

SUSAN

I was so psyched. It seemed like forever since Ginny and I had spent time together. We talked on the phone once or twice a week, and she sounded really good, but I had to see for myself. She certainly had been busy making preparations.

Our plans were to leave Valley Forge on Sunday and stay in Lewes until the day after Christmas. It took some convincing on my part to get Derek to leave work for that amount of time. After working for an advertising agency on the Main Line for several years, Derek had launched his own graphic arts business. Picking up several large retail accounts, his fledgling company had finally taken off. He was working late almost every night. I thought the trip would be good for him. He needed the downtime. We both needed the downtime, together, and away from the pressures of his rapidly expanding business.

I had purchased gifts for everyone, planning to put them under the tree on Christmas morning. I told Ginny I would bake some pies. She suggested, for old time's sake, that we go to the Food Lion in Lewes, buy the ingredients, and bake the pies together on Tuesday. Ginny said the oven would help to heat the house, too. Because the house was drafty, she added that we should pack clothes that we could wear in layers. I was OK with that. It would give me a reasonable explanation for wanting to snuggle up with Derek. He had been rather distant in the wake of his daily stress.

Dan and I had talked in secret over the phone about Ginny's engagement ring. I couldn't wait to see it!

DEREK

I couldn't believe we had to leave for Lewes on Sunday morning. Christmas was not until Wednesday. I had just landed several big accounts. I needed to hire more staff to handle the workload. Until I got that done, I would be working late every night just to stay afloat. Our Christmas jobs were done and out. However, we had one big project that had to be out and invoiced before the New Year, and we were cutting it close.

To the contrary, Susan was so excited. She wanted to leave on Saturday. So, we compromised on Sunday. She had already started packing. I think she was working on her second suitcase by the time we had discussed it. She said we needed to pack layers because the beach house was drafty. I knew that, and as I suspected, Dan had done nothing to upgrade the heating system or add insulation. Honestly, that old house should have been torn down and rebuilt before Dad moved in. I couldn't imagine how Dan was going to keep it inhabitable much longer. He was such a misguided dreamer.

DYLAN

Though it was the busiest time of year for me, I thought it would be nice to get away for a few days and spend time with everyone. I had worked through several nights and days to get all the orders shipped out in time. I had a substantial increase in requests for rocking horses that season. They came in three sizes. That year, everyone wanted the smallest size. I guess there was an increase in toddlers? That was good for me. If Lily had been born, I would have made a very special one for her. I thought about Ginny and Dan every day. I was surprised by how much losing Lily had affected even me. I was getting excited about becoming an uncle and having a little one to spoil. I had often thought of calling them to see how they were coping, but I was never quite sure what I would say. I was reasonably certain that Susan, my sister-in-law, had picked up my slack and had stayed in touch.

Ginny said to dress warm because the house was drafty. I told her I would be right at home. (It was weird saying that to her, because it was my dad's home, which meant that at one point, technically, it was my home, too.) Anyway, I was used to working in the barn all day, and half the night, so I knew I would be OK.

I enjoyed making presents for everyone, but what I detested was wrapping them. So, I figured I would take care of that once I got down there. That way the trip in the back of my truck would not destroy all of my portentous giftwrapping. (I am being sarcastic, of course!)

GINNY

Everyone from the Carter family arrived on
Sunday. Dylan was first. He was here in time for lunch, but
first he insisted on unloading the truck, and we were not
allowed to help. To top it off, we had to hide our eyes while
he made five trips up the stairs and back down. Five. I
counted them.

When Dylan finally sat down, it was good to catch up
with him. He congratulated us on our engagement and told
Dan he would be down every weekend, if needed, to get the
house ready for the big day. He and Dan were making a
fuss about the deck. I didn't get the big deal, but if they
wanted to work on it, that was fine by me.

Derek and Susan showed up after lunch, but in time for
football. Not NCAA or NFL football. We were talking about
the infamous CFFL, Carter Family Football League. After
they got their things moved in upstairs, we all decided we
were in need of some exercise and fresh air. Dylan
inserted, "I've got a football in the truck."

So, there we were, the five of us, once again. Except this
time, instead of looking at death, we were trying to kill each
other. First Dylan called boys against girls. Susan and I
said that was fine, but they would have to play down a
man. So, Derek and Dylan said they would team up and
take on Dan, Susan, and me. One may have thought that
was unfair and that each team should take a girl, but Susan
and I were not wimps. Did I mention the only football the
Carter boys played was tackle? They won the toss—a
clamshell—and elected to kick off to us. We had an
offensive strategy. I pretended to fumble the ball while Dan
and Ginny blocked the other two, giving me space to run. I
found the hole. Dan held Derek back. Dylan picked up
Susan, hoisted her over his shoulder, and started running
after me. All three of us collided in a heap. Dylan jumped
up, performed his signature celebration dance, and then

called a time out. He needed a victory beer, and did anyone else want one?

We waited outside while Dylan went back to the house to retrieve a round of beers. I think that was the first time the five of us had had a beer together in a year. It felt good to clink the necks of the bottles together, which sounded extra bright, perhaps because of the cold, or perhaps because I had not had a beer since I knew I was pregnant. For a moment, I felt sad and guilty, as if I didn't have the right to drink a beer. Susan and Dan snapped me out of it and pulled me back into the huddle.

Our team scored on the next play. Dylan said we needed to stay hydrated.

How did this become a drinking game, and who let Dylan make up the rules?

It was on. Dan came up with our defensive strategy. He said he would take on their quarterback and that Susan and I should double-team the other guy. That meant it was highly likely that Susan and I would be doing all the tackling. Dylan hiked the ball to Derek and then took off running down the beach. Dylan was running with his second beer in his hand. Susan and I came at him from both sides. Susan, being taller and longer than me, reached out and grabbed Dylan's arm. The beer flew out of his hands. Amazingly, I caught it and ran.

"Interception! Run, Ginny, run!" I could hear Dan and Susan yelling over the sound of the waves. It was all about the beer.

Stumbling through the sand at a high rate of speed, I ran as hard as I could. "Touchdown!" Knowing that Dylan was a Penn State alum, I started singing the Ohio State fight song.

That'll show him!

As I was creating my own signature victory dance, Dylan came running at me to either stop my singing or retrieve his beer, or both. As he approached me, I spiked his beer into the sand, neck down, draining out whatever was left. Derek called foul and charged me with excessive celebration. Dan scooped me up and carried me on his shoulders as we danced with Susan around Dylan's spiked and emptying bottle of beer. Unbeknownst to us, Dylan plundered our beers and ran off.

We got a couple more plays in before calling halftime. After all the beer we had consumed, we needed a pee break. Without saying anything, and as if they had practiced it a million times, the guys lined up at the water's edge, unzipped, pulled it out, and peed away. I wished I'd had a camera to capture the moment. Susan and I ran to the house to remedy the matter properly and try to warm up a bit.

After the halftime show, the game continued. We would have gotten four quarters in and we would have kicked their butts, except Dan and Derek ended up in the water. For a show of solidarity, Dylan ran in after them. Soaking wet and freezing cold, the game was called.

The guys headed for hot showers. Derek took the indoor shower upstairs while Dylan took the one outside. In the meantime, Dan stripped off his wet clothes and waited. Shivering with a towel wrapped around his waist, he paced the kitchen floor. Any girl would have been in heaven to be around all of those half naked Carter boys. When Dylan finished, he came running in. Now we had two exposed six packs in the kitchen. With steam rising like a thick fog from his Adonis body, Dylan looked like he was on fire. Dan disappeared into the outside shower as Dylan ran up the stairs to dress. If no one else had been around, I would have joined Dan in that hot shower, indoors or out.

Tired and worn out from all the cold, fresh salt air, we decided to eat out. It took some time, but we were all finally dressed and assembled in the living room. The feeling was beginning to return to our fingers and toes. Derek drove us to Irish Eyes.

There was a good crowd that evening. We were seated at a long table that ran perpendicular to the window. We had a great view of the canal. The waitress took our drink order and we looked over the specials when Dan spotted Dex at the bar. Not only that, it looked like Dex was with a date.

"Hey guys, isn't that Dex Lassiter?"

"Is he with that attorney?" Dylan whispered scandalously across the table, being the second one to notice.

To avoid drawing attention, Derek slowly turned his head.

"Oh. My. God. What is he doing here? I didn't think he would ever come back to this place. He's got a lot of nerve," Derek commented.

I wondered about the brief history Dan had given me. Dylan and Dan gave Derek a scowl that said, "*Ease up.*"

"Don't give me that look. He probably hired that attorney to get him out of his latest mess," Derek spouted, justifying his indignation.

Dan and Dylan got up to say hello. Derek waved them off, electing not to move.

I watched them out of the corner of my eye. Dylan and Dex did the old back slap and handshake that men do.

"Dex, it's been years," Dylan spoke first. "Ms. Sable, good to see you again."

"Courtney, please," she said, redirecting him.

Dex shook their hands and so did Courtney.

"How are you guys making out?" Courtney asked.

"Everything seems to be settling in. Thanks for asking," Dan responded.

"Is your older brother with you?" she asked.

"Yeah, he's over there at our table with Ginny and Susan. Please, come over and meet everyone," Dan said, politely extending an invitation.

Dex and Courtney grabbed their drinks off the bar. Courtney threw her small purse over her shoulder, and then they followed Dan and Dylan back to our table. As they approached, all eyes were on them. They made a handsome couple. Dex was tall and tan. His sandy brown hair was naturally highlighted and on the wild side. I imagined his intoxicating smile would certainly challenge a lady's proper upbringing. With his broad shoulders and his shirt tucked into the slim waistline of his jeans, that man was very handsome in a very rugged sort of way. Perhaps it was the location and time of day, whatever, Dex was exuding an enormous amount of sex appeal that I had not noticed before. It was hard to believe he was still single.

Perhaps, he's a player.

Unlike Dex, Courtney was polished and walked with an air of sophistication. She had beautiful straight, thick brunette hair that reached half way down her back. Like her healthy hair, her skin was radiant. Her big eyes were a soft sky blue. She was wearing a tight sweater that accentuated her endowments. Her pencil skirt showed off her slim figure and long legs. The parts and the sum of her added up to a very sensual look. What was my first impression? She was the type of girl the rest of us love to hate.

"Derek, you remember Dex?" Dan asked.

"Of course. It's been a long time," Derek answered as he stood and half-heartedly shook Dex's hand.

"And, Ms. Sable . . . uh, Courtney?" Dan continued.

"Ah yes. Who could forget? Nice to see you again, Ms. Sable." Derek accentuated the Mzzzzzz with a smirk on his face. I could sense a jab in there.

"Dex and Courtney, this is Derek's lovely wife, Susan, and my fiancé, Ginny."

"Nice to see you again, Ginny." Dex remembered me, making me blush. I felt off-balance.

The "nice-to-meet-you's" and handshakes went around the table. For the first time, I wished I could have flashed an engagement ring. I had an uneasy feeling about Courtney. It seemed to me that she could become a force to be reckoned with.

Dan, being the gentleman that he was, invited them to join us for dinner, and much to our surprise, they looked at each other and accepted his offer. Dan and Dylan found two more chairs and pulled them up. The conversation began with Dan politely suggesting that Dex and Courtney made a nice couple. They both laughed.

"Nope, been there, done that," Dex said, raising his hands in surrender, making the correction swift.

He is a player. My intuition has not failed me.

"We tried dating, but it was too much like kissing my brother," Courtney added.

By his body language, I could tell her comment took Derek back.

"Yeah, we'd rather punch each other in the arm or give a shove rather than cross first base," Dex explained. He winked at Courtney.

"So, Dylan, are you seeing anyone or are you the last Carter hold-out?" Courtney asked, rather bluntly.

"Yep, I'm the hold-out. I figure I'll hang loose for a while and learn from their mistakes," he said, implicating his brothers, and us.

Susan and I protested, claiming that Derek and Dan could not have done better. Though he didn't know us, Dex agreed.

Our orders were taken, and Dan requested a second round of drinks.

"I guess we should have designated a driver, we have so far to go," Dylan cautioned sarcastically.

"Not to worry," Dex assured us. "We have a counselor here who's a great defense attorney and knows her way around this town and its legal network."

"Obviously," Derek remarked. We were not quite sure whether he was trying to be humorous or insulting. Either way, he was out of line.

Something had his boxers in a bunch. Susan later explained that Derek had a lot on his mind with work and all. Dan later confided that he was sure it was something else.

Courtney asked what brought us all back to town. I explained that we were hosting the Carter Family Christmas in Lewes. I mentioned that Dex had been invited. Dex immediately reconfirmed that he would be there. Derek's eyebrows furled and shot Dan a look that expressed strong disapproval.

"Courtney, if you don't have plans, you're more than welcomed to join us."

What was I thinking? I had just invited the alleged shark to our family Christmas. Plus, I invited her without asking Dan, first. There had to be some logical explanation for my impulsiveness. We were all getting along so well, with the exception of Derek. I guess I thought it might make Dex more comfortable if Courtney were there, too?

"Thanks so much for the invitation, but I'm having dinner with my parents. Maybe I'll stop by for dessert or a nightcap, if that's all right?"

We all agreed that was a good plan, with the exception of Derek, once again. I was hoping his protests were not as obvious to Courtney and Dex as they were to me. However, if they were, it didn't seem to faze them. Later, I learned that our now expanded guest list would have kept Derek home had he known before accepting our invitation.

"I have to warn all of you. Dan over here, being the respectful man that he is, invited my parents for Christmas," I interjected.

Susan and I kept few secrets from each other. So she knew full well what the implications were, and gasped.

Dylan cordially said, "Oh, that's nice, we'll get to meet them."

Derek could not have cared less. The holiday was already a bust for him.

Being the perceptive one, Courtney asked, "I take it this is going to create some stress in the house?"

When the evening was over, we stood outside the restaurant and exchanged our goodbyes and added our "it-was–so-nice-to-meet-you's," again. Derek drove us back to the house. I have no idea what happened to Dex and Courtney after that, nor did I care. Admittedly, though, I was curious about them. I wasn't convinced that Derek was OK to drive, either, but it was only a few blocks. Obviously, alcohol was clouding my better judgment. We were piled into Derek's tank of an SUV, the Explorer. It gave him back his need for control, something he had lost earlier that evening and guessed was important to him. It was a quiet ride back.

There was a lot of yawning and stretching when we were back inside the house. We quietly hung up our coats and slowly branched off to our rooms for the night, but not before Susan tapped me on the shoulder and whispered, "See you on the deck in half an hour."

"Are you crazy? We'll freeze out there!"

"Come on, it won't be much colder than it is in here!"

Sarcastic humor is usually full of truth. We were going to need a lot of veiled sarcasm in the next few days.

After slipping into my PJs, I kissed Dan on the cheek to let him know that I was going downstairs to have some girl-time. I think he appreciated that I had an almost sister-in-law like Susan to talk to. Susan, on the other hand, waited for Derek to fall asleep. It didn't take long, thank God. She sneaked out from under the covers, wrapped a spare blanket around her body, and tiptoed downstairs to the kitchen.

"You know what this house needs? A fireplace," she said as I handed her a hot chocolate I had made while waiting for her.

The thing is, Susan and I didn't use those powdered hot chocolate mixes. We went for the real thing, and it had to be made with whole milk and Hershey's chocolate syrup. Marshmallows were optional and, at times, used for ammunition.

Wrapped in blankets, we made ourselves comfortable on the sofas, knowing that going out on the deck would be hypothermic suicide.

"So how do you guys like living down here?" Susan asked as she blew across her mug and took a cautious sip.

"It's a little too early to tell, this being our first winter and all. It's a different kind of cold, and I don't think this house was built for winter habitation," I replied as I pulled my blanket tighter around me, making sure every square inch of my body was covered, including my toes. I continued my thought. "It's a little lonely at times, too. I haven't made many friends. I'm hoping that will change soon."

"That must be hard."

"Yeah.... How are you guys doing?"

"We're doing OK. Derek's business has taken off. He's putting in a lot of hours, though. He leaves early in the morning and doesn't get home until somewhere between nine and ten at night. So, it can get pretty lonely at times. Most nights, I eat dinner by myself. Occasionally, Derek works past ten o'clock, and on those nights, I go to bed without him. Even though we are sleeping under the same roof, I can actually go thirty-six to forty-eight hours without seeing him. Not exactly what I signed up for when I said, 'I do.' He says once he gets some help hired and trained, he'll be able to cut back. I do miss him, though."

DYLAN

On Monday, I decided I had better get serious about wrapping my gifts. The next day was Christmas Eve, and I didn't want to be out there with all the crazies. So, I went to the Rite Aid in Lewes to look for wrapping paper and tape. That pharmacy had probably been there since the first Dutch settlement in Lewes, in 1631. It had pretty much everything you would expect to find in a pharmacy and some touristy stuff, too. And who did I bump into?

"Hey, Courtney!"

"Hi, Dylan, what are you doing in the Rite Aid? Family

giving you a headache so soon?"

"No, not yet. But on that note, I'd better pick up some Tylenol, too."

"Oh, you don't like Christmas much, do you?"

"God, no. I love Christmas!"

"Oh . . . then you don't like gift giving?"

"No, I enjoy gift giving. What I detest is giftwrapping. It's environmentally unfriendly and a waste of time. It will take me hours to wrap everything, and it will all be ripped off within seconds. It's just too much unnecessary work and waste."

"How bad can it be? You wrap the paper around the box, tuck down the corners, add a little tape, and put a stick 'em bow on it. If that doesn't work, throw it in a gift bag. And, if you're really worried about the environment, reuse it next year."

"I wish it were that simple. I made all of my gifts, and they don't fit into boxes or gift bags."

"Wow. That's impressive. Most kids I know stopped making gifts when they reached middle school."

She was tough, and she had a real edge to her. As much as I found it annoying, her wit was equally attractive.

"Laugh all you want. My work is one of a kind, only the best of the best."

Her ears perked up, and her eyes were scrutinizing me. I had her attention.

"What kind of work do you do?"

"Woodworking."

"Like custom woodwork? Like I should call you if I need custom cabinets?"

"Yes, you should. But you'll have to pay for my travel time and expenses."

"Are you any good?"

Wow, does she always put people on the defense? It comes so naturally to her.

"Visit my website. You'll see some of the work I've done."

I pulled a business card from my wallet and handed it to her.

"Yes, maybe I'll do that. Good luck with your wrapping. You must be good with your hands, so I'm sure you'll figure it out. A little tape here and a pair of scissors there . . ."

"Yeah," I said not realizing how much of a heavy sigh I had made until it was out.

"Dylan, listen. I'm an expert when it comes to giftwrapping. Would you like some help?"

"You wouldn't mind? I mean, this close to Christmas? I'm sure you have a lot to do."

"No, I'd be happy to help. Besides, I'd like to see your work."

"Wow, I could really use the help. Would you mind coming to the house? I'm only moving this stuff one more time and that's down to the tree."

"Sure. When would you like to do this?"

"Do you have plans tonight?"

"Oh, my Monday evenings are almost always completely booked," she said laced with sarcasm, which would have been obvious to most people, but I had been rendered unarmed, again.

"Oh, I see. How about Tuesday morning?" I responded, still not realizing that I had taken the bait.

Courtney chuckled, confirming that I was easy prey.

"What time should I stop by tonight?"

"Oh, hey, that would be great. How about 7:00?"

"I'll see you then," she called out as she walked past me, waving over her shoulder.

Oh. My. God. My heart was racing. I really didn't know her, but she sure was intriguing. Who would have guessed that a high-powered woman like her would volunteer for wrapping gifts with a guy like me? She was the type I could picture at the Christiana Mall, outside of Macy's, at one of those wrapping stations, waiting to have all her gifts wrapped by a girl scout or someone like that. Or maybe, during the holidays, she volunteered her time to wrap gifts in one of those stations, in return for a donation to her favorite charity. You know, it's good for public relations because it's the right thing to do.

Great. She thinks I'm a charity case. That's it. She feels sorry for me.

While I was out, Derek and Susan decided they would provide the evening meal. They never disappointed. Derek grilled Cilantro Lime Salmon. Susan made Junky Salad, as she called it. It was made with romaine as the base, and then she added everything she could think of: tomatoes, sweet peas, cucumber, celery, water chestnuts, yellow peppers, carrots, mandarin oranges, dried cranberries, bacon bits (she actually fried up extra crispy bacon), shredded parmesan, and topped it off with a sweet strawberry blush wine dressing. The beverage? Margaritas, straight up.

As we sat around the table, there was complete silence except for the occasional "Hmmmm" and "Ahhhhh." It was synonymous with the moaning and groaning of ecstasy. I waited until then to announce to everyone that Courtney was stopping by that night to help me wrap my Christmas gifts. Ginny stopped chewing and looked at me with her head down and eyes up. She didn't look angry, just surprised and somewhat overwhelmed.

"Dylan, why didn't you tell me? The kitchen is a mess. We've left stuff all over the place."

"Ginny, that's why I didn't tell you. You don't need to worry about any of that. And besides, it just sort of happened. I bumped into her at Rite Aid today, and I mentioned that I had gifts to wrap. I told her I was challenged when it came to that sort of thing, and she took pity on me."

"I'm sure she couldn't resist your charming sad face."

Courtney was right on time, 7:00 on the dot. She had on a pair of skinny jeans, and a pale blue cashmere sweater that accentuated her baby blue eyes and her other attractive features. She wore an awesome pair of leather boots that made her already sculpted long legs look even longer. She left me feeling like a hopeless schoolboy. Somewhere between the soft soothing look of cashmere, the body that filled it, and the high profile of fitted polished leather, I felt a full court press coming on.

After escorting her into the living room to be greeted by everyone, she said, "Take me to the kitchen and I'll show you the first good practice of gift wrapping." She was carrying a large shopping bag that I had failed to notice due to all of her other distractions. The way she took control was kind of a turn on, too.

I obediently showed Courtney into the kitchen. She set the bag on the counter.

"Nice place you've got here, I like it."

"It's not mine, remember? You were there," I said with a scolding grin on my face.

"Oh, yeah," she replied sarcastically. Again, I had to believe she knew what she was doing.

Seeing it through her eyes, I had to admit the place really did have a lot of charm. The kitchen was one large open rectangle that absorbed much of the Bay Avenue side of the house. The floor was old random width oak. It had many scars from burns and spills that added to its character. The cabinets were oak as well. The double porcelain sink was marred with nicks and chips. Each scar had its own story connected to a generation that had vacationed there. The stove was the one originally installed when the house was first built. It was a Roper and a relic at that. The refrigerator was an old Frigidaire. Its corners were rounded and its long door handle worked by pulling down on its lever. It took some getting used to. There was no icemaker, so we kept the freezer full of ice trays. It was probably the least energy efficient appliance remaining on the planet. Tucked away in a corner, the washer and dryer were off to one side of the kitchen. Thank goodness they were a little newer. Luckily, Dan and Ginny had purchased an automatic drip coffeemaker; otherwise, the house would have been full of cranky people.

Courtney set the bag on the counter and pulled out two half gallons of Wawa Egg Nog, a bottle of Pusser's dark rum, and nutmeg. I knew then that I could fall in love with her! Hell, I could have made love to her right then and there on the kitchen floor. Well, not really. First, I was not some horny bastard looking for an easy lay. Second, I doubted very much that there was anything easy about Courtney. Third, I was sure my urges were that of any healthy American boy, but I had to keep them in check. And fourth, I estimated that she was about the same age as Derek or Dex. And fifth, well let's just say she would never be interested in someone like me. I was so out of her league.

"The first thing to know about wrapping gifts," she stated, "is to never attempt it without liquid refreshment, especially during the holidays. You know, things always go better with . . . fill in the blank," she teased. It was hard to believe that I was in that kitchen with the same person I had met at Sable & Sable; the one with those long legs and alluring figure; the one with quick wit and seemed to hold the world on a string; the one that almost ate Derek for lunch. She so confused me. I was almost afraid to be alone with her. She could have done anything she wanted to do with me right then, and in many ways, I wished that she would before the night was over.

We slowly heated up the eggnog, added the rum, ladled the concoction into six mugs, and sprinkled nutmeg on top. Courtney said that Christmas was about the spirit of giving. I thanked her for her generosity, secretly thinking of all the things she could give me that I would have been happy to accept. We carried the tray out to the living room where everyone was pretending to read or work on a crossword puzzle. "It's a Wonderful Life" was on as background noise. It was probably released about the same time the beach house was built. We handed out the eggnogs. Everyone raved and thanked Courtney profusely for her thoughtfulness.

Who are these people?

With the refreshments distributed, Courtney asked, "So where are these presents we need to wrap?"

"Upstairs," I answered sheepishly.

With that, Dan blew eggnog out of his nose. His body convulsed several times as he covered his mouth and nose with his hand, pretending he had inhaled powdered nutmeg. Once he knew he was not going to spew, he removed his hand and took a deep breath.

Derek stared in disbelief, like I was about to sleep with the enemy, literally.

Courtney took it all in stride.

Dan recovered and waved us off with a "you go" grin on his face.

"Come on, Courtney, I'll show you upstairs."

Courtney, unaffected by my moronic brothers, followed me up the stairs.

I opened the door to my bedroom, which was my father's room, and let her in first. I shut the door behind us. Her jaw dropped as she stood and stared.

I had made Derek, Susan, Dan, and Ginny each a rocking chair. I personally selected every piece of oak used. Each chair boasted its own unique design. Each spindle design for each chair was different. I had hand carved the scrolls on the top of the chair backs, arms, and runners. The grain on the seat ran straight from front to back. I stained and coated the chairs to bring out the rich wood grain.

"Dylan, these are beautiful. Where did you learn to do this?

"My dad had a woodshop where we lived in Pennsylvania. He allowed me to watch him work, and I gradually picked it up from him. When I didn't find a job right out of college, I used woodworking as a way to alleviate the stress of being unemployed."

"Wow, this must have taken a lot of time."

"It's what I like to do, and it pays the bills. Like I said, check out my website."

"I will," she said as she walked past each chair,

seductively fondling the wood. Well, anything she did that night appeared seductive and flirtatious to me.

"OK, this wrapping business is going to be much tougher than I thought," she confessed. "If it were I, here's what I would do. I would purchase four uniquely handcrafted bows and tie one onto each chair. I'd make sure the bow is about thirty-six inches wide so it covers most of the chair seat and back. On Christmas Eve, I would wait until everyone was asleep and then sneak the chairs and their attached bows downstairs. Mission accomplished."

All I could think of was her sitting in one of my chairs on Christmas morning. I shook my head to snap out of it. She saw me.

"You don't like my idea?"

"No. . . . I mean, I really do. It's a great idea. But where would I find bows like that?"

"Well, lucky for you, I know a florist outside of town, and I'm sure I could convince her to make four bows for you for a good price. Let's take a picture of these chairs to show her." She pulled out her cell phone to snap a picture.

"Dylan, stand over there so I can give her some perspective on how big these chairs really are."

I walked over and knelt down between two of the chairs.

"Smile!" she commanded and then snapped the shutter. She looked at the picture.

"This is really good." She turned the phone so I could see for myself. *Not bad.*

"OK, now take one of me with *your* phone." She walked over to the chairs. "May I?" she asked, wanting to sit in one of them.

"Of course!"

She sat down and allowed my work to embrace her. In that moment, I would not have minded being that chair. As she crossed her legs, she leaned forward and propped one elbow on her knee and rested her chin in her hand. Her long hair fell forward across her shoulders. Her sweater showed off her heavenly curves. Its V-neck permitted an innocent view of her porcelain skin that formed her soft round cleavage and beautiful neckline. She smiled a dizzying smile and looked right at me as if I were solely responsible for her happiness in that moment. I loved those chairs, and every ounce of sweat was worth it.

I snapped the picture. It was, as I thought it would be, right from the cover of a magazine. I showed her, and she approved.

Before I even gave thought to what I was about to say, the words flew from my mouth.

"Can I have your phone number . . . ? Uh . . . in case I have to call you, tomorrow, so you can help me find this florist."

Good catch.

We exchanged numbers. When she left, I added her picture to her file card in my "Contacts" so it would come up if and when she ever called me.

With the non-giftwrapping decision made. I sat down in the chair next to hers. We struck up a comfortable conversation while we sipped our eggnogs.

We shared our family Christmas traditions and other things. For example, she had lived in Lewes all her life. Her father was the first half of Sable & Sable. She had two sisters. One was a pediatrician, and the other was a dentist. So, she explained, they had two doctors and two lawyers in the family. She said there was a bad joke in there, somewhere. However, none of the girls lived at home at the time. Courtney, it turned out, had a townhouse at Five Points, which is located off Route 1 at the Lewes cut-off. She said it was a small three-story unit with three bedrooms and a loft, adding that it was just right for her.

I told her about Unionville and all the charms of Southern Chester County. She said she had never been to Longwood Gardens, but had heard that it was a very nice place to visit any time of year. She asked if I lived near Winterthur, another sprawling du Pont estate featuring a museum, gardens, and library. Her father had taken her and her sisters there many years ago for a point-to-point steeplechase and tour. I explained that though it's in Delaware, it's within miles of where I grew up. I shared how we would do our shopping in Delaware to avoid Pennsylvania sales tax. My brothers and I would buy our alcohol over the border, drive around for a while, and then bring it back across the Pennsylvania state line, making sure we had not been followed.

I told her how Derek, Dan, and I would spend our summers in Lewes and how Dad eventually bought the house. Although, somehow, I think she already knew that part. I told her how Derek and Dex were close in age and how Dex would hang out with us even though he was a local. I told her the story of how we met Dex at a beach volleyball pick-up game. He had joined our team as the fourth man and together we kicked butt. Then Dex told us about the tournaments at the Rusty Rudder in Dewey. We entered the following year, and the four of us kicked butt there, too. What I did not share with her was how, after the tournament, a group of girls challenged us to the best of three. They sent us away licking our wounds. Then they invited us back to their place where ... let's just say ... they stroked our egos. It was a night we would never forget, but we had made a pact to never talk about it. I think Dex and Derek made several pacts during that formative summer.

I asked Courtney how she knew Dex.

"Well, that's an interesting story ..."

Right then, there was a knock on the door. Dan quietly pushed it open, as you would if you were afraid of walking in on your parents. He could be such a lovable moron, sometimes. He whispered like he might wake us up.

"Hey, guys. We're all turning in for the night. Make sure you lock the door ... you know, the back door, downstairs . ... I didn't mean this door ... uh ... well, you could lock this door ... uh ... never mind."

That boy sure could trip all over himself. When he closed the door, I realized he had just seen the chairs. However, I wasn't sure if he even noticed or had his eyes opened. I chuckled and shook my head. Courtney's reaction was the same.

"I guess I'd better go. Sounds like tomorrow is going to be a big day for the Carter family."

Courtney rose from her chair and I followed her, opening the door that Dan had so carefully closed moments earlier. As she walked past me, it was the closest she had been to me physically. I felt a surge through my body, even though she had not touched me. It was as though I could feel her moving and breathing against me, for just a flash. It was all rather arousing.

Downstairs, as she was putting on her coat, I asked if she was going to be OK driving home. She assured me that she would be fine.

"Don't forget your eggnog and rum."

"You hold on to it. I think you're going to need it."

"Hmmm, probably right. About the bows, where is this florist?"

"Tell you what, I'll come by in the morning, pick you up, and take you there. What time should I be here?"

She had caught me off guard. I couldn't instantly recall what the plans were for the next day.

"Well, what time can you be here?"

"Her shop opens at 9:00. So I'll pick you up at 9:00 sharp."

"That'll be great. I'll have the coffee on. How do you drink it?"

"Strong and straight up. I like everything strong and straight up."

Does she intentionally say those things?

I watched her get into her car, back out, and slowly make her way up Bay Avenue. My eyes followed her car until the taillights disappeared. I honestly don't know which was more thrilling: the woman, or her car. Courtney was driving a white Porsche Boxster S. I told myself that her car was much more appealing; however, the truth was that I found her nearly irresistible. I was really looking forward to the next morning.

I wanted to go upstairs and climb into bed, but Courtney had me all fired up. I locked the kitchen door just as Dan had asked me to, turned out the lights, walked through the living room, and went out onto the deck. I was hoping the December night air and gentle lap of the water would calm me down. I wanted to get my head back on straight.

OK, Dylan, get a grip. First of all, she's way out of your league. Secondly, she's much older than you. And how about she's Dex's best friend, like a sister and all, and we all know what Dex is capable of.

I stood there a while longer and soon realized that my meditation wasn't helping me. In fact, it was only making matters worse. As I looked down the beach, I wondered what it would be like to be with Courtney, there, on a warm summer's moonlit night. My thoughts drifted toward the inappropriate, so I turned to leave the deck and my roaming fantasies.

Inside, I ran into Ginny and Susan. I should've known I would run into those two. They were standing in the living room, in their pajamas, and wrapped in blankets.

"Hey, Dylan. Where's Courtney?" Ginny asked.

"Yeah, we went through all the trouble of sneaking past your bedroom door and here you are down here, alone," Susan followed up.

"She went home."

"She seems pretty nice," Susan suggested. "I mean she did come bearing gifts, and that eggnog really hit the spot."

"Good. I'm glad you liked it. She left the rest of it here, thinking we might need it tomorrow. No offense, Ginny."

"None taken. I have to confess that I'm not looking forward to tomorrow, either. Truth be known, I was really peeved with Dan for inviting my parents. Now there's no getting out of it. He's upstairs sleeping like a baby, and I probably won't get any sleep until they leave on Thursday. You guys will have my back, won't you?"

"Sure, little sister." And with that, I gave her a hug. It

kind of took me by surprise, too. Looking back, I think spending time around Courtney made me all touchy feely. Not that Courtney was that way. Maybe it was because Courtney was the one I wanted to touch, but I knew better. I had vague memories of my mother telling me to grow up to be a good respectable man like my father.

"Well, I'd better turn in," I announced with hopes of making a clean escape.

"Whoa, not so fast, Casanova. You can't crash our pajama party and not give us the details." They both had their hands on my chest so I couldn't move forward.

"Wait a minute, you're the ones that crashed my moment of solitude. The only one I may get for the next forty-eight hours. No offense, Ginny."

"Again, none taken."

Susan jumped in. "Sorry, it doesn't work that way. We're here and you're here, so now you have to spill it."

It was a losing battle, so I finally relented to save us all time. I sat down on one of the living room sofas. Ginny and Susan climbed into the opposite one and stared at me like two journalists who were about to get an exclusive on some breaking news story that would impact the course of western civilization. My life would have been easier that night if they had been more like Barbara Walters and just eased the tough stuff out of me, like squeezing a new tube of toothpaste.

"OK, what do you want to know?"

"So, did you really wrap gifts, cause I didn't hear any wrapping paper?" Susan asked accusingly.

"What, were you listening in on us?"

"No, not really. But you know how thin these walls are. The question stills stands. Did you or did you not wrap any presents?"

"Now you sound like Courtney."

"Just answer the question."

They were having a good time at my expense. I don't know if it was the late hour or that it never took much to get those two started.

"No, we didn't do any gift wrapping. We were . . ."

"I knew it!" Susan stood and shouted, pointing a finger at me.

"SHHHHH! You'll wake the whole house, and nothing happened. We came up with a different plan."

"Ahhhhh . . ." Ginny mused, looking at Susan as if they were about to crack the case of the century. "So you came up with a better plan behind closed doors!" she continued with an insinuating tone to her voice.

I couldn't imagine for the life of me how my two brothers dealt with those two when they started.

"OK, if I tell you what happened, do you promise not to tell Derek or Dan?" I knew that would get them. I have never been married, but I knew when someone asked you to keep something from your spouse, it meant that it was big. They leaned forward, and you could hear a pin drop.

"I'm not exactly sure how it happened. Maybe it was the eggnog. Maybe it was my look of desperation." I demonstrated my "desperate face" for them. They snickered. Perched and sipping their hot chocolates with rapt attention, I continued. "Maybe because we were in my bedroom, alone, with the door shut. You couldn't hear anything, could you? Why do women always have to be so loud? I know, she just couldn't help herself, but she was out of control. I'm sorry you if heard any of that. It's not my usual treatment, but she likes to play rough and by her own rules. Which kind of rubbed me the wrong way, but not really . . . if you know what I mean. There were more than just a couple of sugarplum fairies dancing on my head . . ." I paused as if I was reliving a life-defining moment before concluding with: "She can wrap my gift anytime she wants to." I gave them a cad's wink.

Silence . . . and then they squealed with laughter.

Ginny was hunched over with tears forming in her eyes. She was trying to catch her breath.

"Dylan, you did not . . . you did not just say that!" Susan reprimanded, slapping my arm.

Dan, awakened out of a sound sleep to the screams of his fiancée and the bite of a slap, bolted down the steps. I swear he skipped two-thirds of them. He saw Ginny hunched over, and it looked as though Susan was leaning over her. I stayed in my chair and shrugged my shoulders.

"Ginny, baby, are you OK? What happened? Is she OK?" Dan pleaded.

With an "I-Don't-Know" look on my face, I shrugged my shoulders again, drawing him into the scheme that was spontaneously unfolding. Susan could not look at Dan for fear she wouldn't be able to contain herself, so she kept her head down.

Now, Ginny was pretty quick on the draw and loved a good prank as much as the next person, but I couldn't believe what she did next. She went completely limp with her limbs extended as though she had just bit the big one.

"OH, MY GOD! GINNY, DON'T DO THIS!" Dan leaned in to check if she was breathing. Derek, who had properly put on his robe, came down the stairs to see what all of the commotion was about.

"Dan, is she all right?" he asked, standing on the bottom step tying the belt around his waist.

Dan put his ear to her nose and mouth to see if she was breathing. As soon as he pulled back, Ginny stuck out her tongue. Every muscle in Dan's face tightened. He knew he had been had.

"You scared the living daylights out of me, don't ever do that again! "

He was mad. The fact that the rest of us were laughing didn't help, either. Dan looked around from face to face and scolded each one of us with his livid blues.

"Ginny, what if the next time you *are* really hurt. How will I know?"

"Because the next time, if I'm really hurt, I won't kiss you like this." Ginny wrapped her hands around Dan's neck and locked them up.

"Ughhh, Yuuuuck. Get a room!" we all responded in unison, every one of us clearly jealous that we were not in a relationship like theirs. Those two really were like teenagers.

I stood up.

"I'm going to bed. I have a date in the morning. Don't forget to lock your doors. . . ."

COURTNEY

I was up before my alarm, which was unusual for me on a day off, especially considering that I'd had a restless night. Dylan said he would have coffee ready for us, so I was going to take him at his word. After combing out my hair and taking a closer look at my eyes and complexion in the mirror, I turned on the hot water.

I don't know why I felt so compelled to exam myself in the mirror each morning. It wasn't as though I expected something miraculous—or alarming—to happen overnight.

At the time, it wasn't the aging thing that concerned me. I was almost twenty-seven, so I had a lot of good years left. Yet, I took a close look as if performing triage on my skin, face, hair, and figure, something akin to a full body scan. That morning, I turned sideways and checked the profile of my naked body in the full-length mirror.

Flat stomach, shoulders back—still firm and perky—it all looks good.

With the shower starting to create some steam on the mirror, I stepped in. That morning, I decided on strawberry shampoo, cream rinse, and body wash. Something sweet and fresh to brighten up a winter's day. My bathroom had a skylight that let in the bright warm rays of the sun. During the summer, when it was too hot, I would pull the shade across it. That day, for a little added vigor, I opened the skylight to let some of the cold morning air fall on my wet hair and over my shoulders. The steam started swirling and disappeared as the cold air invaded the space. Finished and completely refreshed, I turned off the water, and even though there was no one there to see me, I wrapped a towel around my torso. There never was anyone there to see me.

I stepped into my dressing room.

Hmmm ... What to wear on Christmas Eve?

I opted for a pair of jeans (my day-off favorite) and a very loose fisherman's sweater that was the color of oatmeal. Its sleeves were long and fell to my fingertips. The bottom of the sweater reached mid-thigh, just covering my bums. I stepped back. It was very comfy. However, I thought a pair of leggings would set it off better than my jeans. So, I changed. I added a pair of Earthie's Seriph ankle high boots with soft socks that peeked out over the top. It took someone tall and thin to pull it off. I turned side to side and looked in the full-length mirror in my dressing room.

Yep, I've got this covered!

I added a little mascara, a touch of blush, a swatch of lipstick, and headed for the door. I wrapped a red and green scarf around my neck and grabbed a pair of mittens that actually matched my socks and sweater. I reached into the hall closet and removed my leather bomber jacket from its hanger, just in case I needed it. I was out the door when a wave of butterflies hit my stomach. I was actually off to spend the morning with the most handsome and charming young man I had ever met.

Because of our age difference and Dex's connection, all that complicated stuff, I knew nothing could come of my attraction to Dylan, but for some unknown reason, that guy really excited me. I wished I were a couple of years younger, like three or four, then ... maybe ... I'd forget Dex.

DYLAN

As always, I was up at the crack of dawn. After taking care of some usual morning rituals, I took a good look in the mirror and decided to let my morning shadow stay for the day. I jumped into and out of the shower and slipped on a pair of jeans. I rooted through my suitcase, trying to find a shirt or sweater to wear. When I had packed, I wasn't thinking about trying to impress anyone. Dan walked by the bedroom door, which I had unintentionally left cracked open. Out of the corner of his eye, he spied me in my hopeless state. He backed up and peered through the crack between the door and its frame.

Again? Is there no privacy in this house?

"Getting ready for your date?"
"Yeah, but it's not like a real date, you know. I was just trying to throw you guys off last night because you're all so lame."
Dan chuckled. He knew I was right.
"I just didn't bring the right shirt to wear."
"Do you want to borrow one of mine?"
"That would be great."
"Ok, come with me, but you have to be real quiet; Ginny's still sleeping. She needs her rest before her parents land."
"What time are they due in?"
"Who knows? My guess is somewhere between lunch and dinner."
We tiptoed into their room and stood in front of the closet. Dan pulled the hangers across the rack one at a time. He examined each shirt to see if it said, "Dylan's a sexy guy with no girlfriend."
He pulled out an off-white oxford shirt.
"I never wear oxford shirts."

"Yeah, OK. Let's check the sweater department," he whispered.

Throwing the shirt at my head, he walked over to the dresser. He slowly opened the middle drawer and pulled out a dark ivy green V-neck sweater.

"This should work."

Ginny lifted her head out from under the covers. Her eyes were slits and her red hair flowed in every direction.

"Seriously, at this hour of the morning? I never knew you to care so much about how you look. Yeah, she got to you, didn't she? She wrapped you, all right—right around her little finger. It was nice knowing you!" Ginny laughed, pulled the covers over her head, and rolled the other way.

The "brother" in me wanted to jump on the mattress, pin her down, and make her pay for her little jest—albeit laced with a heavy dose of truth. However, it would've been too awkward with Dan there, and she knew it! Ginny: 1, Dylan: 0.

Back in my room, I put on Dan's shirt and sweater, and raked a comb through my hair. I grabbed my wallet and looked inside it to make sure I had some extra cash before jamming it into my back pocket. I picked up my watch and wrapped it around my wrist, pulling the buckle to tighten it down. Moving back into the bathroom, I brushed my teeth and checked my smile. I was good to go. Seeing it was 8:00, I ran my fingers through my damp hair once more, then headed downstairs to put the coffee on. While it was brewing, I went out to the living room, turned on Good Morning America, and plopped down on a sofa. The day certainly had potential. Emeril was showing Diane Sawyer and Charlie Gibson how to make an amazing southern pecan pie. I don't like pecans, but it looked sweet and tempting, and that about summed up my hopes. Well, at least for the morning—very sweet and very tempting.

COURTNEY

I arrived at the Carter beach house at 9:00 on the dot. From the outside, it appeared that the entire house was still asleep. I turned off the engine and gingerly walked up the stairs to the kitchen door and tapped lightly. Very quickly, the cold air started to pinch my nose. I blew into my hands and rubbed them together to keep them warm. Soon, the door opened and the aroma of fresh coffee gave me a morning rush, just as Dylan appeared.

Just what I need!

In the morning light, he looked amazing. Definitely a sight I could wake up to every day.

I am playing with matches. This is not good.

"Hi!" I whispered.
"Good morning, and why are we whispering?"
"I don't want to wake anyone," I replied, softer still.
"Ahhh, don't worry about them. They'll wake up soon enough. Today's the big day. We've got to clean ourselves up for Ginny's parents, remember?"
"Are you sure there's enough time for all of that?"
"I don't know, what do you think?"
Dylan held his arms out from his side like I was supposed to check him out. So, I did! And, the verdict? Wow...
"With a little bit of work, there's hope. But first, I need that cup of coffee you promised me."

Dylan filled two mugs with coffee and handed one to me.
"Strong and straight up," he boasted. He does have an

amazing, sexy smile. That morning, I could have jumped right into it.

"You remembered."

We both blew across the surfaces of our hot coffees and took a careful sip.

"So, Courtney, I can honestly say I've never been shopping for ribbons and bows before."

"Well then, today we're going to get in touch with your feminine side."

Dylan grinned and I noticed a vivid depth in his eyes that I had not seen before. Then he took another slow sip of his coffee and looked out over the lip of his mug, right into mine. Transfixed by his gaze, I observed how his lips carefully caressed his mug. Between his smile, his eyes, and the thought of his lips, my legs weakened and I was swept away for a brief moment.

"Did you wear a coat?" he kindly asked with sincere concern.

"Oh, it's in the car."

"Are you ready to go?"

"I think so."

What the hell is wrong with me?

"Well, let me grab my coat and put the lids on these mugs."

Dylan topped off our mugs, leaving the carafe half empty. Everyone else in the house would have to fend for themselves. With his coat over his arm, he escorted me out the door, and closed it behind us. The cold air turned our breath into vapor. Seeing it made me realize how short of breath he was leaving me. I had been through some pretty tough negotiations in my short career, but I had enough experience to know that the best offense is to never let the other side see how thin and vulnerable your case may be. If that had been a deposition, I would have been failing miserably. Unaware of my thoughts, Dylan opened my car door for me. As he crossed the front of my car, I could not help but notice the sexy contour of his body. The thoughts that raced through my mind were totally inappropriate. As he slid into the passenger seat, I put my key in the ignition and turned over the engine.

"Nice wheels, Court . . . uh, Courtney"

"That's all right. All my close friends call me Court."

I backed out and we headed for the florist.

DYLAN

The morning air was brisk, and the streets were quiet with the exception of a few seagulls that were circling overhead in search of breakfast. It was a short ride to the florist who was located on the opposite end of town.

Without the busyness of its summer guests, it seemed all of Lewes was sleeping-in. We passed one middle-aged woman walking her mid-sized dog that was wearing a mid-sized sweater. Otherwise, the sidewalks were vacant. There were few cars on the road and for once you could drive through town without having to stop at a crosswalk. It felt as though we were the only ones who had survived the night.

I have never been a morning person. Normally, it takes me at least one cup of coffee to become hospitable. Yet, we talked all the way to the florist as if we had never parted ways the night before. When we arrived, we had been discussing when each of us had learned the truth about Santa Claus. Simple stuff. I didn't know her well enough to talk about anything heavy, like the things I imagined she would enjoy debating. Things like what defines the right from the left, the separation of church and state, or what continues to fuel wars in the Middle East.

After pulling into the small parking lot in front of the Florist Shoppe, we remained in her car drinking our coffees and chatting a while longer. Courtney had turned the engine off, so the chill was beginning to creep into the cabin. Our hot coffees and bodies were the only things left to produce heat. The windows were noticeably steaming up.

Funny how a little thing like that can trigger a memory that takes you back to a different place in time.

My thoughts turned to my high school days when I ended up parked in a field off Wollaston Road. It was the night I was about to hit my first home run. My date and I had just come out of the movies and we had time left to kill before she had to be home. She initiated what became some heavy making out in the theater's parking lot. Her intensity escalated rapidly. Looking back, I could see that she had had a plan all along. She suggested we drive to someplace secluded, like the field we ended up in. I had a feeling she had been there before, but I was not about to question or care about it right then and there. She was in the present and obviously ready and willing.

After off-roading across the rough terrain in the middle of nowhere, I put my old truck in park. She pretty much led the way with penetrating kisses while moving my hand under her blouse. I began working with her as she unbuckled my belt and tugged at my zipper. This was going to be a big moment. At the age of seventeen, I knew I would have bragging rights after that night. She was practically undressed and I was out and ready to respond to her invitation. Crunched up on the bench seat of my truck, trying to avoid being impaled by the gearshift, I laid my body across hers. I was about to enter the unknown when there came a hard knock on the window. I lifted my head and peered through the steamy glazed-over glass above my feet. I could barely make out the dark looming silhouette of a large figure on the other side of the driver's door. It quickly disappeared behind the illumination of a bright intrusive flashlight. Concerned for our safety and ensuing embarrassment, I tried to pull up my pants. My agile date covered herself with her blouse as I wrestled with her legs and my clothes. The officer told me a second or third time to roll down the window. Crawling back behind the steering wheel as my date sat up in the passenger seat, I rolled down the driver's side window. I tried to fill the space with my head and body, hoping to keep her free from scrutiny. Needless to say, upon checking my driver's license, the officer informed me that he knew my father. He even knew my dad's first name. Peering around my head, he asked my date, by name, if she was OK.

He knew her, too? Maybe she . . .

She said, "Yes," in a tone that clearly suggested she was annoyed by the interruption. Still leaning on the door, he said that this time was only a warning, but if he ever caught us out there again, my fate would be in the hands of the law, not hers.

Did he really just say that?

My thoughts returned to the present. I wondered what Courtney was like when she was in high school. I wondered if she had ever gotten caught.

"Dylan, did you hear a word I said?"
"Uh . . . yeah . . . You said it looks like she's open and we should probably go in."
It was a gift, being able to listen to two different conversations at the same time. Derek said I would really appreciate it if and when I ever got married.

Courtney's friend, the florist, made the most amazing bows. Courtney showed her the picture of the chairs with me kneeling between them. The florist asked Courtney if she was interested in decorating the chairs or the guy in the middle.

I'm standing right here, ladies.

Courtney squinched her eyes and looked me over. I

wished I knew what she was thinking when she did those things.

Before making each bow, her friend asked for background information about each person to receive a chair. Accordingly, she tailored each bow to the short summary I had given her. Each bow was spot on. When she was finished, she put a removable nametag on the bows so I would remember which bow belonged which chair. However, the bows were so perfect, I would have known without the added identification.

Derek's bow was a very stately red, green, and gold plaid. Susan's was more on the playful side with whimsical gold star wiring added to it, making the bow look like the stars were popping out of it. Dan's bow was all about sports. She wired in a few small football ornaments. Ginny's was perhaps the most perceptive and revealing. It was as though she had known Ginny personally. It was a calm silvery blue, trimmed with white lace. There was a snowflake pattern in the ribbon and she added wire with silver and white snowflakes, as well. It was beautiful and serene. In my description of Ginny, I guess I had let on more about my concern for her peace of mind and wellbeing during the holidays than I had realized.

When the florist had finished the last bow, I felt bad that I didn't have a gift for Courtney, especially because she had done so much to help me with my finishing touches. If I had known, I would have brought something special for her, to show my appreciation.

SUSAN

Ginny's parents were due to arrive at anytime. We didn't know if they were coming straight to the Carter beach house or checking into the Rodney Hotel first. We waited . . . and waited . . . and waited. Obviously anxious, Ginny was beginning to pace. Derek and Dan were oblivious to the situation, as they casually watched football, making frequent play calls and raucous commentary. Dylan and Courtney had returned from their morning "date." They said a quick hello, wrestled with several large bags, and trotted upstairs. They were beginning to raise some suspicions among the rest of us.

Maybe he isn't kidding about her giftwrapping technique?

I had to shake the visual . . .

Instinctively knowing what to do for my future sister-in-law, I went out to the kitchen and poured two glasses of Sauvignon blanc. Ginny looked at me cross-eyed as I handed her a glass.

"What? It's past noon," I said, answering her quizzical expression.

At least it got her to stop pacing and sit down. She was just starting to relax when we heard a car pull in. The engine shut off, and a silence fell over the room. It was a silence that shrouded the cheers and curses of our two football fanatics in the other room. It was the quiet before the storm, and the storm was knocking on the back door.

"Oh. My. God. They're here," Ginny whispered with intense fear.

The guys were still glued to the TV. Sometimes, I believe that when they are watching sports, they actually entered another dimension, leaving our universe to escape the inevitable reality.

Telepathically communicating that it was go-time, Ginny and I looked at each other. We raised our glasses and polished off their contents. If that house had had a fireplace, I think we would have thrown the empty glasses into it for effect. Regrettably, for several reasons, there was none. So, we carefully set our empty glasses down on the kitchen counter by the sink. Ginny inhaled deeply, straightened herself out, and then opened the door. A tsunami of frigid winter air rushed in. I felt its force even as I stood on the far side, away from the door.

"Virginia dear, how are you?" her mother inquired as if addressing the rest of the world. She air-hugged her daughter and kept on walking. It was like watching a drive-by hit-and-run courtesy of a flashy redheaded Cruella De Vil, minus the Dalmatian coat and opera length meerschaum cigarette holder.

Her mother came to rest in the middle of the kitchen. Without introduction, she removed her coat and gloves and promptly handed them to me. Relieved of her outer garments, she began surveying the room from wall to wall, ceiling to floor. She was doing a mental evaluation to determine where she should begin her "white glove inspection."

Ginny's father gently and sweetly wrapped his arms around his only child and kissed her forehead.

"How's my baby girl?"

DAN

As soon as I felt the cold air and heard Ginny's parents, I turned off the TV, much to Derek's dismay. With adrenaline flowing, I rushed into the kitchen to greet them. First, I saw Ginny's mother giving our kitchen the visual once over. Susan, seemingly in shock, was holding Mrs. Huff's coat while Ginny was reveling in her father's embrace. (I knew that no matter what came of their visit, the affection of her father was what Ginny would cherish most.) Not wanting to interrupt their moment, I stood back. Her father eventually saw me, broke their embrace, and walked over to shake my hand.

"Dan, how have you been? Again, we are so sorry for your loss . . . for Lily."

"Thank you, Dr. Huff. Ginny told me you called her almost her every day while she was recovering. It meant so much to her."

"Anything for the both of you. I wish we could have

done more. It's so difficult. In pediatrics, when we see children suffer, it is absolutely unbearable. We are strongly cautioned not to become emotionally attached to our patients; however, with children it is next to impossible to avoid. It is heart wrenching when parents have to turn and try to face the world without them. But this? This was too close to home." He had his hand on my shoulder just like my dad used to do. "I was really looking forward to having a granddaughter. I am so very sorry. You and Ginny mean the world to us. You have been in my prayers."

I was blown away. He was speaking straight from his heart. His condolences were sincere. Ginny's father, Dr. Huff, pediatric surgeon, was not all business. He was not a stoic academic. He was kind and compassionate. He cared about his patients, their families . . . his family . . . he cared about us.

"Thank you, sir. I don't know what to say. I'm glad you're here. This visit has given Ginny, and me, something to look forward to."

"And probably a little something different to worry about, too," he added, glancing over toward his beautiful and devious wife.

"And please, call me Stan."

"Yes, sir . . . Stan," I tried. "How was your trip?" I asked to change the subject.

"Our trip was the typical 'get across the Cross Bronx Expressway and into New Jersey and you'll be fine' kind of a trip. But I must say, once we got onto the Route 1 expressway to the Delaware Beaches, things started taking a turn for the best. And Lewes is such a charming town! Here I thought Darien had cornered the market on charm. Driving through Lewes today was like driving into Christmas as it was meant to be. This is a beautiful location, Dan."

"Thank you, Stan. My father loved this place. He had many aspirations of fixing it up. One day, I hope I can make his dreams come true."

Overhearing us, Ginny jumped in. "Daddy, Dan and his dad used to talk constantly about their ideas for this house. You would've loved Dan's dad. The two of you could have sat on the deck sharing Manhattans, fish stories, or out on the beach creating them."

"I would have liked that."

That must have been the man I never got to know during our visit to Connecticut. In some ways, he reminded me of my dad. The difference was that Dr. Huff came from so much wealth. He did seem genuine in his sympathy, and I was beginning to feel more comfortable around him. I definitely wanted to get to know him better and thought that we should try to see them more often.

I could feel Ginny's mother staring at me. I had not acknowledged her. Big mistake. I walked over and extended my hand. It was the kind of gesture that gave her room to hug me, if she wanted to, or just shake hands.

"Welcome, Mrs. Huff. Ginny and I have been looking forward to your visit."

Her only response was, "Yes, thank you." She kind of brushed me off. She didn't step forward to receive my extended her hand. She just let me stand there with my arm out. It was very awkward. I knew she was upset with me; however, I had hoped that she would have been a bit more sensitive after all that Ginny and I had been through. I thought it best to let it all roll off my back and hope that Ginny would be able to do likewise.

With perfect timing and savoir-faire, Derek walked into the kitchen and took Mrs. Huff's heavy coat from Susan and hung it in the small closet next to the washer and dryer. I introduced them as my oldest brother, Derek, and his wife, Susan. Derek, being the statesman that he was, shook hands with Ginny's mother and father. Susan did likewise. Derek asked if they had checked into the Rodney Hotel as yet. They had not. He offered to drive over with them, when the time came, to make sure they got there, parked, and settled in OK. He told them about the parking spots marked for hotel guests behind the building in the bank parking lot. He explained that it was a well-kept secret and would save them from having to park on the street. They thanked him for the information and kind offer. He was ringing up the brownies points. *Cha-ching!* Sometimes, I thought Derek should have gone into politics. However, I just could not picture him kissing random babies, but he sure was kissing up that day.

We moved into the living room where I thought Stan and Victoria might want to relax after their long trip. Stan walked up to the double sliding doors that led out to the deck and overlooked the calm bay beyond the dune.

"This is a lovely view, Dan. If I lived here, I would have my coffee and read my paper right here, every morning."

I could picture him sitting at a small table and chair right in front of the window, wearing a pair of reading glasses half way down his nose, the paper held up in one hand, and a cup of hot coffee in the other—like my dad used to do. I told Dr. Huff how once the weather warmed up, I usually left the doors open so the bay breeze could fill the house with the scent of salt air, the sound of waves crashing on the shoreline, and sea gulls calling as they performed their flybys. I told him how we rarely locked the doors unless we were leaving the house for a day or more.

"I think the last time we locked the doors was when we came to Connecticut."

"Well then, you should get out more," Ginny's mother interrupted with contemptuous commentary.

Clearly, it was time to offer everyone something to drink. Just as I was about to take orders, Dylan and Courtney came bounding down the stairs. When they saw Doctor and Mrs. Huff sitting on the sofa, they came to a dead stop, almost knocking each other down the remaining steps. The rest of us froze, gaping at their folly. They looked like a train wreck. In their surprised state, they appeared guilty as hell. To my knowledge, and probably to Dylan's great disappointment, they were not. Dylan had never openly admitted his interest in Courtney, but it didn't take a genius to read the playfulness in their eyes and in their body language.

I rose from my chair and waved them on down, introducing them as my brother, Dylan, and our friend,

Courtney. I noticed how Ginny's mother raised an eyebrow as she gave them the once over, especially Courtney. She was summing them up and condemning them all at the same time. How sad. She knew nothing about them: Dylan who I loved as my brother, and Courtney who I was starting to realize might not be an insensitive shark, after all.

There may actually be a nice, fun-loving person behind Courtney's tough facade.

"OK.... So, we have beer, wine, and I can make a mean Manhattan ... *my father's favorite.* We also have Coke and Diet Pepsi. I think we have some eggnog and rum, compliments of Courtney, and Ginny makes the best hot chocolate in Sussex County. I could spike it with a little peppermint schnapps, too."

Susan, who had been unusually quiet up to that point, gave Ginny's hot chocolate a big, "A-men!" Having embarrassed herself, she curled back into her seat on the sofa. She and Ginny exchanged stress-filled glances.

"Stan, what would you like?" I asked.

"I would love a Manhattan, straight up, thank you."

I think what a person drinks, says a lot about who they are, even when the selection is limited. My father would have gotten along well with Stan. Good ol' Dr. Stan Huff and David Carter sitting on the deck at the end of a warm summer's day, sharing their Manhattans, perhaps a good cigar, and shooting the breeze. It would have been nice.

In the absence of her mother, I probably could have let my guard down around Ginny's dad. Ginny was sitting on the armrest of her father's chair. I took a mental picture. She was the love of my life and he was becoming a man that I might actually come to admire.

"Mrs. Huff, how about you, would you like something to drink?"

"You wouldn't have a bottle of Albert Boxter Pinot Gris, would you? 2005? That was their best year. Don't you agree, Stan?"

The room fell silent, like a grand pause, a hard stop. No,

more like another train wreck.

"I'm afraid we don't," I said. I had no clue what she was even talking about.

"We do have a bottle of Barefoot Sauvignon Blanc."

Stan glared at his wife and amusingly scolded, "Please Victoria, just politely ask for a goddamn glass of white wine. We're not at your country club. We're not at one of your social events. We're in Dan and Ginny's home. Let go and just relax, for once. You don't need to impress anyone here."

Whoops, now that was a train wreck! I could hear Ginny and Susan gasping for air. Dylan and Courtney buried their faces in each other's shoulders, turning away so Victoria couldn't see their smirks. Inside, I was giving Stan a big chest bump.

Yay, Stan! He gets it. He gets us!

Good ol' Stan had just broken the barrier. It was OK to be us. We didn't need to pretend we belonged to or even had an inkling of how to be a part of her world. She was on our turf now, and she could attempt to lord over it all she wanted, but she would do so alone. He wanted to be with us, among us. He was here to spend time with his daughter and to get to know her friends, not impress them. In many ways, I felt sorry for Victoria.

She settled for the Barefoot. It must not have been too horrific. She was on her third glass by dinner.

I asked Ginny's father if he would kindly come out to the kitchen and help me with the drink orders. He jumped right up as if he were waiting for me to ask. He was more than happy to oblige. Ginny looked pleased and slid into the cushion where her dad had been sitting.

"Don't cause any trouble out there, you two," she cautioned sarcastically. It was just how she used to tease my dad and me. I missed those times when we were together with him.

Out in the kitchen, Stan asked, "What can I do?"

I whispered just loud enough for him to hear.

"Dr. Huff . . . uh . . . Stan, the reason I asked you out here is to . . . ummm . . . well . . . to ask . . . you see . . . I love your daughter, very much. And when I think about the future, she is every part of it, and I pray she feels the same way about me. And I think she does . . . and . . . uh . . . I want to marry her. In fact . . . well . . . forgive me, sir . . . but I have already asked her. . . . But tonight, I wanted to make it official . . . with a ring. . . . She doesn't know that part. . . . But first, I need to know if I have your blessing."

That was painful.

Stan looked very stern, somewhat angry, even. His eyes were drawn tight, staring intently back at me. He was rubbing his chin with one hand and had the other crossed in front of him as if to put up a roadblock. He didn't say anything. He just stared. Perhaps I had misread him earlier. I thought we were getting along. Maybe that business earlier about being happy with "who we are" came with conditions like "as long as you don't marry my daughter." Maybe it was over his line of acceptance because I didn't come up to his standards for his beloved daughter. His stare was burning a hole into my eyes and my heart. I had not thought about what I would do if he said, "No."

Then, he flashed an ear-to-ear grin and gave me a big hug and a strong pat on the back.

"Daniel, nothing could make me happier! And, I know nothing would make Ginny happier than to spend the rest of her life with you."

I exhaled, to the point that I thought my lungs would collapse. I put my hand on the counter to steady myself and thanked him. My body was Jell-O as he shook my hand and slapped me on the back one more time. Harder. Almost knocking me to the ground.

GINNY

I could see how Dan and my dad were getting along, and it made me feel all the more certain of my decision to marry Dan. He was not my dad by any stretch of the imagination. It was not like one was better or worse. They were just different, yet so compatible. And now, they were out in the kitchen making drinks together. I had a flashback to Dan and *his* dad in the kitchen preparing whatever surprise they had in store for me. I felt a bit of sadness come over me, and yet, so pleased with the bonding I had hoped would one day take place. No one could fill the empty space in us that was once occupied by Dan's dad. However, my own father was helping us find our way to appreciate what we had had and to not be afraid of what was ahead. The evening was beginning to feel as if I was gaining two men in my life.

I politely asked Courtney to stay for dinner. She was about to decline, when I whispered, "I'm sure Dylan would like it if you did." I threw in that we were having Dan's baked lasagna. She smiled and accepted my invitation. To this day I am not sure what convinced her to stay. Was it the continuation of a day spent with Dylan, Dan's lasagna, or my mother's entertaining charades? No matter, one or the combination of things had been enticing enough.

Dan, being the great chef that he was, made a big pan of lasagna, complemented by a basket of fresh baked garlic bread, and large bowl of Caesar salad. Everyone was beginning to drool as the heavy aroma of the sweet tomato sauce, olive oil, garlic, oregano, basil, and Parmesan filled the house. Dad and Dan delivered our drinks. Dad made a toast to "Family." Again, Dan swiftly disappeared into the kitchen for a few minutes, then quickly came back out and announced that dinner was ready to be served. He motioned everyone to the table.

Jockeying for position around the table, we did a little

dance for a few awkward moments. Everyone, including myself, was trying to avoid the seat next to my mother. Seeing what was going on, Dan politely announced, "I'll sit right here." It was the dreaded seat. He was such a saint. I already loved him for more reasons than I could count, and yet he kept racking up the points. Derek and Susan cozied up next to each other. Dylan and Courtney shrugged their shoulders, trying to convince the rest of us that they would sit next to each other if there were no other options. *Nice try.* I was not buying it. Fortunately, the chair on the other side of Dan was open, so I could sit next to him.

Those few seconds of "where should I sit" awkwardness took me back to some painful high school days.

* * *

I was a junior with a mad crush on a senior. His name was David Buckley. Because my best friend was his best friend's girlfriend, I got to sit at their lunch table. As the weeks went by, David and I began striking up a strong connection. Soon, we ended up at the same parties. We would see each other at football games. Every once in a while and eventually every morning, he would stop by my locker. It was easy for everyone to see that we were attracted to one another. However, both of us were inexperienced in such matters and afraid to make the first move. There was, however, a certain chemistry escalating between us. I was sure, given time, we would become more than friends, and given the right moment I would have my first romantic kiss.

Then one day, out of nowhere, this girl showed up at our lunch table. She was someone I knew of, but didn't know personally, and like David, she was a senior, too. She sat in *my* seat next to David. She talked to him all through lunch. I tried my best not to show my hurt feelings. I thought the next day would be a different. *"It's probably just a onetime thing,"* I rationalized. I was wrong. The next day, and every day thereafter, she sat at our table and in my seat. Our friends all shifted so I could sit next to David on his other side. It was the worst place to be. I was always looking at the back of his head as she rambled on and held his attention for the entire lunch period.

After the first week of that, her conversations began to include moments when she would touch his hand, his arm, or even lay her hand on his leg. I was sure they had not yet kissed. Perhaps there was still hope?

Then it happened. One Monday, they came back to school holding hands, talking about the great party at her house that Friday night, and how they enjoyed the movie they saw together on Saturday. It was too late. She had seized the moment. No, she had created the moment. David looked back once that Monday before sitting down at lunch. I was not about to let him see how hurt I was. So, I kind of waved him on, as a good friend would certainly do. He followed her over to *their* new lunch table with *her* friends. I had my seat back, but my reason for wanting to be there in the first place was gone.

To this day, I cringe at the thought of open seating.

* * *

After we were seated, Dan asked that we hold hands as he said grace. Now, to my knowledge, this was not always a family tradition with the Carters, but it seemed that Dan was determined to make it one. We always said grace at the Huff house, reciting the same one every night. "God is great, God is good, ya-da, ya-da, ya-da ya . . ." Dan held his hand out to my mother, again. This time, she reluctantly placed her hand in his. We all bowed our heads.

"Dear God, thank you for this day when we can come together as family and friends. Thank you for bringing Ginny and her family into my life. I ask You now for Your special blessing upon us as we begin our journey in this life together . . ."

Oh no! There it was! We had not said anything to my parents about wedding plans, and Dan was praying out

loud for our future together. I was more afraid of my
mother's reaction than God's. I didn't hear another word of
what he said. I only heard what he had just intimated. I
was not sure he knew what he had done.

"Amen."

Everyone responded with a whispered, "A-men."

I was frozen. I was waiting for my mother to
ignite. Nothing. She was too busy to notice. She placed her
napkin in her lap. She made sure her silverware, which was
really stainless steel, was properly arranged. Perhaps I was
being too paranoid.

Dan rose from the table and said, "Allow me to serve
dinner."

After I started to get up to help him, he insisted that I sit
still. I was surprised that none of the others bothered to
offer their assistance.

Carrying only a small butter dish, Dan reentered the
room. He was acting very strange. Something seemed
terribly wrong. I had a flashback to the tray of raw oysters
and another of soft shell crabs. My nerves were shot. My
stomach was uneasy.

Dan approached his chair, pulled it out, and pushed it
away from the table. He knelt down in front of me with his
back to my mother.

Not a smart move.

"Dan, are you OK? Are you sure I can't help?" I
anxiously whispered.

He took my hands into his and looked into my eyes,
drawing me in as he always did.

"Ginny, I love you more than you will ever know. I
never knew I was capable of being this much in love. When
you are not with me, if only for a minute, I am missing
you. You are the one I want to share every good thing
with. You are the one I want to be with when facing the
difficulties of this world. You are the one that shines for me
and lights up my every day. Will you marry me? Will you
give me the opportunity to do everything in my power to

bring you as much happiness as you have brought to me? Ginny, I want us to be together, forever. Please . . . please, marry me."

The world stopped spinning at that moment. We had already decided to get married. But, this? This was not what I had expected. This was a beautiful love story and I was in it. Dan made me feel like I was the only one in the room—in the world, for that matter. I could feel warm tears begin to stream down my cheeks.

Dan lifted the lid on the butter dish and there, in a black velvet box, was a magnificent diamond ring. It was a solitaire that spoke of two people who would never part from that day forward.

"Yes, of course."

Dan placed the ring on my finger. A place he already owned.

We hugged, and I cried happy tears. Dan kissed my forehead and then my lips. Everyone at the table clapped and cheered. Everyone, except my mother, that is. She sat there with no emotion written on her stone cold face. She was perched like an angry gargoyle. Everyone else was congratulating us and toasting us with their glasses. Dylan got up from his seat and patted Dan on the back. Susan came from behind me and gave me a big hug.

She whispered in my ear, "We're really going to be sisters, now!"

I looked at my dad. He was still clapping and gave me a two-thumbs up.

I looked at Courtney. She mouthed the word, "Congratulations!"

I looked at my mother. She was directly behind Dan and facing me. Anger was emanating from every pore in her body. I noticed my father had his hand on her arm, encouraging her to remain calm, hoping she would not ruin the moment. It was official. The cat was out of the bag, and the alpha feline was poised to pounce. I don't remember Derek's reaction. Up to and including that moment, he had been a nonentity.

After things settled down and I caught my breath, Dan got up and went out to the kitchen to serve dinner. I removed the napkin from my lap and stood up to go out and help him. Dylan, sitting next to me, grabbed my arm.

"Oh no, you're not going anywhere. If you go in there, dinner will never make it to the table. I'll help him," he asserted, shaking his head as he rose from the table, smiling back at his sister-in-law-to-be. *That would be me!*

DEREK

The night turned into a nightmare.

First, Dan proposed to Ginny, making the wedding talk official. Don't misunderstand me; I had given Ginny the benefit of the doubt, initially, and Susan adored her. However, I couldn't help but think that Ginny had been trying to maneuver Dan into a proposal from the very start. She had scripted it, including the way she sucked up to my dad. When she said she was pregnant, I had my doubts until she miscarried. Dan had the opportunity to re-evaluate their relationship, but she must have really poured it on once he inherited the beach house. She moved in, and then she invited us all down for Thanksgiving. What a disaster that turned out to be and now, the proposal. She had sealed the deal.

While everyone was eating, the dinner table grew quiet. But, I had a feeling that Mrs. Huff was not going to leave things alone, and I was more than interested in hearing what she had to say.

"Dan, how do you propose to take care of my daughter, give her the things she needs, and raise a family?"

"Mrs. Huff . . . ?"

"Look at this place. Do you really believe you can raise a healthy family here? Do you think Ginny could be happy here, long-term?"

"Mom!" Ginny scolded.

"Mrs. Huff, I think that in time we will be able to make the necessary repairs."

"Repairs? REPAIRS?" Her voice grew louder the second time. "This place is beyond repair. It needs to be torn down."

"Mother, stop!" I thought Ginny was going to jump out of her chair.

Things are going well, I surmised.

"Ginny, open your eyes. This place is falling down around him. He will never get out from under this money pit. It needs to be torn down and rebuilt, which I doubt Dan here can afford."

Oooooo . . . nice touch.

"Or, better yet, sell the property and buy a place in a good neighborhood," Mrs. Huff spouted out and then raised a fork full of Caesar salad to her mouth as if her point was evident to everyone else. It was evident to me, anyway.

I stated, for the record, that I shared her opinion and had suggested the same to Dan, several times. My confession took Susan and Ginny by surprise.

Dan responded as any dreamer would.

"Mrs. Huff, with all due respect, we have only been here a short time. Once spring arrives, we'll begin the necessary repairs. We have dreams for this house and with a little faith and a lot of perseverance, I believe we can make this place something special."

To my surprise, Courtney came to Dan's defense. It was probably more about launching an argument against me.

"Mrs. Huff, there are many people here that would help. Among us, we have the knowhow and the manpower to restore this house. And, Lewes is a close community; we take care of one another. Plus, our cost of living is not as high as it is in Darien. So, respectfully, I disagree with you and Derek. This would be a great place to raise a family."

Dylan jumped in behind her. They were assembling on the front line.

"This house has been in our family for years, and I don't think he should give it up. Dan is an excellent architect. He can do this, and I will come down to lend a hand whenever possible. They could use the property as collateral for a loan, if need be."

Just great. They offer up the property as collateral for a loan they can't afford. It will only be a matter of time before the bank forecloses and the place is gone for good. I have to put a stop to this.

"That's very doable," Courtney followed up.

Ginny reached over and patted Courtney's arm as a sign of solidarity. That was all I needed, a united front between those two. If the Huffs and I could convince Dan that his ideas were a pipedream, then I would have a chance to offer a buy-out. I was biting my tongue. I wanted to raise that possibility, but thought I should pull Dan aside when his defense team didn't have him surrounded. It was the time, however, to let Mrs. Huff wear him down, and Ginny, too. Ginny was probably the bigger issue, after all. I gingerly stepped in.

"Dan, I don't want to sound like a wet blanket, I love this place as much as you do, but the payments on a loan will be enormous. They'll bury you and you'll end up losing it anyway," I said to add credence to Mrs. Huff's argument.

Ginny looked upset. Susan was looking at me like she didn't know who I was. She elbowed me. Hard. I stood down and decided I would fill her in later. She would understand my rationale eventually.

"Dan and Ginny, you're young and this is the time to dream big and work hard. If you don't try now, you'll regret it. I say you should go for it," Dr. Huff said, submitting his opinion. I wished he had not done that. He, alone, made me feel outnumbered. I was smart enough to know that he could be a big piece of artillery.

"Stan, these kids don't need to waste their money on

some pipedream. They could sell this property and live wherever they wanted to. He needs to put together a plan that will give them security and provide for Ginny and her children. He's young. And quite frankly, he obviously doesn't have a clue what it will take to bring this place up to code and make it a suitable residence," Mrs. Huff continued.

I could see Dan bristle. She talked as if he wasn't even there. Good tactic.

"Mother, don't you get it? We want to live here," Ginny asserted.

That made my blood boil. Where did she come off thinking she had or would ever have claim to the Carter beach house? She was unbelievable: a real piece of work. If they did marry and have children, then their children would stand to inherit it all. That would cut me and mine out completely. I couldn't believe what was happening. I couldn't let it happen.

Then Dan gave his puny speech:

"Mrs. Huff, my father loved this place. He gave up everything to keep it in the family. I know he would want us to do the same. He spoke many times of what he thought this place could be. And, he was very fond of your daughter. He was ecstatic when he learned he was going to be a grandfather. If the stroke didn't kill him, losing Lily may have. We plan on staying here. It's what he would have wanted for us," Dan spewed.

I was getting pissed. Why would Dad want that for Dan and Ginny more than he would for Susan and me, or Dylan, for that matter?

Then it happened, I could not have planned it better. Mrs. Huff stood up and slammed her hands down on the table.

"Ginny, you need to rethink your choices, all of them." She was waving her arms around. She was furious. "You two have been nothing but irresponsible. You're not ready for a family. You cannot live like this. It's not all right to live at the beach like a bunch of bums. We put you through Yale. You've been accepted into the doctorate programs at Yale and Penn. There isn't a good medical school within fifty miles of this place. What are you thinking? You have your whole life ahead of you. If you choose to do this, don't come running to us for help when it all falls down around you—all of this, what little there is. And Dan could vanish like most men do these days. Think of what you're giving up. Think of what he's asking you to give up. He could never give you what a doctorate could. If I thought you two could do it, I would be the first to say so. But that's not the case. Come back to Connecticut. Complete your doctorate at Yale. If Dan wants to be with you, he'll sell this place and come after you. But I don't think he will. I don't think he can. He's a dreamer and he's pulled you right into it. If his father had any sense, he would have taken care of this dump rather than hang it like a noose around his son's neck and now yours, too. You're making a huge mistake."

OK, now she crossed the line. As much as I disliked having this place land in Dan's lap, she had no right to stand there and berate my father.

"Victoria! That's enough." Dr. Huff shut her up and grabbed her arm, thank God. She shook him off and left the table.

"My sincere apologies, Dan, and all of you. I am so sorry. I think it best we go, now," Dr. Huff stood and said with great remorse.

"Dad, tomorrow's Christmas, will you be back?" Ginny spoke in a near whisper, looking as though she would cry at any moment.

"Yes, sweetheart. I can't speak for your mother right now, but I'll be back tomorrow. Good night, everyone. Dan, thank you for a wonderful dinner. And, congratulations you two, I am happy for both of you. Hang in there, Dan. Victoria's a tough cookie, but she does have a soft center. She'll come around."

He kissed his daughter on the cheek and shook Dan's hand. Dr. Huff showed himself and his wife out, closing the door behind them. However, Mrs. Huff had just blown Dan and Ginny's doors off with words they needed to hear. I intended to reinforce the damage when the time was right.

DAN

It was not anything that a good night's sleep couldn't cure. Ginny was becoming desensitized to her mother's rants. Her father congratulated us and said he would be there the next day, for Christmas, and that pleased us both.

It was Christmas Eve, and just the six of us remained in the house. I glanced over at Derek wondering why he was so intent on discrediting my ability to take care of Ginny and the beach house. I could only shake my head and hope that I could restore his confidence in me. However, one of the darts Mrs. Huff threw, stuck: How would I ever be sure that Ginny could finish her doctorate if she really wanted to? How would I know that I had not pulled her into a terrible regrettable mistake?

"Well, that was entertaining," Courtney said, removing the napkin from her lap. "Dan, you do have your work cut out for you!"

"I'm sorry," Ginny apologized. "I tried to warn you, but I didn't expect her be that rude."

"She was just expressing her opinion," Derek defended. "She did make some valid points."

"She was out of line," Susan snapped. "And what's the big idea backing her up?" Susan continued with eyes that could burn holes right through him. "This is a fine house. Anyone with imagination can see how much potential it has." She turned to us and seemed to soften. "Dan and Ginny, we'll support you in any way we can. Won't we, Derek?" Using her elbow, she jabbed him to agree. He smiled back at her, or maybe it was more of a sneer.

Susan and Ginny said they had pies to bake and invited Courtney to stay. She said she would stay to help with the dishes, and then she needed to leave in order to spend time with her sisters. They were due to arrive at her parent's house at anytime, and all of them were spending the night there.

When the dishes were cleaned, dried, and put away, Dylan walked Courtney out to her car. She appeared very pleased to have him follow her out the door. They left me wondering who was going to make the first move and how long Dylan was going to be out there. We had a poker game hanging in the balance.

"I have twenty bucks on Courtney," Susan threw out as if she had read my mind.

"Mine's on Courtney, too," Derek agreed.

"I say nothing happens, and he'll be back inside before you can take out your wallets," Ginny countered.

Sure enough, Ginny had it right. Dylan was back inside within the minute. She explained her wager later that night. She noted that they were obviously very attracted to each other. Dylan seemed very happy when she was around. Ginny said she didn't know Courtney well enough, yet, but they seemed to bring out the best in each other. They had a "playful camaraderie," as she put it. Flirting sounded too juvenile, I guess. Ginny believed if Dylan and Courtney took their time, it could lead to something. Or else, they could become sexually frustrated, satiate their hunger sooner than later, regret it the next morning, live in the awkwardness of it all, and lose their friendship. Dylan was too shy to make the first move and Courtney, she believed, was too smart to risk it. Ginny confessed that she hoped they would take their time. She and Susan were beginning to feel comfortable around Courtney, and they had enjoyed watching Dylan trip all over himself in her presence.

Ginny and Susan baked two pies while they rehashed the events of the evening and surmised what they thought the next day, Christmas Day, would bring. We three guys set up a card table and played poker. We knew there would be no sleeping after all of the excitement at the dinner table.

Once in the oven, the warm aroma of pumpkin and apple pies began to fill the entire house. While Derek dealt the next hand, my activated senses conjured up memories of Christmases past. It transported me back to a place in time when I was very young. My mother was in the kitchen baking her own Christmas pies: one pumpkin and the other was mincemeat. Remembering how my dad loved my mother's mincemeat pie made me laugh to myself.

What the hell is mincemeat anyway?

I envisioned them in the kitchen in our Unionville home, she with her back to him, he with his arms around her waist, giving her a kiss on the back of her neck and whispering something in her ear. That was a very happy and secure time for us. The love they had for each other made our family all the more complete. I wondered if Ginny had ever experienced that kind of happiness.

"Dan, your wager. What do you want to do?" Derek snapped me back to the present situation.

I looked at my hand. I made sure to keep my face expressionless.

I wonder if they can tell I'm not in the game?

I laid my cards face down on the table, got up from my chair, and walked out to the kitchen. I sneaked up behind Ginny as she and Susan were admiring the mess they had made and the pies in the oven. Burying my face into Ginny's hair, I whispered, "I love you." She spun around and dabbed flour on my nose and kissed my lips ever so sweetly. Her eyes smiled into mine. She was doing better already. Susan kept herself busy wiping down the counters around the sink so as not to intrude on our moment.

Returning to the table, I threw in my poker hand and decided to help the girls finish up in the kitchen much to the protest of my brothers. The mood was much lighter in the kitchen.

With five people in the house and one and a half bathrooms, it made getting ready for bed a long drawn out ordeal of "who's next?"

Derek and Dylan called out, "You girls go ahead. We men are going to finish our beers."

I knew the implications of their gender specific inclusions.

I acknowledged their teasing and sat back down at the table, giving Ginny and Susan full access to the bathroom and the upstairs, indicating they could take their time. Which was somewhat crazy, because I knew they would be right back down for their "girl time" sometime during the course of the night.

With the girls finally upstairs changing, we had the downstairs to ourselves.

"Dan, your mother-in-law-to-be is a real piece of work. Courtney's right. You're going to have your hands full," Dylan said, restarting an earlier conversation.

"Do we really have to revisit this?" I asked him strongly, implying that we should not go there.

"Dan, we're only here for two more days, and I think we ought to have this discussion before you go and sink a lot of money into this property," Derek said with paternal-like acumen.

"This property? Really Derek? This is more than a piece of property. This was Dad's home. He loved it here. He wants it to remain in the family. I don't understand why he did what he did, but I am sure he wouldn't want me to sell it. I think he wanted me to make his dreams a reality."

"Yeah, well, he's gone, Dan, and his reality didn't include us," he said waving his finger back and forth between Dylan and himself. "If he had split everything down the middle, maybe we could have pooled the insurance money and rebuilt this place. We could have used it as an investment property and rented it out. We could have come down on the vacant weeks or any weekend we chose to."

Derek was letting the elephant out of his closet. I was beginning to understand why he had been so distant. I just wished there was a way to subdue the pachyderm he had been nursing. It felt like he was itching to stampede all over the entire holiday.

"I don't think that is what Dad had in mind, otherwise, he would have left it that way. But, he didn't," Dylan countered.

"No, he didn't. He changed his mind two weeks before he died. So, when did he know Ginny was pregnant, Dan? What did you guys say to him to make him want to cut us out?"

Derek's anger was raising its ugly head. The mastodon was getting ready to slam its trunk down and gore me with its huge tusks, fighting for what he believed was his fair share. He went down a path I did not see coming.

"Susan and I have been trying for years to have children. Does anyone care about us? Maybe one day we would like for our children to have a part of this," he said, waving his hands around, implying the beach house.

I didn't know how to respond. I understood his anger and hurt. I'm sure I would have felt the same way. I just can't say how I would have reacted, if it were me. Not like that, I had hoped.

Derek continued. "Dylan, you can't honestly tell me you weren't disappointed. You have to be suspicious. Do you really think this is OK?"

Dylan was silent. He was staring through the glass doors facing the water. I could tell he was carefully forming his answer, and admittedly, I was fearful of his response. Finally, Dylan took a deep breath and faced us.

"Dan, I don't know what Dad was thinking, either. But, Derek, he didn't completely cut us out. He left us a huge sum of money. Money I actually need to prop up my business. Dan didn't receive any of that. All he has now is this place and a dream that he and Dad carved out for it. Am I a little disappointed? Honestly? Yes. Am I upset enough to accuse Dan and Ginny of manipulating Dad? No. I don't believe for one second that they would have done that. I also don't believe that Dad would want us to be fighting over this. I don't know what you're driving at, Derek. You know Dad would want this place to stay in the family. You know it was home to him, not some investment or rental property. Maybe that's why he did what he did. He knew in the bottom of his heart, and so do you, that Dan would never look at it that way. Dan would make this place . . . no, *keep* this place as a family beach house, and I intend to help him do that. You can do what you want."

Dylan had said his piece and got up to leave the table. Derek grabbed his arm to make one more point.

"Dylan, you know your girlfriend must have had this discussion with Dad. She probably knows when and why this all happened. Ask her. Or better yet, I'll ask her," Derek charged.

"First, she's not my girlfriend. And second, you leave her out of this. You know she can't divulge their discussions. She has more integrity than that. And don't you go and browbeat her either," Dylan warned.

"You know, Dylan, I think she can hold her own. Just like she has you following her around like some lovesick puppy," Derek bullied.

"OK, that's enough. It's Christmas. I don't get to spend enough time with you guys, so I don't want to spend whatever time we have arguing. This is not what Dad would have wanted. This is not what I want. This is not easy for me, either. I need you guys to help me out here," I admitted.

"You have some nerve asking for our help," Derek said, walking away and swiping the air with his hand as if I were some annoying bug.

Dylan put his hand on my shoulder. "You do have your work cut out for you, little brother. You'll figure it out," he said, trying to encourage me. "And, for the record, she's not my girlfriend, and I am not some lovesick puppy."

I thanked him for his vote of confidence, but I didn't comment on his denial. It was just a matter of time.

Later that night, Ginny and I lay awake in bed. I was staring at the ceiling and Ginny had scooted up against me with her head resting on my chest. My left arm was wrapped around her shoulders. We heard someone making several trips up and down the steps. On one particular pass, I heard him curse as he missed a step. I told Ginny it had to be Dylan. He liked to wake up with stuff under the tree, so ever since he returned home from college he had an innate need to play Santa Claus on Christmas Eve. When he completed his mission, he would be thrilled that he had kept the Christmas spirit alive for one more year. I may have been the youngest, but sometimes it felt like Dylan was the baby.

"Are you ladies having girl-time tonight?" I whispered.

"No, we had our girl-time while you guys were arguing."

"Oh, sorry you had to hear all that. How's Susan doing?"

"OK. She's just a little concerned with the way Derek's been acting. She said he's a happy camper at home, but she's noticed how he gets in a funk whenever he's here or whenever our names come up. She said once they return home, it will take him a couple of days to work himself out of it. She loves him so much, but she doesn't recognize him when he's like this. She apologized for his behavior tonight. I hope these debates don't make it too difficult for her to spend time with us in the future."

"I don't think that will be a problem with you two."

"What exactly were you guys arguing about?" Ginny wanted to know.

"Derek let the elephant out of the closet tonight. He's upset that Dad left this house to us."

"No, Dan, he left the house to *you*," she swiftly corrected.

"It's just a technicality. I'm not sure, exactly, what Derek wants me to do about it."

"I just hope this place doesn't drive a wedge between all of us. I love your family far too much for that."

After Dylan completed several more trips up and down the stairs, we enjoyed the silence that finally settled into the old house. The place was becoming our home and our refuge. Over the months, we had come to know its idiosyncrasies. We knew exactly which step was creaking under Dylan's feet. We would wait to hear the shower drip nineteen times before it stopped. We could imitate the squeaking of the kitchen door. We loved the sound of the deck door sliding open and the rush of salt air entering

134

in. We loved the sound of rain on the roof. We loved the way the sun crept across the living room floor during the day and the moon danced on the water at night. Mrs. Huff was right about one thing: I could never leave.

We drifted off to sleep: safe, healthy, in good company, and in a good house, no matter what Mrs. Huff wanted us to believe.

DYLAN

The house was abuzz with morning activity. There was an energy force at work in all of us. Coffee was being poured, and Dan was making pancakes, bacon, and eggs. The rest of us were milling around when there came a knock at the door. Ginny rushed over, excited that her dad had returned so early. (We weren't expecting them before lunch.) She pulled the door open.
"SURPRISE! MERRRRRRRY CHRISTMAS!!!!"
It was Dex and Courtney. All of our activity came to a screeching halt. After a quick mental reset, Ginny invited them in.
"Come on in, you guys. Merry Christmas! What a surprise!"
When they got inside they held up a handle of vodka and two bottles of Bloody Mary mix."
"We come bearing gifts!" Courtney cheered.
"Court said you guys could probably use a breakfast beverage," Dex explained.

He called her Court? And why are they together this early in the morning? OK, it is after 10:00, but it's still morning.

My suspicions were running high and I was crushed.

The story of "Oh, we tried, but never made it to first

base," was just a ruse. But what do I care? I have no claim to her.

"Do you guys do anything other than drink?" Derek asked accusingly.

Courtney and Dex were dressed, and we were donning whatever we had slept in the night before. They looked showered and fresh. We were a mess of shaggy hair and unbrushed teeth. They were all bright and perky. We looked like the walking dead, and I was well aware that I was all commando and swinging free in my sweats. But hey, who cares? We were all like family, all except for Courtney and Dex. I tried not to think about it, my commando-ness, that is.

"Hey, you guys, come look at the awesome presents Dylan gave us!" Susan squealed.

Courtney went out to the living room with Susan and Ginny. We could hear the oooohs and aaaahs. I was glad they liked their presents, and the decorative bows were a big hit, too. Ginny came back out to the kitchen. She poured a cup of coffee for Courtney and scurried back to the living room as if she were afraid she would lose her seat, even though there were plenty of rockers out there.

Us-guys hung out in the kitchen, literally, stealing strips of bacon as Dan removed them from the pan. Initially, he smacked our fingers with the spatula. Eventually, he gave it up.

"So when did you guys plan this little visit?" I directed toward Dex while trying my best to conceal my worst fears.

"I ran into Court and her sisters at Irish Eyes last night. They came out for a nightcap. She said she had dinner with you guys and the lasagna was awesome, but Mrs. Huff was a bit overbearing. *Understatement.* She thought a couple of Bloody Marys for breakfast would be just what the doctor ordered for the house, and I told her I could make it happen, so I picked her up this morning, and here we are."

He looked at me as if he could read my mind.

"Not to worry, Tiger. She spent the night with her

sisters. And by the way, Dylan, if I didn't know better—and I know that I do—I'd say she's very interested in *you*. I'd say that's why we're here so early in the morning," he added, giving me an affirming shove.

Tiger? Really?

No matter, a butterfly flipped in my stomach, but I was not about to let Dex and my brothers know that. I tried to pretend that Courtney meant nothing to me.

I need to practice that cavalier thing.

"Yeah, I think she's kind of fun, too." It sounded ridiculous when I heard it come out of my mouth.

Dan had thrown more bacon into the pan and removed more eggs from the fridge. The pancake batter was ready to be poured onto the hot skillet.

"Yo, Dex, you gonna stand there and shoot the breeze, or make me a Bloody Mary?" Dan barked from his command post at the stove.

"Is he always this grateful?" Dex quipped sarcastically.

"Only when you keep him waiting!" I responded.

I pulled seven tall glasses from the cabinet. Dex pulled the ice trays from the freezer.

"Hey, Dex, make mine a double." Derek barked, finally acknowledging Dex's presence.

"Comin' up!"

"Breakfast is ready!" Dan called out to anyone within earshot, which was everyone because the house was not all that big. Dan left the pans and skillet on the stove so everyone could serve themselves. He always made way too much food. He even warmed up the maple syrup. At this rate, breakfast had the potential to be even better than Christmas dinner. We all sat down in the same seats we had the prior night, except for Dex. He unknowingly chose Mrs. Huff's vacant chair.

"No, don't sit there . . . !" Ginny blurted out. "It's

possessed. . . . Well, actually, go ahead. Just don't point your finger and start lecturing me."

"Must have been some night."

"It was memorable."

They all complimented my rocking chairs and started giving me ideas as to what they wanted for Christmas the following year. Dex and Courtney pouted and complained because they didn't receive a rocker. For a woman as strong and as confident as Courtney had appeared at Sable & Sable, she sure could be a paradox. And the familiarity between her and Dex was a little disconcerting, too.

The conversation stayed lively and entertaining throughout breakfast. Even Dex and Derek were getting along. Within a half hour, our bellies were full and our mugs and glasses were empty. It was Christmas, after all.

"Ugh, I think I hurt myself," Derek bellowed as he rocked back in his chair and held on to his intentionally puffed out belly. The Lion had been fed. He was beginning to return to his more docile and contented self. For Dan and Ginny's sake, I was glad to see it.

"I've got a football," I whispered loud enough for everyone to hear.

"Oh, yeah, game on!" was the collective rallying shout.

We bundled ourselves up in whatever clothes we could find. We decided spouses and soon-to-be spouses could not be on the same team.

"OK, well then, I say I can't be on the same team as Dex and Dylan," Courtney proclaimed.

Just what does that mean?

"It means nothing," she defended.

Really. Can she read my mind?

"Huh?"

Before the game got underway, I learned that Courtney liked to make up her own rules, but I liked her rules. The teams morphed into Derek, Dan, and Courtney against Dex, Ginny, Susan, and me. Poor Courtney: Dex and I took her down numerous times. However, she was no wallflower. She took the legs out from under me on almost every offensive play I ran. She even intercepted a pass right in front of me. There was a lot of physical contact on the beach that morning. I'm a very competitive sort, and I did enjoy chasing Courtney, or having her take me down whenever she could, which was more often than I thought possible. When she tackled me, we were a little slower getting up. Well, I know I was. I loved the sensation of her body on top of mine. I would take an extra roll with her wrapped around me. It wasn't as though I was trying to take advantage of her. I noticed she held on, too. Also, I couldn't help comparing our tumbles to when she and Dex went down. I kept a close eye on their interactions, looking to justify my suspicions, which secretly I hoped were only a manifestation of my misguided jealousy.

It was a physical morning, and my body was feeling all the pluses and minuses of it afterwards.

Courtney needed to leave early, again, to spend the better part of the afternoon and dinner with her family. I offered to drive her back to her parents' house since Dex brought her over in the morning. I had no clue where her parents lived. It didn't matter.

Crossing over the drawbridge, I glanced over at the boats resting below in their icy cold slips. Many more were on dry dock; shrink wrapped in plastic like leftovers in a refrigerator. I noticed Dex's Right Tackle was still in the water. There was only one other boat in the water anywhere near his. In fact, it was right next to his. They resembled two horses huddled in a field on a cold winter's day. The two boats were the same make and model, and looked like identical twins. I wondered how cold it got out there at night.

We made a right turn on to 3rd Street and a few blocks later we were in Shipcarpenter Square. In all the summers I had spent in Lewes, I'd never met anyone who lived in Shipcarpenter Square. Her parents' house was a beautiful colonial saltbox with spruce siding stained a New England blue. The trim was Concord buff and the shutters were a deep blood red. They had a three car detached garage, with an apartment above. The driveway was wide enough to handle all the extra cars. I immediately recognized Courtney's Porsche. It was bookended by a Mercedes C Class and a Range Rover. It appeared her sisters were doing well. She thanked me for the ride, and I reminded her that if she was interested, she was invited to stop back for dessert later that night. She then surprised me by leaning over and kissing me on the cheek.

"Merry Christmas, Dylan. Maybe I'll see you later," she whispered softly.

Courtney hopped down from my truck and ran inside. The scent of her hair and the feel of her lips on my cheek remained with me. I revisited our tumbles on the beach. . . . Yep, none of it was my imagination.

When I arrived back at the house, I saw Dr. Huff's Lincoln Navigator parked in my spot, so I had to relocate.

I hate when that happens.

I remember how in the summer months we would put cones in front of the parking area so beach goers wouldn't park their cars there, barricading the entrance to our property. That was the worst. We had gotten blocked in several times. Fortunately, there was plenty of parking on the side streets during the winter months, so I parked on West Canal Street, just off Bay Avenue, and walked back to the house. The day had warmed up nicely, so I didn't mind the minor inconvenience. It felt like we were the only ones at the beach for the holidays. I wondered how Dan and Ginny would survive on Lewes beach, alone, during the coldest months yet to come.

Indoors, I greeted Dr. Huff and teased him about taking my spot. He laughed, slapped me on the back, and thanked me. I asked for Mrs. Huff, and he informed me that she remained back at the hotel. He was going to pick her up before dinner. I felt it best not to pry any further. Actually, I had a pretty good idea why she didn't want to spend Christmas Day with the likes of us.

Dan had Christmas music playing in the background.

Nice touch!

Everyone was gathered around the tree, sitting in their rocker and waiting for me to return. What a sight. I loved my family and what it was becoming. I knew I would miss them two days later when I had to return home. Knowing I would want to reflect on that moment, I pulled my cell phone from my pocket and took a picture.

With everyone assembled, gifts were given and ripped open. Near the end of the melee, there was one box remaining under the tree that no one recognized. It was labeled: "For the Carter Family." Derek did the honors. Inside was a case of sky lanterns with a note, "To be released on the night of Ginny & Dan's wedding."

The process of elimination told us that Courtney had given the gift anonymously. Perhaps she was more of a romantic than I had originally thought. I wished I could figure her out. I found her mystifying and extremely attractive. I thought about her often in those days.

GINNY

All of the gifts had been opened. I think Dad had as much fun as we did. Dan slapped his knees, stood up, and said he had a turkey to stuff and better get to it. Dex got up and said he was sorry to leave the party, but he had some errands to run.

What possible errands could anyone have to run on Christmas Day?

Dad said he had better get back to the hotel to pick up my mother. I decided I would take a nap while the house was quiet and I could sneak one in. Not wanting to risk missing anything while I was asleep, I grabbed a blanket and curled up on one of the sofas.

I napped for several hours, I think, before I felt Dan nudging my shoulder and asking me to wake up.

"Ginny, wake up. There's another present here, and it's for you."

I opened my eyes and attempted a stretch. At first, I was disoriented. I felt more tired than when I had first laid down. I couldn't remember what day or time it was. It felt like midnight.

Did I miss dinner?

No, it was still light outside. I looked around and saw the decorated tree and rocking chairs. I smelled the turkey in the oven. Then I remembered: It was Christmas Day.

"I'll Be Home for Christmas" was playing softly in the background. I thought of Mr. Carter and Lily. I wondered what they were doing that day. I wondered what Christmas was like in Heaven. I slowly sat up. Dan was sitting next to me and I put my head on his shoulder and closed my eyes. I took a couple of extra seconds to remember them both. When I was ready to shift gears, I opened my eyes. Dex was back.

What's he smiling about?

Then I noticed a big box in the middle of the floor.

"It's for you!" Dan exclaimed, his voice rising with excitement.

I wiped the sleep from my eyes and stared at the box.

Where did that come from?

I scooted to the edge of the sofa so I could reach across

the box and pull off the wrapping.

"No, no. Just lift the lid," Dan instructed.

"OK."

I lifted the lid off the box, and at first glance I couldn't see anything. The box was empty. Then, something scratched the cardboard and moved. It was a little yellow ball of fuzz. Whatever it was, it had its tiny head all tucked in under its paws and was sleeping in a blanket pressed up against a corner of the box.

"Go ahead. Pick it up," Dan coaxed, noticing my hesitation. "It won't bite you."

I reached in and wrapped my hands around its cottony soft sides. As I lifted it out of the box, four little paws dropped limply. It whimpered and opened its eyes. It was a puppy!

"A little yellow puppy! It's sooooo cute! Where did you find it? Is it a boy, or a girl? Is this really for me? Does it have a name? "

I was so overwhelmed by its small size, brown eyes, and wet nose. I pulled it to my face and snuggled into its soft fur. Susan and Dylan were awww-ing and oooo-ing. Dan and Dex were smiling ear to ear like proud papas. Derek was shaking his head in disbelief.

"It's a girl. She doesn't have a name, yet. She's just old enough to leave the litter," Dan said.

"Where did you find her?"

"Dex knows one of the Vet Techs at the Savannah Animal Hospital. They knew of a litter that needed a good home. Dex knew I was thinking of getting you a puppy, so we went to see them and we fell in love with her. We picked her up two days ago and she's been staying with Dex." Dan was obviously proud that his plan had worked out so well.

"Yep, and I got this way cool pink harness for her, too," Dex crowed, holding up a little pink harness and leash.

"She'll grow out of that in a week," Derek snarked.

"And, while you guys were having a fun time at dinner last night, I was out in the cold walking your dog!" Dex continued, trying to lay on the guilt. However, I got the impression that he enjoyed having her with him while he could.

"I think I would have rather been walking my puppy than sitting at the dinner table," I retorted.

"She needs a name. What's her name?" Susan joyfully demanded, reaching out as I handed her my puppy that she was impatiently waiting to hold.

We tossed around a lot of possible names from the sublime to the ridiculous.

"What do you think, Ginny? Dan asked. "She's your dog . . . that is, should you decide to keep her."

Susan handed her back to me, and I looked into the puppy's eyes, nose to nose.

"Gilda. Her name is Gilda."

My father and mother arrived shortly before dinner. My mother was very quiet. I think she was pretending that none of us were there and that nothing had occurred the night before. She wanted nothing to do with Gilda.

Courtney made it for dessert and coffee.

Dan outdid himself. His father would have been very proud. At different times during the night, I could tell that he was missing his father, especially having to roast a turkey without him for the first time, ever. Dylan jumped in now and then to help, especially when it came time to carve. I think Dylan was aware of how much this meal meant to Dan now and in the past.

As the day came to a close, my parents left for the hotel so they could get a good night's sleep. They planned on leaving early in the morning, so they said their goodbyes before leaving the house. Derek and Susan decided to turn in early. Dex thanked us for a great day and said goodbye to everyone. I gave him an extra big hug, thanking him for taking care of Gilda. We invited "Uncle Dex" to come visit her anytime. Dylan and Courtney were just kind of hanging around when I suggested that Dan and I should take Gilda out for one more walk.

Gilda was a little wary of the dark, the noises, the sand, the waves, and maybe us. We sat with her on the beach for a while until she acclimated to all of it. She was soon ready to play. She was all fur and her back feet sometimes got ahead of her front, causing her to crab sideways when she clumsily ran. Her little tail wagged and we heard her bark for the first time.

So that's what our little ball of fur sounds like!

From that moment on, I knew I would recognize her bark anywhere, and she would soon come to recognize our voices as well. We would be a little family. We let her play in the cold air, hoping it would tire her out and that she would sleep through the night.

As we started back to the house, we could see Courtney and Dylan inside, sitting close together, and having what seemed to be a serious conversation. Not wanting to disrupt anything, we hung back.

"I still have my money on Courtney," Dan whispered.

"Could be, looks like emotions are running high in there, and he leaves tomorrow."

Then, they stood up and disappeared into the kitchen.

It was the day after Christmas, and Gilda had cried most of the night. We were all pretty ragged by the time the sun came up. I later asked Dex how he had kept her quiet on the boat for two nights. He asked if I had ever heard of a "three dog night," meaning he let her sleep in bed with him. Mystery solved. Thanks to Dex, Gilda thought she was supposed to be in bed with us. Being alone in a crate was not what she had had in mind. Dan and I decided we needed to be strong. The last thing we wanted was a one hundred pound golden retriever in bed with us every night.

Everyone left in the morning as they said they would. Susan and I hugged and said goodbye. Dylan waved as his truck backed out.

And so, there we were: Dan, me, and one crazy puppy named Gilda who was busy chewing on my pant leg. In subsequent weeks, we allowed Gilda into the bedroom. However, she was not allowed on the bed. It took two nights of shoving her off for her to learn that we had rules, but when it was all said and done, we were so proud of her. As a reward, we ordered a dog bed from LL Bean. She loved it.

The winter marched in and we froze. So did the pipes in the upstairs bathroom. Gilda was the informant. Forgetting the rules, she came bounding up on our bed, and she was cold and soaking wet. We thought she had gotten out and ran down to the beach. It turned out that she didn't have to go any farther than the living room because the water was pouring down the wall. Dan spent that weekend, and several after that, making the necessary repairs. Dex came over and helped whenever he could, which was pretty much for the next two weekends and a few evenings.

We were alarmed one afternoon by a commotion in the kitchen. Gilda's hair was raised on her back as she barked at the washer. It was walking itself across the kitchen floor. She clearly thought it was a monster. We could never get it balanced after that, so we bit the bullet and replaced it.

In the spring, Dan and Dex had to make several repairs to the roof. The faucet in the downstairs bathroom had to be replaced. The ceiling was falling down between the kitchen and the living room, and keeping Dan's Jeep running in the midst of it all was a constant project. Dan and Dex did a lot of bonding over the winter months, and we had Dex over for many beers and "Thank you" dinners.

In April we purchased a beach tag so we could drive the Jeep onto the beach at Cape Henlopen State Park. Gilda loved the ocean. She chased everything that moved: seagulls, sand crabs, and people, especially the small variety. She was getting bigger and clumsier, then. To make matters worse, she didn't know her own strength. When Dex would stop by the house, Gilda would run full tilt toward him. Stopping did not come naturally to her, so she would plow right into his legs. Once, when they were playing chase on the beach, she came up behind him and took him out at the back of his knees. Down he went into a perfect face plant. She happily sat over top of him and continued the assault with her sloppy wet tongue. A few weeks later, she accidentally knocked down a toddler. We decided then that it would be best if we kept her on a leash unless no one else was out and about.

When warmer weather finally began making its guest appearances, Dex had to tend to some of his own priorities and projects. He had the Right Tackle pulled so he could inspect the hull and repaint it below the waterline. That's when we learned that he stayed in the Sable's garage apartment during those times when it was inconvenient or too cold to be on the boat. Dan helped him in return for all he had done for us. The weather was unseasonably warm the weekend the Right Tackle was ready to be launched, so instead of hammering and sawing here at 408 Bay Avenue, the guys took the day off and went with Dex on the Right Tackle's shakedown cruise. I must admit, while I missed having the guys here for the day, it was nice to have a few hours of peace and quiet.

The three of them returned in the late afternoon wind burnt, exhilarated, and talking of future fishing excursions. It had become obvious that Dan, Dylan, and Dex liked hanging out together. I was happy that Dan had made a friend in Lewes, especially because his brothers lived two hours away. If only Susan lived closer.

May arrived before we could blink, and fortunately, we had been graciously spared an extended harsh winter. The plans for our wedding, albeit very small, were in high gear. It was only two weeks away. Dylan had stayed with us the first week of April to help repair the deck. Dex helped on weekends and sometimes in the evenings. I could say they worked for peanuts and a song, but they deserved more than that. I made sure there was a steady stream of beers, snacks, lunch, and dinner. However, above all, I think they worked for the camaraderie. As hammers were pounding and saws were whining with friction, they talked sports, politics, fishing, cars, and boats. They ragged on each other continually. Sometimes, they would take a break and throw the football around. It always ended up in some pseudo-wrestling match. When Dylan was there, Courtney would always show up. I think she and Dylan were staying in touch by then. Their friendship had grown, just as I had suspected it would.

The first weekend in May, with the Right Tackle back in the water, Dex said he would work all day at the house on Saturday if we all agreed to go out on the boat with him on Sunday. I was really looking forward to it. Dex warned us that even though it was May and the air felt warm on land, we should be prepared and dress in layers. He very humbly asked if I would mind preparing a picnic lunch for everyone. I was more than happy to do it and glad he had asked. It gave me something to focus on, other than the wedding.

On Saturday, the guys put the finishing touches on our deck. They replaced the old splintery wood with Trex. It was a material that was made from recycled goods and would probably outlast the house. They built it twice as wide as the original, so the new deck was very roomy. They built a screened-in porch over half of it. I loved what they had done and could not wait to spend summer nights outside without being chased by mosquitos.

Courtney stopped by and helped me prepare the picnic for our trip the next day. We fried chicken, made roasted potato salad with bacon, and a dozen cheddar biscuits. Courtney and I also baked two-dozen chocolate chip cookies. She said they were Dex's favorite. Dan purchased a case of beer.

While we were in the kitchen, I had many moments when I wished Susan were there. With the wedding so near, she called me almost every night. But, I still missed her terribly. Courtney had offered to help on numerous occasions, which was kind. She was OK to hang out with; she just wasn't Susan. I still had my guard up around Courtney, and I was not ready to be completely transparent with her. She reminded me of the girls that would never be caught dead hanging out with me in high school. She was more like the girl that stole my seat at the lunch table. Whether she intended to or not, she intimidated me. She was beautiful. She was smart. And, she made the big bucks.

Sunday morning had arrived. Courtney helped me pack the food into a cooler and a couple of canvas totes. We loaded everything into Dylan's truck and drove the half-mile to the canal. When we arrived, Dex was out on the deck of the Right Tackle straightening the lines. He stood up, fully exposing his bronze shoulders and six pack abs. His arms were chiseled, but not overdone like someone obsessed. He was slender and solid. He was nature's son. He had on an old pair of jeans that barely hung on his hips with the help of a worn leather belt. His tan feet were relaxed and kicked back in a frayed pair of sandals. I became acutely aware that I had just gawked at my fiancé's friend. Momentarily, I felt a self-imposed voyeur's guilt. Looking around, I realized no one had noticed my indiscretion. Throwing on a T-shirt, Dex waved us on down the catwalk and helped us load everything on board.

The Right Tackle really suited Dex. She was every bit as rugged and aptly named for a football position that was part of the offensive line. Right tackles had to be strong and fast off the block. Dex claimed she was all of that. I asked him why he referred to the Right Tackle as a "she." He said it was part of English folklore. Some believed it was because captains often named their ships after their mothers, spouses, or mistresses. Others say ships were named after goddesses. Either way, it was rather ironic, because women onboard were supposed to be bad luck at sea. Dex said we could test out that theory with Court and me onboard that day.

She was beautiful from a distance, just as I had seen her when walking down the dock from Irish Eyes. Up close, she was majestic and proud. Boarding her was electric, like a first kiss. Somehow, I knew I would never be the same. She listed ever so slightly as I took Dex's hand and shifted my weight over and on to her. I moved to the center of the cockpit as the others boarded. There was enough room to have a large cocktail party out there.

With everyone gathered safely on deck, Dex asked if I would like a tour. It was then that I realized I was the only one who was on a maiden voyage. I was the last of the day's crew to lose my innocence to his beautiful vessel.

Dex said she was forty-two feet long and had a beam of fourteen feet. We went into the main salon. It was immaculate, which really took me by surprise. I thought that having a bachelor as her captain, and being a fishing boat, meant that she would probably be messy and fishy smelling. She was clean and in tip-top shape.

Her interior was natural teak wood throughout. Her upholstery was a very light sky blue, setting off a peaceful contrast of color. There was seating for five or six around her dining table, plus another casual sitting area across from it.

Below, her galley contained as many appliances as the beach house kitchen. Dex had all the accommodations he could possibly need and then some. He was living better than we were!

The guest stateroom had a queen-size bed, several drawers and a hanging locker. The color scheme was a very patriotic red, white, and blue. Its bathroom was shared by all guests on board, but could be locked off for privacy.

Dex informed me that a bathroom on a boat is called "the head," and, of course, I asked why.

"The term comes from the early days of sailing ships. Because the wind most often blew from the rear (or stern) of the ship, the bathroom would be located at the front, or the head of the ship, to prevent any spray from blowing back and to carry the foul smell of excrement away from its crew."

"Oh . . . that really makes sense."

His master stateroom was gorgeous with an island queen bed and a private "head." It had two sets of drawers and a much larger hanging locker. It was framed out in teak like the rest of the interior. The spread on the bed was navy blue. Several throw pillows were navy with white cord trim and anchor appliques. Others were made from nautical signal flags. The largest pillow, front and center, featured a large compass. The soft recessed lighting added an air of invitation. However, the best feature was the way the reflection of the water danced across the ceiling in random ribbons of light. I could only imagine what a handsome bachelor like Dex could get into aboard his floating boudoir. The natural rock of the water must have had its own sex appeal. It was making me uncomfortable just thinking about it.

To my surprise, there were a lot of ports below that allowed an ample amount of light and ventilation. Dex said we had to remember to close everything up before we got underway. We made our way back up on deck. The others were standing around and had already cracked open a few beers.

Next, up to the bridge. As I climbed the ladder, with Dex just below me, I could feel the boat sway. I looked down to see those clowns rocking her, intentionally.

Assholes . . .

I smiled because I knew I would have done the same. Up on the fly bridge, we had a picturesque view of the marina. There was a captain's station with a bench seat before the wheel that could seat two to three people. In front of the captain's station was more seating. There was enough room on the fly bridge to accommodate all of us, and Dex said that was the usual preferred seating for us cruisers. The two of us sat down and Dex quickly walked me through the control panel and navigation instruments. He rattled off things like depth sounder, radar, GPS, weather bands, marine radio, autopilot, etc., etc., etc. There was a lot to learn, yet it seemed the boat could pilot herself. Dex proudly stated that she had two 485 horsepower engines and he could run her out at 28 knots. That did not sound very fast to me, but he assured me that on the water it was plenty of speed. He mentioned that when people charter a fishing boat, they were not there to cruise and take in the sights. Their main objective was to get to the fish, quickly.

"Next stop, the top of the tuna tower."

"You mean up there?"

"Yep."

"I thought that was for ... uh, decoration. You really go up there?"

"Of course, and so will you. It's a heck of a lot easier to climb up there now than out in open water, so it's now or never."

As I started up the ladder, the others below were chanting, "Go, go, go!"

I threatened bodily harm if they rocked the boat again. Of course, they did anyway. Who was I kidding? I decided to just climb up strong and steady and not look down. Dex followed right behind me, again, telling me I looked like I had been scaling ladders all my life. I must admit that it was not as scary as I thought it would be, even though I was terrified of heights. Anyway, I was able to override my fear as I climbed up, completely captivated by the aerial view. Dex explained that the tuna tower had a real purpose. It was designed to help the captain navigate and spot fish. The view was magnificent. I made Dex promise that if the conditions were right, he would let me ride up there for at least part of the trip.

After several minutes of savoring the sights and the unhindered breeze, we descended from the tower. Back in the cockpit, Dan had a beer waiting for me. He knew me so well. After I had my first draw, he put his arm around my shoulder and told me he was amazed that I had climbed the tower, and with such ease. So was I! It must have been the adrenaline pumping through my veins.

Back on deck, Dex got down to business. He took no shortcuts in going through the necessary safety information like where the lifejackets were stowed, how to use the flares, and the correct way to deploy the lifeboat. He talked

us through the "man overboard drill." He gave me some
words he called "nomenclature" like bow, stern, port, and
starboard, so I could at least follow some basic instructions.

One more check around the boat, and Dex was ready to
kick over the first engine. I had never heard anything as
powerful as that below my feet. After a minute or so, he
kicked over the second engine. It was exhilarating. The
engines had their own unique sound as they pulled in
seawater as a coolant and expelled it out of the exhaust in
the stern. The exhaust pipes would submerge in and out of
water as the boat rocked, creating a beguiling cadence. The
deck hummed with the horses running smoothly below it.

We prepared to cast off, making sure everything was
stowed away, ports were closed, and the hatches were
battened down. Dan was in charge of the bowlines, Dylan
manned the spring line, and Courtney and I were stationed
at the stern lines. From the fly bridge, Dex gave the signal
to release the stern lines, and as the Right Tackle began to
slowly move forward, Dan began looping the bowlines onto
the large cleats on the pilings on either side of the
bow. Dylan was walking spring line until the pilings were
about amidships. Letting go, he laid the line on the
catwalk. As soon as her stern cleared the last two pilings,
Dex swung the Right Tackle around on a dime, and just like
that we were on our way out. The sound of the water
rushing over the hull was like nothing I had ever heard
before. It was soft and gentle as it rippled across the
smooth massive vessel. She glided effortlessly through the
water. It had an immediate calming effect, and I was
mesmerized by the small wake trailing behind us.

Before reaching open water, we all scurried up the
ladder to the seating area on the bridge. Inviting me to
experience everything from the captain's vantage point,
Dex patted the seat next to him. Dan, Dylan, and Courtney
sat in the bridge salon in front of us. From the captain's
bench, I had a panoramic view of the area where Dan and I
now lived. It looked so enchanted from the water. It even
smelled different as the sea air washed across my face. We
soon left the canal and entered the Roosevelt Inlet. The

water sparkled like glitter and formed a funneled path that led us to the sun that was continuing its ascent just above the horizon. The discoloration of the inlet bulkhead was witness to the rise and fall of the tides. Each thick piling, spaced evenly across the wall of stone, was capped off with a seagull calling out to us as we passed by. People of all ages and genders were standing and fishing on the rocks. I knew none of them, yet many of them waved, acknowledging a connection of sorts. The wake we left behind trailed along the rocks and created a running line of spray.

I looked toward Dan. His gaze was extended out across the water. His face was to the wind and held no expression except that of complete serenity. His heart had all it needed to keep beating for a thousand years. I knew then that that place on the water was Dan's mistress with whom I could never compete. It was suddenly clear where Dan belonged. Now, fully revealed in his youngest son's spirit, I understood Mr. Carter's Last Will and Testament. It was then that I, too, understood that I wanted to be there always, with Dan. Mr. Carter's Will had cast a long lasting and loving power over both of us. Lost and found, my life was on a new trajectory.

When we left the "No Wake Zone" and cleared the inlet, Dex started to throttle up the Right Tackle. The bow began pitching up at an uncomfortable angle and it felt like the stern was going to sink below the surface. Not sure of what was happening, I white knuckled the handrail. As the acceleration continued for a number of concerning seconds, the bow finally began to level off and the stern rose back up. The Right Tackle felt like she was rising up above the water as she picked up more speed. It was like flying. The engine noise was left behind us and became almost inaudible from where we were sitting. Dex opened her up. It felt like we were doing seventy miles per hour. He looked over at me.

"Told you so!" A shit-eating grin covered his proud face.

Dan called for my attention and pointed out the Carter beach house. With a large dune in front and a mile of water between us, it looked so small. It *was* small and surrounded by larger, taller neighbors with long waterfront decks and expansive rooftops. The Carter beach house looked humble and shy, as if hoping to go unnoticed.

"That's your new home, Ginny! How does it look from out here?" Dan asked excitedly.

"Beautiful."

We were soon beyond the seawall and officially out in the ocean. The Right Tackle's deep hull cut through the rollers and her flight felt different then. It was like riding a galloping draft horse with its slow rhythmic gait. It was very sensual. Adding to the experience, sea spray would occasionally reach us on the bridge. Dex mentioned that one time he rode on the bridge through gale winds. He said the waves were huge and when the boat went down into a trough, he was eye-to-eye with the crest of the next oncoming wave. He must have known what I was thinking. He nudged me and chuckled, telling me not to worry. He said we would have clear skies and relatively calm seas all day.

Dylan and Courtney were seated next to each other, just chatting away. Dylan had his arm resting atop the cushion behind her, but not around her. There were flirtatious shoulder leans and arm punches. It was all friendly banter. They were such a cute couple. My guess was that she was four years older than he was, but they certainly didn't look or act as though there was a significant age difference. They obviously enjoyed spending time together. However, Dan was right; Courtney would need to make the first move. At that pace, I was not going to hold my breath.

Dan turned to me with complete contentment in his eyes.

"I knew you'd love it out here!"

He came back and sat next to me, forcing the three of us to squeeze onto the bench. I was the squished lemon in the middle, not that I minded. Dan put his arm around my shoulders and gave me a kiss on the cheek. For once, I didn't turn to meet his lips. I was too intent on everything that was happening around us and didn't want to miss a thing. I had never felt so energized. I was also beginning to understand why Dex chose to live in Lewes and on the boat, despite whatever may have happened in his past.

Miles out, Dex powered-down the engines and kept the Right Tackle headed into the wind. With little to no forward motion, the Right Tackle began to roll a lot more. I looked around. Land was nowhere in sight. Without the instruments, I would have had no idea how to get back. My mind raced with a crazed imagination brought on by the unknown.

Everyone on board was rendered helpless and unconscious. I, alone, had to bring her back to port. As if we were in the Bermuda Triangle, all of the instruments were knocked out. I would have to use whatever resources were available to me. Judging by the sun, I estimated a westerly heading, knowing that on that course, at some point, we would reach land.

There were mumblings around me that shook me from my nightmarish fantasy. Everyone was preparing to leave the bridge.

"Ginny, we're going down to rig up some rods. You want to do some fishing?"

We drifted and fished most of the day. Even when we ate lunch, the lines were always in the water. By the afternoon, Courtney and I had turned our poles over to the guys. We went up on the bow to chat and nap in the sun. It was a gorgeously warm day.

When the sun began its descent, it was time to pack it in and head for home. Dex said we had an OK day as far as the fishing went. We brought home eight sea bass, keeping only as much as we wanted to clean and fillet. The rest we threw back. As for me, it was a day I would not soon forget. With calm seas, Dex and I climbed the tower, and as promised, he allowed me to pilot the Right Tackle from aloft. It was so amazing. We could see for miles and deep down below the water's surface. Once we were cruising, the ride was smoother than I expected. We were running with the current and what little wind there was created enough of an ocean roll that it felt like the boat was surfing the waves. She would pick up speed in front of the wave and then slow down once the crest passed us and we reached the next crest. Controlling her was a little more difficult on that tack. Dex stayed close and showed me how to feel and run with the rollers, taking them on the back quarter without letting her turn broadside. After a half hour, I turned her back over to Dex. I watched him as he lorded over his ship and the sea. With the wind in his hair and his strong hands on the wheel, he wore his love of the sea on the sleeve of his fire-scarred arm. It was becoming all the more difficult for me to believe that he could ever set fire to a boathouse and the nautical relic inside.

Back at dock, the guys went up to the cleaning station to filet the fish while Courtney and I packed and cleaned up the Right Tackle. When the guys came back, they put the filets on ice. We all relaxed in the cockpit with a beer, sharing stories of the day. It was as though we were making sure we would all have our fish stories straight should we speak of them elsewhere. The talk eventually drifted to the guys' memories surrounding their boating pasts. They reminisced about a storm they had all navigated together on a smaller craft many years ago. The boat had belonged to a friend of the Carters. The boys all got in trouble for going out as far as they did in unsettled weather. Everyone back on shore was in a panic as they watched a storm roll in from the west, knowing that the boys would meet it on their way back in. Dex said Mr. Carter later shared that he was very close to sending out the Coast Guard. I asked Dex if his parents were in a panic.

He said it was only he and his mom at the time, but he never really answered the question. However, he did mention that they had moved to Silicon Valley shortly after the incident. Dex added that he rarely—as in never—saw his mother after he had returned to Lewes. From what I could gather, it was a mutual decision. We were probably the closest thing Dex had to a family. His complexities were beyond my understanding, other than he loved the water, and he loved his boat.

My mind again questioned how Dex could have deliberately set a devastating fire. As well, Dan had earlier shared with me his doubts about Dex's culpability in the crime. As the story goes, Courtney's dad had represented him and he was acquitted of all charges. I wondered what Courtney's dad knew and believed. I wondered why Derek seemed so determined to convict him over and over, years later. I wondered how his mother could possibly choose not to see her amazing son. Something just did not seem to add up, making Dex more of a mystery.

But we loved hanging out with Dex. We were so grateful for all of the help he had given us at the beach house.

Before leaving, we hosed and scrubbed down the decks of the Right Tackle. We straightened and secured all of her lines, closed her up, and took Dex to dinner.

DEX

The Right Tackle proved herself on that day. Her engines kicked right over and ran smoothly. Her electronics were all up and running. It may have been the first spring I didn't have to crawl into the bilge to repair a hose, or change spark plugs, or hire a mechanic, for that matter.

We had had a great trip. Ginny and Courtney made an awesome lunch. The fish were running, and the weather was perfect. We all looked a little wind burnt. Ginny said it would take several tries with cream rinse to get the knots out of her hair. She did look a little exotic with her tanned face and unruly red hair. Dan was relieved she had had such a good time, hoping she would come out with us again. He shared that perhaps she may take to fishing after all.

Yes, it had been a great day. We both slept like babies that night, the Right Tackle and me.

DAN

It was a day that bonded the five of us. We worked hard and played harder. Ginny said she learned more about boating than she ever expected, and she wanted to know more. I felt like a new man out on the water, and it was rejuvenating to experience it through her new eyes. She looked radiant with the wind in her hair and the sun in her face. Dex and I teased her about talking like a sailor by the end of the day. Not cursing, she actually learned the nomenclature. I was so proud and in love with her uninhibited sense of adventure. I knew that if and when we had children, they would be very lucky to have her for their mother. In a little more than a week, I would be the happiest man on earth.

Back at the house, Gilda was excited to see us. It was rare that we left her home alone. She still liked her crate and would crawl in whenever we left. I think she felt safe in there. Leaving our coats on, we immediately took her out for a walk. During that time of year, we didn't bother to put her harness and leash on. She pretty much stayed with us, and there was rarely anyone else on the beach for her to chase. She was pretty good about coming when she was called. As we strolled the beach and I threw a ball for Gilda to retrieve, Ginny reviewed everything she had learned that day. She wanted to make sure that if Dex allowed her to take the helm again, she would be able to give proper orders. She had been bitten by the boating bug.

Susan called that night, as she usually did. I could hear Ginny telling her all about the day's expedition. Knowing that they would be talking for a while, I headed for the shower. I had no trouble drifting off to sleep that night with the girls continued conversation in the background. I knew Ginny missed Susan, but she would be coming to Lewes soon. Ginny told me the next morning that when her head finally hit the pillow, she could still feel the boat rocking. She was sorry that the feeling had left her by the time she woke up.

SUSAN

I arrived at Ginny's on Wednesday. She jumped up and down and gave me a hug as soon as I walked through the door. I put my things down and Ginny grabbed my hands and ran me up the stairs to their room. As promised, she showed me the dress she had found. It was even more extraordinary than she described on the phone. It was a simple white dress that made her look like an angel. When she walked, it floated like it was a part of her. She wanted the hem raised a bit so it would not drag in the sand. She intended to walk over the dune barefoot. Her dress also needed to be taken in ever so slightly. I had my work cut out for me with very little time remaining. After we hauled my luggage upstairs, we immediately went to work.

Friday morning, Courtney met us at the house and the three of us went to her florist to pick out flowers for our bouquets. The florist said she would make the boutonnieres for the guys and a corsage for Ginny's mom.

Friday night the boys stayed on the boat with Dex, and the girls stayed at the beach house. Derek was due to drive down from Valley Forge to join us first thing Saturday morning, Ginny's wedding day. I had been praying that his visit would go well, for Ginny's sake ... and mine, too.

GINNY

I woke up Saturday morning to the sound of footprints on the deck. Gilda was barking nonstop. I didn't know whether she was being a watchdog or wanting to get out so she could love all over whoever was out there. I wrapped myself in a robe and ran downstairs with one eye barely open. Susan was stirring and wanted to know what was going on. I was thinking it was Derek, but not quite sure why he would be on the deck rather than coming through the back kitchen door. To my knowledge, he still had a key. But it was not Derek. Not even close. There were men on our deck setting up tables and chairs, and covering them in white linen. Other men were wrapping the deck rails in a baby's breath garland. They had candles and barware. They also thrust torches into the sand over the dune and out to the beach. I called Dan's cell phone.

"Dan, wake up. You need to get over here! Did you know these men would be on our deck this morning?"

"There are men on your deck?"

"*Your* deck, and yes, there are men climbing all over *your* deck."

"What are they doing?" he asked, pretending he needed more information.

"They're setting up tables and chairs. They're wrapping flowers around the rails and sticking torches in the sand. What's going on? Gilda's going crazy!"

"I can hear her."

"Dan?"

"It's a surprise. . . ."

"Huh?"

"It's a gift from your dad. He called back in January and asked about our wedding plans. I told him you wanted to get married at the house and that you wanted to keep it small. He insisted on covering all the costs and instructed me to spare no expense. I told him that wasn't necessary, but he said if it were my daughter, I would insist on the same. I knew he was right, and in a way, I thought we owed him that. I told him how you wanted everything to be outside, and Dex, Dylan, and I were trying to make quick repairs to the deck. Ginny, he insisted on paying for the materials. He set up an account at Lowes for us. Then, he wanted to know what caterer we were using. I think you're going to love what he has ordered. He always called me first to make sure it would fit with your ideas. He just wants to be a part of it all. I hope you'll be happy with it."

"Wait, we worked with the caterer. What about the food we ordered?"

"The caterer kept to your menu, but your dad . . . well . . . he embellished it. I think you're going to love it, Ginny. Your dad is an awesome guy. We should give him the moment every father dreams of for their little girl."

I was a little uncomfortable that everything had been taken out of my control and not finding out about it until the morning of my wedding day. Even though they conspired behind my back, I was touched by the thought of my dad and Dan scheming together.

"Ginny, just tell the girls there will be people in and out of the house all day, so make sure they are decent."

"So, now you tell me. I ran down the stairs half naked. They're all staring at me."

Silence . . .

"Just kidding. They should be so lucky."

"You're right, baby. I am the luckiest man in the world. I can't wait to see you."

DAN

She was absolutely beautiful as her dad walked her over the dune. She had a radiant smile that accentuated her sweet dimples. Her hair reflected the late afternoon sun. Her dress flowed with the gentle on-shore breeze. It made her appear to be floating toward me like an apparition.

Is this really happening?

She was walking toward me. Of all the people on this earth in this space and time, she had said yes to me. I wanted to live in that moment forever.

Derek and Dylan were standing with me. I think I heard them exhale when we got our first glimpse of her. Susan and Courtney were waiting for her on the opposite side. Dex was keeping an eye on Gilda. She was visiting everybody, just happy to be there and off her leash. She stayed clear of Victoria, though. I think she instinctively knew to avoid her.

Courtney's dad had arranged for a Justice of the Peace. Our parents and the Sables were seated in chairs covered in white that had been placed in the sand. The ceremony was short, as requested. We exchanged our vows and the rings. The JP encouraged us to be kind, generous, and forgiving. He advised us to play hard and pray harder. He told us that every day and night we needed to choose love. He reiterated it again; "choose to love each other . . . until death do us part." I thought of my dad and Lily. How I wished they were there. In my heart, I knew they were. The sun was low enough in the sky to create a glistening path across the water, landing at our feet. There were sounds of children giggling nearby. I could see a vision of my dad holding Lily and playing with her. They must be celebrating with us. . . .

After the ceremony and the kiss I had waited for all day, hugs went around and we all started back to the house. As we crossed the dune, we saw that while we were out on the beach getting hitched, a bar and table with appetizers had been set up between the deck and the dune. A string quartet was playing on the far end of the deck while we had cocktails. Out on the beach, the caterer was setting up a trough made of new pinewood. They had several huge steaming pots set up over commercial propane burners. Ginny knew instantly what was going on and hugged her dad around the neck.

"Oh Daddy, you remembered. This is the best!" Her feet were off the ground as she held on to him and he swung her around.

Dr. Huff had arranged for the caterer to make low country stew; Ginny's favorite. It contained jumbo shrimp, crab legs, clams, Vidalia onions, Andouille sausage, and corn on the cob. Once the stew was done simmering, the pots were dumped into the trough, which was angled to drain off the water. What was left was an amazing array of flavors. Sitting along the trough were a half-dozen ladles. We had a great time scooping out the stew, eating, drinking, and being with our family and friends. There was so much food and drink, we invited others walking along the beach to come and join us. We even met some of our neighbors.

GINNY

When the evening was over, the caterer packed up everything and cleaned up the kitchen. They left the garland on the deck rails and the torches in the sand. Other than that, you would have never known they were there. My dad congratulated us one more time as we thanked him repeatedly for a wonderful celebration. My mother did not have much to say, for which I was grateful. After my parents had pulled away, Dan and I went out to the beach with the others. The torches were still burning, creating a warm glow in the night sky. The stars had come out to illuminate the heavens. Dex had built a fire and everyone was huddled around it. Dan and I paused on the top of the dune as if we were looking out over our children—our close circle of friends. Derek and Susan were snuggled together. Dex had a stick and was stirring the fire. Every now and then, a log would pop and a plume of sparks would shatter the dark surroundings. Their conversation was muffled as it blended in with the crackling fire and the sound of gentle waves caressing the shoreline. Occasionally, we would hear a collective laugh. To my surprise, Courtney had her head rested on Dylan's shoulder and he had his arm around her. We stood back for a while to watch the magical moment. Our day had become their day, too. Yep, we felt like parents who, at that moment, knew they had "done good."

"Dan, we forgot the sky lanterns. Let's go back and get them," I whispered.

We ran back to the house and up the stairs. We thought we had put them in our bedroom closet, and just as we had thought, we found them there. I started to leave the room with the lanterns tucked under my arm when Dan spun me around.

"Mrs. Carter, I'd like to have a word with you," Dan growled rather sternly.

It occurred to me that this was our first moment alone as husband and wife. Dan wrapped his arms around my waist and pulled me into his body and kissed me with a sense of urgency. I could feel him rising to the occasion and I wanted him, as well.

"Dan, I think we should wait and save all this pent up energy for tonight," I whispered.

"Ahhh . . . But I recover quickly," he pleaded as his hands began exploring my body, making my resistance all the more difficult.

I leaned into him more and thought I might give him something to think about.

"I want nothing more than to make long, slow, delicious love to you right now, but it will have to wait." I pulled away and started down the steps with the sky lanterns tucked under my arm.

Dan followed, let Gilda out, and caught up with me on the deck. He took my hand as we crossed the dune and made our way through the sand and out to the fire.

"We've got sky lanterns!" I announced, holding them up.

"Did you bring a lighter?" Courtney asked as Gilda ran up and climbed into Dex's lap.

"Yep." Dan held up a little flamethrower he had grabbed from the kitchen.

"Got a marker?"

"A marker? Why do we need with a marker?"

"To send up a wish or a prayer," Courtney said as if we should have known all along.

Dan ran back to the house, again. Gilda leaped from Dex's lap and followed Dan because he had become something to chase. I looked over at Dylan and Courtney and they seemed to be having their own little thing going on as the glow from the fire flickered across their faces. They smiled at each other from time to time, a nudge here and a jab there. They would look away and pretend neither was aware of the physical contact they were now enjoying. It was a romantic night, indeed.

I sat down next to Dex.

"Ginny, the day was beautiful. If I ever get married, I think I would want it to be just like today."

"Thanks, Dex," I said patting his arm. "I'm glad you had a good time. After all, you put a lot of work into this place. Thanks, again, for all of your help." I gave him a hug and a kiss on the cheek.

Oh, the lucky girl that lands this handsome man . . .

"You're welcome. And when you and Dan get back from your honeymoon, you have to come out for a celebration cruise on the Right Tackle."

"Something tells me you are just in need of a good

crew."

"Could be."

"It's a deal."

Dan returned with several markers. Circulating them, we pulled out the lanterns and made the distribution. I wrote "Lily" on mine, and Dan wrote "Dad."

Susan and Derek were working on theirs together. The evening had cast its romantic spell on them, too. I saw them exchange a quick kiss. I was so relieved to see Derek at peace. Dylan was helping Courtney with her sky lantern, and Gilda was helping Dex. Well, not exactly, but they were having a good time. Dex had to get a new lantern because Gilda tore the first one apart.

We gathered at the water's edge and began lighting the small fuel packs. It took the balloons more time to fill out from the heat than we had expected. I thought sure the thin rice paper would catch fire, but to my surprise we started to feel them begin to lift before they ignited into a ball of flames. As soon as the lift turned into a tug, we let them go. Dan watched as the balloon with his dad's name rose and eventually blended in with the stars as we lost sight of it. The other two went up and accompanied it. Next we prepared to launch Lily's. Dan paused for a moment before lighting it. I think he was praying. With tears in our eyes, we lit the fuel pack. As it rose into the night sky, it felt as though Lily was waving goodbye. I wanted to grab her back and hug her, just once. Sometimes, she and Dan's dad seemed so close, yet so far away. We stood there in an embrace as we watched her float up and away, winking at us. How I wished that lantern could have stayed with us for the rest of our lives. A light breeze picked up as she seemingly disappeared into the Milky Way. We all remained there for a time, lost in our thoughts and silent healing. Perhaps this would become a new family tradition, a family to which I now belonged.

Dex began throwing sticks for Gilda who happily ran into the dark water after them.

"If she gets attacked by a shark or some other sea monster lurking out there, I'm throwing you in after her,"

Dan threatened.

"OK, Gilda, out of the water. Daddy's a killjoy. Let's go get you hosed off."

Gilda took off for the house and Dex followed her.

It was time for Dan and me to gather our things, say goodbye to everyone, and head out to our honeymoon suite. We were going to spend our wedding night at The Hotel Blue. In the morning we would leave for the British Virgin Islands.

DAN

The day lived up to and surpassed all of my expectations. Honestly, I really could not have cared if it rained and everything planned was ruined. As long as the Justice of the Peace showed up and Ginny and I were married, then I still would have said it was the best day of my life. Fortunately, none of that happened. It was a perfect spring day. Ginny looked absolutely beautiful. (I know every groom probably says that.)

As we took our vows, I knew I would keep my promises to her. Not because I had to, but because I deeply desired to. I wanted to be that man who all of her friends talked about, saying how lucky she was to have a devoted husband like me. Yes, I wanted to be that guy. Hers.

And within my heart of hearts I knew that Ginny would do everything within her power to uphold her promises, and I had no reason to doubt her. We had shared some truly amazing times, and we had survived a time of heart wrenching disappointment. And yet, it still could not come close to how blessed I felt. Through it all, we had stood by each other.

That night, I wanted her to know that while we had lived together over the past year, that day was the beginning of something new and that our first night as husband and wife was very special. She was more than I could have ever hoped for. She was the answer to all of my prayers. I wanted her to know that I would cherish her and honor her forever.

When it was time for us to leave, we threw our luggage into her CR-V and headed for The Hotel Blue. It was within a half mile of our house, and I could not think of a better place to spend our wedding night. Neither of us had been there before, yet we had heard nothing but rave reviews about it. It was located on Angler's Road, before Irish Eyes. It was comprised of sixteen boutique suites and only adults were permitted to stay there.

We checked in, and as promised, we had a corner suite on the top floor. I slipped the key into the door and pushed it open. Then, I swept Ginny off her feet. Holding her in midair, I gave her a long kiss.

"Mrs. Carter, I love you more than words can say. This night belongs to us. This night, you will know how much I love you, all the way into sunrise tomorrow."

I kissed her again and then carried her into the room. I gently placed her feet on the floor and locked the door behind us. I began working my kisses from her lips down her graceful neck and across her bare shoulders. She pushed back.

"Dan, let me get out of this dress and into something more comfortable. Will you unzip me, please?"

She turned around and pulled up her hair. With great anticipation I unhooked the top of her dress and slowly pulled the zipper down to where it ended at the base of her spine, exposing the two dimples above her buttocks. She gathered her dress, which was now barely covering her body, and slipped into the bathroom.

Our suite had a fireplace that I lit to take off the chill. The dressing area had doublewide glass French doors that opened into the bedroom. It featured a long counter with double sinks, and to enhance the ambiance, the countertops and sinks were made of clear glass and were illuminated by blue lights from beneath. The effect cast a sensuous glow throughout the suite. The king size bed was centered in an alcove created by the tower. Outside and through a full view glass door, more gentle blue lights lit up the balcony. I uncorked the champagne and poured it into two crystal flutes, setting them on the nightstand. Everything looked and felt just right. I undressed and threw my clothes onto an empty chair. Naked, I slipped in between the sheets. I heard the bathroom door open and silently, Ginny stepped out into the dressing area and turned to face me.

"Don't move, Ginny. Don't move. Just let me look at you."

The blue glow from behind turned her body into a magnificent silhouette. Her curves were accentuated, and her see-through negligee allowed me to faintly see all of her delicate details. The flames from the fire cast a glow that flickered across her body, causing the shadows of her topographical features to dance. My excitement could not be contained and I had no intention to do so. She slowly walked toward me without saying a word and without losing eye contact. She sat next to me on the edge of the bed as I handed her a glass of champagne. We kissed and then toasted each other and took another slow sip. Trying to maintain patience as my better virtue that night was nearly impossible. I sat my champagne flute back down on the nightstand, freeing both of my hands to caress every curve and crevice of her body. She did the same and soon found what the anticipation of her had done to me. I rolled her over across the bed and we made slow unrelenting love. My hard body and her soft warm curves moved in a rhythm that became more intense with each penetration and long retraction. I held out as long as I could. When I felt her reaching her limit, I joined her, holding her tight against my body and buried deep within, every part of us expressed what we had declared all that day. Our wedding night was so unimaginable; we had spent the hours waking one another. By morning, we were exhausted and inseparable.

When we could no longer delay leaving our wedding bed, we showered, dressed, and checked out. Throwing our luggage back into the CR-V, we drove straight to the Philadelphia airport. We had a direct flight to St. Thomas to begin our honeymoon.

Remembering how much Ginny enjoyed her day on the Right Tackle, I had chartered a 42-foot catamaran to cruise the British Virgin Islands, just the two of us. I had the boat fully provisioned and stocked with our favorite foods and drink. Ginny knew we were going to St. Thomas; however, she didn't know about the boat. I could not wait to surprise her!

When we reached Middletown, Delaware, I was well beyond tired and having trouble staying awake. I asked her if she was OK to drive. She assured me that she was. I pulled over so we could trade seats before getting on to I-95. Good thing, I don't think I could have lasted another ten minutes.

GINNY

To say we were exhausted is a huge understatement. As soon as we left Lewes and were headed north on Route 1, I felt my eyelids grow very heavy. I asked Dan if he was doing OK driving. I would doze ... then ask ... doze ... then ask. This went on for a while. However, at some point, I stopped asking and fell asleep. When I woke up, we were somewhere between Middletown and Christiana. Dan had nudged me and asked me to drive. He said he could no longer keep his eyes open. We had a flight to catch, so there was no time to waste.

Dan pulled over and we traded seats. Running around the outside of the CR-V, we met at the rear bumper, kissed, and then jumped back in. Dan thanked me and laid back into the passenger seat. I checked the traffic coming from behind, found an open spot, and pulled out. I looked over at Dan and he was fast asleep that quick. I turned on the radio, keeping the volume low. I took the ramp to I-95 north, merged, and found a spot where I could cruise with plenty of room between us and the other traffic.

SUSAN

"DEEEEEREK! DYYYYYYLAN!" I yelled out toward the beach. The two of them had taken Gilda and a football out for one last toss before Dex would arrive to housesit, relieving us so Derek and I could go home to Valley Forge, and Dylan to Unionville.

"Please hurry, we have visitors!"

I had offered the two gentlemen a cup of coffee, but they politely declined.

Both Derek and Dylan came running in from the beach. Gilda slipped through the door ahead of them and jumped up on the young man closest to her.

"Gilda, get down! Bad girl," I scolded. Gilda sat down in front of me, and I apologized for her usual behavior.

"Officers?" Derek asked as he came in and shook their hands. "How can we help you?"

"Are you Derek or Dylan Carter?"

"I'm Derek, and this is my brother Dylan."

My mind began racing.

I didn't hear anything happening along Bay Avenue last night. I think Dex had gotten permission to build the fire on the beach, and I'm pretty sure Courtney said that sky lanterns were not outlawed in Delaware. Oh, my gosh, maybe Dex is in trouble again? Derek says he's nothing but trouble. I am having a hard time believing it. But, who knows?

"Please, have a seat," the officer in charge directed.

"That's OK, how can we help you?" Derek repeated.

"I would prefer it if you all sat down."

He sounded serious. We complied.

"Is there anyone else in the house?"

"Does this have anything to do with Dex Lassiter?" Derek asked accusingly. "Because he's not here. He was here yesterday, for a wedding, and left last night."

"No, no. This has nothing to do with Mr. Lassiter."

The officer paused. We were suspended in our thoughts waiting to hear why they were there.

"Do you have a brother named Daniel?"

"Yes," Derek responded.

Looking down at the floor, the officer withdrew into his thoughts for a moment. He took a deep breath and looked back up, reconnecting with us.

"There's been an accident. We're very sorry. Your brother, Daniel, did not survive."

I could not breathe. I could not move. It felt as if a hundred tons of lead were pressing down on my chest. From somewhere deep inside, I was screaming. Like a nightmare, I couldn't hear my crying out. Filled with choking wet sawdust, I could not form vowels in my mouth. Consonants were guttural kicks like an engine that wouldn't start. Everything was stuck and pounding in my throat and in my head.

The house was filled with inaudible pain that screamed from heaven to hell. Dylan suddenly yelled and punched a hole in the wall. The second officer grabbed Dylan's arms and held them behind his back to keep him from hurting himself. Dylan's yelling continued. His soul in anguish; his hand never felt the impact.

The first officer moved toward Derek and me.

Derek slumped over, his face in his hands. He was sobbing, "Oh, God ... No ... Oh, God ..."

"Ginny, where's Ginny?" I pleaded with the men. "Is she OK?" I was trying my best to get the words out, too afraid to hear their answer. Dylan was drowning in his screams and trying to break free. I could see the muscles of his chest wrenching, his stomach convulsing. Derek lifted his head to hear the answer, his eyes red and the vessels in his forehead pulsating purple.

"She sustained serious, but non-life threatening injuries. She's been transported to Christiana Hospital. She was able to tell the State Police where to find all of you. That's when we got the call."

"Who was driving?" Derek demanded.

"From the information we received, Ginny was driving and Daniel was asleep in the passenger seat. He probably never knew what happened. He most likely died instantly."

"That bitch!" Derek growled under his breath as he pounded the table.

I noticed the officer between us shift as he watched Derek closely.

Staying by, they answered all of our questions, making sure we were able to comprehend what they were telling us. They didn't have all of the answers surrounding the accident. Eyewitnesses still had to be interviewed and a full investigation was underway. I-95 northbound was completely shut down. They said they understood it was a miracle that Ginny survived.

"Has anyone called her parents?" I asked through my sobs as I was holding on to Gilda. I pulled her into my lap and held her tight, feeling like she was my last and only connection to Dan and Ginny.

"I don't know. Apart from Ginny, we understand you are Daniel's only living relatives. Is that correct?"

"Yes." Derek answered. "We ARE his only living relatives."

Is he trying to exclude Ginny?

Derek kept his head down. He was hurting. He was angrier than I had ever seen him.

"Where is Dan? Where is he now?" Dylan asked. He had calmed down enough to speak, so the officer had let up on him, but remained close by.

"He should be at the coroner's by now. I will provide you with the phone number and address so you can make the necessary arrangements. We are very sorry."

"Oh, my God . . . they just got married . . . yesterday. . . .

They were married yesterday," I choked out.

"Yes, we were told. We are very sorry. We know this is a terrible shock."

The officers remained with us for a while longer to make sure we were not going to harm ourselves, each other, or someone else. They gave us their cards before they left. One was a Delaware State Police officer and the other worked in the Special Victims Unit. They encouraged us to call with any questions at any time. They said they would be in touch.

As they were leaving, Gilda happily followed them to the door with her tail wagging. She had no clue. One of the officers knelt down, scratched her behind her ears, and patted her on the head. I think I heard him whisper his condolences to her, telling her it was going to be all right. He had not said that to us, because he knew nothing would be right. The door closed behind them. Death had let itself in and consumed the house.

I couldn't breathe. I couldn't speak. And I could not stand. I knew my legs would give out. Grief was weighing me down, crushing my lungs, and sucking the life out of me. The world had changed. In the flash of a few words, it was turned upside-down. The air was heavy and the house smelled stale. The room was dark, despite the bright sun outside.

How dare the sun shine on this day? God of mercy, my ass. How dare he allow this to happen? Hasn't Ginny been through enough? How dare he allow this to happen to Dan?

Dylan dragged himself over to the couch and was now laying face down unsuccessfully trying to keep his emotions in check. Derek staggered up the stairs and slammed a door.

I still could not catch my breath, but I had to. I wished Ginny were there. She would know exactly what to do. She always did. So did Dan.

Oh, God, I need them here . . . now. How could you allow

this to happen?

I looked over at Dylan, again. I had no idea what to do for him. I didn't know how to care for myself, let alone Dylan. Derek had obviously shut us out.

I needed help. I picked up Dylan's cell phone where I felt sure I would find Courtney's cell number.

"Hi, Dylan! How are you . . . ? Dylan . . . ? Are you there?"

"Courtney. . . . Oh, my God, Courtney, I need you here . . . now," I choked out between sobs and tears.

"Who is this?"

"Courtney, it's Susan . . . Susan Carter."

"Susan? What's wrong? Are you OK? Where are you?"

"I'm at Dan and Ginny's. . . . Oh, my God, I'm at Dan's. I don't even know where that is right now."

"Susan, is Dylan there?"

"Yes."

"Is he all right?"

"Yes. . . . He's . . . He's . . . Courtney, we need you here."

"I'll be right over."

I turned my eyes toward the water, looking for something sure, something predictable, like the waves that rolled endlessly onto the shore. I knew the tide would eventually change, but I couldn't think beyond the moment. Any thought of anything beyond it was impossible. As I looked out, I was held captive by the wedding garland still wrapped around the deck rails. My heart cried out for Ginny and Dan. They were . . . so happy. They loved like few I had ever known. I cried for Ginny. She was so young. She was too young to have death constantly knocking on her door.

DEREK

*Bitch . . . that fucking bitch. She killed my brother. She
fucking killed my brother. I cannot believe what she has done
to this family. Nothing good has come of her trying to be a
part of it. She may have legally succeeded, but she won't last
long, and she will never be a part of this family.*

*Dan was the glue. He was the one that made the three of
us work. I should have warned him sooner. I should have
told him that she was no good. I saw it coming. I thought it
would pass like the others. But no, she trapped him by
getting pregnant. She probably didn't even try to prevent
it. It was all a part of her plan. As soon as she could, she
convinced Dan to marry her. She probably thinks everything
is hers. She took everything. That bitch, she even took Dan's
life. She's the one that should have died in that accident. She
was the one at the wheel.*

*I'll destroy this place before I let her have it. Dan was
right. Dad wanted it to stay in the family, and she is not
family.*

*Oh, and she has sucked Susan right in, too. All this girl-
time stuff, all this crap about hanging out and visiting.*

Where the hell is Dan?

My nerves were shot. My stomach was full of bile. My
mouth was dry. Susan was downstairs, probably feeling
sorry for Ginny. What about us? We were the ones that
had known him forever.

COURTNEY

As I ran out to my car, I used speed dial to call Dex.

"Dex, meet me at Dan and Ginny's. Something's terribly wrong over there."

He said he was just getting ready to head out to their place anyway and would meet me there.

I sped through town, stopping only once for a group of pedestrians. They yelled at me to slow down as they took their time crossing the street while cursing at me. So I sped off as soon as they had crossed the double line. When I reached the beach house, I parked, jumped out of my car, ran up the steps, and burst into the kitchen. I didn't see any signs of trouble.

So far, so good.

Gilda ran out to greet me, jumping around as if she were starved for attention—which she wasn't.

OK, that's nothing new.

Hunched over as I continued to pet Gilda, who trotted and jumped alongside me, I crossed into the living and dining area. I had no idea what I was about to walk into.

Susan was sitting at the table, staring into space. She had been crying . . . hard. Dylan was lying face down on the sofa. He was breathing, but I couldn't tell what condition he was in. I thought it best to assess the overall situation before approaching him.

"Susan, where's Derek?" I whispered, needing to account for everyone, first.

"He's upstairs."

Dex came running into the house.

"Courtney, what's going on?"

"I don't know. I just got here."

I knelt down next to Susan.

"Susan, you need to tell me what's happened," I summoned.

Susan told us of the accident. She told us of Dan. She told us of Ginny.

Hearing the horror all over again, Dylan rolled over. His eyes locked onto mine. There was nothing there. They were devoid of the Dylan I thought I was getting to know. Suddenly, he lashed out. With a deep, throaty yell from within, he picked up the rocker he had made for Dan, and tried to throw it through the deck door. Fortunately, Dex saw it coming and tackled Dylan from behind before he could release the chair. Both men fell to the floor. Dylan started swinging at Dex.

"Get off of me you mother fucker! Get the hell off!" Dylan shouted as he landed a solid punch into Dex's left jaw. Dazed, Dex tried to hold him down.

"Dylan ... Dylan, cut it out. ... Stop!" Dex yelled back at him.

They were wrestling, and Dylan repeatedly tried to land another punch.

Barking wildly and nipping at their elbows and ankles, Gilda was running around both of them. Susan tried to get the attention of Gilda and the boys. Dex pulled Dylan up to his feet. Anticipating what was coming next, I scooped Gilda up in my arms. She continued growling and clawing to get free. Out of sheer desperation, Susan was now crying and yelling at Dylan and Dex to stop, but to no avail. Alerted by all of the commotion, Derek came downstairs right when Dex connected with the side of Dylan's head, putting Dylan down for the count. Without hesitation, Derek launched himself into the melee. Grabbing Dex by the arm, he swung him around and threw his fist into Dex's left eye. Susan couldn't react fast enough to stop him. Providentially, Dex hit the floor at Susan's feet. She stood over him, thereby preventing him from getting up and taking another swing.

"Stop! Just stop it or I'll call the police," Susan shouted, warning Derek to stand down.

I was preparing to dial 911, as well.

"What? Are you defending him? Who the hell does he think he is coming over here? He doesn't belong here. Not now, not ever!" Derek roared back at Susan, pointing at Dex who was getting up from the floor and holding the left side of his face.

"He did what he had to do," Susan screamed back at Derek. "And where were you? You went upstairs and left us. You left us when we needed you the most." Susan was shattered. Her nerves were frayed and raw, and she was not holding back.

Dylan got up, staggered out the deck door, and stormed down to the beach.

Derek froze. He was paralyzed by Susan's bold and uncharacteristic indictment of his behavior, yet his eyes remained filled with anger and hate.

I ran over to Dex. "Dex, are you OK? I'm so sorry."

"I'm going to be fine, but you'd better go out and check on Dylan."

I looked over at Susan and Derek. Derek had lowered his fists. Susan had her hand on his shoulder and he sagged down into a chair. Susan looked up at me and motioned for me to go after Dylan. Moving to the other side of the room and staying away from Derek, Dex also waved me on.

"Go on. I'll get Dex some ice," Susan mouthed and half whispered as reassurance.

Somehow, I knew the altercation was far from over.

I ran out the door and down to the beach. I kicked off my shoes and left them in the dune. I could see Dylan a short distance down sitting in the sand with his knees drawn up and his head in his hands. I ran down to him.

"Dylan?"

He looked up at me. He was emptied out. His eyes were asking me to tell him that none of it was true, that it had all been a terrible case of mistaken identity. He wanted me to tell him so that he could go back to the way things were.

I knew I could never give him what he so desperately

wanted.

"Dylan, I am so sorry . . ."

"Oh, God, Court. This is such a nightmare. I can't believe this is happening."

"I know. . . I wish I could say that it wasn't so."

"I lost control in there. I am so sorry. "

Reading his eyes, I sat down next to him and placed my hands on his arm.

"Dylan, you have no reason to apologize to me. I just don't know what to say or do. We're all devastated. Dan meant the world to all of us."

Dylan put his head into my shoulder and sobbed. I wrapped my arms around him as best I could. I stroked his hair and kissed the top of his head. Feeling overwhelmed, he opened up and cried. He trusted me enough to cry in my arms. His defenses were down, obliterated, and I had never felt closer to him, or anyone for that matter. Why does it take a tragedy to make us realize how much we need each other? Or, how much we need to be needed? His cry was deeper than anything I had ever known of a man before. It was not the cry of someone who was weak. It was the cry of a strong man who had realized that he had no power over his circumstance, and there was nothing at his disposal to turn it around. It was a loss that could never be repaired or replaced. His cry equaled the love he had for his brother, his best friend. He had just lost everything.

Dylan gradually quieted. The shaking in his body had subsided. He was not accepting what had happened; rather, he was slowly preparing himself to face it. Right there in my arms, I could feel him gathering what strength he could. Gathering strength to handle it the way he knew Dan would have. When he was ready, his eyes met mine.

"I'm ready, Court. I need to get back to the house. I need to check on Derek."

I stood up and took his hand, pulling him to his feet. I wrapped my arms around his waist as we walked back up to the house. He covered my hands with his. Before we went up on to the deck to go inside, I stopped him. Moving my hands to both sides of his face, I turned his eyes to meet mine, once more.

"Dylan, before we go in, I want you to know that I am here for you. Once you leave Lewes, you may be an hour and a half away, but I am here for you. I'm just a phone call away. I will drop whatever I am doing, and I will be where you need me to be. Do you understand what I'm saying?"

He hugged me, thanked me, and took my hand in his. We walked up the new steps and onto the reconstructed deck that Dan, Dex, and Dylan had built. Before going inside, we paused once more so Dylan could take one last deep breath.

SUSAN

Derek was seething with anger. He was carrying on like Ginny had intentionally caused Dan's death, which was completely irrational. I could understand how he might put the blame on Ginny because she was the one behind the wheel, but he didn't know how it happened. He certainly didn't have all the details. Poor Ginny, I could only imagine that being the driver made her pain all that more unbearable. The last thing she needed was Derek coming at her with his acts of accusation. I could understand Derek needing to be angry with someone; he just lost his baby brother, but how could he be insensitive to the reality she was facing. She had just lost every dream for every day going forward. The one person she had waited for all her life would never be beside her again.

In some respects, Derek was probably lashing out at Ginny because he thought, absent their father, he was supposed to look after Dan. I was beginning to believe he felt as though he had somehow failed, so for the time being, I excused his behavior.

Courtney and Dylan came back inside. With everyone in the same room, Courtney took control of the situation and went into lecture mode. Her point was that Mr. Carter

182

would have never wanted them to behave that way, and Dan would have wanted them to make Ginny their first priority. In an almost scolding tone, Courtney said we needed to pull it together. Derek must have been whipped to allow her to have the upper hand like that.

As we began making plans for the next twenty-four hours, Gilda came loping happily into the room carrying a chewy bone. Yes, there was the matter of silly Gilda. Dex said he would stay at the house and take care of her, as planned. That meant that Derek, Dylan, and I could get on the road quickly and get to Christiana Hospital.

DYLAN

When we arrived at the hospital, Ginny was in recovery. She had bruised ribs and had broken her right leg in two places. Once she had been moved to her own room, we were allowed to see her. We stayed with her until her parents arrived.

"I'm sorry, I'm so sorry. I tried to get out of the way. I couldn't get out of the way," Ginny apologized over and over saying she was sorry she had lost him.

"Ginny, what are you talking about? It was an accident," I reminded her.

"Dylan, I didn't see it. I didn't see it. It was too late. I couldn't stop."

Courtney hung back. Not wanting me to drive my truck alone, she had tagged along with us.

"What happened?" Susan asked, sensing that Ginny may have been ready to talk. Sitting on the side of Ginny's bed and taking her hand, Susan moved closer to her. Ginny slowly turned her head back and forth as if she was trying to clear it.

"Oh, God, Susan. I can't remember. It was a huge truck. I don't know where it came from. I just remember hearing glass shatter all around us, and metal crumpling. It

was awful. The air bags exploded. Dan was
sleeping. Susan, I don't think he saw it. He never saw it.
Oh, my God, what am I going to do? Do you know where he
is? Have you seen him?"

Drifting in and out, Ginny was repeating herself over
and over. Her voice was drowning in anguish. There were
no words that could do justice to her pain. And if there
were, few would be able to fully comprehend them.

In denial, she was asking for Dan. She tried to rip out
her I.V., the leads to the monitor, and the B.P. cuff. Several
nurses came running in and forgivingly instructed us to
leave.

We regrouped in a small private waiting room. Derek
had been stoically quiet during our initial visit with Ginny,
but once in the secluded room with the door shut, he spoke.

"I'm going home. Susan, are you coming?"

"No."

The air was tense and charged. I could almost see a
physical wall separating them.

Susan elected to remain at the hospital with us.

After Ginny's parents arrived, Courtney drove us to my
home in Unionville. She offered to take Susan on to Valley
Forge. Once again, Susan refused. Not wanting to impose
on Courtney for an additional forty-minute trip each way,
Susan insisted on staying at my house.

"Susan, I have no right asking this . . . today has been a
very difficult day, to say the least . . . but here goes. Do you
think Derek needs you to be home with him? I don't mind
driving, really." Knowing that she was sticking her nose
into their business, Courtney was trying to be helpful, yet
very cautious with her counsel.

"I get what you're saying, but Derek doesn't want
anyone around. He is the one who drove off and left me
without transportation. I don't know who he is right
now. He's probably sleeping it off and doesn't want to be
disturbed, anyway."

"But this is a very vulnerable time for him," Courtney

spoke softly, knowing she was probably crossing the line.

"It's a vulnerable time for all of us."

I gave Courtney credit for trying. I didn't know what it was like to be married, and neither did she. I didn't know what it meant to say you would be there for someone, for better or for worse. It just seemed his leaving her, and her not going to him, wasn't it. However, I also knew that these were extenuating circumstances. That day, in a split second, Derek had become my only brother. I felt like I should have been doing something to make sure he was not alone; however, I did not have the right to interfere in his marriage, either.

When we arrived at my house, I gave Courtney a quick tour so she could find what she needed. Once she got "the lay of the land," she took control, again. It was a good thing, too. She made up a bed for Susan and demanded that she take a nap. She also suggested that I should do the same.

"Court, could we just talk for a minute? I think I just need to talk."

"Just talk . . . ?"

"Yes."

"I can be a good listener," she whispered.

Courtney stayed next to me.

COURTNEY

His home said a lot about him. It was an old house with a massive amount of character, yet simple and warm. While furnished in antiques and period pieces, it was absent clutter and every piece of furniture was selected especially for its particular location.

Once Susan was asleep upstairs, Dylan and I shared a couch. He was the only thing that mattered to me at that moment.

"Dylan, are you doing OK?"

"Not really. I just want to see Dan. I want to see my brother." He turned and looked at me with sad eyes that had aged ten years in the last ten hours."

"I don't know if that's a good idea."

"I didn't get to say goodbye. He left and I didn't get to say goodbye."

I knew there was nothing I could do to make him feel better. The best I could do was to listen patiently and allow him to talk it through.

"We had plans, Court. I was going to try to get down to Lewes on the weekends. We were going to get in some beach time together. We even kidded around about entering the beach volleyball tournament this summer. What a hoot that would have been. We had a list of projects we were going to try to knock out before next winter. And Ginny wanted to sail on the Kalmar Nyckel. We were going to make reservations and surprise her. For all I know, he may have already made them. I was going to ask you to go along, too."

"That would have been nice," I added to let him know he had my attention and that everything he was feeling was important to me.

He stopped talking and stared out across the darkened room before finally relaxing his shoulders and closing his eyes. He disappeared back into his thoughts. Drifting in and out of the present, he shared a few other reflections. His head bobbed as he tried to fight off his drowsiness. He looked like a schoolboy struggling to stay awake at his desk. After several rounds of that, I gently took his shoulder and lowered his head onto a pillow across my lap. He fell sound asleep as I stroked his hair.

"I'm so sorry, Dylan." I whispered as I watched his chest rise and fall. "Dan was someone very special and he loved you so much. We're all going to miss him."

CHAPTER THREE

GINNY

It was good to be on my way back home. However, I knew I would have to face the inevitable: walking into the beach house for the first time without Dan. As we drove onto Bay Avenue, the harsh reality started slicing through me. It was razor sharp and its sting was intense, reaching deep where it grabbed and serrated my gut.

Susan had picked me up at Christiana Hospital. Dylan, Dex, and Courtney were waiting at the beach house. They tried to anticipate what I might need when I arrived. As we pulled into the parking area, it was comforting to hear the familiar sound of gravel, shells, and sand under the tires of Susan's Explorer. Dex was waiting outside to carry me up the steps and into the kitchen while Dylan retrieved my wheelchair. Courtney was inside holding Gilda by the collar. There was a general concern that Gilda might get too excited and jump up on me. Susan followed behind the parade and brought in my small bag of clothes.

As we ascended the steps, anxiety began pressing in. I tried my best to conceal it. I didn't want to upset everyone else. I didn't want to take us back to where it all began. Despite their own needs, they had already given me so much. I owed it to them to be brave, I thought.

I didn't know why Dylan had cared for me the way he did. After all, I was the one behind the wheel. Dan and I had not been married for more than twenty-four hours, so in my mind, Dylan had every right to turn his back and abandon me. How could he continue to see me as his sister-in-law? Apparently, it never crossed his mind to think or feel otherwise.

Susan held the door open as Dex carried me in.

Oh, dear God, please let all of this be one terrible nightmare. Please, have Dan waiting inside for me. A miracle . . . Dan believed in miracles . . .

But, it was not to be. The empty kitchen was overwhelming. Even the aroma of Dan's cooking had dissipated. He was gone. He was not at Christiana Hospital, and he was not at home. He was really gone. I had lost him, forever.

The most beautiful people in the world were surrounding me, and yet, I was there and so alone. I would never see him again. I would never feel his arms around me. I would never kiss his lips, or hold his hand, or run my fingers through his hair. I would never hear his voice, his laugh. His whispers would never fall upon my ears. That night, I would sleep alone. I would wake in the morning and he would not be there. I would never again feel his rough morning shadow brush up against my cheek.

Every part of my body was focused on holding it together, yet every part of me was falling apart.

God, if you can hear me, I need him . . . now. Why have you done this? Why . . . ? Dan's faith was so much stronger than mine. He trusted you. . . . Why not take me?

Dex set me down in the wheelchair and then adjusted the leg rests. He remained kneeling next to me while I tried to be brave. I looked up and realized we were all in tears. All of us felt it. Dan was absent, yet his spirit was hovering among us. It was as if he was in the room stroking my hair or patting Dylan on the shoulders, telling us he was all right and that we were going to be OK, too.

Oh, how can you be so sure? I miss you so much . . .

The day was warm and sunny with a light on-shore breeze. Dex broke our silence and suggested we go outside. He wheeled me out onto the deck. Courtney allowed Gilda to sit next to me. Gilda promptly laid her head in my lap as if she understood. I petted her head and wondered how all of this would affect her. When would she realize Dan was never coming home? With time, would she forget him altogether?

It was so good to feel the sun on my shoulders and the bay breeze in my face. Someone had been thoughtful enough to remove the garland from the rails and the torches from the sand. Our wedding presents had been neatly put away. Later that night, I realized our suitcases had been unpacked. Dan's clothes had been taken care of as if he was still living there. Only Susan would have known not to remove his belongings from me. She knew I would cherish the memory of him, forever. There were some things I needed to do at my own pace.

DEX

After we were able to bring Ginny home, the healing process began, and the summer started to pick up some traction. Everyone chipped in to help Ginny recover and make sure she was not alone. Susan stayed with her the first couple of nights. Courtney stayed over the remainder of the first week. Her second week, Ginny asked us to let her stay on her own. She said she had to face the music. We reluctantly agreed. However, I must confess: her first night home alone, I walked the beach, constantly peering up at the house to make sure everything looked OK. Gilda knew I was out there and barked wildly each time I passed by. I saw Ginny wheel herself over to the window and look out. I hid in the shadow of the dune and thought of her loneliness.

Back on the Right Tackle, I called her.
"Hey, Dex."
"How are you doing?"
"Pretty good. Gilda was barking at someone outside,

but other than that, it's been very quiet."

I wondered if she saw me and was waiting for me to confess.

"Do you have everything you need for the night?"

"Yep, I got my pillow, a blanket, my cell phone, and Gilda."

"Good. Call me if you need anything."

"Dex, thanks for everything you've done. I don't know what I would have done without you guys."

"Yeah, well, you owe us big time," I replied kiddingly. "I'll stop by in the morning and make sure you're OK. I still have my key, but I'll call before I come in." (Dan and Ginny had given me a key before they left for their honeymoon. I was supposed to housesit and take care of Gilda while they were away.)

"You really don't have to do that."

"Yes, I do. I need to do this. I'll stop and pick up some coffee on my way over. When I get there, I'll run Gilda down to the beach. Then, I'll have to leave for work."

"OK, Dex. I'll see you in the morning."

"Keep your cellphone nearby. Good night."

Later that night, I drove by her house one last time. It was dark except for a small light left on in the kitchen. I went back to the Right Tackle and tucked myself in.

In the morning, the summer heat and humidity were rapidly on the rise. The day promised to be sweltering. I decided to start early on a job down the road from the Carter house. It involved replacing a roof, the last place anyone would want to be on a day like that. I stopped at Wawa and picked up two coffees, a gallon bottle of spring water, and a 64-ounce bottle of Gatorade. I arrived at Ginny's and called her cell phone.

"Are you decent?"

"Dressed? Yes. Decent? That's a matter of opinion. Come on in."

It was good to hear Ginny's sense of humor making small reappearances every now and then.

I slipped my key into the lock, opened the door, and was

instantly greeted by Gilda.

"Good morning!" I called out. "Has Gilda been out yet?"

"Not yet. I was just going to let her out to run on the beach."

I walked in and let Gilda out the deck door. Ginny was on the couch looking like she had just attended a high school sleepover. My guess was that she didn't get much sleep the night before, either. Her hair was tied up on her head and she was still in the pajama pants and T-shirt that she had worn the day before. Her casted leg was stuck straight out. She swung it around and rested it on the blanket chest that worked as their makeshift coffee table. I handed her a coffee.

"Careful, it's hot," I cautioned her. "Now, if I remember correctly, you drink it with just a little cream, no sugar."

"How did you know?"

"I remember these things. How did you sleep last night?"

"Not well. This cast wasn't comfortable in the hospital bed, and it's even worse on this couch."

"Do you want us to bring a bed downstairs for you?"

"I don't know. I'll give it some thought."

Gilda was at the door barking to come back in.

"Well, I'd better get going." I let Gilda in. "What are you doing for lunch? I'm working right down the beach from here."

"Oh, I thought I'd go for a run up to the canal, have lunch at The Lighthouse, and then run back," she answered sarcastically.

"I'll stop by."

"I'll have something ready for us."

"How are you going to do that?"

"I'll figure it out, you just be here!"

The summer heat was draining. I drank water and Gatorade throughout the morning. When we took an hour for lunch, I immediately sought shelter from the heat and needed to get rehydrated. Too hot and tired to walk, I drove the short distance back to Ginny's.

GINNY

I had developed a love-hate relationship with the cemetery where we were going to lay Dan to rest the first weekend in June. He would be right next to Lily, and his parents were on her other side.

My parents came down that Saturday morning, as did Derek and Susan. It was the first time I had seen Derek since the wedding. He looked tired. He was very cold toward me, not that I blame him. I could understand it if he held me responsible.

My mother was back to her usual begging me to come home and work toward my doctorate. Everyone backed away when she started. However, when Susan saw that my mother was upsetting me, she came to my rescue.

"Come on, Ginny, let's go upstairs and get you ready."

I looked at her like she had six heads. First, how was I going to get up the stairs? Second, I had not planned on getting dressed up. It was difficult enough just getting sweats over that cast.

"Derek will carry you up the steps, and I'll help you get dressed."

Derek was not happy about that, but he carried me up anyway, and sat me on my bed. Leaving the room abruptly and slamming the door behind him, he made it obviously clear that he had been put out.

"Susan, he is really mad at me, isn't he?"

"Honestly, I don't know what he is right now."

She started looking through my closet and drawers for something that I could wear.

"I can't blame him for holding me responsible. Do you think he will ever forgive me?"

"Ginny, it wasn't your fault. The accident report clearly states that witnesses saw the semi suddenly change lanes and pin your CR-V up against the guardrail. You had nowhere to go. It's a miracle you survived. You are not to blame for the accident, or Derek's bad behavior. It's hard to say what's up with him. It might be frustration. So many things are going on at home. He's been working sixty to eighty hours a week. We're still not pregnant, and I know that upsets him. He won't talk about fertility treatments. And... well... some other stuff. Do me a favor, Ginny; don't leave this place. Don't sell it. It's rightfully yours. Dan and Mr. Carter would have wanted it that way."

"Why do you say that?"

"Just tell me you won't do anything, not immediately, anyway."

"I don't know if that's possible. I don't know how long what little money I have will hold out. I'm beginning to wonder if maybe I should go back to Connecticut."

"What will you do with the house?"

"I don't know. I haven't talked to Derek or Dylan about it, yet."

"Ginny, Dylan has his business in Unionville. He seems very happy there. And Derek... well... if you give him the chance, I'm afraid he will try to steal this house out from under you. I wouldn't feel right if that happened. When Mr. Carter died, Derek suggested that we contest the Will. When Dan died, Derek immediately stated that we should take rightful possession of the Carter family beach house. I love him, Ginny, I really do. But ever since his dad died, something has changed."

She was right about that, I had noticed it, too. I also agreed that I should not make any big decisions, not right away. However, something was just not sitting right, and I knew my lack of funds could force the issue.

"Ginny, don't overthink it. Listen, Derek and Dylan received their inheritance: a pile of money that they both needed. Dan received the house. It's yours. Dan would want that for you."

My head was starting to hurt.

"Did you find anything for me to wear?" I asked, looking to change the subject.

"OK... here's a nice pair of shorts and a top. This should do it," Susan said as she held them up.

"OK, girlfriend, get over here and help me get dressed."

Dex, Courtney, and Dylan had arrived by the time Susan finished dressing me. Susan called for Derek to come up and get me, but Dex immediately volunteered. He must have read the look of disdain on Derek's face.

So, we made another trip to the cemetery. Unbelievably, I think I was out of tears. I think we all were. My dad said a few words, stating that Dan would have been a great son-in-law. Dex shared a couple of stories about their glory days at the beach. Dylan, bless his heart, said a prayer. He prayed for me. He prayed for all of us. Dan would have liked that.

Back at the house, my dad said that he wanted to take me for a drive.

"We need to talk," he said, sounding unusually serious.

Everyone else agreed to hang out at the house until we got back, even though Derek, as usual, was in a rush to get home. Dad dropped my mother off at the Rodney Hotel, in town, and then he and I drove back over the canal, making a left onto Cedar Street. We followed it to the end where he parked the car, facing the inlet, so we could watch the boats come and go. A couple of them were drifting with the current, their fishing lines in the water with hopes of a bite. My mind flashed back to our day on the Right Tackle.

"What are your plans, Ginny? Are you going to be OK?"

"I don't know, Dad. I'm taking everything one day at a time. It's about all I can handle, right now. But I know I'll have to face forward, someday soon."

"Hmmmm ... What do you want to do?"

"I don't really know. I just don't have medical school in me, right now. No offense, but I don't think I want to live in Connecticut, either."

"None taken, I understand."

"I love it here. I really do. I don't know how I'll feel about being here without Dan, though."

"Anything else keeping you from staying here?" he asked, and somehow I think he knew the answer.

"Dad, Dan and I were barely keeping ahead of the bills. I had plans to get a job after we returned from our honeymoon, but obviously, that has all changed. I don't think I can afford to keep the house, and even if I could somehow manage the bills, Derek and Mom were probably right about one thing: the place will fall down around me."

He studied my face for a few moments, and then he took my hands in his.

"Ginny, you were very young when your grandfather passed away. You were his only grandchild, so he left you a trust fund and named me as the trustee until you turned twenty-five. Until that time, I can distribute the funds as I see fit. Then, it becomes yours."

"Huh? I don't understand."

"I thought it best to keep it quiet until you were twenty-five, allowing you time to grow up with some sense of self-responsibility. The fund has grown quite well over the years, just like you." He chuckled as an afterthought as his hand touched my shoulder.

"Why are you telling me this?"

"Because with the help of those funds, you could stay here, if you wanted to."

"And you think the Carter beach house is the best use for that?"

"I think your grandfather would be pleased if it made a way for you to stay in a place that felt like home to you. My intention was to hold on to it, and let it grow. However, all the interest in the world is not worth what you and Dan had. I can see how happy you have been here, and, admittedly, the property is a great investment."

"Dad, if I sell the house, get a job, and reinvest in something small and affordable, I should be OK."

"Do you really believe that? You and Dan loved this place. I saw how you loved each other. If you need to leave because it's emotionally too hard to stay, then you should go. But, if you want to stay, you have the means to do so."

"Dad, what are we talking about?"

"Ginny, there is enough in your trust to not only pay the bills, but to make Dan and Mr. Carter's dreams come true."

My head was spinning. I wished my grandfather were there so I could give him a huge hug.

"Ginny, don't make any permanent decisions, not yet. This is not the time. You are right to take each day one at a time. So for today, do you want to come home with your mother and me, or do you want to stay here?"

"I want to stay here," I whispered, and for the first time, I knew I meant it. Without the obstacles and stress, I knew in my heart that Lewes was where I wanted to be. "I want to stay here, Dad."

"Then I will write you a check to hold you over until you are ready to make a final decision. If and when you decide to stay permanently, then I think we should get to work on the place."

The cast on my leg was heavy and awkward, but it could not hold me back. I unbuckled my seatbelt, leaned over, and hugged my dad around his neck.

"Thank you, Daddy. I love you so much."

"I love you too, baby girl."

We pulled up to the house, and I called Dex's cell phone, asking him to please come out to get me. (I didn't want my dad to try to carry me up the steps.) I gave my dad another hug. He said that he and my mother would stop by before leaving the next day.

Dex skipped over several steps on the way down, opened my door, and lifted me out of the car. My dad waited until we got up the steps and in the door before driving away.

DEREK

When Dex carried Ginny back inside, I thought, *"Good, now we can get out of here."* But, she had other plans. With her parents out of the house, her mood had lightened dramatically. I would not go so far as to say she was smiling, but the heaviness that held her down all day had disappeared. Her head was up as she scanned the room. Her relief was palpable. The edgy anxiety that had pervaded her day had left. She seemed "settled." Even the dog sensed it and was trotting alongside her wheelchair. It was obvious to me what was going on. Dan was buried, and she was OK with it. She even suggested that the guys grill something up for dinner, adding that that was what Dan would have wanted if he were there. She was probably right about that, but what were we celebrating? I was disgusted. Susan pleaded with me to stay through dinner and then we could be on our way. I was curious to know what was going on, so I reluctantly agreed. I rationalized that the turn of events might give me the opportunity to feel Ginny out regarding the house. I was certain she would not be able to hold on to the place for much longer. I wanted to make sure she knew that I had first rights to it. Well, that would include Dylan, too, of course. But I really didn't think he was in a position to consider it, and I was fairly certain he was happy where he was.

Dylan and Courtney announced they were going out to pick up some steaks and asked if we needed anything else. Susan and Ginny went out to the kitchen and began making a salad. That left Dex and me alone in the living room.

Great. Just great.

It was awkward, to say the least. Grabbing the remote from the table, I turned on the TV.

"Derek, we haven't seen a lot of you lately. What have

you been up to? Susan tells me you've started up a graphic arts company," Dex asked, trying to strike up a polite conversation.

I thought about ignoring him. He really got under my skin. I could still picture him in the boathouse making out with her, on top of her. He knew how I felt about her, and she wasn't completely innocent, either. By all accounts, it looked like she was making all the advances. But still, he knew how I felt about her. So, I set the fire.

He got her out in time, and then, like an idiot, he tried to put out the fire and got caught. He took the rap, but my dad sure was suspicious. He knew I wasn't home at the time it had happened.

Dex's mom hired the Sables to represent him and with all her money and influence, he was acquitted. My dad's skepticism led to a lot of questioning at home, but I wasn't going to fess up. It was Dex's fault, after all.

"Yeah, we're doing OK. It pays the bills."

"That's good."

I could hear the girls out in the kitchen chatting it up and even sharing a few laughs.

"Hopefully, you'll be able to come down and visit more often. I still owe you a fishing trip, you know."

"Yeah, right. Big time. Are you still living on a boat?"

"Yep. Really, Derek, you need to come out with us sometime. When was the last time we all went fishing together?"

I'd rather not remember.

"I really don't remember."

"Well, like I said, you'll have to come out with us, sometime."

I was channel surfing but could not come up with anything worth watching, so I left it on ESPN. Anything would be better than listening to Dex's chit-chat. Seriously.

Ten years later—or so it seemed—Dylan and Courtney got back with the steaks and some bar supplies. They immediately went to work on happy hour. I passed, reminding them that I had to drive home. I think Dylan was waiting for an invitation to stay down and drive home the next day. If I didn't know better, I would have said that he had a huge crush on Courtney, and she was leading him on, for whatever reason. She was supposed to be so successful, yet she was such a leech. Go figure. Though, I knew the ladies found Dylan very attractive, it was all just another train wreck waiting to happen, and Dylan's heart would be left in the rubble.

Dex volunteered to do the grilling. Courtney put the salad, dressings, and condiments on the table. When everyone started on the second round of Bloody Marys, dinner was ready. I thought it might be the perfect opportunity to coax information out of Ginny regarding her intentions for the house. She was not drinking, but she was grieving and on pain medication, so I surmised she might be in a vulnerable state, anyway.

"So, Ginny, are you going to be OK in this house all by yourself?"

"Well, I really haven't been alone all that much, so far. You know, Susan comes down on most weekends. Dex and Courtney stop in every day. Dex stops by for lunch more days than not. I think he does it to take advantage of my air conditioning and cold shower. It gets him out of the heat."

I hated it when she referred to the place as hers, as if she had lived there all her life.

"Are you going to be able to keep this place up?" I asked gingerly, trying to sound genuinely concerned for her, which I wasn't. Susan kicked me under the table.

"I think I can. I just haven't decided."

Admittedly, everyone looked a little shocked by her answer.

"Ginny, that's great. You shouldn't make any big decisions for awhile, anyway," Susan said to encourage her. I could have kicked her; she and I had already visited that topic. I knew how she felt, and she knew where I stood. It had become a point of contention in our home.

"Well, if you need to sell it, promise you'll come to Dylan and me first. I'm sure you would want it to stay in the family," I said, adding a pinch of guilt to however she may have felt that day. Hopefully, she was touched by my concern and generosity.

Courtney put her fork down and looked at me like she wanted to burn a hole right through my retinas and out the backside of my skull. She was getting under my skin, too. I didn't need her to become a problem. I decided to leave it lay. In front of all those witnesses I had made my point.

GINNY

Derek and Susan left after dinner as Derek said they would. The rest of us retired to the deck.

"Look! It's the Milky Way!" Courtney squealed excitedly, pointing through the black sky.

She was right. It was a new moon and every star was visible. Floating across the sky was a beautiful ribbon of lights. It was so close; it appeared as though you could touch it if you reached up on your tippy-toes.

"Dan once told me that God spoke to him in lights," I whispered up to Dex, who was standing beside my wheelchair.

It hurt deeply to speak of Dan in the past tense. Dex leaned down to me and put his hand on my shoulder. I think he sensed my loneliness at that moment.

"Perhaps he is speaking to you, right now," Dex whispered back, finishing my thought.

"I think so . . . I would like to think that."

Everyone pulled up a deck chair and we sat in a close semi-circle. Our conversation drifted around the vastness of space, and I wondered silently if Dan and Lily's spirits could be found up there . . . somewhere.

Sometime after 10 PM, I was having trouble staying awake and announced that I needed some sleep. I had invited Dylan to stay the night. It seemed silly for him to drive home or stay at a hotel. He accepted with much appreciation.

"Ginny, why don't I stay on the couch tonight, and you sleep in your own bed. I will be here in case you need anything," Dylan suggested.

"Oh, I don't know. I haven't slept in that bed since . . . well . . . since Dan."

"This might be a good time to try, especially because you won't be in the house alone," Courtney said, and as always, she had made a good case.

"OK . . ." I paused to gather my thoughts. "You guys have been so good to me. I'm so glad you're here. There is no way I could have survived this without you."

I shared how blessed we were to have each other. It was rare for a biological family and its in-laws to remain so close.

"Thank you, Dan, for bringing me into your family. I wish you were here to share this night with us."

"Dex, could I bother you for one more lift up the stairs?" I asked.

"You're killing me!" he replied.

"Will you need help?" Courtney asked politely.

"I'll call you if I do. I'll take my cell phone with me."

Dex wheeled me into the house. I hobbled myself into the powder room. That maneuver I pretty much had down. Dex waited outside while I went to the bathroom, washed my face, brushed my teeth, and tied up my hair. While I was in there, I remembered the night that Dan and I told his dad that I was pregnant. At the time, I was able to run into that small powder room. Little did I know then that a worse night was looming in my future. My eyes filled with tears as I choked back the grief that was trying to rip at my throat. When I came out, Dex was waiting for me. He scooped me up in his arms and stared down at me with pity written on his face. As we ascended the stairs, sure enough, that one step gave a mighty squeak.

"Oh, Dan, you have the funniest way of letting me know you are here . . ."

"We're going to have to fix that," Dex remarked.

He carried me into my room and gently sat me down on the bed, unlike Derek who practically spiked me like a football.

"Do you need anything before I go?" Dex asked.

"Would you mind handing me those shorts and shirt hanging on the door?"

"Ginny, you are one of the bravest people I know," he said as he handed them to me. "Dan would be very proud of you. I'll stop by tomorrow. OK?"

"Thanks for everything, Dex."

With that, he leaned over me and kissed the top of my head.

"Good night, Ginny."

I think Dex left the house after he got back downstairs. I fell asleep to the sound of Dylan and Courtney talking. It sounded like they were sitting close together. Definitely on the same couch. I'm not sure if Courtney went home or stayed the night. Either way, I was glad they were there. It was good to be back in my own bed. I slept on my side of the mattress, out of habit. I could feel Dan in the room. I could still smell him in the sheets and in the air. I missed him terribly. I turned on my left side as I would have done, and then he would have wrapped his arms around me and we would have spooned together throughout the night. I prayed I would dream of him that night and every night thereafter.

Despite my glum existence, the summer came and brightened the skies and warmed the sandy beaches. In fact, the summer weather was so incredibly perfect, it made me feel all the more heartbroken. The better the weather, the more I missed Dan. He should have been there to share it with me. Dan was never one to sit still or stay indoors. I knew if he were there, we would have been taking all kinds of outdoor adventures: hiking, biking, fishing. We may have set up a volleyball net on the beach. No, we definitely would have done that. We would have played a lot of CFFL football. Gilda would have had a grand time chasing everyone and everything. Instead, she spent her days lying next to me while I stared out at the Bay. I wondered if she realized Dan was gone. I wondered if she missed him, too. I wondered if she stayed close because she knew how heartbroken I was. I would like to say that I did things other than sit out there on the deck, but that about summed up my existence.

From the deck, I could see and hear children playing in the water. Sometimes they squealed as the cool water washed up somewhere between their ankles and kneecaps. Their dads lifted them up out of the water and spun them around, plopping them right back down into the next oncoming wave. I saw the women with their sunglasses, floppy hats, and loungers, relaxing as they sat in the heat, reading the latest romance novel or People magazine. They reapplied sunscreen from time to time, hoping for a bronze tan without the risk of skin cancer. Meanwhile, I could not bring myself to pick up a book or a magazine. I used to love reading steamy romance novels on hot lazy days. After the accident, I didn't wish to summon up any juicy romantic notions. All of my romance left the road on that tragic day in May. I didn't listen to music, either. For our wedding we had made a playlist of our favorite songs. However, I could no longer listen to any of them. If I heard one of our songs, my lungs would feel like they were being sucked in to collapse by a force over which I had no control. As I would try to contain my tears, I would reach a state of near panic. I was frightened by what would happen if I allowed the music to take me to that place and time when his arms were around me and his lips were on mine. Gone forever were his seductive lips. He was gone, and I could not run after him. I loathed looking through the mail. Letters and bills addressed to Dan continued to arrive at the house. Then, I had to make the dreaded call, telling the sender that Dan had passed away, and they needed to either discontinue the subscription or change the name on the invoice. Or, "For God's sake, please take us off your God forsaken list. Dan is not here to enter your damn contest. He is not here to make a contribution to your all-important charity. Not now, not ever."

I gathered up all of the pictures I had of Dan. I cherished each one of them. In fact, Dex and Dylan gave me some that I had never seen before. Dex had pictures that were taken in years prior to my knowing any of them. He gave me pictures of Dan playing beach volleyball. He gave me pictures of Dan and Dylan sailing away from the beach in a Sunfish. Dan always said, "If you can sail a Sunfish, then you can sail anything."

Dylan's pictures included several of Derek, Dan, and him when they were all much younger. One of my favorites was of the three of them standing beside a tree swing that flew out over a creek. Dylan said it was taken during a canoe trip down the Brandywine Creek in Chester County, Pennsylvania. They were flexing their muscles and showing off their rib cages. Dan could not have been more than twelve years old. Their grins were priceless. If my guess about his age in that picture was correct, then it was taken about the time their mother was very ill or had passed away. I had come to believe that the three of them must have pulled together to cope, as evidenced by that picture. They must have been like the three musketeers, roaming the countryside in search of a cause worthy of their heroism. Sadly, there was nothing they could save at home; the war was over.

As I spent my days and nights alone, I often wondered what the future would have been. I was beginning to resign myself to believing that perhaps it was never meant to be. And despite the pain, I knew if God had introduced me to Dan and said, "I have a terrific husband for you; however, he will die before your marriage is twenty-four hours old. Will you still receive him?" I would have said, "Yes." Yes, yes, yes. Not ever having met him, not loving him, not being loved by him, would be worse than losing him.

DEX

The summer got off to a rough start. Losing Dan was devastating for all of us. Dan and I had hung out a lot after he and Ginny moved down from Connecticut. They were such an amazing couple. I never felt like a third wheel around them. They were more like family to me, and Dan reminded me so much of his dad. With Mr. Carter and Dan gone, I had this instinctive need that I still cannot explain. It was a sense of responsibility toward Ginny to make sure that she was taken care of. Courtney was not as close to Ginny as I was to Dan, and Susan was two hours away. So that summer, I felt it was my duty to look after her.

In June, while she was still bound to her wheelchair, I stopped by every day and tried to get her out of the house. Taking her to happy hour and dinner at Irish Eyes every Friday night became a weekly ritual. The waitresses were beginning to treat us as if we were a couple. On the rare occasion that I would show up for a nightcap without her, they would look for her and ask where she was and how she was doing. It was easier to let it go than try to explain our relationship and all that had happened.

On our Friday nights out, we would often bring Gilda along with us. Dogs are welcomed on the outside deck of Irish Eyes, and Gilda was becoming a regular. She loved the attention she received from the staff and patrons. She also didn't mind the separate meal we would order for her: a plain hamburger with a side of fries. Ginny said I needed to stop spoiling Gilda because she was beginning to expect special treatment all of the time.

Getting ready for Friday night was more manageable at Ginny's than on the boat. Showering, for one, was much easier at Ginny's. So, on Fridays, I would finish work, go straight to her house, see if there was anything that needed to be done, get the job done, and then go jump into the outside shower. I started keeping a change of clothes there, as well as shampoo, soap, toothbrush, and toothpaste. One weekend when Dylan and Susan were down for a visit, they had a field day seeing my things in the powder room and the spare bedroom. They just would not let it go. Derek did not make that trip, thank God. He didn't come down very often. In fact, he had not been there since Dan's interment. It was just as well. He had a way of creating walls between all of us. Susan tried to come down every weekend. More often than not, Dylan made the trip as well. We purchased beach tags for Dan's old Jeep and Dylan's truck. Add a couple of fishing poles and beach chairs, and we were off to Henlopen whenever the weather cooperated. Courtney usually tagged along.

The girls usually napped or chatted. Courtney read a lot. Dylan and I tossed around the football when the fish were not biting. Those were the times Dylan and I really missed Dan. I could hear him yelling at me to go long. He would have me chase his throws into the surf, my body slamming into the water like a dolphin tail. We would get sand in our bathing suits and the crevices of our bodies, and salt water in our eyes. Occasionally, when Dan was feeling particularly ornery, he would throw the football in front of a vehicle coming down the beach. One time, before Ginny, I remember we spotted a topless Jeep with four girls in bikinis coming down from Herring Point and looking for a spot to pull in. When they had no luck finding something that they liked, they turned around by the towers and headed back toward us. We didn't have to huddle up for that one. It was an audible at the line of scrimmage. Dan sent me long, right in front of their Jeep. His timing was perfect. I caught the ball, rolled across their hood, and off the other side. As anticipated, they screamed and slammed on the brakes. It was perhaps one of the stupidest things

I've ever done in my life. Needless to say, the girls put it in park and stayed with us for the remainder of the day. They shared their food. We shared our beers. They parked with us a lot that summer. Dan was a crazy man back then, and Derek was pretty wild, too. If I remember correctly, it was the summer Derek earned his bragging rights, as he put it.

There was one summer weekend during Ginny's rehab that sticks in my mind the most. It was late June. Ginny was due to get her cast off that Monday. Susan and Dylan couldn't make it down because there was a wedding in the Carter family—a cousin, or someone like that. Ginny was invited, but she said she felt as though she would have put a damper on the celebration. She had never met most of them, and she thought her presence would only serve as a reminder of all they had lost, not to mention a distraction, stealing the bride's day. So, she declined the invitation and sent a gift.

That particular weekend began with our usual Friday night happy hour and dinner. During past Friday nights we talked mostly about my week at work. Ginny would fill me in on what was newsworthy, locally and globally. She stayed up on the headlines around the world by reading the newspaper and having CNN on as background noise during the day.

We shared similar political views, Ginny and I. We clung to the left side of center. So the right-wing-nuts were great fodder for our entertainment, and it was open season as far as we were concerned. Occasionally, we batted around religion. We both believed in God. We just could not understand why he would allow such terrible things to happen in the world if he loved us as much as his Bible claims he does. That conversation brought us down. So, we generally tried to avoid it.

Anyway, that particular Friday night, Ginny was very quiet. I had not seen her smile much at all that night. Not leaving Ginny's side, even Gilda was calmly behaving.

"Ginny, are you OK? You haven't said much tonight. You haven't eaten much, either." She didn't respond, so I continued to carefully dig.

"Did I say something wrong? Did I forget something? It isn't your birthday or something like that, is it?"

"No, no, it's nothing like that."

"Well, when is your birthday, anyway?"

"It's March 19th. You have plenty of time to get me a fabulous present and the best chocolate cake on the face of the earth."

"Now, that's more like it. So then, what's bugging you?"

"I guess I have really come to depend on Susan coming down on the weekends, and without Dylan here, I don't expect I'll see Courtney, or you, for that matter."

I felt a little lame for not figuring it out sooner. As she played with her French fries, I quickly tried to mentally run through my calendar for the next couple of days. I had promised an elderly widow who happened to live two doors down from Ginny that I would fix a dripping faucet in her house. Other than that, I was pretty sure my weekend was free.

"Tell you what, tomorrow afternoon we'll go out to the beach or find something to do. I have to stop by Mrs. Pollock's in the morning to fix a leaking faucet. We can go after that."

"Dex, you know you can't babysit me for the rest of your life. There is some awesome girl out there waiting to meet you, and you're going to miss her if you're hanging out with me all of the time."

"There is? Who is she?"

"I don't know, but there's a special someone for everyone, and you're not getting any younger. As a matter of fact, you're not getting *any*, as far as I know," she teased.

"Well, neither are you!" I returned fire, as a friendly spar. However, after it came out of my mouth, I realized how cruel my return was. Poor timing. Insensitive.

"Ginny, I'm so sorry. I didn't mean to . . ."

"It's all right, Dex. It's kind of funny when you think about it. Here we are: two healthy—well, almost healthy— attractive young adults, hanging out together every Friday night because we're so hopeless," she said smiling; allowing me to see that she still had a sense of humor.

"Yep, that about sums us up."

"You're probably the only person in the world who could get away with kidding me about something like that," she said cautiously.

"Well, you can dish it out too, you know!"

Right then I had the impulse to put her in a headlock and give her nuggies. It was also then that I realized there was no one else I would rather spend my Friday nights with. Since Ginny arrived back in Lewes to heal and recuperate, I had seen her every day, sometimes more than once. I thought it was out of obligation, or because it was the honorable thing to do. That night, I realized it was because I wanted to, and I felt a bit uneasy about it, too.

Saturday morning, I woke up with the sun streaming through one of the portholes above my bed. I stretched and threw on some shorts, shirt, and sandals. I grabbed a set of tools out of the Right Tackle's stern locker and headed out to the truck. Remembering I had promised to take Ginny to the beach in the afternoon, I went back below and grabbed a pair of swim trunks and a beach towel. I was psyched about spending some time with her that day, rather than alone cleaning the Right Tackle, or something like that. On the other hand, I was a little apprehensive, as well.

Mrs. Pollock was an elderly woman who lived on Bay Avenue, two houses down from the Carter beach house. Over time, the Carter clan had become her adopted grandchildren. When she heard of Dan and Ginny's accident, she sprang into action, as did many residents of Lewes—well, as much as a 76-year-old widow can spring. She brought meals down to the house almost every day for the first week. She made a mean pot roast, heavenly chicken 'n dumplings, shepherd's pie, and loaded mashed potatoes, just to name a few. She also baked an outrageous strawberry rhubarb pie. She was the Queen of Comfort Food. We finally convinced her to stay one evening and eat with us. That was when we learned her story. She and her husband had been married for fifty-two years when he suffered a massive stroke. "He was here one day and gone the next," she said. He was declared brain dead at Beebe Hospital, and in accordance with his Living Will, she had him removed from the respirator. They never had children. She and Ginny bonded quickly over their losses. After that night, I tried to stop in and see Mrs. Pollock whenever I could. On warm evenings, I would wheel Ginny up to spend time with Mrs. Pollock on her deck. The three of us would share dessert as the sun was in the process of setting.

That particular Saturday, Mrs. Pollock needed a leaking faucet repaired in her upstairs bathroom. It was probably something as simple as replacing the washer. While there, she said she had something she wanted to show me. When I finished the repair, she escorted me out to her garage. It was detached from the house and set at the back of her lot. She walked very slowly, so it took a while to get out there. On the way, we walked through her gardens. She named each variety of annual, perennial, and shrub as we passed by, as if she was introducing me to her old friends. When we reached the garage, she asked me to raise the door. As I pulled it up, light from the late morning sun crawled across the concrete floor and illuminated a worktable on the far wall. The garage was a treasure trove of tools and machinery. It was the ultimate workshop. She insisted I have the whole lot. I told her I had no place to store any of it. So, she offered to keep it all in the garage and give me "unfettered access" to it, as she put it. Reading the puzzled look on my face, she said she missed the sound of a hammer banging and the screaming saw as it cut through whatever her husband was working on at the time. At first, I declined her offer, suggesting it was far too generous. But then I saw her tear up, saying she had no one to leave it to. I took her hand and gave her a gentle hug, thanking her. I asked her to please call me if she ever needed anything fixed around the house. She seemed pleased.

Ginny, Gilda, and I spent the remainder of Saturday on the beach at Henlopen. I threw a couple of beers in the cooler, gathered towels, beach chairs, and a blanket and threw it all into the back of Dan's old Jeep. Ginny couldn't bear to part with that wreck of a vehicle, and I promised I would keep it running as long as possible.

It was kind of nice to spend a relaxing day, just the two of us. I didn't have to run after Dylan's football thrown deliberately into the water or in front of an SUV. It was a day to relax and "just be." I had set up the chairs and placed the cooler between us as a table. It was a convenient way to grab another cold one. Gilda chased the waves for a while and then came back and lay down in front of us. Ginny had brought a book along, thinking she might be ready to read again. She never opened it. We had talked for about an hour when she said she was ready for a nap. I had to help her down onto the blanket, and without Susan there, it was my job to put sunscreen on her back. Massaging it in, she was asleep within minutes. In many ways, she reminded me of a wounded bird I had tried to save when I was in the first grade. I was devastated when it died. We had a burial service for it and everything. This time, I was not going to let anything hurt this wounded one. I watched her sleep.

By August, Ginny was free of her walking cast. She couldn't wait to try out her new freedom. She walked more and more each day, building up her stamina and strength. She went to physical therapy three days a week and was making great progress. She began driving again, too. She even began talking about finding a job.

Ginny decided she needed to get into an exercise routine of sorts. Her weapon of choice was a bicycle. So, she and I visited the Lewes Cycle Sport Shop on Savannah Road. She explained to the owner what type of cycling she might enjoy. I could tell that she was making it up as she went along. However, as it turned out, she just wanted a bike to ride for the fun of riding. She was not out to race or participate in any "Bike to the Bay" type marathons. She just wanted to take leisurely rides around the area. The owner recommended a seven speed cruising bike. She took it for a test spin and was sold. I had not seen her that happy since her wedding day. She was giddy as she dismounted the bike. The thought of getting out of the house whenever and however was giving her an oxygenated high. She made the purchase and he told us to stop by the next day and he would have it assembled and ready to go. She also asked him to add a rear view mirror, water bottle holder, and a removable basket.

GINNY

I finally got out of my walking cast. I was a little cautious the first couple of days. I wasn't sure how much weight or stress my right leg could carry. I continued with physical therapy, but I was hoping that it would end sooner than later. It felt so good to be mobile again. As soon as Dex left the house, I waited a few minutes and then took the Jeep for a drive. The tires were still aired-down from our last beach trip, so I did what any normal person would do; I drove it out onto the beach at Herring Point, in Cape Henlopen State Park. With the top down, I cruised up and down, listening to the waves while feeling the salt air on my face and the moist wind in my hair. I felt like the bald eagle we had spotted gliding high above the ocean on several occasions. With no particular destination in mind, I was just driving the beach because I could. When I drove off the beach, I aired the tires back up. I drove back past Cape Shores, past the Cape May-Lewes Ferry Terminal, past the Dairy Queen, and up Bay Avenue to our house.

"Oh, Dan, where are you . . . ? You should be here to celebrate this moment with me. I am so sorry, baby. I am so very sorry."

I parked the Jeep and went inside. It went much better than I thought it would. I was able to summon the courage it took to embrace my independence. Gilda was at the door wagging her tail, always happy to see me. I grabbed her head with both of my hands and rubbed her ears wildly, celebrating our success as independent women.

"Your Daddy would be so proud of us."

I took her outside and let her run the beach for a while, while I carefully walked through the sand. I felt like a caged animal finally set free. I could move around on my own, and I was obsessed with the need to keep moving. I didn't want to stop, but the sand was making my little hike a difficult task. So, on a whim, I went out and bought a bike. I remembered how much I loved riding my bike when I was very young. I still remember the first time I had found my balance and learned how to brake. My dad never gave me training wheels. He said training wheels were for sissies. He would run behind me, holding me up until one day he let go and stood still as I rode off. The stopping was a little rough, but it didn't matter. I had found a new freedom. I remembered how strong my legs would feel and how I could ride my bike for hours at a time. I wanted my legs to be that strong again. I remembered the sound of the wind rushing past my ears as I would fly recklessly down the hills of Darien with no hands. I longed to hear that sound again. I remembered the burn in my legs as I pumped my way back up. I wanted that glorious painful fire again. The day I bought my bike, I felt that surge of freedom once more.

I didn't realize Dex was going to buy a bike as well; he surprised me with the news. I was thrilled. It meant that I would not have to ride alone. He was in such good shape; I only hoped that I would be able to keep up with him. During my convalescence, he had carried me up the steps or out to the beach like I was a bag of feathers. I had seen him outrun the other guys when we played football. Sheesh, the stakes were high.

We picked up the bikes the next day. I insisted on riding

mine back to the house. He loaded his into the back of his truck. Once I was out on Savannah Road and headed back for Bay Avenue, I just was not ready to stop. I rode past the house, noting Dex's truck in the drive and the bike gone from the truck bed. I knew he was probably out riding around, testing out his new wheels as well. I rode up Bay Avenue to the Children's Beach House, making a left and then a right onto Cedar Avenue. I rode up to the inlet, and there he was. His bike was on its kickstand, and Dex was standing on the rocks looking out across the water, just as I had seen Dan do so many times before. If I didn't know he was gone, I would have sworn it was Dan. Their silhouettes were almost identical.

I pulled my bike up beside his, leaned it on its kickstand, and walked up behind him. I don't really know why, but when I reached him, I surprised him by wrapping my arms around his body.

"Thank you," I whispered.

"Hey! I wasn't quite sure who that was," he said, as he spun around. We were now face to face, and his hands naturally went around my waist.

Suddenly, an alarm went off in my head, alerting me to our closeness. I had become acutely aware of the electric charges that were flowing between us. I dropped my arms and took a step back, but I didn't want to lose the moment. Something needed to be said. The words poured from me before I could stop them.

"Dex, I don't know what I would have done without you these past several months."

"Oh, someone would have looked after you, like Mrs. Pollock," he teased, flashing his handsome grin.

"Right, I'm sure I wouldn't starve to death if that were the case."

"Aaaahhh, so I probably should have fed you more. That's why you're all skin and bones," he said sarcastically, pinching my upper arm. I responded with a jab to his solid biceps.

"Seriously, she wouldn't be able to carry me up the stairs or out to the beach. She wouldn't be able to take

Gilda out for a run. She wouldn't drive me out to Cape Henlopen and share a couple of cold beers with me. She wouldn't take me to happy hour and dinner every Friday night."

"True, true . . ."

"I'm going to miss all of that. I mean, I may be physically mended, but I just don't know if I'm really ready to be completely on my own."

"Your recovery doesn't mean we can't hang out from time to time."

"Time to time?"

"It's been really nice to spend time with you, despite the regrettable circumstances. It's been nice to be needed every once in a while. It's given me a purpose in life."

"That's what I've been? I'm a 'purpose' to you? A welfare case?"

"No. You know I didn't mean it that way."

"Dex, don't hang around just because I'm some charity case or because you feel obligated to do so."

"Yeah, well it's easy to accuse me of what? Martyrdom? Sure, now that you don't need me anymore. Maybe you were just using me? Am I right?" He cocked his head and squinted one eye, studying my face and scrutinizing my motives.

"No. And how dare you suggest I would do that. If I had to, no matter how difficult, I suppose I would have found a way to manage."

"True, you could have gone back home to your mother's. Or, you could have stayed with Susan, but we all know how Derek would have felt about that. No, you chose to stay here. Why did you stay, Ginny?"

Why did he even have to ask me that? What was he expecting me to say? I needed him? This is bizarre.

I started to feel dizzy and a little sick. Though he was standing right next to me, it felt like he was ten miles away. Yet, I wished he were closer. I wished he would put his arm around my shoulder and steady me a bit, just as he had done for the past three months.

"I have to go before we say things we don't mean." And then, he left. I didn't hear from him after that.

The weeks ticked by.

DEX

Maybe she was right. Maybe I was just trying to be some kind of martyr. Maybe I was hoping the Cape Gazette would get wind of it and do a full-page story on my heroism. Good Morning America would fly me to New York and interview me on national TV. I would be named World News' Person of the Week. Right.

Maybe I did it out of obligation, which was not totally wrong. Dan and I were becoming good friends. I knew that he would have wanted me to take care of her. He would have been devastated if I had turned my back on her. I knew how much he cherished her. She was his entire world.

He would have done the same for me and mine, except there was no "mine." I missed Dan, but I knew my hurt was nothing compared to the pain Ginny was living with every day. And now, I missed seeing her, too. Perhaps my motives were not so noble, after all. I mean . . . I really missed her. . . . I really wanted to drive over there and see if she would want to go to the beach, or happy hour, or bike riding. That was the other thing: I could not believe that I actually bought that stupid bike. Never in a million years would I have bought a bike. I bet Dan would have bought a bike if it meant he could cycle alongside her. Is that why I bought the damned bike? It wasn't like she had replaced Dan as my friend, or that I expected to replace Dan as hers.

I never took a shower or got changed before hanging out with Dan. We just hung out, a sweaty stinky mess. I never called to make sure we had plans. We just did. I never stopped over to have lunch practically every day. I don't believe we ever did that. I never had butterflies when I thought about spending time with him. I never found it difficult to leave. We never had a disagreement about motives. The relationship with Ginny was feeling wrong. However, it was a relationship that was hard to end, or even change, for that matter.

What was wrong with me? Nothing good could come from what I was feeling. Nothing could ever come of it, either.

I visited with Mrs. Pollock several days a week, just to check in on her like I always did.

"So, Dex, I haven't seen you at the Carter beach house lately."

"Yeah, Ginny's out of her cast, and she can pretty much do everything on her own now."

"Oh, I know. She stops over a couple of times a week for coffee. She said I had to stop with the desserts. She said we girls need to maintain our girlish figures."

"That sounds like Ginny. Is she riding her bike much?"

"Yes, just about every morning she rides up and down Bay Avenue. I don't think she has ventured very far, yet. I told her I had heard that there was a lovely trail ride between here and Rehoboth. She didn't think she was up to it just yet. She suggested that I should borrow your bike and we could ride the trail together. Imagine that!"

I shook my head. Ginny was always the kidder.

"She did, huh?"

"Yes, she did. I thought she meant a motorcycle! But she said you bought a bicycle."

"Yes, I did."

I still could not believe it myself.

There was a pause in our conversation.

"How's she doing, Mrs. Pollock?"

"She looks like she's surviving. She has Gilda to keep

her busy. That dog has a lot of energy that needs expelling, and Ginny looks like she's getting stronger every day because of it!"

"That's good. Gilda's a good dog and Ginny's a strong person. They'll make a good team."

"They will at that, but Ginny has been through a lot. I wish she had more friends her age around here. If she was lonely or depressed, she would never admit to it, now would she?"

"No, I guess she wouldn't. She was the one that held us all together. She was the one who could always make us laugh at ourselves, or mediate our disagreements."

Another pause.

"You know, Dex, she has asked about you, as well."
"She has, huh?"
"She has. What happened? Did you two have a disagreement that she couldn't, as you say, mediate?"
"Not really. I guess she needed some space."
"That's funny. She said the same thing about you."

Back at the boat, I realized how much I had missed her and I was worried about her, too. I was tempted to call. I was tempted to drive over there. However, my motives scared me. I never felt like that when Dan was there. I didn't want to be that guy that moved in on his best friend's girl . . . his wife, for that matter.

Would I be acting like this if he were still here? Am I that guy? Is that what Ginny thinks? What do I care what she thinks? She's made it clear that she doesn't think too highly of me, anyway. Did she always think of me in this way?

I was restless and needed to get off the boat. I called Court.

COURTNEY

Those two were a mess.

Dex asked me if I'd like to get together for a drink. He said he had not seen much of me lately and thought it would be nice to catch up. I told him I should finish up at the office at about 7:00, and then I could meet him at Irish Eyes.

"Court! Thanks for coming!"

As I approached the bar, he stood and gave me a hug and a kiss on the cheek.

"Hey, Dex, good to see you, too."

My God, he's good looking!

"Should we get a table?" He grabbed his drink from the bar as his buddies whispered a few remarks. The hostess escorted us to his usual table by the window. I caught her studying me. She appeared confused.

Does he really spend that much time here?

"So Court, thanks for coming out to meet with me. How have you been?"

"Great. I know this is not about me, so what prompted your call?" I was never one for small talk.

"I don't know. I just thought it might be nice to catch up. I was so consumed with taking care of Ginny. I kind of lost track."

"Uh-huh. By the way, where is Ginny? I thought she'd be here?"

"You know, I don't have to do everything with her. She can take care of herself now."

"Oh, I thought you guys were good friends. I didn't realize it was an obligation thing for you."

"Yo, where is that coming from? We were . . . I mean . . . we *are* good friends. I needed some space. You know. And she needed space, too. I didn't want her to start depending on me for everything."

"Heavens, no. And you don't want to depend on her for anything either, right?"

"I don't like what you're insinuating," Dex said as he rose from his chair.

I grabbed his arm and pulled him back down just as a waitress approached us to take our order.

"He'll have another and I'll have a Manhattan straight up. Oh, and add an order of loaded cheese fries, please. I haven't eaten all day. It will keep me from chewing this guy up and spitting him out."

Dex glared at me. He was truly annoyed with me. I loved it when I got under his skin like that. Despite his tough exterior, he really is a cupcake. He could be so vulnerable, at times. I liked vulnerable.

"Dex, once in a while, you should try owning up to your stuff."

"Courtney, I didn't ask you to meet me here so you could get into my head and make all these false accusations."

"Then why did you ask me here?"

He didn't respond immediately. He knew the answer, and at that moment, so did I.

"She got to you, didn't she?" I asked leaning closer and at a near whisper. I knew I had cracked the dam and the truth was ready to spill out. It would take a little while, but I could wait. My drink arrived and my fries would be served up soon.

"You know, Court, you and I have been through a lot together. I have always been honest with you. Your family has been like family to me. And who knows where I would be if it weren't for your dad and Mr. Carter.

"You mean my dad, and *your* dad, don't you?" I whispered, still leaning in to keep our conversation private.

"Stop answering everything with a question," he snapped.

"Then let's back up and start with the truth of what we're talking about here."

It was the one secret Dex and I shared. It was information we were never meant to have. However, I had uncovered the truth years ago when Dex was accused of burning down a boathouse. My dad had taken his case and one night rummaging through my dad's office, looking for who knows what, I came across Dex's file. I had seen Dex around and always thought he was so handsome. When I saw his name on the file tab, my curiosity got the best of me, as it usually does. I opened the file and read through it, and there I learned the truth about Dex. I also learned the truth about Mr. Carter. I learned how he had continued to support and look after Dex from afar, according to the wishes of Dex's mother. Mr. Carter was a good man. However, at the time, Dex's mother's wealthy family did not want it known that she was having a baby out of wedlock. Unbeknownst to David Carter, Alicia was engaged to be married to someone else. Alicia made it clear that her parents would demand an abortion if they found out that the baby was anyone's other than her fiancé's. After much pleading from Alicia, David Carter agreed to keep her secret and keep his distance. To the delight of her parents and breaking David Carter's heart, she did marry into the Lassiter family. She had the baby and lived with her husband in a sprawling Victorian house on Savannah Road.

Many years later, after the boathouse fire and acquittal, the Lassiter family moved to California. Dex, who was a teenager and her only child, moved with them. Two years after the move, Dex was at an all-time low. He and his "father" were coming close to blows. Alicia called David Carter and said she was sending him back to Lewes. Though devastated, she believed it was best for her son. She asked David to keep an eye on him while not giving up his identity.

Back in Lewes, things seemed to be working out for Dex. His heart had always belonged to the water. Before moving to California, his summer jobs were around the docks and charter boats. When he was young, he dreamt of one day having his own charter company.

As I continued to read through his file, I began to understand that David Carter was a man who dearly loved his wife, the mother of Derek, Dylan, and Dan. However, he never forgot Alicia and Dex. Privately, he never denied his responsibility as Dex's father. Publicly, he kept his promise to Alicia. So when Alicia called, several years after the death of David's wife, and Dex was on his way back to Lewes, he did not balk at the request. David sent Alicia the money to make a large down payment on the "Right Tackle," and she then co-signed the loan for Dex. When it was all said and done, Dex never knew David Carter was involved.

Once back in Lewes, Dex and I did meet up. Of course he remembered my dad, and we did become good friends. The dating thing didn't work out for us, as much as I had hoped it would. Through our late night talks though, I learned of his rocky relationship with his so-called father. And despite his mother's cajoling, he never flew back to visit them. Sometime later, she suddenly stopped making partial payments on the loan. Fearful he would lose the boat and determined not to make a reconciliation trip to visit his mother, Dex fell into another downward spiral. That was when I decided it was time to let Dex know the truth about a very remarkable man named David Carter.

"Yes, Court, she got to me, and I know it is so wrong on so many levels, but I also know that I didn't always feel this way. It isn't like I was moving in on Dan. It just happened along the way, after the accident, after Ginny came home. I just got used to seeing her every day. It wasn't a chore. It never was. I really looked forward to seeing her. Now, I can't see her at all."

"Why?"

"We had an argument."

"Over what?"

"The long and short of it is that she called me a purposeful martyr and I accused her of using me."

"Do you really think she was using you?"

"Never. I don't even know why I said it."

"Great, Dex. She's already been through enough, and you accused her, your friend's, no, your half-brother's wife, of using you?"

"I really messed up, didn't I?"

"Yeah, you fucked up big time. What were you thinking?"

Dex, put his head down into his hands and started running his fingers back through his hair. I put my hand on his arm so he would not close me out.

"Court, it all got so confusing."

"You fell for her, Dex. There's nothing confusing about that."

And why is it that he never fell for me like that? It is painfully clear to me that he is in deep: hook, line, and sinker.

"Huh . . . ?"

"Dex, it's so obvious to everyone, but you. You've fallen for her."

"Court, what do I do? This is all so wrong. I can't stop the way I feel. It's like trying to stop time. And, if I could stop time so none of this would go any further, I don't think my heart would cooperate. And worse yet, even if I could, I don't think I want to go back in time. If Dan were here today, then . . . am I that guy?"

"And maybe that's why we have 'time.' It is the one thing that is completely out of our control. Without time, we wouldn't learn anything because we would go back and undo whatever needed to be undone. Then we'd do it all over again, repeatedly. If we could control time none of us would need any sense of responsibility or decency. Without time, this world would be in worse shape than it is. And, come to think of it, I'd be out of a job. There'd be no injustices because you could just go back and undo what was done."

"Court, that's a real stretch and you're making my head hurt."

"Dex, it sounds like you're concerned with a moral issue, which, when you come right down to it, is not relevant. None of this, not even your own thoughts and feelings toward Ginny, happened when Dan was here. You haven't done anything wrong because at the time—their time—Ginny was nothing more to you than a friend and your friend's fiancée. Your feelings for her came at a time when you were doing what was noble and right."

"I wish I could believe that. God, I wish I could believe that."

"You looked after her. You cared for her. You essentially gave her the last several months of your life. You think the rest of us didn't notice? We all knew you were acting out of the kindness of your heart, your generosity, and your obligation to your friend and brother. Well, I was the only one that knew about the brother part, but all of us were witnesses to what was happening. Even Dylan and I talked about it."

"You did? You and Dylan? How much did you tell him? What's up with you two, anyway?"

"Don't try to change the subject. We're not here to talk about Dylan and me."

Thank God, my French fries arrived.

"Look," I said as I grabbed the ketchup bottle and squeezed out a large puddle into the basket, "it was bound to happen. No one is accusing you of having bad intentions, now or ever. You are doing that all on your own. You are your own worst enemy when it comes to women, you know that?"

I should know. He never gave us a chance.

I picked up a hot fry and dipped it into the ketchup.

"Jeez, Court, could you spare me some feelings here?"

"No," I said as I popped the fry into my mouth. "Share these with me before I eat them all."

At least, for now, Dex was no longer denying his feelings. Of course, I had no suggestions for him going forward. I basically left him hanging, telling him he had to work it out with her. After all, it is Biblical that a man should take in his deceased brother's wife. Actually, the

Bible says that he should marry his deceased brother's wife, except I didn't dare go there. I knew it would throw him over the edge, especially coming from me.

I did confess that I was almost tempted, once, to share Dex's biological relationship with Dylan, but felt it best not to divulge that unless Dex was OK with it first. I did tell Dex that I thought the truth should come out, and soon, all of it, including why he was back in Lewes. Those were the kinds of secrets that could destroy a family.

When Mr. Carter was alive, we were honoring his wishes. Now that he was gone, we were harboring a secret; one I did not wish to live with much longer, not if I was going to continue seeing Dylan, in whatever capacity. It was information I wished we had shared with Dan before he died. It was one Dex needed to share with Ginny, should he really consider pursuing his real feelings for her.

CHAPTER FOUR

GINNY

It was September. A chill was in the air and the back door was coming off its hinges, literally. I was feeling a little unhinged myself. I had not seen or heard from Dex in weeks. Every time I crossed the drawbridge over the canal, I looked to see if the Right Tackle was in or out. If it was in, I would strain to see if Dex was on board.

I really could have used his help then. Who was I kidding? I missed seeing him, too. The truth was that the door could have provided me with the perfect excuse to call him. But then he would think that he was right, that I was only using him, when in fact, I really enjoyed his company. I truly appreciated everything he had done for me. I just wished there was a way I could have made him realize how sincere I was about that, and that I was never taking advantage of his kindness. My one hope was that Dylan would be in Lewes for the weekend. I knew Dylan would fix the door, and maybe it would be a reason for all of us to get together. I gave Dylan a call.

"Hey, Dylan, how are you doing?"

"Hi, Ginny, I was just thinking about calling you. Is it OK if I crash at your place this weekend? I'm going to tag along on one of Dex's fishing trips."

"Sure, that would be great! Are you going to see Courtney?"

"I think so. Maybe the four of us should go out to dinner or something."

"Mmmmm . . . that sounds good. Though, I haven't seen Dex in a couple of weeks. I think he's upset with me."

"Really? What could he possibly be upset about?"

"I'm not really sure. I wish I knew. I think I offended

him."

'That doesn't sound like you."

"It didn't feel like me at the time, either."

"Ginny, I'm sure you didn't upset him. He's probably feeling a little stressed now that charter reservations are picking up, and he's still working full-time for that construction company, right?"

"True. Speaking of construction, there's a door here that is coming off its hinges and I could use some help. Would you mind fixing it while you're here?"

"I don't know. Will I get a discount on my weekend rate?"

"Same one you always get."

"OK. I'll take care of it, and I'll give Dex and Courtney a call and make arrangements for all of us to get together for dinner."

"Dylan, why don't you let me cook dinner for everyone, kind of my way of saying thanks."

"That would be nice, Ginny. I'll see you sometime Friday night."

The realization of spending a winter alone was beginning to set in. Things around me were changing. The vacationers had gone home. Owners of the summer rentals had closed up and left town. Even the Lewes Farmers' Market would be ending soon.

The weekend could not come soon enough.

Dylan arrived late Friday night. First, he stopped at Irish Eyes to meet up with Courtney. I tried to wait up for him, but I couldn't keep my eyes open, so I left the light on and headed up to bed.

Sometimes, it felt weird having him stay over, but I enjoyed the company and liked knowing that someone else was in the house. I also liked that if someone were casing the place, they might discover that a man was staying here with some frequency.

Before going up to bed, I set the coffee pot to brew at 5:00 AM. Dylan had mentioned that he needed to meet Dex at 6:00.

When I came downstairs the next morning, Dylan was just about out the door. He was going to stop at Wawa for coffee and sandwiches. I poured freshly brewed hot coffee into a thermos and handed it to him saying he and Dex were going to need more than just one cup of coffee from Wawa. I reminded him that we were all to meet at the beach house for dinner after their trip.

I knew they would have a great day. The weather was looking very favorable. Full sun with just a light breeze was expected all day. I heard the fish were starting to run, and I also heard that Dex was pretty good at finding them. I remembered his telling me how he would venture miles out to the wrecks where the fish liked to feed.

I also handed Dylan a bottle of suntan lotion.

"Yes, Mom," he teased.

Around 8:00 AM, I rode my bike over to the Lewes Farmers' Market. The outdoor market materialized every Saturday morning in the summer months following Memorial Day and closed down at the end of October. The vendors would assemble at Shipcarpenter Square, which was a small area just off the canal. It was a step back into time in many ways. The original houses that stood around the square marked an era when women waited for their men to come home from the sea, as evidenced by the many widow walks atop the waterfront homes.

The purveyors of fresh produce, seafood, baked goods, flowers, and arts and crafts lined the promenade. The centerpiece was a workshop where small wooden boats were still being built. With its double barn doors opened wide, observers were transported by the sight, sound, and the smell of fresh hewn wood to an earlier time in the town's romantic history. The men gathered around the unfinished hull of the skiff and admired its shape and size. Its lines were voluptuous to the seasoned sailor. She was wide enough for comfort and deep enough for a smooth ride. This mistress would soon be a finished sailing vessel. The whole event was a photographer's dream. I could hear camera shutters snapping away to capture a Rockwell-like Saturday Evening Post magazine cover.

In the midst of my stroll, I stopped to admire all of the ripe colors and greet the kind people who made me feel as though I had known them all my life.

What I needed to do was focus on finding a couple of items for the evening's side dishes. That autumn day, the market was filled with apples, hot apple cider, homemade applesauce, peach cobbler, vibrant peppers, squash, and huge displays of pumpkins and chrysanthemums. As always, I searched for something different each week. Back at the beach house, I would experiment and try to create something new. Dan and Mr. Carter would have been so proud of me.

Sometimes, when I was in the kitchen, I could hear Dan and Mr. Carter laughing. Other times, I could feel Dan standing behind me and wrapping his arms around my shoulders. He would lean over and kiss my cheek. There were times when we just stood in an embrace. When that happened, I was afraid to move, hoping he would materialize. Standing as still as I could, I didn't want the sensation of him being that close to leave me. I would stand motionless until my back hurt, and then he would slip away. Staying at my feet, Gilda would look up and cock her head like she had felt his presence, too.

I was strolling casually through the different displays and looking for something unique when I came across a large variety of squash. I couldn't think of anything more appropriate for an autumn meal than acorn squash. I would halve them, scoop out the seeds, and bake them with butter and brown sugar. For an appetizer, I found some beautiful mushrooms to stuff with crabmeat and sausage. I selected several greens and vegetables for a fresh salad. I bought two Granny Smith apples and a small pumpkin to make pumpkin crème brûlée with caramelized apple slices on top. I had my work cut out for me as I carried everything back to my bike. I took a deep breath and readied its basket for the short ride home. The idea of working with fresh produce in the kitchen always gave me butterflies.

As I crossed the drawbridge, I noticed that the Right Tackle was out. I prayed that Dex and Dylan would have a safe trip. I also prayed that we would have a nice evening and that Dex and I could put our misunderstandings behind us.

My plan was to grill the fresh fish that they would undoubtedly bring home. In the unlikely event that they would return empty handed, my back-up plan was to grill pork chops. I had purchased red and white wines and was prepared for either scenario.

At 11:00, I texted Dylan and asked if they had fish to bring home for dinner.

[Yes. Blues]

[Good. Filet pls]

[K]

That afternoon, Courtney called—as a courtesy—and asked if I needed anything. I told her I was in pretty good shape, except for unscented candles and that I couldn't locate my cooking torch for the crème brûlée.

"Ooooo, fire! That sounds romantic. I'll bring mine, and I'll pick up some candles. Can I stop by early to help?"

I told her that would be great. She was there within the hour. I put her to work setting the table. The acorn squash was scooped and ready to go. The salad was ready to be assembled. The pumpkin crème brûlée was baked and chilling in the fridge. I would add apple slices, sprinkle with sugar and torch them just before serving. All we needed were the guys and the fish.

Courtney and I had time to kill, so we uncorked the first bottle of wine, poured each a glass, and sat down to relax. She asked me how I was adjusting to the cooler weather on the Delaware Bay.

"It's OK. Though, I have to admit: I am missing New England."

* * *

Autumn was so beautiful in New England. When the leaves turned, the mountains would become a quilt of color. The vivid contrasts would set off the white church steeples that peeked out from the valleys. Raking leaves and jumping into the wispy piles was a favorite pastime of children, and earthy smells would fill the air. It was a time of year when families began baking pies and canning fruits and vegetables. Homemade applesauce and hot cider were staples. Wool sweaters were pulled out of their cedar chests, and summer clothes were packed away. Wood was stacked and ready for the winter's fires. Snowplows were reassembled, and school buses flew down country roads leaving a flurry of leaves in their wake. It was a beautiful time of year in New England.

* * *

"Have you thought about going back?"

"Permanently? From time to time, but it always comes down to this: I have no one to go back to."

"Ginny, I don't mean to pry, but what keeps you here?"

"Memories, I think . . . perhaps Dan . . . memories I made with him." I carefully constructed my answers as I stalled for time to think them through. She had me, though. Was I ready to share with her how I felt about Dex? I sat staring at my glass of wine and took a deep breath.

"Because of you, Dylan, and Dex, I feel most at home here in Lewes. I love this place and this house, especially when it is filled with people. Gilda likes it here, too."

At the sound of her name, Gilda, who was lying on the floor next to me, picked up her head and wagged her tail. I reached down and patted her head.

"Ginny, how are you and Dex getting along, if I may

ask?"

I sighed heavily. I was not sure how to answer her, because I didn't know myself, and I didn't know how much she knew.

"Dex has been so good to me. We were like best friends."

"Were?"

"I did use the past tense, didn't I? When I got my cast off and started getting my feet back under me, I think we said some things to each other that I know I regret. I haven't seen him in weeks and it's been lonely around here without him stopping by all the time. Admittedly, I am very nervous about seeing him tonight. The fact that he accepted my dinner invitation is a good sign, right?"

"Sure it is, and I don't think you have anything to worry about. Quite frankly, I think he's starting to develop feelings for you, more than two people would share as just friends, and I think it scares him. I think he is wrestling more with himself than with you."

Smelling of fish and beer, the guys arrived around 5:00. Coming our way to give us hugs, we fended them off and sent them to the showers. Like old times, Dex took the outdoor shower, while Dylan went upstairs. Courtney and I assembled the salad, and then we finished the squash and slipped them into the oven to bake. When I shut the oven door and turned around, Dex was coming in the back door with one towel wrapped around his waist and rubbing his wet hair dry with another. He stopped, then backed up and studied the door.

"Ginny, this door needs to be repaired. Why didn't you call me?"

"I wanted to, but . . ." I was trying to find the words for my explanation when he interrupted me.

"Ginny, you should have called me. This looks like someone tried to break-in. Did you hear or see anything?"

"Oh, God, no. Other than Dylan coming in late last night, I don't remember Gilda barking at anything. Are you sure that's what happened?"

Dylan came downstairs, dressed and wondering what everyone was looking at.

"What's up?"

"Dylan, did you notice anything about this door last night, or this morning?"

"Nothing more than what Ginny has told me."

"She told you?"

"Yeah, she called me earlier this week and told me it was coming off its hinges and asked if I would fix it while I was here."

Dex stood and stared at me with scolding eyes. I was not sure whether I was seeing hurt or anger.

"Ginny, why didn't you call me?"

I could see his pleading pain and hear it in his voice.

"This is nothing you should have let go. This door and frame need to be replaced. It looks like someone tried to jimmy the lock and push their way in." He was clearly upset.

He looked at his watch and surrendered to the fact that it was too late to do anything about it that night. He and Dylan surveyed the damage a little longer, and decided they would make the repairs in the morning. Dex left the kitchen. I heard him go up the steps, presumably to change into clean clothes he had kept in the spare room. I prayed he would not discover that I had gone in there to check and see if he had removed everything after not hearing from him. I had to see if he was so upset with me that he had moved everything out. With a few of his clothes still there, in my mind, there was always some hope that he would return. On the other hand, it was difficult to have clothes in the house that belonged to two men who seemed to have vanished from my life: one I knew would never return, and the other I had not been sure of.

When Dex came back downstairs, it was time to grill the fish fillets. I watched as he laid each one in aluminum foil and coated them with butter, leaving a few pats on top. Next, he spritzed each filet with white wine and then dusted them lightly with Old Bay. He sealed the foil packets tightly. As Dex was working, he would occasionally glance my way as if he was about to say something. Then he would turn back to his work. When the fish packets were ready, Courtney suggested that she and Dylan be the ones to take them outside to do the grilling. Gilda trotted happily after them. That left Dex and me in the kitchen. It was the first time we had been alone together since our disaster at the inlet, the day we had picked up our bikes.

"Dex, I'm so sorry."

"Don't. . . . Don't apologize. You have no reason to. I'm sorry for what I said and the way I've acted."

"I'm sorry, too, Dex. These past few weeks have been . . . awful . . . and lonely."

"I'm sorry about that, too. I should have thought about what you've been going through. I should have thought about your being here, alone . . . and your safety, too. . . . I am so sorry."

I walked over to him, inviting him to naturally pull me in for a much-needed embrace. I put my arms around his waist and laid my head on his warm chest. All of my muscles that had been stressed for so long just let go, and I relaxed. I could hear his heart beating fast. I wondered about the rate of my own pulse. It was good to be held by someone who cared, someone who cared as much as Dex. Fearful of what I felt tempted to do next, I did not dare look up at him.

COURTNEY

"What was that all about?" Dylan asked when we got outside.

"They're having issues."

"Issues? What issues?" he further inquired as he lit the grill.

"I'd tell you, but it's not my story to tell."

Facing me, he leaned back on the deck rail. The sun was about to set behind him, casting a deep red-orange backdrop laced with streaks of silver and blue. He raised his beer to his lips and took a draw.

"Court, are we keeping secrets now?"

Ouch, that was something I didn't want between us, and I was haunted by the bigger secret that was looming on the horizon.

"Hmmmm ... I really don't know for sure about any of this, but watch them and tell me if you think Dex has fallen for Ginny. And why have they avoided each other for weeks? I think he's afraid of how he feels and she's confused and vulnerable."

"Should we be concerned?"

"I don't think so."

"Doesn't it seem a little fast to you?"

Dylan lifted the lid of the grill, laid the fish packages on the rack, and then lowered the lid back down.

"Yes, except that he took care of her every day. I don't think it's anything he planned. I think it just happened along the way," I explained.

"I don't know; I feel like I should have watched out for her. She is my sister-in-law ... my brother's widow. Dex is a great guy and all, but I just don't want anyone getting hurt or taken advantage of."

"Do you think Dex would take advantage of her? Really?"

"No. Not intentionally, anyway."

"You know what I think, Dylan? I think it's a good thing Dex was here and that they got along so well. It was a blessing that he was willing to look after her the way he did. And, if something happened between them, who are we to judge? Besides, other than you, who would Dan want to look after her?"

"Crap, Court, if I'm ever in trouble, will you argue for my defense?"

"Depends on the crime."

We ended our conversation with a stare, or was it a gaze? Was it a wish? Where was our relationship going?

Where are we, Dylan? Friends? It feels like more than just friends. Why do you make me second-guess myself? Dammit. Nothing can happen until he knows the truth, anyway. I don't want to explain it after the fact.

Who am I kidding? There will never be an "after-the-fact."

DYLAN

Dinner was the best home cooked meal I had had since my dad passed away. Ginny's menu was as good as any Dad and Dan had created, and that was saying something. It took something extraordinary to concede anything having to do with those two. Ginny was someone special. It felt weird thinking that I was glad Dan had met her, knew her, fell in love with her, and married her. And yet, if they had not met, Dan might still be with us. It wasn't her fault. I'm not laying blame. Just stating the facts. Though, Court could probably find a way to make a case against that thinking, too. Court could take a web of confusion and straighten out each strand, one at a time, so everything would appear as though it should have been obvious all along. On one hand, I was glad Dan and Ginny had met. On the other, I sometimes wished they had not.

Having dinner with Dex and Ginny showed me a few things, and Court did manage to put others into perspective. Dex really did care for Ginny. He had checked in on her at least once a day when she was recovering. He even got her out of the house from time to time. He had made sure she got to all of her doctor appointments. He had filled her prescriptions. He promised we would get on the damaged door the next day. He talked about looking into a security system for the house because he was concerned about Ginny being alone at night. With winter coming, he talked about looking into what storm windows were in place or available and if any sealing needed to be done. He talked about the need for insulation.

Dex and Ginny made a pact to try to ride bikes at least three times a week as long as the weather held up. Then there was some mention of him not riding his bike since the inlet affair? They laughed. Obviously a private joke they shared.

They even have private jokes?

They wanted to tackle the Breakwater Trail from Lewes to Rehoboth. It might not sound like much, but I knew that Dex was working fulltime for a construction company, plus still taking bookings for weekend fishing charters. He was really going out of his way for her.

I noticed that a playful banter had developed between the two of them. By the end of dinner, they were both a little buzzed. They had managed to polish off a bottle of Pinot Grigio, not that I was keeping track. It probably didn't mean much, but added to Ginny's fondness, Gilda loved Dex, too. He fed her that night, and later in the evening he took her out for a run. Courtney was right. It was fairly obvious that Dex had fallen for Ginny.

I wasn't sure how Ginny felt. She was trying to be so brave and independent; however, I thought the suspected break-in might have given her second thoughts about staying in the house alone. I would be there with her that night. We would call the police to report the incident in the morning and then fix the door.

COURTNEY

After dinner, I volunteered Dylan and me to do the dishes and clean up the kitchen. My mistake was that I had forgotten that their kitchen did not have a dishwasher, so it meant that we had to wash and scrub everything by hand. We poured ourselves another glass of wine to make the task less painful. Dylan washed the dishes, pots, and pans, and I rinsed them and then set them on the drying rack. We were splashing soapsuds and spraying each other with the hose. Actually, I had the hose, so Dylan got the worst of it. That was until he grabbed me, wrestled the hose away, got his revenge, and then some. I thought sure Dex and Ginny would come to my rescue, if only for the sake of the old kitchen floor. When we finally gave up the fight and declared a truce, we discovered why they had not appeared.

Dylan was headed upstairs to get towels for us, and the floor. He stopped short before entering the living area and waved me over. Peering in, we could see Ginny and Dex sitting side by side on the sofa with their backs toward us. Dex had his arm around Ginny's shoulder and they were talking quietly. It looked serious. Dylan and I withdrew back into the kitchen, not wanting to interrupt their conversation. Soaking wet and standing in a wide puddle of water, we looked at each other.

"What do we do now?" I whispered.

"Find some towels, somewhere."

I checked the dryer, but it was empty.

"Tell you what, I'll drive back to my place and bring back some towels."

"Don't leave me here with them!" Dylan pleaded. "This could get embarrassing."

"OK, then we have to at least mop up some of this water before we leave."

We made quick work with a mop we had found by the washer, some dish towels in a drawer, and a roll of paper towels under the sink. We peeked into the living area one more time and saw that they were still talking. Dex no longer had his arm around her, but they were still enjoying each other's company. We quietly left and drove to my place.

DEX

From stuffed mushrooms to the pumpkin crème brûlée, Ginny had prepared an amazing dinner for us. After dinner, Courtney and Dylan volunteered to take care of the dishes. Ginny asked if I would be more comfortable sitting on the sofa than at the table. As Ginny moved to a sofa, I opened the deck door to let Gilda out, and then I sat down next to her.

After being in the sun and wind all day, the wine was like a warm vapor coursing through my veins and affecting many things, including my inhibitions. Being that close to Ginny raised every red flag I had ever been taught to respect. I was doing battle with my natural desires and my deferential upbringing. Sometimes, doing the right thing exhausted me.

All day I had been longing for time alone with Ginny. There was so much I wanted to tell her. I wanted her to know how much I had missed her for the past several weeks. I wanted to apologize, again, for being so thoughtless. I wanted to tell her that I would like to start spending more time with her, not because she needed me, but because I needed her. Yes, there it was. Finally, I was ready to admit to her, and to myself, that I would like to be more involved in her life.

I knew it was too soon for her. I knew that rushing her would have been a terrible mistake and would only lead to our demise. Plus, I needed to tell her who I really was. If Courtney and I kept our secret much longer, when it finally came out—and it would—it would appear that Court and I were playing a hurtful game of charades with all of them. I would be right back from where I had started: an outcast in the midst of my own brothers. I couldn't bear the thought of Ginny seeing me the way Derek did, and perhaps still does. I didn't want to let it go on for one more day, let alone another minute.

Regardless of how I felt, I knew I couldn't dive in with my heart. I had to be smart. I had to wait. I decided I would strategize the announcement with Courtney. For the time being, I would just enjoy Ginny's company and the moment.

As she talked, I could feel the crackle of energy between us. It was like two magnets being drawn together. I had to stay far enough away that I wouldn't be pulled in beyond my ability and inner strength to fend off her attractions.

Her eyes were as beautiful as sapphires set in diamonds. Her hair illuminated the evening with hues of cherry wood and hazelnut. Her voice sounded like a song that I had just discovered. I wanted to take her hand, but I dared not for fear of getting sucked into a zone from which I could never return. I didn't know which was more intoxicating, the wine or the woman. I only knew that at that moment, the mixture was dangerous.

DYLAN

I had been at Courtney's place many times before. This time, there was something romantically comical about running in dripping wet, especially because there had not been a cloud in the sky all day. I stood in the kitchen while she ran upstairs to get some towels. After a minute or two, she came back down wearing a robe and carrying two towels, both for me.

"Here you go. Why don't you go upstairs. My room is the first door on the right. Change out of your wet clothes and I'll throw them into the dryer."

"Sure, but that leaves me with nothing to wear?"

"Pity," she said with a glint in her eye. "Don't look so worried. I laid out a big old sweatshirt. It used to be my dad's, until I confiscated it."

"And ... ?"

"Ah, yes ... and a pair of pajama pants. They might be

240

short, but I think they'll cover the essentials."

The essentials?

I went upstairs and into her room for the first time. It was very erotically inviting. The soft recessed lighting, a big cherry canopy bed with white lace sheers, the long cherry dresser with full mirrors that ran the length of the wall behind it, the double doors with brass fixtures which I imagined led to her dressing room and bath, a comfy lounging chair and lampstand all made for a potent environment. Unfortunately, I also wondered how many others had visited her sanctuary.

Positioned on her dresser were pictures of her taken with her, mom, dad, and two sisters. Several of them were taken in different parts of the world. I recognized the Eiffel Tower behind them in one of the shots. There was a beautiful picture of her and her sisters by a magnificent waterfall in a tropical setting. I remembered her telling me about a trip they had taken to Africa.

Then my eyes landed on a picture that must have been taken in the last several years. It was in a small gilded frame. I picked it up to take a closer look. In it was Mr. Sable, my dad, and Dex, all holding up tuna they had just caught. They were smiling proudly, like old chums having the time of their lives. My dad had his arm around Dex's shoulder and Mr. Sable was pointing at them with his free hand in a "get a load of these two" kind of way. It looked as if it had been a moment that was very natural and familiar to the three of them.

Why didn't I hear about this fishing trip or any other? You would have thought Dad would have told us if he had caught a fish that big.

The three of them were standing in the cockpit of Dex's boat, the Right Tackle, and my guess was that Court had taken the picture.

On the other side of the dresser, next to a jewelry box,

the one I had made for her birthday, was the picture she had taken of me on Christmas Eve kneeling down between the rockers I had built. I stared at it wondering if it was something she might gaze at from time to time, or was it just a part of her room's decor? Was I just a friend to her; more like a family member? Or was I someone that she might . . .

I was feeling a little dizzy. Perhaps it was the wine and the chill that was beginning to set into my body. Perhaps it was because I was in her room. It smelled like her hair and combined with the soft recessed lighting, it had a very sophisticated and sensual feel.

Get it together, Dylan.

A sweatshirt and a pair of pants were laid out on her bed, as she had promised. I removed my wet clothes and threw them into a ball on the floor. I pulled the pants on and lowered the sweatshirt over my head. Yes, the pants were too short. However, as stated, they covered what needed to be covered.

I have to admit that being in her room was somewhat arousing. I needed to leave before I thought too much about it. I gathered up my ball of wet clothes and carried them downstairs just as she called up, questioning what was taking me so long.

"If those pants were any smaller we'd have a problem!" she teased as I came down the stairs.

"Well, I could remove them, but I don't think you're ready for that."

She hesitated. Her wheels were spinning. I was on the roller coaster of right and wrong, self-control and unrestrained desire. I took a step toward her. She took the wet clothes from me, stared into my eyes as if she was going to take me, as well. Then, with second thoughts, she turned and said we had better get back to Ginny's. I wanted to ask her so many things. My questions would have to wait, and I knew I was in for a sleepless night.

We were silent on the drive back. Each of us knew what

the other was thinking, I was sure of it. Yet, when I was near her, I was sure of nothing.

GINNY

After a while, it got awfully quiet in the kitchen.

"What do you think is going on out there?" I whispered close to Dex's ear.

"I don't know, but I sure don't want to walk in on anything."

We sat still for what seemed like minutes. We didn't hear lips. We didn't hear the rustle of clothes. We didn't hear any whispers or moans of ecstasy. Without warning, Gilda barked at the deck door, scaring both of us. Dex got up and let her in. When he crossed back in front of the sofa, he whispered, "I can't stand the suspense any longer. I'm going in."

"Not alone. I'm going with you."

We crept through the living area and past the dining table. Like international spies we were pressed against the wall, we peeked around the corner, and scanned the kitchen. Nothing. No one. Gilda, clueless as ever, trotted happily past us and over to her water bowl and began lapping water in her usual sloppy way. I stepped into the kitchen and slipped on the floor. Dex tried to catch me and we both went down, landing in a heap. I fell on top of him.

"Oh, my God, are you all right? My feet went right out from under me."

"I'm fine, but if your elbow had landed a few more inches to the left, there would have been some serious damage to report."

We carefully untangled ourselves and got back up to our feet.

"Dex, this floor is wet, and we're not anywhere near Gilda's bowl."

"Yeah, and the culprits are clearly not here, either."

"And they didn't bother to say goodnight."

Dex and I grabbed some paper towels and tried to do a better job with the floor.

"Do you need me to wait here until Dylan gets back?"

"No, who knows when he'll come in? And who says he'll even come back?"

"Well, I should go. I promised Charles I'd get up early and go out for a spin with him in the morning before his first party shows up. He ran into some engine trouble yesterday and had to limp in on one prop. He said he thinks he's got it fixed, but he wants to take her out and open her up before he heads out again with a boatload of people."

"Do you have a trip to take out tomorrow?"

"No, it all worked out so Dylan and I can get some things done around here. I'll see you sometime in the morning."

A silence fell between us. Then he moved forward.

"Listen, Ginny . . ."

He was stalling, looking into my eyes and then looking away.

I was frozen. "What is it, Dex?"

"Ginny, I need to confess something to you."

He carefully placed his hands on my arms and pulled me in.

"I love you. I really do love you. These past few weeks have made me realize how I feel about you, even though you may not feel anything for me. I know this might be scary to hear, but please don't let it scare you away. I don't care if you feel nothing for me other than as a friend. I just don't want to hide from you anymore. I just need to let you know how I feel. Please don't push me away or hide things like a broken door from me again. I'm here, and I'm not going anywhere."

I had frozen at the words "I love you." Then, my glacier of denial melted away when I realized he had said it twice. He basically said he did not care if he was on a road that led to nowhere. I couldn't hold it in any longer. I had to confess, most of all to myself, that I wanted to be on that road with him. I reached up and touched his face. Up on my toes, I reached his lips with mine. As soon as we touched, he held on to me. First, a quick brush, he drew back and looked into me to make sure it was OK. Assured, he took me with long, soft, and slow movements of his mouth, his tongue curling around mine. I was lost, thoroughly lost. He had managed to stop time.

"Ginny, I have to go," he whispered. "I don't want to, but I have to. I love you too much to stay." He lingered a kiss on my cheek and left.

DEX

As I drove away, I swiftly regretted leaving, and I slowly grew to regret the terrible mistake I had just made. I had crossed the line. I had crossed the line without letting her know my relationship to Dan, first. Now, there was no going back.

I didn't regret telling her how I felt. I didn't regret showing her what I was feeling, not in a million years. What I did regret was that she didn't know, fully, who I was. It simultaneously left me flying high while feeling like crap. I was afraid of the truth and the things that I couldn't change. I was more afraid of the truth than I had ever been in my life. What if the truth felt like betrayal to her? Worse yet, what if she believed I not only betrayed her, but Dan as well. I loved her and I loved my brothers, and for that I ended up hating what I had just done.

At 4:30, I woke up to my exceptionally annoying alarm. The first thing I remembered was the kiss I had shared with Ginny the night before. My lips, and a few other things, tingled at the memory. The second thing I remembered was the remorse I felt for not sticking with the plan. Third, and for the time being, I needed to put those thoughts on hold and fulfill an obligation I had involving a good friend and mentor.

Charles owned the boat next to mine. It was a Bertram and a twin to my own. Built in the same year, they were practically identical, except his had way more hours on its engines. He had way more fish pulled on to his decks and way more stories written into his Captain's Log.

Charles was my mentor. After a rough first year in the charter business, Charles took me under his wing. He helped me rig out my boat, told me of his best fishing spots, and sent customers my way when his trips were booked. I would have guessed Charles was about twenty years older than I was. He and his wife, Becky, had two sons that were a hand full. Once when Charles had to take Becky to Beebe Hospital, they asked if I would be kind enough to come over and stay with the boys. They were asleep, Charles said, so there should've been nothing for me to deal with other than being there so social services would not pick them up for negligence.

After Charles and Becky left, all hell broke loose. As if he had radar for that sort of thing, the oldest one started screaming, waking the youngest. I never quite figured out what all their fussing was about, other than to make me completely miserable. I had a choice to make: allow them to ruin a promised quiet evening, or find something enjoyable that the three of us could do until they fell back asleep. I found a book about pirate ships on the coffee table, took it up to their room, set them back down into their beds, and began reading. It was not long before they drifted back to sleep. However, unaware of all the shipwrecks off the Delmarva coast, I was thoroughly engrossed in the book and its stories. When Charles and Becky returned, I asked if I could borrow it. Charles was pleased.

Charles knew David Carter. He knew Mr. Sable. Recently, he had met the Carter boys, and Courtney. By August, he had seen Ginny on board the Right Tackle several times. Last week, he mentioned that he had not seen my lady friend lately and wanted to know what I did to scare her off.

If he only knew . . .

When I came up on deck, Charles had just started the engines of his Morning Starr. (His last name is Starr.) He made some smart remark about my being a lazy ass and getting my butt in gear. Announcing that the coffee was on and that he didn't have all day, he made it clear that he was ready to go. I loved the way Charles rode me on anything that felt like fair game. With coffee in my hand and the feeling of revival coming over me, Charles didn't waste another minute. We cast off the lines of the Morning Starr and left the dock. I looked back at the Right Tackle, resting and abandoned in her berth. I rarely got to see her from that vantage point. High above the water, her wide bow flanged out and around. The ripples of the small wake we had left behind created a reflection of watery sunlit ribbons on her smooth glossy fiberglass contours. She seemed sad that I was leaving with another.

Once past the breakwater, Charles started throttling up the Morning Starr until she planed over and reached cruising speed. I swear, I baby my boat, but there was no one that knew how to care for and maintain a mistress like Charles. Doing what she was designed to do, the engines of the Morning Starr were humming as she cut through the water like a knife. Watching Charles at the helm, it was easy to recognize the special connection he had with his Morning Starr. He cared for her the way a knight looks after his lady. Some say Charles was so meticulous about the Morning Starr that one could eat off the bottom of her bilge.

I'll take their word for it.

I wished Ginny was with me and that we were on the Right Tackle, cutting through the water, riding the fly bridge together, just the two of us. With the sun coming up, the sky was changing to welcome the new day. It was so peaceful as pelicans glided above the rollers and three dolphins raced us off the starboard bow. Ginny would have loved it, and I would have loved to share it with her. However, after the prior night, and the truth that was laying in wait, I was less than hopeful that we would ever be more than just a dream.

GINNY

I could still taste Dex on my lips. I could smell him in my hair. I wanted him to stay. I wanted to pull him back inside. Why was he in such a hurry to leave? Getting up early with little to no sleep never seemed to bother him before. I adored that he was so considerate and respectful. It was one of the many things I found so attractive about him. Perhaps he was thinking of Dan, as I should have been.

When his head clears, will he think less of me because of my actions? After all, I initiated the kiss.

I hoped he would return the next morning, as promised, to fix the door. Was it possible that I was only looking for someone to take care of me? Was I thinking of my physical needs? Was it a mere physical attraction I had for him? Did it make me unfaithful to Dan? Was it lust, or was it love? My heart swelled when I thought of him and hurt at the thought of losing him.

Should I think with my heart, or my head? Does my heart count in any of this? Will I ever love again the way I loved Dan?

I walked out onto the deck that Dan, Dex, and Dylan had rebuilt. It felt safe and secure under my feet. Walking up to the rail, I looked out across the water. It was a new moon much like the night we almost touched the Milky Way, the day we had sadly laid Dan to rest.

248

Beyond the sand, there was nothing but a large chasm of still black water. Miles out, there were a few visible lights from freighters at anchor waiting for a pilot to come and steer them up the Delaware River. It was like looking out to Dan and Lily, waiting for me to come and join them, but I could not. In the meantime, there would remain an endless reach between us: one that I could not cross until it was time, and one that they would never cross again.

All the way to our very end, so many things happen from which there is no turning back. I had had my share.

I went up to bed. I didn't want to see Dylan and Courtney, if and when they returned to the house. I undressed and slipped into my PJs. I thought of calling Susan, but it was far too late. On my nightstand was a picture of Dan and me. His dad had taken the picture the day after we had told him that he was going to be a grandfather. Most nights, I gazed at Dan's proud smile and talked to him, and most times I knew how he would have responded. That night, his confident countenance and my confusion made me miss him all the more. That night, I couldn't bring myself to ask his advice on the matter. It felt wrong.

I reached out and touched Dan's face.

I'm so sorry, Baby. I miss you so much . . .

I looked at the picture again, thinking how Lily was a part of me when it was taken. She was in the picture, too.

Look how happy Dan is.

Dan was a man on top of the world. How quickly things had changed. How temporal things in my life had been.

I'm sorry, Mr. Carter. I'm sorry that I didn't make your dream come true.

I heard Dylan come in the door. Gilda ran downstairs to

greet him. I pretended I was asleep, which was not far from the truth. I must have drifted off shortly thereafter.

I woke up with the sun, remembering Dex was due to arrive sometime in the morning after his test ride with Charles. I later learned that Dex did have a fishing party booked for the morning, but turned the reservation over to Charles so he could spend the day with me. It specifically had to do with the door and the attempted break in. He had made the call to Charles when he was upstairs changing before dinner. Sometimes, I thought of Dex as my reluctant knight in shining armor.

I put on a pot of coffee and made some buttermilk biscuits. I vaguely remembered Dex saying he liked biscuits with honey or jam. I had eggs and a pound of bacon that could be fried up when the guys were ready. Soon, Dylan emerged from the guest room and stumbled down the stairs. The poor guy looked like he was up wrestling with his pillow all night.

"Good morning, Sunshine!" I chortled.

"Morning."

"You OK?"

"I'm fine, just exhausted. I didn't sleep much."

"Neither did I."

I thought about Dex. I thought about Dan. I thought about the day ahead. And actually, until I got past that one day, I could not envision the future with any certainty.

Dex arrived about thirty minutes later. With everyone there, I called the Lewes police and reported the attempted break-in. Dispatch said they would send an officer over, most likely within the hour. While we waited, the boys measured the door and talked about what they needed from Lowes. Dex told us about the tools and workspace that Mrs. Pollock had willed to him. He said that after breakfast he would walk up and get what he and Dylan needed to get the job done.

"You know, I'll walk up with you and spend a little time visiting with Mrs. Pollock, if that's OK? That way, I don't have to be here when you guys start hammering away."

"Sounds good."

Dylan poured the coffee. I had the bacon sizzling in the pan and biscuits warming in the oven. As soon as the bacon crisped, I fried the eggs.

We had just sat down for about five minutes when a knock came at the door. Gilda barked and snarled. Once Dex opened the door, she became the visitor's best friend, in her mind. It was not like she knew the visitor. She just didn't like it when she couldn't see who was on the other side of the door.

"Hey, Dex. How are you doing?"

"Good, Pratt. Glad you could come out."

"You two know each other?" I asked, surprised by their familiarity.

"Yeah, Pratt and the force usually come out on a fishing trip once or twice a year. Pratt organizes the trip and holds a couple of the Right Tackle's records."

"Yeah, Dex sure knows how to find the best fishing holes off the Atlantic coast."

After everything Derek has intimated about Dex, I was surprised to see him acquainted with the right side of the law for the right reasons.

"Did you make the call?" the officer asked Dex.

"Only at my prompting. This is Ginny Carter. She owns the place."

"Nice to meet you, Ginny," Officer Tom Pratt said, tipping his hat and shaking my hand.

"And this is her brother-in-law, Dylan." Officer Pratt also shook Dylan's hand. Then he asked the question for which we were not prepared.

"Mrs. Carter, is your husband home?"

I became instantly cognizant that I was still wearing my wedding ring. My head spun. Not quite sure what to say, I know I stammered. Dex, as always, came to my rescue.

"He died in a car accident last May, Tom."

"Oh, Mrs. Carter, I am so sorry for your loss. I do remember that call. I was one of the officers on duty that morning when the call came in from the State Police

Barracks. We were all devastated."

"Thank you, officer. It's been a rough year."

I looked over at Dex.

The officer turned his attention back to the door. He took down the information and a brief summation of what had happened, which wasn't much, because we really didn't know all that much. He surveyed the door and agreed with Dex: it looked like someone had tried to break in. However, he went on further to say that something had made whoever it was give up. He said that the door and its frame were in such bad shape it should have been fairly easy for the perpetrator to break through with one final shove. He explained that given the circumstances, there was not too much that could be done. As far as we knew, nothing was stolen, and the door was the only thing damaged, that we could see. Officer Pratt said that they would patrol the area more often. He said he would personally keep an eye on the house.

After the officer left, Dex assured me that Pratt was a good guy, and if he said he would keep an eye out, he would carry it through. Then Dex shared with us how during the winter months, it was not uncommon for the vacant houses on the beach to be broken into.

So, we talked about ways to make the Carter beach house look obviously occupied. We talked about a security system; however, I vetoed that. We had a security system at my parents' house in Darien. It would go off for unknown reasons and scare the living hell out of me. An overactive security system could potentially scare me more than any possible perp. Besides, I had Gilda. She was probably the one who chased off whoever it was in the first place.

The guys went to Lowes, and I went on ahead to visit with Mrs. Pollock.

DEX

We fixed the door, Dylan left for home, and I delivered
Ginny's new key to her. She was still visiting with Mrs.
Pollock when we wrapped up, so I met her there after I
finished putting the tools away in Mrs. Pollock's
garage. Handing Ginny her new key, she invited me to stay
for dinner, but I had to decline. The night before, I had
asked her not to allow my feelings to scare her away. I had
not counted on them scaring me away from her. Until the
truth was out, I feared moving ahead. I returned to the
Right Tackle and called Courtney.

"You have to meet with me."

"OK, I'll meet you at Irish Eyes, half an hour, and you
buy dinner."

"No, it can't be Irish Eyes. It's too close. Ginny might
see us there."

"What did you do now, Dex?"

"I'll pick you up, and we'll go to Big Fish Grill in
Rehoboth."

"Nice, but you're still buying."

"Half an hour, be ready."

When I got to Court's, I was tempted to blow the horn. I
would have done that had it been any other good friend, but
not with Court. There would be serious
consequences. First, she would ignore me and I would end
up having to go to the door anyway. Then, she would
lecture me about the death of chivalry. *I know, I know . . .*
So, I walked up and rang the doorbell.

"Hey, handsome loser who's obviously gotten himself
into some kind of trouble, again! Let me get my coat."

I hate how she enjoys exploiting my predicaments.

On the way to Big Fish, I told her what had happened
after Ginny and I realized that she and Dylan had left and

the house was empty. I had to tell her three times that I left after the kiss. She was deliberately making me repeat myself. So, I asked her what happened with her and Dylan. She admitted nothing, and said that I needed to realize that not all heterosexual relationships were based on one's primal need for sex. I couldn't believe she said that after the raft of crap she had just given me. I had to chuckle at the thought that the two of us were debating the possibility of platonic heterosexual relationships. How ironic.

After we were seated and our drink order taken, I told Court we needed to get the truth out, and soon. I made the case that because it reflected on both of us; we should break the news to the surviving Carter family, together. Then kiddingly, I suggested she announce it to everyone as my legal representative and spokesperson. She ignored me.

We discussed bringing everyone together for the event; however, Thanksgiving would be the soonest that could happen, *if* Ginny was hosting the family dinner. There were too many *"ifs,"* and possibly too late for my liking. The final plan was that the two of us would break it to Dylan and Ginny, first. Dylan was due to come back to Lewes that weekend.

"Are you sure nothing is going on between you two?" I asked, knowing full well that Courtney was not going to answer me.

"Ha, don't drag me into your mess, and thanks for dinner!"

I wondered if she rode Dylan as hard as she rode me. The rest of the evening we discussed how we would accomplish our mission. Courtney was much more cavalier about it than I was. She was, after all, more of an innocent bystander. I was the consequence of my biological parents' actions. I was the issue at hand, and now the culprit for overstepping my bounds. I had let my heart override my head.

We decided that as soon as Dylan arrived on Friday night we would get Ginny and him together. At first, I suggested that we have the discussion on the Right Tackle. However, boats are not very soundproof and in case it was not well received, no one else on the dock and the restaurants nearby needed to be entertained by our mess. I would rather have Ginny throw me out of her house than watch her storm off of my boat. Exactly *how* we were going to announce it and what we were going to say was a much longer conversation.

GINNY

When they had finished installing the new door, Dex stopped by Mrs. Pollock's to give me my new key and relay that Dylan had said "thank you" before heading home. Dex did stay and chat a bit with Mrs. Pollock about some of the tools they had used for the door and how appreciative he was for the workspace in her garage. Of course, he asked how she was doing and said he would stop by, again, soon. He claimed that he needed to get back to the Right Tackle, and then he abruptly left. No hug. No "I'll call you later." No "I'll see you soon." He just left.

I stayed a while longer at Mrs. Pollock's. I'm not quite sure what we talked about after that. My mind was trying to replay and understand Dex's actions. He was doing it to me again.

Monday morning came and I thought Dex might stop by before he went to work or in the afternoon for lunch. But he never did. In the late afternoon, I went up to the spare room to see if he still had a change of clothes or other things left behind. I was looking for something to give me hope that he might return. Nothing. But then again, he had changed into clean clothes after their last fishing trip. Perhaps it was the last of what he had left in there. I walked over to Dan's drawing table. Lost in my thoughts, I spread out the last project that Dan had been working on. I ran my fingers over it hoping for some divine inspiration.

"Dan, why do things have to be so hard? Why am I always the one left behind?"

How I had hoped that I would not to be left alone again. Then I became aware that without any forethought, I was actually talking to Dan about Dex, and it felt OK.

"I am so sorry, Dan. I hope my feelings for Dex are not a betrayal. I never meant for things to turn out this way. Just let me know that I'm going to be OK."

I looked at the drawing board again and realized that the plans were not for a job proposal. The plans were drawn up for Bay Avenue. The exact address was 408 Bay Avenue. It was our address. I started looking through the layers of pages. It included some of the things I remembered hearing Dan and his dad dream about. The drawings represented something razed and something new. The plans for the new dwelling showed an expansive house that sat higher, making way for a double garage underneath. A wide staircase that rose to the deck on the second floor separated the two oversized garage bays below.

The second floor housed the sleeping quarters. It had four bedrooms, two on the waterfront side and two on the Bay Avenue side. Each bedroom had a private bathroom. There was a den/study between the two bedrooms on the waterfront and a laundry room between the two rooms facing Bay Avenue. Each bedroom had a double sliding door that led out to the deck that surrounded the house.

The top floor was the main living area. It was a large open space with high vaulted ceilings. The waterfront side was all glass. There was a fireplace in the middle of the glass wall. The kitchen was as large as the living area and featured seating capacity for six around the counter that separated the kitchen from the dining area. It had an additional long center counter with a produce sink on one end. The appliances were all commercial grade, complemented by a spacious walk-in pantry. The outside wall of the dining area included a long granite wet bar that featured a dual-zone wine and beer cooler.

The top floor also included a master suite. The master suite shared a see-through fireplace with its luxury bath. Between the master bath and its bedroom was a large cedar lined walk-in closet and dressing area. The master bath showcased a large double shower, a Jacuzzi opposite the shower, and a heated tile floor. There was an outside deck that surrounded the top floor, as well. The plans included every accommodation I could remember Dan and his dad ever talking about.

That room had been Dan's sanctuary. It was where he laid out plans for our lives and honored the dreams of his father. The spirit of both of their imaginations was right there on all of those pages. I checked the drawers for other things he may have left behind. Nothing. I looked in the closet. Nothing. I began to wonder if I was looking for things Dan had left behind, or things Dex might still have had there.

What is wrong with me?

As I was about to shut the closet door, my eyes had adjusted to the dark space and saw that there was a black box on the very top shelf, in the back corner. The darkness and an extra blanket made it easy to miss and had kept it concealed for who knows how long. I moved the blanket and pulled down the box. It was a very curious old tin box. Perhaps it was the sign I was looking for.

I took a deep breath and carefully opened the lid. It was filled with documents. On top, I found a copy of Mr. Carter's Last Will and Testament. Dan told me he had a copy of it, but I never thought much about it. I really had no reason to. The box contained his parents' marriage certificate and the boys' birth certificates; however, there was one certificate too many. I pulled out the extra certificate and unfolded it. It was for Poindexter Thurman Lassiter.

Who names their child Poindexter Thurman?

According to the date, this person turned twenty-eight on May 10th.

Poin-DEX-ter Lassiter?

Is this possible?

Then I read the father's name and it knocked the wind right out of me. His father was David Grant Carter. Dan's dad had another son? The mother's name was Alicia Marie Lassiter. I didn't recognize her first name. I didn't remember Dan ever talking about her. The date on the birth certificate was about eleven months before the date on Mr. Carter's marriage certificate.

Oh, my God, Mr. Carter, what did you do? Dex is Poindexter. Dan had a half-brother. Did he know? Does Dex know about this? Whose box is it, anyway?

I dug through it looking for pictures and other clues. Then I came across another shocking surprise: the title to a 42-foot Bertram convertible sport fishing boat. It was registered to Poindexter T. Lassiter. The documented name was "Right Tackle."

What the hell? Did Dan know about this box, or did Mr. Carter hide it here? Who put the copy of Mr. Carter's Will into the box? It had to be Dan, didn't it? Or was it his dad's copy?

I sat down in the chair. I didn't know whether I should cry or scream. All of a sudden, it was as though I never knew the Carter family. I didn't know whose house I was living in. How many other secrets were there? What did these walls know that I didn't? What did this town know that I didn't? I walked downstairs carrying the box. I set it on the table and stared at it, as if it would talk to me and spew out every sordid detail. Nothing. I thought back to the day Mr. Carter's Last Will and Testament was read to the boys. Nothing was ever said about Dex. Dan never mentioned his name. Furthermore, Dex didn't come to the cemetery when Mr. Carter was laid to rest. My head felt like it was going to explode. My heart felt like it had been played.

Is he a player? Oh, my God, and I fell for him and kissed him. I allowed him to make me feel...

The thought of what had happened was making me nauseous. I needed air. I stood up, put on my coat, and took Gilda out for a walk. With anger and tears streaming down my face, I talked to Dan as Gilda pulled me along.

"Dan, did you know about this? Did you keep secrets from me? Do you know I fell for your half-brother? You have a half-brother. Did you know that?
If you were here none of this would have happened. You would be right here walking Gilda with me. We would be planning Thanksgiving and Christmas, together.

I hated myself, and I knew I would never get past it.

DEX

I could not stop thinking about Ginny. The fact that we were waiting until the weekend to tell Dylan and Ginny the truth was killing me. It made me feel as though I was lying to her every minute of every day past and present. I needed to tell her the truth. I could no longer wait, so I decided to stop and see her after work.

I called Courtney and told her that I was going to go ahead and tell Ginny everything that evening. Courtney was not happy.

"What about our plan? How am I supposed to let Dylan know when he's two hours away?" she whined, saying it was not something she wanted to share with him over the phone. "Are you sure this can't wait? Aren't you being a little selfish?"

"Yes, I guess I am, but I can't go on avoiding her the rest of the week."

"No, I guess you can't."

"Please, don't ask me to keep this from her any longer."

There was a pause . . .

"OK, I'm going to call Dylan and let him know I'm coming up for a visit—tonight. Stay in touch and let me know how it goes for you, OK?"

"OK. Be safe . . . and Court, thank you."

I drove to Ginny's. Good, the Jeep was parked in the drive. I ran up the stairs and knocked. She didn't answer, and I didn't hear Gilda bark. I inserted my key, a new key I had kept, and let myself in. No one was home. They must have gone for a walk. There was a curious old tin box, about legal envelope size, on the table. I picked it up, and the lid fell open, spilling its contents onto the floor. I scrambled to put the papers back into the box when I noticed that I was holding my own birth certificate in my hand. It clearly spelled out my parents' names. I also found the loan papers and the documentation of my boat. It was all there. It was like looking at myself in the mirror, yet I didn't recognize the reflection. Instead, I saw a man who had been hidden away, left to live out the lies surrounding his genesis. I was looking at someone I felt sorry for. It reminded me of the person I wished I could have been—a man with a real father.

I was startled when I heard Ginny and Gilda come in through the deck door.

"So, you found the box," she said with her arms crossed in front of her.

"Well, kind of. It was sitting here on the table. I picked it up, and it spilled open."

"So, you know what's in it?"

"Ginny, I didn't know about this box."

"Dex, did you know about the things in the box? Your birth certificate? The documentation of your boat? Your brothers?"

"Ginny, please . . . I came here to explain, but I didn't know about the box."

I pointed to the sofa, beckoning her to sit down. She did so reluctantly and I sat down next to her. I tried to take her hands into mine, but she yanked them away.

"Ginny, I wanted to tell you. I wanted to tell you before our kiss the other night."

She slid farther away from me. "About that kiss, Dex, and everything you said . . ."

"Ginny, I meant every word of it, except I hadn't planned on the kiss. You initiated that."

"Oh, no, you're telling me now that you just went along for the ride? "

"No, no . . . Ginny, I meant everything I said and did. I've been thinking about you and our kiss since the moment it happened. That's why I'm here, now, to tell you everything before this goes any further."

"After this revelation, how much further did you think this could go?" she asked, waving at the box.

"Ginny, I didn't know about the box."

"And how does that make it any better? You still hid the truth from me, from all of us."

"Ginny, look at me. . . . Please. . . . I meant every word I said, and I wanted to tell you everything. You have to believe that."

She didn't respond. She didn't move. Something was wrong. I could see it in her eyes. They were changing color. Her spark was leaving them. They were agitated and hurt.

"Do they know?" she asked solemnly.

"No. I don't think they do."

"But you knew all along, didn't you?" she spoke slowly,

examining every move of every muscle in my face.

"Yes."

This is not going well.

"And you felt it was OK not to tell them?"

"Only because Mr. Carter asked us not to."

"There are others? Who else is involved in this, Dex?"

"Courtney and her dad."

"What? You told the Sables, but not your own brothers, or even me for that matter?"

"No. Mr. Carter made us promise never to speak a word of it. The Sables knew for legal reasons. I didn't tell them. Mr. Carter did."

"What kind of games do you people play around here? And now that the truth is out, as you had so fortuitously planned, what comes next? Drag me up to the bedroom and carry on like none of this matters?"

"Ginny, don't. Please don't lessen what the other night meant. Please, try to understand. I've fallen in love with you. I didn't plan on it, but I couldn't avoid it, either. I kept the secret prior to this because Mr. Carter asked me to, and he was honoring the wishes of my mother. The ironic thing is, I don't even know where my mother is. She turned me out when I was eighteen years old. I struggled for years, until I finally hit rock bottom. That's when Courtney filled me in on a file she had found that spelled things out. Ginny, I thought I was doing the right thing. I'm sure Mr. Carter thought he was doing the right thing, too. Anyway, once I faced my feelings about you, I knew I couldn't continue unless you knew everything. The other night, I wanted you to know how I felt. I never expected what happened to happen, and now that it has, I don't want to lose you. I do love you."

"I was falling for you, too, Dex. I really was. I was beginning to believe that there might be something to look forward to, for us. I had all the butterflies and everything. But now all I feel is hurt and betrayed."

"Ginny, I am so sorry. Hurting you is the last thing I

ever wanted to do."

"What about Derek and Dylan? What about them?"

"Courtney is on her way to tell Dylan, tonight. I don't know about Derek and Susan. We haven't thought it through that far."

"So you and Courtney really did have this all planned out."

"Ginny, I never meant to hurt you or upset you. I just wanted you to know the truth. I told Courtney I couldn't wait any longer. Believe me, she wants the truth out, too."

Ginny got up from the sofa, walked over to the table and opened the box.

"Here, you can have your birth certificate and the documents concerning your boat. Now, please go. Leave your key on the table and go."

There was nothing left to be said. I placed my key on the table as she had requested, patted Gilda on the head, and walked to the same door I had replaced just days before.

I turned and looked at her one last time. "I'm so sorry. I wish you could believe that I never ever wanted to hurt you, or Dan, or anyone else. I was only trying to carry out Mr. Carter's wishes. He was my dad, too, you know, but I could never speak of it."

She said nothing. In fact, she looked away from me. I could tell that the sight of me conjured nothing short of a conniving liar. Closing the door behind me, I left. As I reached my truck, I heard the new dead bolt that I had installed turn over and lock me out.

COURTNEY

I called Dylan to tell him that I was on my way to Unionville. He didn't answer, so I left a message. I drove above the speed limit, but thankfully not enough to get pulled over. I hit traffic at Christiana, where Dylan had said it always backed up. Another half hour and I knew I would be at his door.

Shortly after 8:30, I pulled into his drive. I knocked on the door, but there was no answer.

"Out here!" I heard him call from the barn.

I walked into the barn and obviously caught him off-guard.

"Courtney? Oh, my God, is everything OK?"

He walked over to me and rubbed my arms up and down as my father used to do when he would try to console me. (Dad began doing that in my teenage years when I refused to allow him to hug me or pull me onto his lap, especially in front of my friends.)

"Here, let's go inside the house where it's a little warmer." He picked up a few logs on the way and opened the heavy front door for me. He showed me into the living room and threw a log onto a fire in the fireplace that made the room so perfectly cozy.

This will be a good setting.

"Would you like a beer, wine, tea, water?"

"I think I could use the bathroom, actually. Then, I'll take you up on a cup of tea."

After we settled ourselves in, I explained the reason for my trip. I told him about Dex's relationship to him and his brothers. I told him how Dex's mother had requested that it not be made public and because his dad was our client, we were bound to confidentiality. I told him how my dad had taken Dex's case when the boathouse burnt down. That was when I came across the "Lassiter/Carter" file. I told Dylan how—at one time—I had found Dex intriguing, so I looked through the file and discovered that his dad was Dex's biological father. I told him how I had arranged for the two of them to sit down in my office when Dex was in dire need of financial aid. I told him that because Dex was developing feelings for Ginny and because I valued our friendship, Dex and I had decided that it was time that the truth came out. With both of the Carter parents gone, we felt it was no longer a matter of honoring his dad's wishes; it was a matter of our own integrity.

Dylan didn't say anything, at first. I wondered if he was contemplating his relation to Dex, or that I had actually admitted to my initial interest in his half-brother? Dylan seemed stunned as he tried to sort it all out. I could see that he was replaying all of the possible cues he may have missed along the way. Then, he turned to me.

"You mean to tell me his real name is Poindexter? I wouldn't tell anyone who I was, either, if my real name was Poindexter. Who names their son Poindexter?"

I was so relieved. I had not laughed that hard in a long time. It was definitely worth the trip. He asked a million questions late into the night. I took him up on that glass of wine, stayed over, and drove back home the next day.

GINNY

I could not stay in the Carter beach house that night. All of its secrets were closing in on me. I was afraid that in my own weakness, I would call Dex. Then, what would I say? I had no clue. I had no words for what I was feeling. I called my dad and said that I was coming home for a little while. I planned on driving up and bringing Gilda along with me. He asked how long I could stay, and at that point, I really had no idea. With hopes that the long drive would help to clear my head, I told him that I would explain everything once I got there. As always, he begged me to drive safely. It could have been my imagination, but ever since the accident, he sounded even more worried about my driving, especially because I was making the long trip alone. He asked if I wanted him to come down and pick me up. I told him it was not necessary, and I would see him soon. I packed, checked to make sure the house was clean and secure, filled my travel mug with coffee, and threw my luggage into the Jeep. Retrieving my sole passenger, I opened the door for Gilda who jumped into the front seat and then, at my insistence, reluctantly crawled into the back. One final look around, I locked the door to the Carter beach house, and left for Darien, Connecticut.

DEX

The next day, I tried calling her every hour. She was not answering. I would have texted her, but that would have been too impersonal for what I needed to say. I left messages and received no returned call or reply. Finally, after work, I drove over to the house. The Jeep was gone. I knocked on the door and Gilda didn't bark to announce her presence on the other side. I no longer had a key, so I couldn't go in and check on Ginny, or the house. Defeated and deflated, I walked back down the steps and to the truck. I decided I would stop back and try again a little later.

My second visit produced the same results: no Jeep and no Gilda. Once again, I returned to the Right Tackle and tried calling her several more times. No answer. I decided to drive over to the house, again. Still, no Jeep and no Gilda. In fact, they were not at the house all night, unless she and Gilda were inside and in trouble.

I called Pratt and explained the situation. He warned that if I went in without a key, I could be charged with breaking and entering. He strongly advised against it. He asked if there were other people who might know her whereabouts and suggested I call them first. In the meantime, he would go right over and walk around to see if there were any signs of foul play.

I called Courtney. No answer. I called Mrs. Pollock. She had not seen Ginny since my last visit. Now, she was concerned, too.

Great, now I've upset Mrs. Pollock.

I promised Mrs. Pollock that I would keep her posted and told her not to worry because the police were on it and patrolling the area. Telling her that the police were involved was probably not a good idea, either. It made her worry all the more.

Finally, reluctantly, not wanting to scare them too, I called Dr. and Mrs. Huff. With great relief, and yet sadly, I learned that Ginny was on her way to Connecticut. Dr. Huff didn't know how long Ginny planned to stay, but he thanked me for my call. He said it was comforting to know that there was someone who would miss her so quickly, especially given that she lived alone and so far away from home.

He has no idea . . .

I called Pratt and Mrs. Pollock to let them know that Ginny was OK and on her way to her parents' home in Connecticut. Pratt made a smart remark about my ability to cope with independent women, though he reinforced that I had done the right thing by calling him. Mrs. Pollock simply said, "Thank heaven."

To the contrary, I intentionally neglected to tell them that I was not OK. Ginny had broken my heart. For many years, I had become all too familiar with how it felt to be ignored and unwanted. Somehow, Ginny's rejection was far worse than all the heartaches I had ever experienced before that day.

GINNY

On my way north to Connecticut, I pulled over at the site of the accident. The tire marks were gone and the guardrail had been replaced. One would never know that a terrible tragedy had occurred at that very location. It was the place where I lost Dan, and my life had been changed, forever. I whispered to Dan, telling him how much I missed him. I said a short prayer and then got back into the Jeep where Gilda was happily waiting for me. When there was a lull in the heavy traffic, I pulled out and continued north.

I arrived at my parents' house at one in the morning. I was exhausted, and Gilda was confused and anxious after her confinement in the Jeep's back seat for so many hours. My dad, bless his heart, had stayed up to wait for us. He greeted us outside and helped me carry my bags inside. Gilda ran circles around us as if to say, "Look at me! Look at me!" My dad made a remark about how much she had grown since he last saw her. It was true: in just the time that Dan had been gone, Gilda had sprouted from a clumsy puppy into a full-sized, sleek golden retriever, albeit with too much energy and still lacking grace, good manners, and coordination.

Dad and I carried my cargo upstairs. Setting the payload down inside my old bedroom door, I asked if he would meet me in the kitchen in a couple of minutes. He obliged and took my overly rambunctious dog back downstairs and outside for a quick romp.

In the kitchen, as my dad was pouring each of us a cup of tea, I pulled a chair up to the counter. He sat down next to me, sighed, and asked,

"So what brings you home, Ginny?"

"Dad, I don't even know where to begin."

Still too hot to drink, I blew across the top of my tea, sat it back down onto its saucer and brushed a tussle of my tired hair back behind my ear, all in a grand effort to stall for time.

"Do you remember Dex, the gentleman who looked after me while I was recovering at home?"

This is weird. Up to this moment, "home" has always been my parents' house, here in Darien, the very place I have just run to. My heart is speaking before my brain can edit my thoughts, and now I know, without a doubt, that Lewes has become my refuge. So why did I just flee from there to here?

"Vaguely, yes," my father responded. "We met him over Christmas, right? And he's answered your cell phone more than once when I've called."

"He's the one."

I went on to tell my dad how Dex and I had become great friends, and how Dex recently confessed that he had feelings for me. I think I even expressed Dex's "feelings" as "love."

"How do you feel about him?"

"I don't know, Dad. I mean, I do know, but things have changed."

"Yes, Ginny, things have changed. It's going to take a long time. You don't have to rush into anything. If he loves you, he'll wait."

"I know that. But I just found out that I didn't know everything I should have known about him."

I explained as much as I could about Dex's relationship to Dan and his brothers. I told my dad how it was an honored secret until I had stumbled upon the papers. I told him that Dex had planned on telling me, but the point was that he hadn't bothered to in all the time that he had known me. Worse yet, in all the time that he had hung out with his half-brothers, he never told them, either.

"Ginny, does it really matter if he's a Carter, or not?"

"I don't know."

"He was going to tell you, when?"

"He said that day. That's why he came to see me."

"Hmmm ... And you're worried about his integrity?"

"Well, he said he couldn't tell his brothers before, because he promised his dad—their dad—that he wouldn't."

"So, he kept his promise to his father all those years."

"Yes."

"That must have been hard."

"I suppose so."

"He kept his promise . . ." echoed in my ears.

We talked a while longer, and I found myself beginning to soften. Dad also told me that Dex had called before I had arrived, very concerned, and wanting to know when I reached Darien, and if I would be returning to Lewes.

When I finally crawled into my bed and pulled the covers up around me, I was consumed by my loneliness. I was missing him. I wanted to call Susan, but it was way beyond our definition of "it's never too late." And what would I say? Was it my place to tell her and Derek? I decided that I needed to talk to Dylan, first, and ask how he thought it should be handled. Gilda gave a big yawn and stretched out at the foot of my bed. I drifted off to sleep with a million unresolved questions swirling around in my head that was already crammed with doubt and confusion.

It was 10:00 AM when I finally got out of bed the next morning. The last thing I wanted to do was face my mother, but I thought that I should just get it over with. I pulled on my robe and went downstairs to get a cup of coffee. She was not around.

Whew!

I was spared for the time being. I let Gilda out and kept an eye on her until she was ready to come back in. I felt bad for my lack of attentiveness those past few days. Hoping my poor neglected pup would understand, I went back upstairs and called Dylan.

"Ginny, where have you been? Dex is a mess. He's worried about you. Why won't you take his calls?" Dylan barked.

"Dylan, did Courtney come up and visit you yesterday?" I asked.

"Yes."

"So you know about Dex?"

"What about Dex?'

"You know . . . being a Carter and all."

"Yes."

"And you're OK with that?"

"Pretty cool, huh?"

I could imagine him smiling from ear to ear.

"And you're all right that they never told you before this?"

"Ginny, I am always the last to know anything that goes on in this family. Besides, would you admit to anyone that your name is Poin-DEX -ter?"

I heard him laughing.

"Arrrgghhh! Dylan, be serious, you're driving me crazy!"

"I am serious. Promise me if you two have children, you will never name my nephews 'Poindexter the Second,' or 'Poindexter the Third,' or whatever it might be. "

"Dylan, stop! There's nothing going on with us."

"Keep telling yourself that."

Dylan, because of his innocent naiveté, can find humor in the worst situations.

"OK, I will when you admit to what's going on between you and Courtney."

"Yeah, well, you know she stayed here last night, right?"

"She did?"

"Psych! Nothing happened."

"Dylan, please, I called you because I need your help."

"OK . . . shoot."

"Do Derek and Susan know about Dex? Have you told them, yet?"

"Nope. It's not my place."

"Did Courtney tell you that?"

"No. And what if she did?"

"Because she usually gives good advice."

"And, I don't?"

"No, you're usually the one who needs advice."

"Ginny, you know I love you, but this time it seems you're the one that needs the talking to."

"What are you saying?"

I couldn't believe that I was talking to the same guy who second-guessed everything.

"Can't you see? Dex is crazy about you. It's probably the only reason he decided to break the promise he made to Dad in the first place. From where I sit, he made a promise and kept it as long as Dad was alive. He never got to have the father/son relationship that he wanted, but he didn't retaliate or even play the martyr. He's been completely selfless, and more so now that he has fallen for you. You're the reason. Otherwise, he probably would have carried his promise to the grave."

Oh . . .
What have I done?

DEX

Despite my boss's disappointment, I took the day off. Making an effort to face the music to a song that I didn't write, I needed to meet with Derek and Susan. On my way to their home in Valley Forge, I rehearsed the uncomfortable lyrics over and over. I knew this was not going to go well, no matter how much I prepared for it.

When we were teens and the Carters were in Lewes during the summer months, Derek and I used to pal around together. In our minds, we ruled the beach. However, the summer after the Carters lost their mother, everything had changed in dramatic fashion. Derek grew angry and annoyed with me. I had hoped it was just a phase; however, phases have a beginning and an end. For this, there seemed to be no end.

Susan sounded puzzled when I called to say I was making the trip. She probably assumed that my visit had something to do with Ginny. She immediately invited me to stay and have dinner with them, something I was sure she should have cleared with Derek, first.

When I arrived in late afternoon, Derek was not at home. Over an open bottle of wine, Susan and I chatted while she made dinner in their large kitchen. Derek said he was held up at the office, and each time he called, Susan restated that we would wait dinner. It did not take a genius to figure out that my visit had become a point of contention.

Derek finally strolled in around eight o'clock, announcing that he was very tired and would have an early start the next day. I could read between the lines; my stay would have to be brief.

Over chicken cordon bleu, garlic mashed potatoes, and spinach salad, I shared my reason for being there. With great painstaking caution, I explained my relationship to the Carter family. Susan was stunned. Derek didn't flinch. When I said all that I thought needed to be said, Derek held his fork up in the air and pointed the tines in my direction.

"Dex, that's a really good story, so what exactly do you want from us, now?"

"I don't expect anything, Derek. I just thought you should know."

"Well, you've managed to keep it a secret all these years, so why now?"

Even though I had anticipated that this question might come up, I was not completely prepared to explain my timing.

"I know this is going to sound . . . uh, wrong, but . . ."

"Dex, as far as I'm concerned, everything you've said tonight sounds wrong."

"Well, it involves Ginny."

"Why am I not surprised?"

I explained how over the time that I had cared for her, I had fallen for her, as well.

"So you had the need to come all this way and tell us your sad story because you have feelings for Ginny? That. Is. Pathetic."

"Derek!" Susan scolded. "What is wrong with you? Dex, I'm so sorry." Puzzled, she asked, "Dex, are you sure about all of this?"

Derek ignored Susan's rebuke and jumped back in.

"Susan, my father's name may be on his birth certificate, but my mother's blood does not flow through his veins. My father and his mother were never married. You know what that makes him, don't you?"

That stung. Then he addressed me directly.

"And why are you here, Dex? You've moved in on my brother's wife, and now you want to move in on the beach house. What more could you possibly want from us?"

I had no idea how to respond. Ginny had left me. The half-brother whom I once considered a good friend and co-conspirator had all but called me a bastard.

"I'm sorry for upsetting your evening. I should probably go."

I folded my napkin neatly, laid it beside my half-finished plate, rose from the table, and left the room. Derek didn't budge from his seat. Susan walked me to the door.

"Dex, I apologize for Derek's rude and uncalled for behavior. He's under a lot of pressure at work and probably needs a little more time to adjust. On the other hand, I am thrilled to know that you are part of the family! Thanks for coming all this way. I'm so glad you told us.

She gave me a big squishy hug.

"Yeah, I'm not sure where all of this is leading."

"So, what's this with you and Ginny? I haven't talked to her in the past several days, which is really unusual, come to think of it. I should have known something was up. You sure move fast."

"Oh, please don't say it like that. I didn't mean for it to happen. It just did."

"I know. But what exactly *did* happen?"

"You should probably ask Ginny. Just know that no matter what, I really do care about her. Thanks for dinner, Susan. I hope in time Derek will forgive me and believe that my intentions have always been good."

"I believe you, Dex. And, I don't think any request for forgiveness is necessary."

"Thanks, that means the world to me."

I gave her one more hug before turning to leave.

"Dex, drive safely."

"I will."

Later it dawned on me that she probably thought I was driving back to Lewes, when instead, I was on my way to Darien. I knew if I left then, I would not arrive until one or two in the morning. No matter, I was half way there with no better place to go.

SUSAN

"So when were you going to tell me?" Those were the first words out of my mouth when Ginny answered the phone.

"Susan, I've wanted to call you. So much is going on."

"Tell me about it. Dex was just here."

"He was?"

"Yes.... Wow ... who knew? ... How are you doing with all of this exciting news?"

"Me? How are *you* guys doing?"

"That depends on who you ask. Dex stayed for dinner and tried to explain his history and circumstance. Derek was not having it; he was very rude. As soon as Dex left, Derek went upstairs to bed. I don't think he took it very well. On the other hand, I think it's kind of cool!"

"Yeah, it's taking me some time to get used to, too. Does it bother you that he never told us?"

"No.... Should it? I mean, he did what he was asked to do. His mother obviously didn't want anyone to know, and Mr. Carter, bless his soul, honored her wishes, yet he still came through when Dex needed him. I kind of feel sorry for Dex and Mr. Carter. They never had the opportunity to develop any sort of meaningful relationship. It's amazing that Dex has survived it as well as he has!"

"Yes, I guess you're right."

"So, what's up with you two?"

"Oh, Susan, I think I've fallen for him, and he said he loves me, but I didn't handle that news very well, either. I wouldn't be surprised if he hates me, now."

"I don't think he hates you, not by a long shot. I think he cares deeply for you."

"Susan, where is he?"

"He left here about a half-hour ago. He should be back in Lewes in an hour or so."

I could hear a sigh of relief on the other end of the phone.

"Susan, do you think I'm doing the right thing? I mean, I do miss Dan, terribly. But I am . . . well . . . kind of . . . I don't want to lose Dex."

"Ginny, I think as long as you're honest with yourself and honest with Dex, then you'll be fine. Remember, he lost a friend—and a brother—too. I'm sure he'll understand and give you all the time you need."

"I feel so selfish and self-absorbed."

"No. You're just two people trying to find their way through an imperfect world."

I went upstairs to bed as soon as I was done catching up with Ginny. Derek was already sound asleep. He looked so peaceful; unlike the agitated man he was earlier. Whenever Derek was around Dex, or even at the mention of Dex's name, Derek would turn into someone I was unable to recognize. Unfortunately, that was nothing new. It had developed into an easily anticipated pattern. I wished it were different, especially if Ginny and Dex were to get serious. My imagination ran with all kinds of scenarios. It made me happy and scared, all at the same time, to consider all the possibilities the future could hold. However, I knew nothing would please Derek, unless it concluded with the eventual demise of their relationship.

GINNY

After I finished speaking with Susan, I decided to leave Darien immediately and head for Lewes. It was late, but I knew my chances of finding sleep were little to none. Why waste time idling and rethinking everything that had transpired when I could be on the road to repairing the damage I had done. While repacking and gathering up Gilda, I decided that I would drive straight through and be on board the Right Tackle by sunrise. Knowing my parents would be furious, but not surprised, I left a note on the kitchen counter by my dad's first stop every morning: the coffee brewer.

Hours later when I arrived in Lewes, it was still dark and quiet on the streets and over the water. It was also very cold, and the town appeared to be on lockdown, giving me an irrational sense of isolation.

I wanted to surprise Dex, so I quietly boarded the Right Tackle, trying desperately not to rock her. My efforts were for naught as Gilda leaped over the gunnel and landed on all four. Her nails were clicking furiously on the fiberglass deck as she danced about excitedly, looking for the captain, no doubt. I opened the cabin door, went in, and turned on the main salon lights.

Why he never locks the cabin doors, I'll never understand.

Gilda jumped up on a sofa, began panting, and looked up at me, wondering what we were going to do next.

"Sit. Stay."

We had been working on those two commands, and it was about time for the payoff.

It never ceased to amaze me how well Dex took care of the Right Tackle. Everything was neat, clean, and secure. Leaving Gilda behind, I made my way through the galley and knocked on the master stateroom door. No answer. I quietly called his name. It gave me butterflies to think that he would be ecstatic to hear the sound of my voice. I was disappointed when I heard no response. I slowly pushed the door open. My heart was set on curling up next to him and telling him how sorry I was. I had hoped that whatever amount of love had survived would be enough to offer me a second chance. My heart was racing. I looked in, and to my disbelief, he was not there. Tired and depressed, I sat down on the edge of his bed. I gathered up the blanket that lay across the bottom of the mattress and wrapped it around my shoulders. I made my way back up to the main salon and curled up on the sofa opposite Gilda. She climbed down, lay on the floor next to me, gave a big yawn, and promptly fell asleep.

Sometime later, Gilda began barking and nudging my shoulder.

"All right, all right, let's go out."

I opened my eyes, stretched, and immediately concluded that I was not at home in my own bed, and it certainly was not Gilda nudging me.

"You were sound asleep, Missy! Where's lover-boy?"

"Charles? What time is it?"

I grabbed Gilda by the collar to settle her down. Happy to see Charles, her tail was wagging out of control as she jumped around him.

"It's 7:00. I saw the light on and thought I'd see if Dex wanted a cup of coffee. That's what we do around here, you know, share a cup of coffee." He leaned down and scratched Gilda behind her ears.

"Where's Dex?" I asked, trying to brush the cobwebs from my mind.

"I was going to ask you the same thing."

"He was supposed to come back last night ... I think ... I was waiting for him ... I guess I fell asleep," I managed to sputter out of my scrambled state.

I was trying to get my head around what I was doing there and why Dex wasn't there and why Charles was offering me a cup of coffee.

We stared at each other.

Then a wave of panic washed over me.

"You don't think something happened to him, do you?"

DEX

I had driven to the Stamford Marriott Hotel, just off I-95. I was dead tired and knew not to disturb the Huff household in the middle of the night. So, I stopped to get a little shuteye, shower, and then I would continue on to Ginny's in the morning.

Several hours later, my cell phone jolted me from a sound sleep.

"Hello?"

"Dex?"

"Ginny? What time is it?"

"Oh, Dex, thank God. Where are you?"

"Uhhh ..." I scratched my head and tried to get my thoughts together. "I'm in Stamford. Where are you?"

"Stamford? What are you doing there?"

"I was hoping to see you."

A telling pause followed.

"Oh ... well, I'm here ... on your boat."

"You're where?"

"I'm on the Right Tackle, waiting for you."

"Ginny, I'll be there. Stay put."

Ginny said she was going to finish her coffee with Charles and then head back to the house where it would be warmer for her and Gilda.

When I reached Lewes, six hours later, I drove straight to Ginny's, ran up the outside stairs, and into the old drafty kitchen. There she was, waiting for me. I grabbed her up in my arms and told her that I was so sorry and that I never meant to hurt her. She said something about being sorry for jumping to conclusions and for not trying to understand what my life had been. I was so relieved, and hoped that we would be able to put it all behind us.

Time actually moved backward and erased all the damage that had been done. Her kisses were sweet and delicious like milk chocolate truffles, and I wanted to savor each and every morsel. I wanted to make love to her for the first time, but I knew I had no right, and if I truly loved her, I would wait. For me, the moment was like trying to stop a herd of stampeding horses, but this was not something to be rushed into or forced. I wanted to make sure that when it did happen, it was when she was ready and at her pace. I didn't want us to wake up in a bed of hurried regrets.

DEREK

It certainly did not take him long to move in. Together, Dex and Ginny made a perfect pair of manipulative gold diggers, and they had Dylan completely snowed. As for Courtney, I was sure there was something in it for her. Why else would she have been so interested in Dylan? He was much younger than she was, not to mention that she was one of Dex's best friends. There was some sort of scheming play going on, and I had to get ahead of it, especially after the screw-up with my father's Will.

I loved Susan for the same reasons she so easily fell prey to those connivers. In everything we did, she was completely selfless, always putting me first. She waited dinner for me almost every night. She had coffee and breakfast ready for me every morning. Even in the little things, like when she bought Girl Scout cookies, she always selected my favorites. We always watched the movies of my choosing. We had a subscription to the Wall Street

Journal because that was the paper I preferred to read. She stopped going to Ginny's every weekend because I told her I needed her at home. She never grilled me about my business trips, or questionable hours. She loved unconditionally, and she gave completely. How do you protect someone like that?

Then there was the matter of my dad. I think that may have been what pissed me off the most. Ginny took advantage of him. She came off like the daughter he never had. Plus, she was his youngest son's girlfriend. How can you compete with that? Then, to cap it off, there was the whole pregnancy thing. Try to tell me that wasn't a trap that was sprung. I would have sworn she was making it all up, had it not been for her miscarriage.

GINNY

Thanksgiving came quickly. Susan invited us up to their house in Valley Forge, but given the way Derek had shunned Dex the last time he was there, Dex was a little perplexed by the invitation. We debated our two options at great length. We went back and forth between going to Susan and Derek's, or staying home and having a quiet dinner, just the two of us. Dex called Dylan to see what he was going to do.

Meanwhile, I was quietly angry with myself for letting Derek intimidate me enough that I would possibly consider not spending the holiday with Susan. Thankfully, Dylan said he was going to have dinner in Valley Forge and then drive down to Lewes for dessert with the Sables.

"Oh, and by the way," he went on, "ask Ginny if I can crash at her place afterward?"

"I don't know how I feel about you staying at my girlfriend's house," Dex mused. "I think you should stay on the Right Tackle."

"With you and your snoring, plus freeze my ass off? No,

thank you! Besides, Ginny always has coffee and breakfast ready for me in the morning."

"I wouldn't know about that."

"Sure, sure . . . And, what do you have on the Right Tackle? Some guy named Charles that lets himself on board."

It was decided. The three of us were going to meet at Susan and Derek's for Thanksgiving dinner and then make the trek to Lewes for dessert. Susan suggested that we spend the night before Thanksgiving at their house rather than drive up and back in one day. Dylan passed, saying he was behind in his holiday orders, and I said I didn't want to leave Gilda with someone else overnight. Susan knew that the Sables and Mrs. Pollock had offered, repeatedly, to watch Gilda. I could tell that she had detected my avoidance. I told her I just didn't want to burden anyone with a seventy-pound hairy dog while trying to enjoy their Thanksgiving dinner.

I was looking forward to spending time with Susan, but I didn't want to face Derek.

I had to admit, aside from the family issues, I knew it would be a difficult week because it also marked the anniversary of losing Lily, and it would be my first Thanksgiving without Dan. I pondered what life would have been like if Lily had survived. She would have been without a father, and I would have been left a single mother. Who knows why things happen the way they do, especially those things over which we have no control?

On the ride to Valley Forge, Dex and I had almost two hours of uninterrupted downtime. We talked during the entire ride, mostly about our families. Dex was usually the one who listened while I talked, but on that day, he opened up about what he knew of his family history.

Dex shared the nightmare of living with a man he feared. He was very young, but remembered hearing his father (or who he thought was his father) and his mother argue and her being slapped around. He used to put his pillow over his head and pray that his father would die.

Other than that, he didn't know what else to do. When he was about seven, the man beat him with a belt. When his mother tried to defend him, the man turned on her. Dex ran to a neighbor's house for help. For Dex's sake alone, they called the police. He remembered it took two officers to place the man in handcuffs and remove him from the house. That night, his mother packed what she could, and they left for his grandmother's.

Dex's maternal grandmother lived in Lewes where Dex believed Mr. Carter had met his mother several years before his birth. Because of Courtney's curiosity and fascination with Dex, he was able to learn the facts about who he was, and realized then that the man whose last name he had inherited at birth may have known all along that Dex was not his biological son.

Dex said that he and his mother lived with his grandmother until he was sixteen years old. During the summer months of their earlier teenage years, Dex and the Carter brothers would hang around together on a regular basis. Derek and he, the older two of the bunch and only a year apart in age, were best buddies back then. Dex also remembered when Mrs. Carter was deathly ill and how her loss was such a blow to the Carter boys and their father.

Derek ramped up their adventures during that time. Looking back on it, Dex believed it was probably Derek's one escape from the reality of his mother's suffering and inevitable death. Dex also remembered that was when Derek first began showing signs of lashing out. Their adventures were no longer innocent as they began taking on more sinister missions. They set boats adrift in the Bay; threw firecrackers at passing cars; in the dark of night, they boarded boats that were resting up on dry dock; and they inflicted some costly property damage along the way. His last summer in Lewes was when one of the acclaimed boathouses along the Lewes-Rehoboth Canal had gone up in flames. Sustaining burns to his right arm, Dex was taken to Beebe Hospital in a police cruiser. At the time, he thought it odd that both his mother and Mr. Carter showed up, expressing concern about his wellbeing. With the legal representation of Attorney Dean Sable, Dex was acquitted of all charges, including arson. However, he lost his best friend that night. Derek no longer wanted him around and avoided him at all costs. To make matters worse, Dex's mother was seeing a man whose job would eventually take them to California. Once Dex's trial was over, they quickly packed and left. His new stepfather turned out to be no better than his mother's first husband, except this time when Dex was old enough to protest his stepfather's aggressions, Dex was asked to leave. He was thrown out. His mother gave him Mr. Carter's and Mr. Sable's addresses and phone numbers and said they would help him reestablish himself in Lewes. Dex was eighteen years old, thrust into a world with an unknown future, and told to seek help from men outside his family. He remembered the Sables, especially their daughter, Courtney, who had shown an interest in him during his trial. Years later, Courtney was the one who convinced Mr. Carter to share the truth with Dex. He remembered that day clearly. He said he was grateful to know that his real father was an upstanding man, unlike his stepfathers. What he could not understand was: why the big secret? Mr. Carter only replied that it was the way Dex's mother had wanted it and he would have to ask her to explain the reasons why.

* * *

When we arrived in Valley Forge, Derek was as cold as ice toward us. I witnessed first hand, with new eyes, the loathing he had for Dex. I'm not sure Derek acknowledged or looked at him even once. He only spoke to us when necessary, and when he did, it was with as few words as possible. It was easy to see that he wished we were not there, ignoring us, and trying to make us invisible.

Dex and I brought the appetizers: shrimp cocktail, crab dip, crackers, salsa, and tortilla chips. I stayed with Susan in the kitchen while she was putting the finishing touches on dinner. When the turkey was ready, she summoned

Derek to carve it. When he came into the kitchen, he swung Susan around and landed a kiss on her lips—a long, wet lusty kiss. I think I heard him whisper how much he loved her. Rarely, in the past year, had any of us witnessed a public display of affection initiated by Derek. Susan then stayed in the kitchen to help him. Feeling like a third wheel, I went out to the family room with Dex and Dylan.

"Three's a crowd in there, if you know what I mean," I commented.

"Really? You've got to be kidding. That's a huge kitchen," Dylan remarked. He took me literally. He could be so naïve, at times.

"Never mind. But don't say I didn't warn you when dinner isn't served until midnight."

Fortunately, and unfortunately for Susan, it was not long before she called all of us out to the dining room. We gathered around the table, strategically plotting our seats. We said grace, and then Susan asked that we go around the table and share the top three things for which we were thankful.

As luck would have it, I would go last, thank goodness. I was conflicted and needed time to think about my "blessings." I was grateful for Dex, but would that imply that I no longer mourned for Dan? Would it imply that Dan's passing was effectively a blessing for me? Of course not, but I was uncertain of how the others would interpret my sentiments. I couldn't say that I was thankful for Dan *and* Dex. That would just feel wrong, and not sit well. I could have said that I was forever grateful for the time I had with Dan. However, I didn't want Dex to conclude that he would be forever living in Dan's shadow if he decided to stay with me. I had no idea how to put my current state into words without the possibility of offending someone at the table.

Dex went right before me. He slipped his arm around my shoulder and held up his wine glass.

"I am grateful for the truth; that it will always prevail, and that it has allowed me to be part of a family that I have always longed for. I am thankful for a father who kept the wishes of my mother, yet never abandoned me." Then he kissed my hair and finished with, "And I will always cherish you, no matter where we land. I will cherish you forever."

I leaned over and met his quick kiss, releasing with a blush because I realized that it was the first time I had kissed him in front of his half-brothers.

Then, it was my turn. I could not sum up what I was thankful for without bringing up the pain that bore it. I couldn't put any of it into concise thoughts without the risk of being misunderstood. No one had lived in my shoes. I was living in a state of confusion. So, I excused myself and left the table. I walked through the family room and out onto the deck that overlooked the valley below lit up with homes filled with families having celebrations of their own. I soon discovered that Dex was right behind me.

"Ginny, are you OK? Did I upset you?"

"No. Not in the least. In fact, I loved what you said in there. I just can't put into words where I am right now. I'm just sort of lost . . . drifting. I am thankful for so many things, but they're all attached to so many painful events that make it impossible for me to express without sounding like a hypocrite. For example, I am so happy that you are in my life. I am so in love with you, yet at what cost? So, is it right for me to be truly thankful? Will I ever be able to fully appreciate where I am or the good things in my future without the pain of guilt and loss? Does that make any sense?"

"It makes perfect sense. You wouldn't be who you are if you didn't feel the way you do."

"Do you ever think it will change?"

"Probably not. Dan was an amazing man, and he loved you very much. You can't expect to go through the remainder of your life as if the past never happened. Dan was here. He was alive, and we are better people because he was a part of our time on earth. He will always be a part of you, and in many respects, a part of me, too. I believe the thing we each need to do is learn how to accept our past and move forward with it intact. We should try to take the best of it into the future with us, and do what we can to make sure the worst of it never visits us again."

"Dex, if anything happened to you, I don't think I could survive it."

"I feel the same way about you."

"On the other hand, you should know that I don't think I can ever let go of Dan, either."

"I would never ask you to."

"And you never have. You have been the one person I have been able to talk to. You are the one who seems to understand the most."

Dex took my hand and gently kissed it before wrapping his arms around me to hold me close. We didn't say anything further. We didn't need to. We just stood against each other, sharing the view of the black sky and valley below, visible only by the tiny sparkle of each house and a faint trickle of car lights moving across a ribbon of road in the distant valley below.

When we went back inside and rejoined the feast, I could tell Susan was examining me to make sure I was OK. I could sense her concern. It made me feel self-conscious in a very strange way.

What is happening to us?

We arrived back in Lewes by 9:00 PM. It was good to be back home and spend the remainder of the evening with the Sables. They were known for their spread of rich desserts and specialty coffees. Dex said I would be amazed and indeed I was. I chose the hot dark chocolate lava cake. Dex and Courtney opted for a piece of warm apple pie topped with Breyer's vanilla ice cream. Mr. and Mrs. Sable's plates looked as though they were having a little of everything, including a 1,000 calorie slice of New York double dark chocolate cheese cake.

The interaction between Dex and Mr. Sable provided the entertainment for the evening. They were like two old fishing buddies trying to outdo the other's story. They had us in stitches, and I was not sure my facial muscles would ever return to their natural state.

After consuming my decadent selection, I began to tire quickly. It had been a long day, and it was catching up to me. Courtney said she last looked in on Gilda at 5:30, so I was also becoming concerned about leaving her home alone much longer. I think Dex read my mind and asked if I was ready to go. He stood from the table, pulled out my chair, and thanked the Sables for a wonderful evening.

Watching Mr. and Mrs. Sable, the way they loved their daughters, and interacted with Dex made me wish I had had that kind of family experience. Maybe, one day, I could provide the same for the people in my life.

Dex delivered me straight back to the beach house. Half of me wanted to invite him in, and the other half was afraid he would misread my invitation. It was an awkward moment as he leaned my way across the front seat of his truck and quietly said he would see me later the next day. He explained that he had a big fishing party to take out early in the morning; it would be his last for the season. I knew that was what he did for a living, but because of the exceptionally cold weather and the higher than normal velocity of the autumnal winds, I was especially concerned about his safety during his seasonably late expedition.

Friday, I spent the day making Christmas lists and cleaning the house in anticipation of putting up the Christmas decorations. As I went to work, I tuned the radio to a station playing Christmas music. That lasted about two minutes. The music brought back too many memories of my Christmases past with Dan.

As the afternoon wore on, the clouds rolled in and the winds picked up, as expected. The sky was turning dark as I paced impatiently, waiting for Dex's call. I kept telling myself that he would be OK. Charles had said that Dex was one of the best on the water, but this was later than his usual return to the dock.

Due to my intensely anxious state, I startled and jumped high when my cell phone finally rang.

288

"Hey, Babe."

"Dex, I'm so glad to hear your voice."

"I'm more glad to hear yours. What a long day. We had to fight a head wind all the way back. I'm cold and wet and I need some attention."

"You're such a baby."

He was so cute when he was needy.

"Well, come on over. There's a hot shower and a comfy sofa waiting for you here."

I so enjoyed hearing the shower run, or his whistling when he undressed, or the sound of him walking around upstairs. I loved the rhythmic canter of his footsteps dancing down the steps even better. For dinner, I made his favorite—a grilled New York strip steak with mushrooms and caramelized onions, and a baked potato topped with broccoli and bacon cheddar cheese sauce. After dinner, we relaxed in the living room. He fell asleep on the sofa, using my lap as his pillow. My thoughts wandered to what could be.

With Thanksgiving behind us, Christmas was fast approaching. Anticipating another holiday without Dan was more difficult than going through the actual event. Because we were working together through our loss of Lily, Dan and I had stayed quietly close to each other as we prepared for our first Christmas as grieving parents. Thankfully, the following year, Dex was there to encourage and give me hope for brighter days. He helped me bring the decorations down from the attic. Memories of Dan seemed to be boxed up with the ornaments and the small collection of Christmas trimmings. After all, Dan had helped me pack it all up a little less than a year before. As I opened the boxes, I was reminded of how he had to eat crow over the blue lights. I remembered our looking and shopping for items that would carry the beach theme I was so determined to capture. I remembered our arguing over the balance of ornaments. Dan would place them all in one area and I would move them in an attempt to space them evenly around our asymmetrical tree. I remembered sending him down to the beach in the frigid air to fill a large bucket with sand. I remembered our sitting in the dark with our glasses of wine and enjoying the glow of soft lights.

Dex asked me about all of it. He genuinely wanted to know, as if he could relive a moment with Dan who he was now missing, too. He allowed me to do what I needed to do most: remember all that was good.

I remembered all of us being at the beach house on Christmas Eve, except Dex who was dutifully babysitting my little Christmas surprise. I craved the eggnog Courtney had made for us. I laughed as I told Dex about how Courtney and Dylan had locked themselves away in his room on Christmas Eve to wrap our presents. I did remember Dex and Courtney showing up on Christmas morning with Bloody Marys and the awesome breakfast Dan had prepared for the hungry and slightly buzzed mob. We both spoke openly about how much we missed Dan and all that he had meant to us.

That night as I lay down in my bed, I kissed my fingertips and gently laid them on the photo of Dan that was perched on my nightstand. I truly missed him. I loved Dex for allowing me to express all of my feelings; however, there was one memory I didn't share: the first night Dan and I made love after losing Lily. It was the night we had decorated the house, and he later asked me to spend the rest of my life with him. It was the beginning of something that was never meant to be.

Then, strangely, I removed my rings and laid them on the nightstand below Dan's picture. My heart broke, but I knew it was another curative step I had to take in the healing of a very deep wound that would, over time, become an everlasting scar I would learn to live with.

Indeed, I had come to love Dex in a very profound way. In some respects, he was like Dan. Yet, in many other ways, he was not like anyone I had ever known. He promised not to rush me, and he had kept to his word. We would sit close and cuddle during movies or on a cold night when we were immersed in whatever books we were reading. We had begun to hold hands in public. We would go grocery shopping and have dinner together almost every evening. He would bring his laundry to the house, and quite frankly, he kept a drawer full of clothes in the spare room. He had shampoo and soap in the outside shower, deodorant, toothbrush and toothpaste on the powder room vanity. And yet, he had never shared my bed. Believe me, there had been many times when I just wanted him to carry me upstairs, but I had promised myself, until I was ready to remove my rings and take Dan's picture from my nightstand, I would not cross that threshold with Dex.

I could feel myself moving in that direction with each passing day.

I was not quite sure how he did it, but Dex convinced me that we should spend our first Christmas with my parents. My dad was thrilled. My mother probably felt imposed upon, but nevertheless, she agreed. So Christmas Eve morning, we loaded up the Jeep and headed north to Connecticut. It was somewhat surreal having Dex sitting next to me and behind the wheel of Dan's old Jeep. Gilda, as usual, was in the back seat and fast asleep. Though Dex had suggested and advocated for the trip, on the way up he asked a million questions about my parents. He had met them before, and Lord knows Dan and I had our share of stories, but Dex wanted to be accepted by them even though he knew he had a rough road ahead, especially where my mother was concerned.

When we crossed through New York and reached Connecticut, it was snowing. The flakes were large, about the size of a nickel. Large blobs of white raced toward our headlights and smashed silently into the windshield as we raced north on I-95.

Gilda perked up as soon as we started up my parents' drive, her tail wagging excitedly. Once the Jeep was in park, Gilda danced wildly and then bolted over my seat and out as soon as I opened my door. The air was still, not the slightest breeze. The snowflakes, falling heavily down from the gray sky, "shushed" as they descended through the stoic trees.

My dad greeted us at the door with a huge bear hug. My mother, as usual, waited inside so she could make her grand entrance. After a late lunch, the snow shower had stopped, leaving a fluffy white blanket to cover the frozen ground. My mother said she had a few last minute errands to run and asked if I would like to accompany her. I looked at Dex. He was already waving me on. Dad said he and Dex would find something to keep them occupied.

Great.

One would have expected my mother to bombard me with a million questions about Dex. Perhaps a few about how I was doing in my first year without Dan. Maybe even give me the fifth degree about bringing another man to the house within the first year. Not a peep. All she wanted to know was if I liked the shade of nail polish she had selected at the spa. That's right, one of our first stops on Christmas Eve was to her favorite salon. She asked if I would like a manicure or pedicure. I really didn't have a choice. Either I said, "Yes," or I would sit around for most of the day, waiting for her. No matter how you looked at it, that was going to sum up my entire day, anyway.

When we arrived back at my parents' house, I was overwhelmed by the sight of my dad and Dex in the kitchen drinking manhattans and cooking up a storm. They sent us out and into the den to relax in front of a fire that Gilda was already enjoying. (She had not even bothered to greet me when I came in.) My mother kept moving, and I assumed she went straight up to her room. Gilda and I were left in peace to quietly enjoy the comforting crackle of the warm radiant heat.

Soon, Dex appeared with a platter of shrimp cocktail and another filled with veggies and dip.

"Vegetables? Really, Dex? Where is this coming from?"

"Your dad! I could get used to this. The man knows

how to entertain!"

He put the tray down on the coffee table and sat next to me.

"I missed you while you were gone, but your dad's a blast to hang out with. He gave me a tour of the house. I now know that you used to play the piano, and quite well from what I understand. He showed me the theater room downstairs where you two used to watch Disney and Nickelodeon together. He showed me your room, which quite honestly, I think is bigger than the Right Tackle and the beach house put together. And oh, he showed me his Shelby. We took it out for a spin, and he let me drive it!"

Dex was rambling on like he had just met his new best friend. I was so happy to know that the two of them had hit it off.

And, I was sad to think that Dan had barely gotten past the front door . . .

I cursed my mother, Christmas and all. I knew the day was still young enough for her to dig her talons into Dex and our young relationship. I wanted to caution him, but I didn't want to spoil his moment, either.

Dinner was somewhat stressful, mostly because my mother put Dex on the spot two seconds after we had sat down at the table.

"So, Dex, where are you from?" she asked with a glint of delicious judgment in her eyes.

"I've spent most of my life in Lewes."

"And where are your parents, now?"

And there it was. I felt a level of anxiety well up inside me while Dex remained as cool as a cucumber. My dad just sat back, savoring his "seven fishes over linguini," as he liked to call it.

* * *

I had forgotten how much I had enjoyed that meal. We were not Italian, or Catholic. We were not any denomination, for that matter. But my dad loved the idea of seven fishes. Anything that included massive quantities of seafood was on the top of his list. So, he made up his own recipe to cover the doctrine properly, at least in his mind. He would make a white wine and garlic sauce and then throw in crab, shrimp, clams, smoked tuna, mussels (except when I was home. I don't like mussels.), lobster (except when Uncle Frank was there. He's allergic to lobster), and scallops. The rich sauce was then served over linguini with shaved pecorino over the top. That night's rendition did not disappoint.

* * *

"My father died a little over a year ago. And my mother, honestly, Mrs. Huff, I don't know where she is."

"You don't know where your mother is?" I heard her snap at Dex with a snarl on her lips, hoping she had easily uncovered a weak spot.

"Unfortunately, that's correct. She turned me out of the house when I was eighteen, almost nineteen. She moved and left no forwarding address or phone number. I don't think she wants me to find her."

There was a brief pause before my dad spoke up.

"Dex, do you have any desire to find her?"

"Not really, Dr. Huff. It was just too painful watching her enter into one abusive relationship after another. The night I tried to intervene was the night she threw me out."

That night, as I drifted off to sleep in my old bed, I could hear my mother arguing with my father. I could hear her stating that *"he"* was obviously not highly educated. *"He"* may have inherited abusive tendencies and that they had better be vigilant about it. I had no idea whether Dex could hear them at the other end of the hall, or not. Part of me hoped he could so he would know what he was up against. It might explain why I was hesitant about making the trip in the first place, and wouldn't care if we never did it again. It was Christmas Eve for God's sake. Wretched memories were flooding back.

I guess in some ways, Dex and I grew up in the same environment, with one huge exception: I had never heard or witnessed my father slapping my mother. In fact, I never heard him raise his voice to her. I never lived with people I feared. I was just in pain, hoping my mother would at least try to understand me, show some affection, or act like she cared about me, in any way.

Christmas morning arrived. I woke up to Gilda scratching at the door to get out and someone tapping on the other side. I slid out of bed and into my soft terry robe. After tying it around my waist, I opened the door. Dex was ready to step in when Gilda bounded out, knocking him over. She was so excited to see him. As I laughed and told Gilda what a good girl she was for protecting me, I extended my hand to help Dex stand back up. He took my arm and pulled me right down into his lap. Gilda was bouncing in circles around us. As soon as his lips touched mine she began barking wildly.

"Shhhhhh, Shush, Gilda . . . stop!"

She continued barking and bouncing, waking up my dad who was now coming out of his bedroom, closing the door behind him.

"What's all the commotion about out here?" He walked right up to our little heap, shaking his head and smirking as he patted Gilda on the head. "I think she needs to go out, and you two need to get dressed."

Dad was still smirking when he led Gilda down the stairs.

"But, we didn't . . ." I tried to defend what never happened before my dad cut me off.

"I'll see you two love-birds downstairs." My dad padded away with Gilda happily following him.

"Well, that was awkward." I looked to Dex for confirmation, but I couldn't read his grin. "Let's get downstairs before my mother comes out and catches us like this." I whispered.

"Not until I get the kiss Gilda so adequately robbed me of."

There on the hallway runner, right outside my bedroom door, I stole a luscious kiss from Dex. It was the kind you never want to end. It was the kind that would certainly lead to something else if it didn't end. It was the kind that sends shock waves through your body and tingles below your belly button. The jab in my thigh let me know what it was doing to him. Just his mere kiss was making the adult in me want to drop my moral compass and take all of him. It was also the kind that made the schoolgirl in me jump up and flee back into my room, shutting the door behind me.

"I'm going to get dressed, and then I'll see you downstairs," I said from the other side of the closed door.

"Okay." I heard him sigh and walk back down the hall.

Alone in my room, I was fired up and ready to spend the day with him. I knew that soon enough I would be ready to go home with him as well.

Dad was downstairs in the kitchen with the coffee on and the bacon sizzling.

"How do you want your eggs?"

"Over easy."

"And how do you want your mimosa?"

"A mimosa?"

"Yep, you and I are starting a new tradition—mimosas on Christmas morning."

I wondered if that was really true. Would I ever spend another Christmas morning with my dad? Recently, I had been cut-off from Susan by Derek and cut-off from my dad by my mother. It was something I knew Dex understood all too well. I knew it was only a matter of time before my mother would try to cut me off from Dex, just as she had tried with Dan. It was something Dex didn't deserve and I didn't want to put him through. Lewes had become my home. It was the one place where I could escape it all and live in peace.

As the stragglers, namely Dex and finally my mother, made their way downstairs, my dad cracked more eggs into the fry pan and I made another round of mimosas. My dad ate last and we all had another cup of coffee. I was wired, buzzed, and ready to distribute and open presents.

We all moved out to the living room where a large Christmas tree occupied the center window. It was ten to twelve feet high, stretching up to the vaulted ceiling. The perfectly spaced white lights cast a soft glow, illuminating all of the carefully placed ornaments. Pine boughs and sprays embellished each large picture frame that held some remarkable, original artwork. Peering through the archway that announced the center hall, one could see pine garland and white lights wrapped around the bannisters that ascended to the next floor. It continued across the balcony above. The deep windowsills were covered in greens and brass candle sticks with red silk ribbons. Byers' caroler figurines were arranged on every table. The usual couch pillows were replaced with Christmas cross-stitched pillows. There were red, green, and gold plaid throws hanging over the arms of the winged back chairs. The fireplace mantel was decorated with pine garland, candles, and red and gold bulbs.

On the end table, between the two winged back chairs, was my favorite snow globe, which came out every Christmas. It was nine inches tall and very heavy. I remember how I was not allowed to pick it up when I was little because I might break it. So, I would enlist my dad to lift it, wind up the music, and shake it for me. After he would set it back down on the table, I would gaze into it, watching the snow swirl around the horse drawn sleigh and the family that were mounted inside the globe and snuggled together under a blanket, enjoying their ride. As its music played, "Sleigh Ride," by Leroy Anderson, I dreamt that I was a part of that family.

I also recognized the antique music box that I also loved as a child. Sitting on top of its large cherry wood lid was a Christmas tree that would light up and spin as the music played, "O Tannenbaum." These were the two things I looked forward to every Christmas.

Looking around the large meticulously furnished space, I was reminded that the Nerry Group decorated my parents' house each year. Every December they would come in and take over for a day. My job was to stay out of their way. I thought about my own little tree back in Lewes. It was small and sparse in comparison. However, it was filled with handcrafted love. It was put into its stand and decorated by two people who laughed and shared stories as they worked to create the right atmosphere. Yes, my home was decorated by two people whose main goal was to express who they were as best they could. No doubt, the Nerry Group was dedicated to expressing the wishes of my mother. However, my mother's goal was to impress, rather than express. I couldn't help but think that somewhere along the way, I had arrived as another pawn in her chess match where winning was the checkmate of social status.

Dex sat next to me, and Gilda was at our feet as we exchanged gifts. Recalling that Dex had commented several times about getting a motorcycle, I gave him a leather bomber jacket, a pair of leather gloves, and a scarf. Seeing him try on the jacket got me surprisingly hot and bothered. For the moment, I allowed my thoughts to drift toward how irresistible he was becoming to me. I had to restrain myself from touching the soft leather wrapped around his hard body. Once again, I had to put my desires on hold. Yes, I gave him the jacket, but I prayed the motorcycle would never come to fruition.

In her stocking, Gilda found a large bone and a squeaky toy. I reminisced on the first time I saw Gilda just one year ago. She was a little bundle of yellow joy in a huge box. Now, she would no longer fit into that box. Thank goodness the bone was keeping her occupied. She was in that stage where she was full of energy and still on the clumsy side. The combination could turn her into a wrecking ball if the mood struck her. I chuckled to myself as I remembered how Dex had cared for her those three days before Christmas. It was no wonder she was so attached to him.

I was not prepared for Dex's gift to me. It was a small

velvet bag containing two small boxes. I opened the smallest one first. It was a beautiful pair of sapphire and diamond earrings. The second box contained a matching necklace. They were the most beautiful gems I had ever seen.

"Dex, this is really way too much."

"Probably so," he smiled, totally pleased with his purchase.

As silence filled the room, Dex stood up and took both of my hands and pulled me to my feet.

"Would you please excuse us?" he politely asked my parents. Upon receiving my father's permission, he escorted me out to their large solarium.

"Ginny, you are the best thing that has ever happened to me. There are no words to express what you mean to me. These gems, as beautiful as they are, cannot begin to match what I see in you. I really do love you."

"I love you, too, Dex."

The visit with my parents was nice, but I was glad when we arrived back at my small drafty house with my unassuming Christmas tree and sparse decorations. On the way home, Dex gave me another surprise. We were going to spend New Year's Eve with Courtney and Dylan, and Susan and Derek at the Lewes Yacht Club. I don't know how he had arranged it, but I was so super excited. It also meant that I had to find a dress to wear. I couldn't remember the last time I had gone dress shopping. Fortunately, with the many outlet malls between Lewes and Rehoboth, one didn't have to go far to find every retailer known to the avid shopper.

DEX

Our big night had arrived. I had worked all day, and I was bone tired, but my heart remained focused on spending New Year's Eve with Ginny. I was running on adrenaline and probably a few other things I can't quite describe. I returned to the Right Tackle, grabbed my tux and went over to Ginny's to shower and dress. When I arrived, she was upstairs and had just stepped out of the shower with only a bath sheet wrapped around her body. I met her at the top of the stairs.

"Hi! How was your day?" she asked, adjusting her towel and making sure everything was tucked in. Her hair was wrapped up in a second towel, her smooth bare shoulders exposed.

"Perfect, now." I stole a quick kiss from her still wet lips.

"Good. You're just in time. The bathroom is nice and steamy hot . . . like you." She poked my shoulder. "I laid out some clean towels for you. Enjoy, and I'll see you downstairs."

I shaved and jumped into the shower. After working outside all day, the hot water felt great as it massaged my overworked body. The weather had been an unusual sixty degrees for the past two days, so my crew and I started early and worked late to make the most of the favorable conditions. After getting thoroughly shampooed and lathered, I stood under the hot water while my muscles loosened up. When finished, I turned the water off, pulled the curtain back, wrapped a towel around my waist, wiped steam from the mirror, and ran a comb through my hair. All that was left to be done was get dressed. It had been years since I had worn anything that resembled formal attire. I wasn't crazy about buttoned up shirts and ties; however, I wanted to do my best to impress Ginny. I had to admit, no matter how uncomfortable I thought it was; I rocked that tux.

After checking myself in the mirror one more time to make sure I had done my best, I went downstairs. I could tell Ginny was still in her bedroom behind its closed door. Quite honestly, I couldn't wait to see her on our first big night out. I already knew she would look fabulous. But knowing Ginny, she would be the kind of fabulous that would drive me crazy. I reflected on how beautiful she was on her wedding day, and how happy she and Dan were. He lived a million years in that way. I caught myself whispering to him that I would take the best care of her, as I knew he would want me to. I did that a lot lately as Ginny and I spent more time together.

I made myself comfortable in the living room. Staring at the Christmas tree and the view of the water behind it, and thought of what could be.

From within my reverie, I heard Ginny's bedroom door open and each of her footsteps coming across the small upstairs landing. It was the unmistakable sound of high heels on an old wooden floor. As she descended the staircase, I turned and saw the woman with whom I had played tackle football, the same one who rode her bike around town, the same girl who normally spent her day in jeans and a comfy sweater. In her natural state, Ginny was one of the most beautiful women I had ever known. That night, she was absolutely and irresistibly gorgeous. She was a stunning vision of elegant beauty and sophistication.

What is she doing with a guy like me?

Ginny was wearing a strapless midnight blue dress that clung to her slender body, wrapping her curves in glamorous gathered silk. Her ravenous red hair was up with several gentle strands that fell around her face, bare shoulders, and back. She was wearing the earrings that I had given her for Christmas. My heart was pounding. The sight of her was sending a series of shock waves through my body. I had never felt that vulnerable in the presence of a woman, ever. I was completely unarmed and she was wearing down my ability to restrain myself.

I was coming to know Ginny in a potent way that was fast approaching equal parts reverence and lust. I felt no guilt or shame. I knew it was right. I knew that if this was how it had to be, Dan would have been relieved and happy for Ginny and me. How bittersweet our lives had become.

"Ginny, you are absolutely beautiful," I whispered.

"You're pretty damn handsome in that tux, yourself. Wow . . ."

She walked toward me. Handing me her necklace, she turned her back to me.

"Would you please put this on for me?"

Her heels must have been at least three inches, making her almost as tall as I was. After clasping her necklace, I turned her back around and gently held her waist with my hands and reeled her in for a kiss. Comfortable at my height, she ran her fingers through my still slightly damp hair. The shock waves roared through my extremities like a tsunami. Waiting for the right time was becoming more difficult with each passing day and night, and each minute of every hour.

I held her coat for her as she slipped it on. We walked outside, and to her surprise, she discovered that I had borrowed Mr. Sable's Mercedes for the night. (He was so in my corner.) With each move, her scent wafted through the air, giving me an added rush. Everything about her was acting like an accelerant to an already smoldering fire. At the car, I opened her door, and watched as she gracefully slipped her legs into the passenger side. She was so intoxicating. She seemed to move in slow motion, her stunning gracefulness made my heart race.

Inside the club, we zeroed in on Dylan and Courtney. They were already enjoying a cocktail. We gave the usual hugs and compliments all around. Dylan asked what we would like to drink and then headed for the bar. Courtney said that Susan and Derek were staying in town at the Rodney. They had checked in and should be arriving soon. They did manage to join us before dinner was served. We shared our round table with two other couples.

They were somewhat older than us. I would have guessed they were in their late forties, about Charles' age. We introduced ourselves and tried to explain our relationships, which generated a few raised eyebrows. Later, when the girls left the table to visit the ladies' room, one of the gentlemen leaned over to me stating that it was obvious to him that Ginny was completely enamored with me, and I would be a fool to let her go.

"Tell me about it!"

After we had finished dinner, Ginny asked if I would dance with her. I figured, what the heck, I needed to work off a few pounds that I had accumulated over the holidays. Dylan and Courtney, Derek and Susan later joined us on the dance floor. Just when we were ready to sit down, the band began a slower set, and Ginny and I slow danced for the first time. It was like visiting heaven. Without forethought or the need for an explanation, I was given the perfect, public opportunity to hold her for more than just a few seconds. Her cheek was against mine and her lips were just a few inches away. Our bodies moved in time as we savored the lyrics of a love song. I pulled away from her, still close enough to look deep into her eyes, and whispered, "I love you, Baby."

"I love you, too," she responded and laid her head back on my shoulder.

Shortly after midnight, we told the others we were ready to leave, explaining that I had had a long hard day. Susan said they would see us in the morning. Dylan said not to wait up; when he and Courtney leave the yacht club, they had plans to continue the celebration with the Sable family.

Ginny and I drove quietly back down Bay Avenue. Her left hand was tucked into my free right hand. Her fingers were soft and tangled in mine, gently moving to let me know she wanted to remain close and as intimate as we were on the dance floor. Arriving at her house, I shut off the engine.

"Would you like to come in?" she invited with a coy

smile on her lips.

"Actually, no."

While what she had asked sounded like a clear invitation, I was not convinced "there" would be the best place for us to continue what had begun on the dance floor. We needed to find ourselves in a neutral place, free of memories, and safe for both of us.

"Ginny, come back to the Right Tackle with me."

"What? I'll freeze."

"The cabin's heated. It's such a beautiful night. It's perfect for star gazing on the water."

"What 'll I do about Gilda?"

"She can come with us."

"Well, that's against my better judgment. I'll need to let her out, first."

"I'll help."

After letting Gilda out for a run, we loaded her into the Jeep, leaving the Mercedes behind, and headed for the boat. I had left the heater on low, hoping to keep some of the chill off while I was out. The night air felt good after being indoors for the better part of the evening. We scurried on board and opened the cabin doors. Gilda raced in ahead of us. She loved the Right Tackle and sometimes I believed she considered it hers.

"Ginny, on a clear night like this, there will be billions of stars out, once we get away from town and all of these dock lights. Let's take her out to the Bay. What do you say?" It was my turn to offer an invitation.

"Dex, if it gets too cold out there, I will freeze and make a terrible crewmate. I will be of no help."

"No help is needed. There's no wind, just a clear night sky. I can manage her on my own tonight," I stated convincingly, I had hoped.

For reasons I have yet to comprehend, Ginny trusted me. I wrapped her up in a blanket, leaving her and Gilda in the cabin. Putting on a heavy coat and gloves, I turned over the engines and let them warm up for a few minutes. Once all preparations were complete, I cast off the bow and stern lines, and in one seamless move I dropped the spring line and eased her away from the dock. The water was perfectly still, like a sheet of black glass. The Right Tackle sliced through the dark silk as if she were a sharp pair of scissors that met no resistance through the delicate fabric. Beneath her decks, the engines hummed a happy monotone song as the water rushed over her hull. Continuing out through the inlet, I could see the party was winding down at the Yacht Club. Out beyond the bulkhead, one could not tell where the dark water stopped and the night sky began. It was like night flying. It was where I belonged, out there with no jacket and tie, no airs to put on, and no road to follow. I was home.

The cabin door opened and Ginny emerged with the blanket wrapped tightly around her, dragging behind her and across the deck.

"Where are we going?"

"Away from the lights, where every star in every direction can be seen."

She pressed up against me to stay warm. I pulled her up onto the captain's bench and wrapped my arm around her.

Half way across the Delaware Bay, between Lewes, Delaware and Cape May, New Jersey, I cut the engines. The Right Tackle lurched, as her wake caught up to us, raising the stern and pushing us forward as its inertia rushed forward from beneath us. Once the wave passed her midship, the Right Tackle settled back down. It didn't take long until we lost all forward momentum and lay silently adrift. It was a slack tide with no wind, so there was little to worry about. There was an absence of sound, except for the rapping of ripples on the hull. It left us feeling as if the rest of the world had ceased to exist. We sat in silence.

"Are you ready?"

"Ready? For what?"

"Here, let me out."

Ginny scooted off the captain's bench. I took her hand as I slid past and escorted her to the center of the open cockpit. I sat down on the deck, pulling her down with me.

"Now lay down on your back and enjoy the view."

She lay down next to me with her head on my shoulder and shifted until she was comfortable and saddled up against me. The deck was still warm from the engine heat, making it cozier than one would imagine.

"Oh, my gosh, Dex, I don't know that I have ever seen anything as beautiful as this. It's even better than the night we almost touched the Milky Way!"

I remembered; we had laid Dan to rest that day. I raised her hand to my lips, kissed it, and gave it a gentle squeeze to let her know that I had recalled it too, and appreciated all that night had meant to her."

"So, I bet you've had a lot of girls out here to see this cosmic spectacle."

Was she teasing or searching?

"Actually, no. You're the first."

"Really?"

"Yes. You're the first."

As if on cue, Gilda lay down on my other side.

"And, she's the second."

Ginny rolled her eyes and then rolled on her side to face me. I knew she was no longer looking up at the stars.

"Dex?"

"Um?"

She wrapped her body into and around mine. A series of deep sensuous kisses began that lasted a decade. We both knew where it was leading. With the moves of her body and my physical response, we were about to chart a new course under the stars and heaven above.

"Ginny, let me take the Right Tackle into shallower water and throw out an anchor."

There was not another boat out that night except for the tankers, miles away and lit up like distant Christmas trees. I took the Right Tackle back toward Lewes and dropped anchor about one hundred yards off the Lewes beach, well beyond the sand bar. From there we could see the blue and white Christmas lights wrapped around the deck rail of the Carter beach house. It was one of the few houses on the shoreline with lights still on. In the summer, the entire coastline would have been lit up. From the water that night, the town looked empty, as if it had gone into hibernation, with the exception of one old tiny beach house.

After letting out a long length of line and reversing the Right Tackle to insure the Danforth was sufficiently buried, I cut the engines and turned on the anchor lights. Ginny had already retreated into the cabin. I went below, but she was nowhere to be found. I walked through the galley and still there was no sign of her. Opening the master stateroom door, I peered in and found her sitting on the edge of my bed.

Without a spoken word, I received her invitation. There was no need to rush. The night was ours. The sun would not be up for several hours.

"I have wanted you for so long. It feels like a thousand years have passed since our first kiss," I whispered.

She wanted the same, her request made known with her lips pressed into mine, and her hands removing my shirt. Following her lead, I removed the blanket from her shoulders and reached around her back to unzip her dress, knowing that beneath was something more spectacular than all the stars in heaven. The next hour was filled with slow, timeless exploration. Once every constellation had been charted and committed to memory, we came together as a storm gathers over the horizon and roars across the water. Starting as intense white caps and spray blowing across the surface, the water depths were soon stirred deeply, throwing wave over wave, and every part of us was alive. Throughout the night, our turbulence pressed on and circled around several more times. There was no turning back . . . into the wee morning hours . . .

As Ginny slept, I took the Right Tackle back to her slip. Once her lines were secured, I went below and curled up next to Ginny and joined her in beautiful silent peace. At last, my restlessness had been tamed.

GINNY

"What's that?" I whispered, nudging Dex with intense urgency. It was definitely not how I had envisioned waking up next to him on our first morning together. However, something startled me out of a sound sleep. The boat was rocking and I could hear footsteps on the deck above us. Gilda was crouching at the foot of the bed, hair raised on her back, and growling a deep, throaty, yet barely audible warning. She was alerting us and preparing herself, still not letting the intruders know we were below. My ears were zeroed in on the noise above and my eyes were fixed on Dex, naked and lying beside me. Dex was groggy, and I really didn't know how he was going to react to this rude awakening after being up all night.

I nudged him a little harder.

"Ginny?"

"Shhhh . . ." I put a finger to his lips. "Someone is up on deck."

Dex stilled to hear what I was talking about.

We heard several voices, male and female, snooping around.

"It's Courtney and Dylan," Dex whispered.

"Oh, my gosh, we were supposed to get together at the beach house for breakfast."

"Yep, it's them all right, and I hear Derek and Susan, too."

"Oh, this is just great."

As if she knew the jig was up, Gilda opened up with a full out alarm.

"Stay here. I'll go topside, let Gilda out, and let them know we're both on board, everything's OK, and we'll meet them in half an hour," Dex calmly suggested.

"I think they know we're here, I'm pretty sure they know everything is OK, and a half hour is just fine with me. Oh, and please don't let Gilda run too far."

Dex slipped on a pair of jeans to go up and greet our beloved band of pirates. I could hear their somewhat muffled voices. The dialogue lasted only a minute or two, and then I felt the boat rock again as the marauders disembarked. Several minutes later, Dex reappeared below with a happier Gilda.

"You got dressed! I just bargained for another two hours," Dex raved, trying to convince me that he was serious and disappointed that I was fully dressed.

I had been so hungry for Dex for so long that I honestly wished he had bargained for those extra two hours. It would have been so nice. But if ours was to be a lasting relationship, we needed to do the family thing. It was time to buck up, face the real world, and go meet up with the rest of the gang. I kept reminding myself that I only got to see Susan every couple of months and Dylan only on the weekends when he would make the trek to Lewes. Hopefully, I would be able to see more of Dex, now, every day and every night.

As previously arranged, we all met at my house for a quickly put together brunch. God bless Susan and Courtney; they dropped the guys off at the house before Dex and I got back, and then they left to pick up bagels, cream cheese, and OJ. Coffee was on by the time we had arrived.

Derek and Dylan were in the living room talking about who knows what. Susan greeted me with a huge hug and her all-suspecting smile. After we broke away from our embrace, I looked at Courtney. I didn't know what to say or do. For the first time, I seriously considered how far her earlier relationship with Dex had gone. I wasn't sure if she was really OK with what was transpiring between Dex and me. She was staring at me, and then her hands beckoned me in for a hug.

"Ginny, Dex is a really special guy, and until this morning, I was always afraid of how I would react when some lucky lady landed him. It was bound to happen sooner or later, and if it had to be, I'm glad it's you."

That was Courtney, always calling it her way, to her satisfaction. I'm sure it was her way of genuinely endorsing me. At least that was my hope.

"Thanks, Courtney."

The six of us sat in the living room as we spread cream cheese on our bagels and drank several cups of coffee. It was a new beginning in a new year.

DEREK

It was sickening. First, we were on Dex's boat. Of all the places I'd rather *not* be, that topped the list. Then to think that the two of them were below, going at it, was even more repulsive. It had not been a year, yet. She was such a tramp. The boat, the two of them, nothing could have been more disrespectful to my brother. To me, it proved that she was in it only for herself. She took my brother's life and then she took the house that was rightfully mine. Worse yet, I had to sit there and tolerate the two of them climbing all over each other and acting like they were the best thing that's ever happened. I was tired of pretending that I was OK with any of it. It was not OK. It was so far beyond wrong.

Susan had been sucked in, and Dylan was so obsessed with Courtney that he was oblivious to anything else going on around him. And Courtney? Something was not right about the way she was stringing Dylan along. There had to be something in it for her. Those three: Ginny, Dex, and Courtney were schemers, and I for one was not having it. It was time to take my wife and my younger brother and get out of there.

SUSAN

I knew it was only a matter of time. I could tell the second weekend she was home from the hospital that there was something about Dex and her that just clicked.

Ginny had loved Dan with all her heart. I remember all the times we had stayed up together and talked into the wee hours of the morning. She was head over heels in love with Dan, and she would light up at the mere mention of his name. She was so excited when she called to announce that they had gotten engaged. I will never forget how brokenhearted she was when he died in the accident. I was not so sure she would ever survive it, either.

Ginny deserved to be loved and to be in-love. And Dex was a great guy. I could not have been happier for them. In fact, I was kind of jealous of all the newness and puppy love that surrounded them. And, it appeared that they had consummated their relationship that night aboard the Right Tackle, and she was over the moon the next morning.

I remember when Derek and I were like that. He was such a romantic when we were dating. He would give me so much attention it was almost alarming. He always held my hand or had his arm around my shoulder. He would take me out to dinner and a movie, or show up with tickets to a Broadway show and whisk me off for a weekend in New York City. Surprise get-away weekends were not uncommon with Derek. To top it off, he really cared and listened attentively when I shared anything and everything that was on my mind. That was then.

Years later, I was no longer sure he heard me at all. I must have done something—or did *not* do something—to push him away, but what? Until last night, I couldn't remember the last time he had embraced me. I couldn't remember the last time we had made love—a month, two months ago? Until last night, I wasn't sure he still loved me at all.

Ginny had endured so much pain in such a short period of time, but she had found a way to live through it and press on. I was beginning to believe that she would actually be able to go on with her life and that Dan would have been very proud of her. I, on the other hand, was about to fall off a cliff without knowing how far down the plummet was going to take me. I couldn't fathom which would be worse: the fall or the landing?

Honestly, it was to the point where I didn't recognize Derek anymore. I thought he would have enjoyed being in Lewes more often, away from work, and spending time with his brothers. To the contrary, ever since his dad died, Derek could not stand being there. I guess that made some sense. Maybe it brought back too many memories. Although, when at home, something might trigger a memory and he would occasionally share a funny story about when he and his brothers were growing up together, so I can't blame his resistance on the proximity to the past with his father.

On the rare occasion when Derek was in Lewes, his walls would definitely go up, and he would become a fortress of solitude. I had noticed that even around Dylan, Derek would become quiet and vigilant of his thoughts. If I mentioned Dex's name, Derek would tense up. Concerning Ginny, if I wanted to visit her, he would have an excuse; and if I could make the trip, it was always by myself. Perhaps he was more depressed about losing Dan and his dad than I had originally thought. With all that said, I couldn't figure out why he had agreed to go down there for New Year's Eve, but I was so glad he did. It was good for him. It was good for us.

COURTNEY

Wow, they finally did it. Dex and Ginny rounded the bases. And to think I had such a crush on him at one time.

I was so excited when he had returned to Lewes almost ten years ago, and so hopeful when he had contacted me after he made landfall. Sadly, he never felt the same way I did. I guess it was just never meant to be. Though, I must admit, I would not have minded if he had stolen home plate in my ballpark. We did go out a couple of times, only because I had asked him. I remember the time I tried to kiss him. I could tell he wasn't feeling it, and my failed attempt to steal first base made everything so awkward the next time I saw him.

"Lesson learned, Court. You can't steal first base!" he *teased many months later when I was ready to laugh about it.*

He was at least gracious enough to notice how hurt I was. I remember he took the time to explain that he didn't want to lose a friend. I remember, of all things, it was afterward that he started calling me occasionally to have dinner or meet for a drink. It was confusing, at first. I was beginning to believe that he must have been gay. I had never seen him with another girl, but he never seemed interested in guys, either. He did have a girlfriend or two in high school, or so he claimed.

Later, it was so awesome to watch him connect with his dad, Mr. Carter. He was hurt at first; yet very grateful to know that his biological father was not anything like the other men his mother had eventually married. Realizing his biological provenance, Dex gained a new sense of pride and dignity; he had something, or someone, worth living up to. He really enjoyed being around Dan and Dylan. However, for as long as I had known him, he had always been troubled by his relationship with Derek. I think deep down inside, Derek believed there had been some foul play along the way. In fact, something told me Derek had always known more than he had let on.

When Mr. Carter died, Dan and Ginny moved into the Carter beach house, and all of a sudden, Dex, Dan, and Dylan became best buddies. I am sure that made Derek real happy! Oh, and the day I first met the Carter boys in my office, what a hoot! Dex told me they would be a trip, and just as he had said, Derek was "the man in charge," Dylan was in a state of confusion, and Dan was a kind and humble gentleman. Dex was so right about all three men. He had made it almost too easy for me.

To my surprise, and something Dex did not predict, I was immediately attracted to Dylan. I saw how he was watching me, as well. He was obviously into me, too.

So why, at a much later date, were we still not giving in to what we both knew to be true? Why was I so scared of Dylan? When we were together, especially when we were alone, my skin tingled, my stomach was full of butterflies, and my heart was in my throat. Why did I think about him almost every minute of every day and then do nothing about it when I had the opportunity?

Yet, I must confess, the thought of Dex giving himself to another made me depressed. It seemed that New Year's Eve had sealed the deal. Dex and I would never be. I had to surrender to the fact that I would never get over him.

Men.

DYLAN

I missed Dan so much. There had been so many times I wanted to ask him about something, usually involving Court or Derek, and then I would remember that he wasn't here. And Derek was no help. He had been so aloof since Dad and Dan had died. Sometimes, I worried about him,

314

but I knew Susan had everything under control ... or at least I thought she did.

Then, there was Ginny and Dex; they made such a perfect pair. I was so happy for both of them. Ginny had always been like a sister to me. And Dex, it turns out, is my half-brother. How comical is that? I wished Dan had known. Anyway, I was happy for them. My family was rapidly changing shape in those years. It had been tragic, losing Dad, then Dan, and even Lily. To think, I almost became an uncle. But out of all that tragedy, something good was being built: Dex and Ginny had found their way through all of the destruction.

Then there was Court. She was such a mystery to me. I just could not navigate my way around her. I really enjoyed spending time with her. OK, truth be known, I was crazy about her. She was smart. She was level headed, yet very funny at times. She was very secure in who she was and where she was headed. In many ways, she was all of the things that I was not. Perhaps that explains why whenever the opportunity arose for me to show her how I really felt, I was so intimidated that I never got up the nerve, and she would continue to drive me nuts.

Then, there was just the pure physical attraction, as well. Let me be honest about this—she knocked me out the very first time I saw her. In her office that first day, I was a bowl of mush. It's embarrassing to think back on it. Thank God, Derek took the lead, like he always did. It's safe to say that she has occupied my mind ever since that day.

Oh, and the way she looked New Year's Eve?

She. Was. A. Knock-out.

Her little black dress and those long legs were making my head spin all night. Her perfume, so faint, but when we were slow dancing and I was a breath away, it was so hard to maintain my cool. Who knows what would have happened had I not fallen asleep on the Sables' couch. I had no idea what time everyone else went to bed. The only thing I remember was waking up with the sun shining through the den windows, my head pounding, and the drool I had innocently left on one of their throw pillows. The next thing I knew, Mr. Sable was standing over me, handing me a Bloody Mary, saying it would cure whatever had bit me the night before. Little did he know that it was his daughter who had turned me into a bite-size morsel; though, I think he had figured it out.

Thankfully, it was a new year. Who knew what it would bring? In the meantime, I was happy for Ginny and Dex. I was glad it was working out for them. I could see it lasting a long time. Their ties were good for me, too. They were my link to Court. I had a reason to come down every weekend, a place to stay, and not have it look too obvious. Well, apparently it was obvious to everyone, except Courtney.

DEX

I had never felt that way about any other person in my entire life. In fact, Ginny had become the world to me, and I was prepared to give her everything I had to offer. In some inexplicable way, I realized then that my heart was under siege long before I was ready for it. Looking back, I believe I was taken captive the first time I had carried her wounded soul up the steps and into the beach house. Eight months later, she gave herself to me, and I knew in my heart of hearts that I would never be the same.

Over the next several months, I slowly moved in with Ginny. I had stayed with her every night since New Year's Eve. The clothes I had kept in the spare room, and more from the Right Tackle, eventually took up residence in a small dresser we had relocated to her room. I occasionally asked Ginny if she would like some space, as in, should I spend more time, including nights, on the Right Tackle? She insisted that she liked it better when I was there, with her.

We celebrated her birthday in March, and I was really nervous about purchasing just the right gift for her. Christmas was going to be difficult to top. I can't remember ever being that concerned about giving the right gift. Quite frankly, other than my mother, I've never had anyone special to shop for, and you can guess how that turned out.

* * *

When I was about nine years old, I had saved up money doing odd jobs like walking dogs, raking yards, and weeding gardens. I used the money to buy my mom a sweatshirt and matching coffee mug that had "Best Mom Ever" imprinted on them. I wrapped and gave them to her for Christmas that year. I remember how the morning after, she was sitting in the kitchen with her sweatshirt on and drinking coffee from her new mug. She gave me the biggest smile ever when she saw how happy it made me to see her in that sweatshirt and drinking from that mug. I curled up in her lap thinking that it was a new day for my mom and me. However, it was not too long after that that her first husband, who I thought was my biological father, claimed that he accidentally broke the coffee mug. The sweatshirt seemed to disappear too, and for that matter, so did we.

* * *

I only hoped that the gift I purchased for Ginny would adequately convey my feelings for her. I wanted to give her something that would not break and make her wish that I would not disappear any time soon.

GINNY

Dex was always so attentive, and to so much more than just my physical needs. He took the time to listen and made an honest effort to try to understand all the things that would make me happy and put me at peace. On my birthday, he gave me a present that I would've never thought to ask for, yet it was the perfect illustration of how well he knew me. It was the first Saturday in March, and Dex had given me a certificate to get a pedicure. Strangely enough, the certificate came with a date and an appointment time already reserved.

Dex should have known that I was not crazy about such things, but I graciously accepted his gift and kept the appointment.

Maybe he likes painted toes?

When I arrived back home with my newly painted

dactyls and raw de-calloused scraped feet, I was happy to see Dex's truck parked in the drive. I was hoping he would be waiting inside so we could spend the day together. Wearing flip-flops and sporting the separators still crammed between my toes, I walked into the kitchen. Thinking it odd that I didn't hear Dex coming out to greet me, I hung my jacket on the hook by the back door.

And where is Gilda? He must've taken her out to the beach for a walk.

As I entered the family room and made my way to the deck door, something dark and ominous caught the corner of my eye. The large alien object startled me.

In my disbelief, I had to blink and refocus twice. It was a piano, and not just any piano; it was a Bosendorfer. I walked toward it as a kitten might investigate its first moth.

Surely this piano must be lost. Where's Dex? What does he know about this?

At that moment, I heard the deck door open and Gilda came bounding in like she had something to tell me. She sat in front of me, wagging her tail, her tongue hanging out as she panted. Removing his shoes at the door, Dex was right behind her.

"Oh, I see you found her!" he said as I patted Gilda's head.

"Dex, what is this doing here? Do you know what this is?"

"Of course, I do. It's a piano."

"This is not just any piano, and what is it doing in this house?"

"It lives here."

"Dex, this is not my piano."

"It is now!"

"What? Are you kidding me?"

"It's all yours, kiddo. Happy Birthday!"

Gilda jumped up placing both front paws squarely on my shoulders. I stumbled back, struggling keep my balance against her weight and my overwhelming bewilderment.

"Dex, this is a Bosendorfer. It's arguably one of the best pianos in the world. Where did you find this, and how can you afford it? This is way too much."

"You're right. It is one of the best pianos in the world, and I can't afford it. However, a friend of Mrs. Pollock's passed away recently. Her friend didn't want her family to argue over the estate, so she dealt out the family heirlooms several years ago. She then named Mrs. Pollock as the executor with instructions to sell everything that was left and divide seventy-five percent of the revenue among her three children, and for her efforts, Mrs. Pollock was to receive the remaining twenty-five percent. I helped Mrs. Pollock inventory and move everything before it went to the auction house. When I saw the piano, I asked if there was any chance I could purchase it. The rest is history. While you were out this morning, I had the piano movers bring it in."

Dex was obviously proud of what he had accomplished. It was a gift that would last a lifetime, and I was overwhelmed by it.

"Oh, and set your alarm tonight. The piano tuner will be here at 8:00 tomorrow morning."

"Dex, I don't know what to say. I have never in my life received anything as beautiful as this."

I fell into his arms and just held on to him while keeping the piano in my sight.

"Would you like to play it?"

"I don't know. I haven't played in years, and I'm not used to playing in front of other people."

"Well, I have some errands to run, so how about I go and let you two get acquainted."

"Dex, will you be gone long?"

"I can be, if you want me to."

"No, no. I was hoping we could spend the day together."

"Then I won't be gone long. By the way, I have reservations at the Buttery for 6:30 tonight. I'll be back in about an hour. Just about the amount of time you are required to practice young lady," he said, shaking a finger at me as if I were a protesting child.

After I heard his truck pull out and start up Bay Avenue, I gingerly sat down on the bench and slid into place. I placed my fingers lightly on the keys as if I was about to crossover and enter into another realm. It would be the first time I would hear her sing. I played a C major arpeggio.

Wow. She sounds beautiful.

She was bright, but not brash. Her lows were rich, crisp, and clear. I started playing several progressions and threw in a few embellishments and turns. Closing my eyes, I was back in the zone. I had no music; I was simply playing whatever I felt in my heart. How I had missed sitting down at the piano and working out all of the stresses of my daily life.

Playing non-stop, moving from one improvised piece to another, I had no idea how long I had been sitting there. Fast asleep, Gilda was lying on the floor at my feet. I also had no idea how long Dex had been standing in the doorway between the kitchen and the dining area. When my hands finally came to rest. I heard a soft sort of choking sound. I turned around to see him leaning against the doorframe, tears in his eyes.

"Dex, are you OK? Is something wrong?"

"No, Darling, everything is beautifully right. I have never been more in love with you than at this moment right here, right now."

I stood and walked over to him. In his arms, we shed tears of joy and sweet kisses, our thoughts and emotions completely in sync. We shared how the presence of the instrument and the music it produced had touched both of us. We silently agreed that music speaks and heals in profound ways. Oddly, the house seemed to be smiling again.

I took his hand and led him upstairs.

DEX

It was like seeing a treasure map for the first
time. Ginny had invited me upstairs, but it had nothing to
do with what I had suspected. Instead, she directed me to
the spare room, the one with Dan's drafting table. She was
filled with electricity and I was being zapped by her
giddiness. I could tell she was making a great effort to
contain herself.
"Dex, I think I could actually stay here. I survived the
winter, and spring is almost here. The days have gotten
longer, the snow geese are leaving for home, and I want to
stay here!"

*That is good to know. I wasn't aware that she had been
considering other alternatives.*

"And, if I am going to stay here, I need to start making
this place into a home, rather than some temporary shelter
over my head."
"OK, so what do you have in mind?"
"Well, come and take a look at this."
I followed her over to the drafting table. She very
carefully rolled out a set of blueprints. We fought with the
edges, trying to keep them from rolling back up. Once they
were fully unfurled and secured, she stepped aside so I
could take a closer look.
I examined the first drawing of a seemingly large house
with two wrap around decks. After skimming over the
page, I peeled it back to the second layer, which showed the
floor plan for its ground level: a two-car garage with work-
and storage-space. I peeled it across to the next layer, the
second floor, showing four bedrooms and four baths. The
final page, the third floor, obviously depicted the area
where everyone would spend most of their time: the
kitchen, living, and dining areas. The top floor also

included a massive master suite. I threw the pages back to the top. Because the drawing was on Dan's drafting table, I assumed it was his work. I wondered when and where the house was going to be built. It was a masterpiece, and I thought how sad it was that Dan would never get to see it come to fruition.

"I guess you should give these back to the architectural firm. I'm surprised they haven't called looking for it."

"No, it's OK. They belong to me."

"Ginny, I can only imagine how much these drawings might mean to you. They're Dan's work, after all. I get that. But I don't think you have the legal right to keep work Dan was contracted to produce."

Ginny pointed and I glanced down at the first page for a second time and there it was: "408 Bay Avenue, Lewes, Sussex County, Delaware." It was her address—her property. It was a magnificent dream. It was their dream. Those pages detailed the vision of the brother I had become closest to and the father I had wished for. They captured everything Dan and Mr. Carter had talked about.

"Would you like to have these preserved?" I asked.

"Preserved? Like framed? Hell no, I'm going to build it. We're going to build it!"

The room went silent. I knew I was supposed to say something, but I had no response. If she had not looked so serious and appeared so confident, I may have laughed at what I thought was one of her little jests. However, it appeared to be no joke, and therefore, it was no laughing matter. Underneath all of her excitement, I could see that she was clearly resolute about it.

"Ginny, these drawings are amazing, as you would expect from Dan. And you know I loved him as a brother. However, you are not obligated to carry this out. It was just a dream, Baby . . . a big, beautiful dream. A dream he shared with his dad. A dream I am sure he wanted for you. But things have changed. He would never expect this of you."

And, I could never afford to give it to you . . .

Instinctively, I had reached for her upper arms, holding on to them as if I needed to steady her.

"Ginny," I pleaded, "neither one of us has the resources for a project of this magnitude."

"But that's just it, I do!"

"Do you realize the scope and cost of a project like this?"

"No, but it's worth researching."

"Ginny, please don't get your hopes up. I don't want to discourage you, but I also don't want to see you hurt and disappointed."

GINNY

I understood Dex's initial reluctance to get excited about my proposal. He should've questioned my intentions and the financial feasibility of the project, as he called it.

I wasn't sure how much I should tell him. I loved him dearly, but I wanted to make sure that my financial situation didn't cloud our relationship in any way. Then again, if I went ahead with my plans, I would have to tell him, or he would become very suspicious. It would crush him when I eventually confessed the truth. It would prove that I had not trusted him with full disclosure when I had made my decision.

"Dex, on my parents' last visit, my father told me of a trust my grandfather had left for me. I'm to receive it when I turn twenty-five. However, as the trustee, my father has the right and he did decide to go ahead and sign it over to me now. It's more than enough to fix up the place. In fact, it's been supporting me over the past several months."

As if I were carrying some contagious disease, Dex took several steps back. He was looking right at me; however, I didn't like what I thought he was seeing. He took another step, to the side this time, as if he could not decide which way to turn. He moved toward the door and used the frame to steady himself. His reaction caused me great angst.

"Dex, are you OK? This is good news, isn't it?"

"Sure. Sure it is. It just caught me a little off guard."

"Why? It was a gift. I think my grandfather would have thought that developing this property was a good investment. Clearly, my dad does. It's what Dan and Mr. Carter talked about all the time. I believe they would have done it, too. Eventually, they would have found a way."

"I can't argue with that. If I had a boatload of cash, I'd invest it in something like this, too."

I detected a bit of resentment in his voice.

"Boatload? That's a strange choice of words. Seems to me you received an early boatload, as well, from the same man that left this house to Dan, speaking of boatloads."

"That hurt. . . . I didn't ask for it."

"Neither did I."

"Ginny, it's hard to love a woman who is taken care of by so many other men."

Hearing the humor in what was wrought by his overblown male ego, he hung his head down and began laughing at himself. I gave him a jab in the arm.

"You are such a stubborn, hardheaded, ego-maniac Carter man!"

"Ginny, I think that is something I have waited to hear all my life."

"You *are* a Carter, through and through. You just have a different last name."

"Well, if anyone would know, it would be you."

Seated at a table on the Buttery's enclosed porch, the conversation about the renovation continued. Once again, I had to reassure Dex that a substantial amount of money was available to me. What I needed to know from him was how to pursue the dream. His ego still bruised, he followed my thoughts. We talked about asking Dan's former employer to seal the plans. We debated the pluses and minuses of contracting the construction company that employed Dex to head up the project. Then there was the matter of where to move while demolition and construction took place. Dex suggested we talk to the Sables' about renting their garage apartment.

To further celebrate my birthday, the pending plans, and the Bosendorfer, we decided to splurge and order double dark chocolate dessert to share with two spirited coffees. We rationalized that it would help us cope with the bottle of wine we had just polished off. As we took the first dip into the divine chocolate decadence, we heard fire engines screaming our way. Flying by us at a high rate of speed went three large trucks, blasting their horns as they barreled down Savannah Road, past 2nd Street. Once over the drawbridge, we could still hear their sirens as they approached the beach. Our waiter, holding his ears, stopped by the table to ask how we liked our dessert. With the ear piercing blasts past us, he said that he heard there was a house fire on the beach, not far from the Dairy Queen.

Fear shot through both of us. Only a few of those houses were occupied year round, and one of them was the Carter beach house. Dex jumped up from the table, reached into his pocket, pulled his American Express card from his wallet, and handed it over to our waiter.

"Charge us what you like," Dex directed.

He grabbed my hand and pulled me toward the door. As we exited the restaurant, we could see a large orange glow in the sky. It was reflecting off of the sea mist and low hanging clouds.

Dex sped toward Bay Avenue. Turning left, we could not get any closer than Market Street at the Breakwater House and Reed's Cottages. We parked the truck and ran down Bay Avenue toward the beach house. The smoke was choking us and ash was falling into our hair and eyes. We could feel the heat as we approached the first fire engine. We crossed the path of a fire fighter who recognized Dex and grabbed him by the arm.

"Dex, you can't go in there."

The Carter beach house was fully engulfed, and that was

when I heard Gilda shrieking.

"Oh, God, Dex, it's Gilda. She's in there."

Dex shook the fire fighter loose and bolted. The fire fighter was not quick enough to stop him, but he did grab me as I tried to follow.

"Let me go, she's my dog. You can't leave her in there. She's crying. She can't get out. She'll die in there."

I could barely hear her above the roar of the fire. And then, she went silent. As I screamed for her, coughing and choking, I stopped fighting the man who was holding me. He let go, and I sank to my knees.

Through the sobs and smoke now burning my throat, I looked up and asked if he could see Dex.

"No ma'am, I can't see much of anything."

He looked toward the house. We peered through the smoke and silhouettes caused by the bright spotlights from the trucks. He radioed to alert the crew of a man, about six feet tall with sandy brown hair near the building.

"You know, Dex . . . Dex Lassiter. He ran toward the house. I'm here with his girlfriend. I had to hold her back or she would have followed him in there."

The radio crackled back. "Sorry, we didn't see Dex or anyone that looks like him."

The man looked down at me. He didn't need to ask. He knew my next question.

"What about the dog, were you able to get to the dog?" he asked his crew.

"No. We couldn't get close enough to it."

I didn't wait for an explanation or apology. I don't remember removing my shoes. I shot up and sprinted up Bay Avenue before he could grab me again. I crossed back through Mrs. Pollock's lot. I could no longer hear the man yelling for me or following me. My feet were getting torn up from the rough macadam of the road. I had to get on to the sand. As I rounded the front corner of her deck, I saw Mrs. Pollock directly above me, leaning over the rail and wrapped in a blanket. With a towel over her face, she was straining to see the fire down the beach.

"Ginny! Dear! Don't go down there. Stop!"

She was crying, I could hear it in her voice.

I kept running. My lungs and calves were burning now. The cold March air and smoke were sucking the life out of me. I crossed over the dune and turned down the beach, running back toward the beach house through billows of thick black smoke. I tried to call out for Dex, but my voice was nothing but a raw rasp. My legs were giving out, and I was losing my vision. I was struggling to stay on my feet and continued to run as I staggered in and out of consciousness. Clearly, I had inhaled too much smoke. I could no longer feel my feet beneath me.

I don't know how long I was out. I only remember something wet and warm moving across my face. My body was wracked with pain as I sat up and began coughing and gasping for air. I tried to open my eyes, but they were covered in sand. My face was plastered with a mixture of sweat and soot. I tried to wipe off what I could. My eyes were on fire. Reacting to something I heard moving closer to me, I slightly opened them again to see Gilda staring back at me. She was bloodied from her head, down her chest, and to the tips of her front paws. She had open wounds on her nose and the top of her head. As I hugged her, I realized she was covered with small shards of shattered glass.

"Oh, Gilda, don't move, girl. Don't move."

Staying low, I slid my body closer to her so I could get a better look and make sure there was no glass lodged in her skin. God, I was cold, covered only by the dress I wore to dinner. I could hear someone approaching. It was Mrs. Pollock.

"Ginny, are you all right?" She threw a blanket around my shoulders.

"Mrs. Pollock, what are you doing here? Have you seen Dex? He ran toward the house to save Gilda, and now, I don't know where he is. Have you seen him?"

She leaned her frail body down toward me to get a closer look.

"I think I saw him about an hour or so ago," she answered, brushing my hair from my face. It was matted and full of sand.

"Have I been out that long?"

"No, dear, I know I'm slow, but it didn't take me that long to get here."

"Where is he?"

"He was headed up the beach. I called him, but he didn't respond."

"It couldn't have been Dex. We were at the Buttery."

"Oh, I thought it was him . . ."

My brain was scrambled, but I think hers was, too.

"Ginny, I'm calling an ambulance."

Mrs. Pollock stood back up. Coughing with the towel still covering her face, she started back for her house.

"Wait! Use my . . ."

That was when I realized that somewhere along the way, I had dropped my purse. I looked back to Mrs. Pollock. She had stopped in her tracks and was staring back beyond us. I turned my head, and Gilda started whimpering as she caught sight of something shadowed by the smoke and the fire's glow behind it. A tall silhouette was coming across the dune. It was Dex! He staggered up to us and dropped in a heap. He was wet, exhausted, and breathing heavily.

"I couldn't get close enough. I didn't think she was going to make it. I called and called for her, and just when I was about to give up, she came crashing through a window. She hit the ground and just kept going. I couldn't catch her. She just kept running. Thank God for those old, thin, brittle window panes."

"Dex, are you OK?"

"Yes, are you?"

"Yes, I'm going to be fine. However, I think we should get Gilda to a vet," I said as I lightly brushed Dex's face and ran my hand down his arm to make sure he was not an apparition. I tried to cover him with part of my blanket, but he refused it.

"We're probably blocked in by now," Dex speculated correctly.

"Take my car," Mrs. Pollock offered. "I'll call the

Savannah Animal Hospital to make sure they have a doctor there waiting for you."

Powered by adrenaline alone, Dex carried Gilda back to Mrs. Pollock's house. She went inside and brought out her car keys and a blanket for Dex and wrapped another around Gilda.

The Savannah Animal Hospital was located out by the Lewes cut-off. They had 24-hour emergency service. They had always been the most caring group of doctors, and that night was no different.

Sure enough, a doctor arrived just as we were pulling into the lot. Mrs. Pollock had obviously filled her in.

"I am so sorry, Mrs. Carter."

Mrs. Carter . . . rarely have I been addressed as Mrs. Carter. I never had the time to be "Mrs. Carter."

I was immediately stricken with thoughts of how devastated Dan and his dad would have be if they knew what had just happened.

What did happen? Did I leave the stove on? A candle lit? Did I use a bad extension cord? The old electric wiring in the house didn't allow for many outlets. What did I do?

"Let's get her inside where I can get a good look at her and hopefully make her more comfortable."

As she unlocked the door to the hospital, she asked if we were OK. She was genuinely concerned, and we felt some relief beginning to pour over us knowing that we were in the presence of someone who cared. She introduced herself as Dr. Sherri Strong. I would have guessed that she was in her late twenties, early thirties. She was probably new to the practice.

After providing Gilda with a large bowl of water, which Gilda lapped up rapidly, Dr. Strong confidently moved around the table as she examined Gilda's eyes, nose, mouth, and body for wounds, removing glass as she went along. She listened to her heart and lungs. She excused herself as she left the room to pull Gilda's chart. Dex and I talked quietly, continuing to sooth Gilda who was lying still on the table. She was falling in and out of sleep then. Dr. Strong came back into the room and handed water bottles to Dex and me.

God bless her.

"Mr. and Mrs. Carter, I would like to sedate Gilda so I can remove some of the remaining glass and debris in her skin and hair, and clean and stitch a couple of these wounds."

I looked down at the chart.

"Gilda Carter. Owners: Virginia & Daniel Carter."

At that time I didn't have the energy or emotional stamina to make the needed correction to her records. Dex gave me a nod to indicate that he thought it was best to let it go.

"I am going to call a tech in to assist me, and I recommend that we keep her overnight for observation." Then Dr. Strong took a deep breath. "I can't imagine what your next several days are going to be like. I understand your house was a total loss?"

"Burned to the ground," I whispered, confirming the news.

"We can keep her here for several days. We won't charge you for her stay. It will be our way of trying to help. You could come and visit with her any time."

I looked at Dex. I was in no shape to make any decisions. I could feel my body and mind shutting down as her words reintroduced the reality of my situation. I was homeless.

Dex answered for me.

"Thank you, Dr. Strong. Please do what you think is best for Gilda. Can we call you in the morning once we figure out what we need to do?"

"That will be fine. We'll take good care of her. We'll talk

to you sometime tomorrow."

Before we left, we gave her another cell phone number to call. In the process of adding to the file's information, I was so moved by her kindness toward us that I felt the need to tell her the truth about my marital status. Dr. Strong's eyes filled with tears as she stepped forward and gave me a much-needed hug. She added Dex's name to the list of contacts and said she would make the correction to the records the next day. I believe she didn't want to remove Dan's name in my presence. The world should be filled with more people like Dr. Sherri Strong.

DEX

When we arrived back at what was once the Carter beach house, Courtney and her parents were there and speaking with Tom Pratt, the same officer who inspected our possible break-in. Mrs. Pollock was there, too, looking bewildered and shaking her head in denial of what had happened. As soon as Courtney saw us, she ran to Ginny and wrapped her arms around her. It was then that Ginny finally released a long tearful exhale filled with emotion that had been bottled up inside since we had left the restaurant. Leaving her in Courtney's care, I walked over to Mr. Sable. He was already assessing what needed to be done. Pratt seemed anxious, shifting his weight from side to side. I could tell he had something he needed to tell us. Mrs. Pollock continued to look like a deer in the headlights.

Courtney had her arm wrapped around Ginny's shoulder as she walked her back toward us. As I studied her face, I could see that Ginny was holding up with a strength that was inspiring. I noticed that her arm was wrapped around Courtney's waist. You could almost see the spirit of encouragement passing between the two of them.

"I guess the piano tuner is going to be disappointed," Ginny quipped.

That's my girl!

"Ginny . . . Dex . . . may we speak privately, please?" Pratt sounded seriously official.

I looked over at Mr. Sable who gave me the nod. We followed Pratt to the back of a large fire truck; the same place the fireman had restrained Ginny earlier.

"Dex and Ginny, one day you and I are going to meet for better reasons."

"Let's hope so, otherwise, I'm staying clear of you," Dex sarcastically warned.

Pratt snickered nervously and then regained his somber demeanor before continuing:

"I need to inform you that the fire chief believes this fire was set. He has called in the fire marshal."

Pratt then turned and looked squarely at Ginny.

"We have to declare your property a crime scene. I am sorry, but you will have to stay off the premises until the fire is completely extinguished and we have had the opportunity to fully investigate." Pratt delivered the news and then waited for Ginny's reaction or questions.

"Why would someone do this? Why would someone want to burn down this little cottage?" Ginny asked.

"I don't know. We're hoping that the two of you can help us find that answer."

"Can it wait until morning?" I asked.

"No, I'm sorry. I'm sure it won't take long."

I returned to where the Sables and Mrs. Pollock were waiting and let them know that Ginny and I had to go to the police station for questioning.

Mr. Sable approached Pratt.

"I am Dex's attorney and Courtney will be representing Ginny."

"I really don't think that will be necessary," Pratt asserted.

I really didn't see the need, either, at first. That is, until

I had a flashback to the first time I had met Mr. Sable. Mr. Carter had called him to represent me when I had been accused of setting the boathouse fire. The recollection filled my stomach with bile, and I was beginning to feel nauseous.

This can't be happening to me again. I can't bear the thought of Ginny having to entertain for one moment that I was in any way responsible for this.

After speaking with the fire chief, who assured us that the area would be secured, we left for the police station. Pratt was right. It didn't take long. Each of us gave our statements and they were able to confirm with the Buttery that we were there when the fire was set. We were free to go, but Pratt told us he would be in touch after the initial investigation was completed.

Standing outside the station, Mrs. Sable asked if we had thought about where we were going to stay.

GINNY

The Sables graciously offered us the use of their garage apartment for as long as we needed. Dex had stayed there many times before when it was "just too damn cold to stay on the boat," as he put it.

Our plan was to spend the first night on the Right Tackle where we would have a few creature comforts that we needed like blankets, towels, and whatever clothes Dex had left on board. However, we reeked of smoke. It was in our eyes. It saturated our clothes and our hair. It coated the insides of our nostrils, making the acrid burning smell inescapable. The roar of the fire and the sound of collapsing beams still rang in my ears. Even though we were a mile away from the scene, remnants of smoke and ash still hung heavy in the atmosphere surrounding

Lewes. We wanted desperately to make it all disappear.

We badly needed showers, so we decided to go to the garage apartment, taking soap, shampoo, towels, and two pairs of Dex's sweats with us, to wash away what we could and change into clean clothes.

We quietly pulled into the Sable's driveway. Out of the truck, we stripped off our outer layers and left them on the ground at the bottom of the steps. We swiftly climbed the steep narrow stairs with what little we had on. The apartment, though small, was furnished with everything we could possibly need. The Pullman kitchen was fully equipped, including cookware, dishes, glassware, and eating utensils. The dinette included a small table and two chairs. There was even a small deck off the dinette. The living space accommodated a loveseat, one recliner, two lamps, and one wall mounted flat screen TV, which Dex proudly announced he had purchased and installed. The bedroom had a queen size bed and two dressers.

The tiny bathroom became my sanctuary as I stripped off my sooty underwear. My skin, especially my face, felt like it was covered with a thin sticky tar. I felt immediate relief as the hot water poured down over my aching head and weary body. Feeling safe, my muscles began to relax. I started to believe that we would survive and a trickle of hope set in as I thought about rebuilding. Sadly, we would have to construct it without Dan's plans. They were gone ... and we would have to do it without Dan.

Out of the shower and dressed, I shuffled into the living area and plopped down on the loveseat next to Dex. Now, I could really appreciate how much smoke we had been in. It was choking me just sitting next to him. Poor Dr. Strong, the three of us must have smelled toxic to her. She had never let on.

After Dex made his way to the shower, I went back downstairs, gathered up our clothes, and quickly threw them into the compact washer. I found a pad of paper and a pencil and sat back down on the loveseat to compose two lists. The first was an inventory of what we should look for in the rubble and potentially lost in the fire. The second was a list of things we would immediately need to sustain us at the apartment. Not having Gilda lying next to my feet as I scribbled away was odd. Wondering what she was doing, I hoped she was comfortably sleeping it off.

When Dex came out of the bathroom, he was dressed and rubbing his hair with a towel. He leaned over the loveseat and kissed the top of my head.

"How are you doing, kiddo?"

"I think I'm OK," I said, grabbing his right arm. I pulled it toward me and lightly skimmed his old burn scar, brushing my fingers back and forth over it. Seeing it as I never had before, I gently kissed his forearm.

"We're going to survive this, Dex—you and I. We are going to get through this."

He nodded, circled around, sat down next to me, and eyed my lists.

"I'm making a list of things we need to find. As soon as we have permission, we'll get right in there and salvage what we can."

"I'm assuming the place was insured?"

"Yes, but I don't know what the coverage includes."

"We'll call the insurance agent in the morning, and I'm sure Court can help us with any of the legalese."

"Who would do this? I can't imagine why someone would do this? Do you think there's some crazy arsonist out there? Were we targeted, or some random hit?"

"It's hard to say, but it's another good reason not to disturb anything that could provide clues."

As I continued talking, I got up to throw the wet clothes into the dryer.

"We should visit with Mrs. Pollock, the poor thing looked so distraught and confused. I'll go visit with her tomorrow and make sure she's OK."

"That would be a good thing to do."

"But the first thing I am going to do tomorrow is visit Gilda."

I could see Dex was starting to nod off as I jabbered on. I gave him a nudge.

"Dex, are you ready to go back to the boat?"

"Yeah, I'm falling asleep here."

Leaving the dryer to run, we gathered our things and drove back to the dock.

On board, we headed right for bed. Spooned up against me, Dex immediately drifted off to sleep. However, I was unable to relax. My mind was running at warp speed. I slipped out from under Dex's arm and went up to the main salon. Looking out across the bow, the canal was so calm and peaceful, unlike the turnings of my mind. There was a soft breeze that created fragmented ripples across the water, and the reflected lights coming from the far bank of the canal sparkled as if to say, *"I'm here. You're going to be OK."* I could feel Dan's reassurances all around me. I wrapped my arms around my body as if he were holding me. I could feel him breathing into my hair. I closed my eyes, making sure nothing would interrupt his visit. Peace fell over me, the adrenaline stopped pumping, and my heart slowed. I could hear the water gently lap against the Right Tackle's hull as if he had passed by, stirring it.

And then he was gone.

I poured myself a small glass of wine. Hoping Dan's visitation would help, I sat down at the table to recreate every detail I could recall of his plans. Time was ticking into the wee dawn of morning before I realized I had been working for several hours. I had managed to capture most of what I could remember. The sun would be up soon, and I thought it best to try to get whatever sleep I could.

CHAPTER FIVE

DEX

When I awoke the next morning, I was glad to see the sun shining and Ginny sleeping peacefully next to me. In fact, she was sound asleep. Thinking it best not to wake her, I went up to the galley to see what was available for breakfast. It had been several months since I had had breakfast on board, so all I found was an old can of coffee and that was about it. I decided I would leave Ginny a note and run out to Lloyd's Market to pick up a few provisions. When I went up to the main salon to grab my jacket and keys, I found numerous drawings spread out across the table. It didn't take long to realize they were sketches that Ginny had made, trying to recapture Dan's drawings lost in the fire.

When did she do this? No wonder she's sound asleep.

My heart went out to her. She had not exhibited much emotion . . . only sheer determination. I was wondering if it would crash in on her all at once. I moved quickly. I wanted to be with her if and when it happened.

At Lloyd's I was greeted by an overwhelming wealth of sympathy and encouragement. Everyone in town and around the area knew of the fire and its exact location. That was how we operated in Lewes. Many offered whatever we might need in the way of clothing, materials, and muscle. They asked where we were staying and if we needed meals prepared to get us through the first couple of weeks. Several even asked if Gilda was OK, but no one had seen or heard anything suspicious. Nothing seemed out of the ordinary in their mid-March preparation

338

for summer, that is, until a fire broke out on Bay Avenue.

Back on board, I checked on Ginny. She was still sound asleep, but had obviously tossed and turned while I was gone. As I started back up to the galley, I heard her raspy whisper.

"Dex? Where did you go? I rolled over and you were gone. What time is it?"

I sat down on the edge of the bed.

"I went to get a few things for breakfast. You don't sound very good."

"My throat feels like it's on fire. I must have inhaled more smoke than I thought."

"Can I get you anything?"

"A strong cup of black coffee would be nice," she mewled.

I leaned down to give her a kiss, but she had other things on her mind when she pulled me down into the bed. Her kisses were soft, warm, and deeply sensuous. Breakfast would have to wait. It was my turn to assure her that I would be there for her . . . always.

GINNY

After my first cup of coffee and breakfast on board the Right Tackle, I took a deep breath and decided to call my dad. I had to use Dex's cell phone because somewhere in the middle of it all, I had dropped my purse. Over the course of the next several days, we looked for it, asked around, and reported it missing. It never showed up. I had to cancel and replace everything.

I told my dad of the fire that ignited while we were out celebrating my birthday. I told him about Gilda's escape from the inferno. I let him know that the Sables offered their apartment for as long as I needed. (I intentionally said "I" instead of "we" because I wasn't quite ready to admit that Dex and I were, for all intents and purposes, living together.)

I told my dad how the fire chief believed that the fire was arson. After his gasp, I told him the property had been declared a crime scene, so I had no access to anything that might have been spared. As I expected, my father asked if I needed him to come to Lewes. I assured him that I had enormous amounts of support. He begged me to let him know of anything I needed. After our conversation ended, I realized that I had neglected to tell him about the piano Dex had given me for my birthday. I would have to tell him later, albeit gone. Though I had only played it once, of everything lost in the flames I knew I would miss the piano the most.

My next call was to Susan.

SUSAN

When Ginny called that morning, I was still in my PJs and Derek was in bed dead to the world. I was confused and concerned when Dex's name popped up on caller ID. I had no idea what was about to hit me. After Ginny's initial customary greeting, all I heard was silence, which was eventually broken with words spoken in such a way that I knew the reason for her call was not good.

"I have something to tell you."

"What's up?"

"The beach house burnt to the ground last night?"

"What? Are you OK? What happened? Did everyone make it out?"

"We're all fine. Gilda is at the vet's now, but she's going to be OK, too."

"What happened?"

"The fire chief seems to think it was arson."

"Oh, my gosh! Ginny, who would do that? Do they know who did it?"

"They don't know. There's an investigation going on right now. They hauled us in for questioning last night."

"You?"

"Yes, Dex and me."

"How was Dex with all that, given his past arson acquittal?"

"He seemed pretty calm about it. Our whereabouts checked out, so I don't think they are considering us as suspects."

"Where are you now?"

"We stayed on the Right Tackle last night. However, the Sables have offered us their garage apartment. We're going to take them up on it."

"Were you able to salvage anything?"

"I don't know, yet. They won't let us near the place because it's been declared a crime scene. We're going to head back later today after we visit Gilda."

"How is she?"

Ginny went on to describe the events of the evening and how Gilda saved herself by running through an old thin pane of glass. As she continued, I began to get a better picture of how awful it must have been for all of them and what she might have been coping with.

"Ginny, when Derek wakes up, we'll come down and help."

"Well, call first. I don't know if there's anything that can be done right now. I don't know when they are going to let us back on the property."

"OK, you need to let me know as soon as it makes sense for us to come down and help."

Derek slept in that morning. He did that every now and then. When he finally came downstairs, it was almost noon. I didn't know whether to make breakfast or lunch. Our schedule could be pretty hectic at times, but this threw me way off. I studied him to see how he was going to work through the late start to his day. I didn't know what mood I would find him in, and I didn't want to drop the news about the Carter beach house until I was sure he was ready for it. Somehow, I knew it was going to be a bomb, and he was going to target Ginny, or Dex, or both. I expected him to go into a tirade about how irresponsible the two of them were. He would give me the whole speech about how they shouldn't have been living there in the first place. I envisioned his face turning beet red from escalating blood pressure. I suspected he might pound his fists on the counter and storm out. He had done that before. The more I thought about it, the more I became hesitant to tell him at all, but I knew I had to tell him soon so he would not suspect me of hiding things from him. He would eventually hear about it anyway.

To my surprise, all of my preparations to break it to him gently were for naught. Derek received it relatively well. He was shocked and angry; however, a shitstorm fueled by his prejudice toward them never came. In fact, when I suggested we make the trip down to help out for a day or two, he responded by saying he thought it was a good idea. I was so relieved. I was fearful he would lash out at Dex, as he had in the past. I was afraid he wouldn't permit me to go be with Ginny, as he often did. Instead, he suggested we leave for Lewes the next morning.

Ginny called later that evening and said there was nothing that could be done for several more days. She asked that we wait until things settled down. She sounded strong, so I waited for her call, and surprisingly, so did Derek.

Her call came two days later. Derek made the trip with me.

DEX

Two days later, we were able to bring Gilda home and allowed back on the property. The wonderful place known as "the Carter Beach House" had been leveled to nothing but a charred mess. I thought about all it had witnessed through the years and why it was so special to several generations of Carters. Now, it would never be the same.

Dylan came down to Lewes to help. He arrived on site shortly after we did, around 10:00. We had just arrived after picking up Gilda from the vet and letting her out of the Jeep. We were curious as to how she would react. The vet techs at the Savannah Veterinary Hospital had fawned over her, giving her a good bath and spa treatment. However, Gilda managed to undo all of their fine work within five minutes. At first, she gingerly stepped toward the ruin. Her nose twitched at the assault of acrid smoke still hanging heavy in the air. She seemed unsure of the dangers that might still be present around the shell of a house that had held her captive during the blaze. She seemed to recall what had happened to her. However, it was not long before she cautiously joined Ginny and me as we culled through some of the surface remnants. Finally, Gilda was happiest when she received Ginny's permission to dig. Her paws and nose turned black and her glossy fur coat dulled, turning a sickly looking yellow-gray. She sneezed frequently as she hunted.

Derek and Susan arrived shortly after 10:30. Derek jumped out of his Explorer, adjusting the narrow waist of his jeans while scanning the devastation. He walked right up to the mess and curtly said his hellos, sorry for our loss, and began surveying the area. Susan, on the other hand, was a complete mess. She sat in their Explorer a few minutes longer. When she slowly emerged, her shock was visible as she tried to process what had happened. She was probably unaware of her chanting, "Oh, my God . . . oh, my

God," over and over under her breath. I watched her as she slowly made her way around the outline of the house that once stood. Noting his movements, I kept Derek in the corner of my eye. Susan was in tears. Derek was annoyed. Susan walked slowly around the ruin and eventually intercepted Ginny, who was standing on the far end of the property with Gilda, who was still excavating.

"Who would do such a thing?" Susan asked.

"You guys have any leads on who did this?" Derek asked sternly.

"No, it's still under investigation. They don't have much to go on." I didn't have much information to give him.

"Well, they probably won't have to look far to find him," Derek remarked.

""What are you suggesting?" Ginny snarled.

Is she looking for a fight?

"Look, Ginny, if you think I'm suggesting Dex is an arsonist, well, it just doesn't matter because he was acquitted and you two were out to dinner at the Buttery, anyway." Derek fired back.

"I never mentioned Dex. You did. I never said we were out to dinner. You did," Ginny shot back at him, trying to corner him into what, I was not sure.

I intervened. "This is not helpful. Let's move on."

Ginny excused herself, saying that she was going to take Gilda for a walk up the beach. Susan went with her.

SUSAN

The house was gone. It had literally burnt to the ground. I could only imagine how fierce the fire had been. With its old wood construction, it must have been a large unforgiving inferno, consuming everything in its path. Just as intensely, Ginny and Derek began nipping at each other. Ginny turned and left for the beach. I went after her.

Catching up, I had no magic words to offer, so I continued to walk with her in silence. I could feel Ginny's anger.

The beach was empty. Half way between the Children's Beach House and what used to be their home, Ginny stopped and sat down in the sand. In the past, I would have slid right in beside her. That day, I felt like I needed permission to enter her personal space.

"Can I sit down next to you?"

"Sure."

We sat in silence. The tide was out and the waves kept rolling onto shore with the same regularity since the beginning of time. The sea gulls were gliding over the water, letting out an occasional call just like it was another ordinary day. Eaten by the voracious flames, no longer was the house or its charred timbers in sight. Cape May was faintly visible on the horizon. The Cape May–Lewes Ferry was beginning to make another crossing. Everything was so familiar except for the small gaping hole in the coastline. We were in new territory.

"Susan, how did Derek know we were out to dinner at the Buttery? Not even you knew that. I don't remember telling you that part."

"Maybe it was in the newspapers, or online? I don't know. Derek reads all that stuff when he becomes obsessed."

"Perhaps. I wish he would give Dex and me just one

break."

"I'm sorry, Ginny. I really don't know what's come over him."

"Do you think someone wanted to kill us? It was obvious the house was occupied. If it was an arsonist, why not set fire to a vacant house? Someone wanted to hurt or even kill us."

"Is it possible Dex has any enemies down here that would want to hurt him?"

"Then why not go after the Right Tackle?"

"Does he have a furious old girlfriend you don't know about? Maybe you should ask him."

DEX

Armed with shovels, picks, heavy gloves, and facemasks, Derek, Dylan, and I went to work. Not wanting to break something that might have been spared beneath the rubble, we stepped carefully. The only thing worse than inhaling smoke was inhaling the damp dust from two day-old ashes. It was heavy, rank, and burnt as it stuck to the back of our throats and seemingly clogged our lungs. Mixed with the moist ocean spray, the ash and dust crept into any space available between our skin and clothes.

Once back from her walk, Ginny would not relent, no matter how many times I suggested that she take a break. Though trying to stifle her emotions, it was easy to see that she was angry and determined. I watched as she searched for photographs, jewelry, and other keepsakes. The rockers that Dylan had built were gone; they had become part of the ash. She stood over the burned out hulk of a piano that was priceless to her . . . and me, for that matter. About all that was left of it was the brass plate, gnarled strings, and scorched pedals. She stared as if lost in time. Two days ago, she played songs that were a reflection of her. Now, the music had gone silent, and Ginny was without words in her exasperation.

We worked until dark. Once the sun sank below the horizon, Ginny had no choice but to give up. We finally loaded up our little family into the truck and headed for our temporary quarters. It was time to introduce Gilda to her new digs and settle in. Dylan left with Courtney. Susan and Derek went over to the Rodney where they were staying the night. We offered to take everyone out to dinner, but they declined. We instead agreed to meet up at Irish Eyes, around eight, for a nightcap.

Ginny was quiet on the ride back to the garage apartment. Before going inside, we bathed Gilda with the outdoor hose. We stripped off our clothes once more and ran up the stairs in our underwear. Ginny showered first and then went straight to bed. It was the first time I had felt closed out and totally alone in her presence.

I caught up with the others at eight. We ordered appetizers to munch on and a pitcher of beer. We didn't have much to say as we pretended to watch the game on a large screen TV over the bar. Something was smoldering, somewhere.

CHAPTER SIX

GINNY
Four Months Later: July

Dan's former employer recreated and sealed the plans for us. Courtney helped us obtain the few variances needed to enlarge the footprint. The construction firm Dex worked for was contracted to run the job, so Dex was there every day. After the property was cleared of debris, the dozers that lifted everything to be hauled away were used to push sand and level the site. We felt like we were finally moving forward when they had dug and planted the pilings. That was the part Gilda liked the best. She wanted to help in the worst way. It was hard for her to understand that her area of expertise was not needed, so I had to keep her on a leash. I was sure, in her golden retriever mind, the large heavy pilings were sticks from heaven sent just for her!

Once the pilings were set and approved, the framework went up quickly. It was a young girl's fantasy to go over to the job site and watch the men work. Under the hot sun, their shirts were off and tan backs exposed. Cut off jeans, work boots, sometimes work gloves, and hard hats were the crew's appropriate attire. Being the property owner, I had every right to stand by and watch as long as I needed. Women of all ages, and sometimes men, walked by slowly to observe, trying to be discreet about their interests, whatever they may be. For me, it was watching Dex. It really surprised me that his boss assigned him to manage this particular job. Even Courtney said it was a conflict of interest and bordered on being unethical. However, Dex seemed to be earning the community's admiration. He was tough and demanding. He commanded the respect of his crew, the architect, and the subcontractors. He had a way of making sure everything went according to schedule and arrived on time. He knew how to synchronize the progress of each phase so that crews and machinery were not sitting around waiting for someone else to finish up or make delivery. Dex knew how to negotiate changes that needed to be made by the architect and subcontractors in order to comply with building codes and best practices, and he knew how to keep my expectations in check.

I watched him as he moved around the site, directing his men and working alongside them. What once was our Friday date-night became their private TGIF happy hour. While I had every right to be on the site, I was not allowed to join them for that weekly event. For as hard as they worked under the hot July sun, I could only imagine how hard they "played" at the bar and under the roof of the Irish Eyes deck.

By August, we were under roof. Electricity and plumbing were in, inspected, and approved. Drywall, windows, and doors were on their way. Everything was three-dimensional and the house looked even bigger than it appeared on paper. The plans were becoming tattered and worn. My goal at the end was to have everyone I could find that worked on the house sign the plans, and then have the pages framed.

I was so excited about the house, and I was so in love with Dex. I learned so much watching him work, and I listened at night as he explained the day's progress and the expectations going forward. It certainly was not all roses for him. Not by a long shot. He had several huge hurdles and challenges that had to be met and resolved while keeping the project on schedule. The worst may have been when one of the trucks arrived from one of the mills. Dex was very unhappy with the condition of the lumber. He said he regretted not having gone to the yard and selecting the 2x12 beams himself. When he called the lumberyard, they suggested he go through the delivery and select what he wanted to keep and to send back what ever he rejected. One look at the load on the truck, estimating the time it would cost him to unload and reload, he sent the entire order back and called another lumberyard. This time, he made the trip to inspect and select the lumber himself. No more surprises. It arrived on site the next day. Even I could see the difference. To Dex, the savings were huge. The project stayed on track.

Another time the plumber had missed a measurement by an inch. Dex said it would affect everything down the line. Concrete was due in two days, and he didn't want to risk that delivery being pushed back. Dex said that once a job falls behind, it's like an exponential domino effect. He made the plumber and his crew come back that night to fix the problem.

Dex was very mindful of the budget, too. We tried to build everything into the plans up front. He said anything that added one hundred dollars to the original plan would add five hundred to a thousand dollars in extra costs if amended later. He said it was not a case of being ripped off, either. He said additions and adjustments cost time, and each came with a verifiable price tag. However, we still made a few upgrades along the way. Once the house took shape, my vision became clearer. There were several additions I needed to make so the dream would become a reality. Dex, after a long day's work, was very patient with me as he steered me through the decision-making process.

One evening we did come to a battle of wills between the property owner and the construction manager. After the windows were installed, I decided I didn't like the ones I originally chose for over the Jacuzzi in the master bath. I decided I really wanted glass blocks so I would never have to close a curtain or worry about some pervert up the coast with a telescope. The window installers had left the site, as in "they're not coming back," Dex scoffed. Insulation and siding were already completed on that side of the structure. Dex said to make that change would be very time consuming and expensive. For the sake of my paranoia and privacy, I was willing to pay the price. He then reiterated the amount of time it would cost and how far it would knock the project off schedule. I was not readily buying it. However, as he had repeated for my benefit several times, those subcontractors were done and gone. Floors, painting, and installation of appliances had begun.

I was very unhappy. He was very tired.

Dex slept on the Right Tackle that night. He said he needed his rest. I think he needed to get away from the whole project. I believe, most of all, he needed to get away from me.

The next morning, I had his coffee, bagel, and bacon ready. As soon as he arrived, I planned to fry up his eggs just the way he liked them. But, he never showed. He didn't call. Alone in that small apartment above the Sable's garage, I began to realize how shallow and spoiled I had acted. I recalled Dex saying it would be best to finish the job, come back later, and install new windows. He had suggested that I should first give what was there a try. I knew he was right. I had picked it out; I should live with it for a while before jumping ship. Ugh, I had become my mother. I drove to the work site to apologize.

Of course, I had to hear it from his crew when I arrived. I knew they loved me, and I was used to their banter, except this time I was a little raw around the edges and knew their sarcasm was pretty much a bull's eye. They meant no harm, but I was in a vulnerable state.

"Hey, Dex, your girlfriend's here!"

"La-dee-da," they seemed to be singing.

Dex strolled over. He was not his usual "so-happy-to-see-you" or "you-came-at-the-right-time" self. He looked more annoyed than ever. He offered no hug. He barely looked at me. I had obviously stopped at a bad time. Maybe I was the "bad time." I wanted to turn and run, but it was too late.

"Ginny?"

"Look, Dex . . ."

"Please don't start. The day is not going well. The flooring for the kitchen and the baths was sent to the wrong address. It took them all morning to locate the shipment and admit their error. Outside of incompetence, I don't know how that happens." He lifted his hat and combed his fingers back through his sweat-dampened hair. Already the morning heat and humidity were promising a very steamy day. "So, we will lose about two days. I had to call and push back the cabinets."

He was not making eye contact. His eyes were scanning the site as he continued.

"I lost the morning and two days on that one issue alone. But that wasn't enough. One of my guys fell down a flight of stairs when he was carrying light fixtures up to the third floor. I lost another guy because he had to drive the first guy to Beebe Hospital while I was arguing with the flooring company. And now you want me to replace the windows over your precious Jacuzzi."

"DEX, forget the damn windows. Forget the floors. Forget it all if you want. I don't want to fight with you."

He didn't respond. Even his body had pivoted slightly away from me.

I turned and walked back to the Jeep.

The worksite had quieted, except for one guy in the back part of the house hammering away at something. Everyone else had witnessed it all. As I was l pulling out, two guys were returning from Beebe Hospital in Dex's truck.

"Hey, Ginny! How's everything looking today?" they asked. They didn't have a clue. I couldn't look at them. I was afraid the tears welling up in my eyes would spill down my face.

I drove back to the apartment. Gilda was disappointed. She had had her heart set on cruising the worksite for the better part of the day and playing catch on the beach while we waited for Dex to finish up. When I pulled into the Sable's drive, Gilda didn't even bother to pick up her head and look out the window. I was beginning to hate that apartment. I was feeling trapped. Trapped in what was supposed to be my sanctuary until our dream house was completed.

I grabbed a book and sat on the small balcony to read. It was too hot to sit in the sun. I thought of Dex working in the heat. I hoped he was staying hydrated. I went inside and began cleaning. I was reminded that Dex had not spent the night there. His toothbrush, toothpaste, shampoo, and soap were gone from the bathroom.

Normally, I would have stood my ground, but this time I had to be big enough to admit my mistake. Around 4:00, I called Courtney and asked what she was doing after work. She sounded surprised to hear my voice on the other end of the phone and even more surprised to hear me ask if she would like to meet for a beer after she had finished for the day. She said she needed about a half hour and she would meet me at Irish Eyes.

"Oh, not there. I think I'd like to meet someplace different. How about The Lighthouse?"

"Uh . . . sure. See you in half an hour."

"OK, thanks. I'll see you then."

COURTNEY

Well, that was different. It was the first time Ginny had called and asked me to join her for happy hour, just the two of us. Sadly, it smacked of the time Dex called when he was questioning their relationship.

Just as I was about to leave the office, Dylan called.

"Hey gorgeous! How was your day?"

"Just peachy. Yours?"

"Same."

"Do you have plans for the weekend?"

"The entire weekend?"

"Yes, the entire weekend."

"Uh . . . let me look." I put him on hold. I knew darn well I had no plans. I just didn't want him to know that. After a sufficient amount of time had passed, I came back on the line.

"It looks open for the most part. Why?"

He started stammering. Though I couldn't see him, I could tell he was nervous about asking me whatever it was he wanted to ask.

This must be big . . .

"Well, I finished an order of custom cabinets for a vacation home in the Poconos. My client loves the finished product, but now he wants to know if I would do the installation."

"Oh . . . and . . . ?" I knew this was painfully stressful for him, but either he was going to ask me as if he meant it, or I was not going along.

"Well, it's beautiful in the mountains. There's lots to do, like hiking, sailing, canoeing . . . It should take us most of Saturday to install the cabinets and then we'll have the use of the cabin for the remainder of the weekend and into next week, if we want."

"Oh, that sounds nice!"

"Well, would you like to come along?"

"To help you install the cabinets?"

"Well, no. Derek is going to help me with the cabinets. Susan is coming along, too."

"Oh. When are you leaving?"

"Friday, as soon as you arrive at my house."

"Sounds good."

"Great."

"I have to go. I'm meeting your crazy sister-in-law."

"Really?"

"Yeah. She wants to meet me for happy hour, at The Lighthouse, no less."

"Sounds like there's trouble in paradise."

"Could be . . . We'll see. I know Dex is flippin' crazy about her."

"Well, work your magic!"

A weekend with Dylan . . . We rarely had a moment alone. It had been virtually impossible to develop any kind of relationship with everything that was swirling around us. I wanted to burst! I knew I had to conceal my excitement from Ginny. I was afraid to speak of it. It could jinx the whole weekend.

At the time it seemed ironic how Derek was willing to go to the Poconos to help with that job, when he did everything possible to avoid time with Dex and Dylan in Lewes. I thought it would be best if Dex didn't know about the Pocono plans. He would be hurt.

I met Ginny at The Lighthouse, at 5:00.

"Hey, Courtney, thanks for meeting me."

"Sure. Though, it's not like you and I do this every week. In fact, we've never done this."

My tact, or lack thereof, was showing. It was any wonder I did not have any really close girl friends.

What is wrong with me?

"I know, Courtney. I'm sorry. It's just . . . well, I'm not very good at all the mingling and social stuff."

"Come on, Ginny, you were raised in Darien, the Gold Coast, for Christ sakes. Who are you kidding?"

"Well, quite frankly, I'm intimidated by you."

"Whaaaat? I am about the most socially inept person you will ever meet. You, on the other hand, you know how to engage everyone you meet."

"I just have trouble initiating things."

The small talk was unproductive and quite boring. It was time to move on.

"Well, we're here now, aren't we? What's up?"

"Courtney, I need your help."

"It's Dex, isn't it?"

"Is it that obvious?"

"Why else would you call me?"

"OK, yes and no. We had a spat and he elected to stay on the Right Tackle last night. How's that?"

"Oh . . . ?"

"I went to see him on the building site today, but he really didn't want to see me."

Ginny continued to pour out her heart, and all I could think about were the possibilities of a weekend with Dylan. Although, the thought of Dex being back on the market . . .

Get a grip, Court.

"Ginny, did you know that Dex and I had a meeting just like this several months ago?"

"You did?"

"Yes, the two of you were arguing. About what, I can't remember. All I can tell you is that he adores you. Why don't you give him some time? I can imagine this job with your house is quite stressful. Whether he'll admit it, or not, he can never get away from it. Never. And that explains why he stayed on the Right Tackle last night and may need to for a while. Frankly, I'm surprised it hasn't happened sooner."

"So, *I'm* the problem?"

"No. *You're* the one he cares about. Trying to please you is *his* problem."

"Oh, so I demand too much."

"No. He cares too much. Once again, it's *his* problem."

Why was I never Dex's problem?

GINNY

After leaving The Lighthouse, I looked to my left where the Right Tackle was just visible through the buildings and other boats. The cabin lights were on and everything seemed to be buttoned down. My heart sank. It probably meant that Dex would not be spending the night with me, and I would have to ride out at least one more night alone. With hopes of catching just one glimpse of him, I never took my eyes off his boat as I hopped into the Jeep. Driving back to the garage apartment in a mental fog, I tried to recall what food was there so I could rustle up a dinner for one.

As I pulled into the Sable's drive, Gilda raced out to greet me.

Oh, my God, I must have left her outside while I was gone. I am really falling apart. It's a good thing Dex didn't see that; it would have topped off his day.

I gave Gilda a huge hug around the neck and roughed her up a bit.

At least someone's glad to see me.

Gilda trotted alongside me as I approached the steps, then rudely butted her way to the front before I could begin my ascent. Acutely aware of my indefinite isolation, my dejected feet weighed a ton and each step became a major effort.

On the top landing was a pair of work boots, and standing in those boots was the man I so desperately needed to see. Not sure what his visit was about, I braced myself for the worst.

What if he's going to tell me that he wants off the job? That's one thing. If he wants out of our relationship, I will die a thousand deaths before the night is over.

He was looking down at his feet. As he lifted his head, he took a deep breath.

Oh, God, here it comes . . .

He looked at me with deep sadness in his eyes.

"Ginny, this is too hard. I can't get away from you or even the thought of you. I'm drowning."

"Dex, I . . ."

"Let me finish. When you are not a part of my day, when I am fighting to keep you at arms length, I'm miserable. I'm lost and find it impossible to focus. When I have you to look forward to, everything stays on target. I miss you terribly."

He isn't leaving me . . . I don't think.

I stood up on my tiptoes and kissed him. He lifted me up onto the landing, never losing the touch of his lips pressed into mine. It felt like it had been a lifetime. I kissed him like it might be my last and I would want to remember it forever. Dex set my feet on the landing and signaled his invitation to join him in private quarters. We let Gilda inside, and once the door was closed and locked behind us, Dex carried me into the bedroom.

His lovemaking was gentle, sweet, and attentive. He moved over me with slow even strokes that elevated me quickly. I tried to wait which only served to increase the intensity of the inevitable. Dex knew, and spared me no mercy, bringing wave after wave. He then let go in a way that spoke of his own relief that we were there, together. We stayed tangled and connected in our moment of serenity. I don't remember falling asleep, but when I awoke, he was still wrapped around me. I was starved and knew he would be, too.

Gilda was overdue for her supper. As I untangled myself from Dex's clutches and climbed out of bed, Gilda began wagging her tail. Stumbling out to the kitchen, I found her food bowl in its usual spot by the kitchen door. I ladled in two cups of food and added a few extra treats because she had been such a good and patient girl, unlike her "mother."

When Dex finally woke up, I threw his pants at him, hitting him square in his sleepy head.

"Come on, you're taking me out to dinner."

DYLAN

The cabinets were loaded and secured in the truck. I double-checked the shop to make sure all of the pieces were on board as well as the tools I would need to get the job done. I gave the driver directions and sent him on his way. The owner of the cabin, Mr. Robert Kampler, was to meet the truck on the other end. He said he would insure that the cabinets were unloaded into the dining hall before leaving.

Courtney arrived at my house around 6:30, looking relaxed and ready to enjoy a weekend away. I wasn't sure that I could ever be that relaxed, especially around her. Just the thought of her kicked my inclinations into overdrive. The realization that I would actually be alone with her for the weekend had my adrenaline infused testosterone pumping out of control. If I had been a teenager, I'm sure my face would have broken out from the super concentrated mixture of everything that made a young man dream his dreams and cause his pulse to race. Trying to make sure I did nothing to embarrass myself, I was keenly aware of every move I made.

Settle down, Dylan. She's just a girl. She could be your big sister.
Ok, that little lecture didn't help.
She's smart, beautiful, sometimes funny, and sometimes without mercy.

Sometimes, when we were boys, we would get our kicks by daring each other to test the limits. We wanted to see how clever we could be and how much we could get away with. This was nothing like that. No one was pushing me or taunting me; I had dared to believe and the possible actualization of my dream was definitely taking me out of my comfort zone.

The little talk I was having with myself was not really helping. I was floating high without a flight plan or a parachute.

How do I land this thing?

She has undone me.

Courtney packed light. She came carrying one duffle bag, which really surprised me. I had expected that she would bring at least one large piece of luggage for her clothes, another for shoes, and another for whatever products she would want to care for her beautiful skin and hair. I had greatly miscalculated. Instead, she had one duffle bag and a coat. I had packed no more and no less than she.

She asked to see the cabinets I had built.

"They're already in transit. In fact, if we get on the road, we may even pass them on the way."

"Really?"

"Yep. Let me close up the shop and lock down the house."

On my way out, I swung her duffle bag over my shoulder and grabbed mine off the floor. I took one final look around to make sure nothing was left behind, and locked the doors.

"What about your tools? Aren't you taking any tools?"

"They're gone. Loaded onto the truck with the cabinets."

"So that's all you have is the one duffle bag?"

"Yep."

"Then let's take the Porsche. We'll leave the top down and you can drive."

As always, she had hit a soft spot. Her car was such a blast to drive, so much more than my truck. She treated it like a newborn kitten and drove it like a fast, agile cat, which was so appropriate because there were few things on earth that purred sweeter than her wheels.

When I opened the trunk to throw in our bags, I also

noted that she had packed a couple bottles of wine and a small cooler that she said contained a six-pack and a variety of cheeses. Once again, she had thought of everything, and we were on our way to something good. Pulling out of my drive, Courtney was all smiles as we headed north on Route 82. The direction I chose would probably add another fifteen minutes to our trip, but I thought she might appreciate the scenery if we cruised through the rolling hills of Southern Chester County, rather than the interstates.

With the top down, keeping a conversation going was not a requisite. We simply enjoyed each other's company as we drove north toward the mountains.

Watching the sun as it set in the west while we headed north, the sky turned a fiery orange and red.

Red sky at night, sailor's delight . . .

Courtney took out a camera and snapped pictures of the sunset. She snapped pictures of me driving her car. She leaned in and snapped a picture of the both of us. I continued to drive with my eyes on the road. She was completely at ease and seemed to be having a good time.

It was going to be a great weekend. I allowed my defenses to drop slightly. After dusk faded to dark, a tunnel through a mountain later, and up a long dirt drive, we had finally arrived at the cabin.

"What are all these cars doing here?" I whispered, thinking aloud.

Derek's Explorer was one of four cars parked in front of the house. That was the only vehicle I had expected to see there.

Derek didn't ask if he could bring friends. What's going on here?

Courtney was silent. The cabin was lit up like a Christmas tree and it didn't take long to realize that it was full of people, too.

"Dylan, let's put the top up before we go inside, OK?" Courtney calmly asked, trying to take my mind off of my apparent state of shock.

"Huh...? Oh yeah. OK." This was not what I had expected. And worse yet, as we raised the convertible top, I heard the squealing of children's voices coming from inside. It was definitely not what I had expected.

COURTNEY

Dylan neglected to tell me that the house would be full of people, and small children, no less. Do not misunderstand me; I enjoy children. I love to play and interact with them because it makes me feel young again. I just don't have many opportunities to do so. I had no nieces or nephews, so I only encountered ankle-biters, little shavers, and teenyboppers when I was visiting someone else that had them, which was almost never. Anyway, this was not how Dylan had billed the weekend, and it definitely was not what I had expected.

Dylan looked rattled. He took my hand and suggested that we go in and meet everyone. There was an "I'm sorry," in there somewhere, too. We walked up the front steps and as we stood on the expansive front porch, ready to use the doorknocker, the front door flew open. A very handsome, though slightly overweight, jovial man greeted us.

"Dylan!" he yelled. "You finally made it! I was afraid you were going to stick us with all of these cabinets, though it was generous of you to send along your brother and all of your tools! And who is this lovely young lady you've brought with you?" he asked, pointing his drink in my direction.

"Oh, this is a very good friend of mine, Courtney Sable." Then Dylan turned to me with a look of fear in his eyes.

"Courtney, this is Rob Kampler. He owns this Pocono

retreat and is now the proud owner of my custom cabinets."

"Pleasure meeting you," I said, proffering a friendly handshake.

He, instead, took my hand, turned it over, and laid a wet smackeroo kiss on the back of it.

Yuuuuuccckk...

"Believe me, the pleasure is all mine." He turned his chauvinistic eyes toward Dylan. "Whoa, Dylan." And he winked at him. I guess that was his thumbs up.

Creepy Bastard. I don't care if he owns this whole mountain, this guy is skeeving me out.

"Mr. Kampler, I'm sorry I didn't tell you about Derek and Susan coming along, but I need Derek to help me hang the cabinets. Of course, his wife wanted to come with him. I just didn't realize..."

Kampler cut Dylan off.

"Dylan, my boy, don't worry about it. The more the merrier! Come on in and meet everyone."

Mr. "Please-Call-Me-Rob" Kampler escorted us into a large family room and introduced us to everyone: his wife, Gillian; his daughters Margot, 6; Juliet, 8; and Sienna, 10. He introduced us to his brother, Marc, and Marc's wife, Laura. Marc and Laura had three boys: Hunter, 10; Michael, 14; and Joshua, 18. He then introduced us to Gillian's younger sister, Cindy, and Cindy's newborn, Kira. Derek and Susan were buried in the middle of the pack, looking rather perplexed.

Dylan was quite shell shocked, and I was sure he was playing over and over in his mind how he could have gotten it so terribly wrong. He was shook up, but he did what any good socially skilled person would have done, especially when he was introduced to the baby.

"She's really cute!" he said to Cindy.

"Oh, why then, she's all yours," exclaimed proud Mama

Cindy as she handed her bouncing baby over to Dylan.

Now it appeared that Dylan had never held a baby before in his life. He looked over at me, and it was all I could do to contain myself.

He did his best to entertain Kira, who was pulling at his nose and trying to put her fingers in his mouth. That was when Rob Kampler asked me to help him at the bar. He was sure Dylan and I could use a drink after our long drive. I saw that Derek and Susan were already working on theirs. I wondered how long they had been there.

Mr. Kampler escorted me into the bar area. From there, I realized that the place was not a cabin at all. It was more of a lodge. From the bar, I could see into the dining hall. In the center was a long trestle table that had to accommodate at least thirty people. On the floor, lining the perimeter of the room were the cabinets that Dylan had built for the kitchen. They were beautiful. They were finished pine, which is not an expensive wood; however, it was a perfect fit with the rustic ambiance of the lodge. Unconsciously, I drifted into the dining hall to get a closer look. As I walked past each piece, I brushed my hand across it as if it were possible to connect with the man that had crafted the handsome cabinetry.

"They are perfect, don't you agree?" Rob whispered close to my ear as he handed me a glass of wine. He had sneaked up behind me and caught me fondling Dylan's craftsmanship. I stepped away from him.

"I knew Dylan was good. I just didn't realize how good," I admitted. "When did he do all this?" I asked, remaining civil.

"Oh, I'd say he's been at it for about a year now. We invited him up to take a look at the kitchen two or three years ago. I think it was just before his father had passed away. It took a while to get him to sign on, but we were patient. After visiting and checking references for several other woodworkers, we decided it had to be Dylan if we were going to go through the expense of custom built cabinets."

"I see."

Mr. Kampler followed me around the cabinets and moved in a little too close for my comfort. He was in my personal space, something that made me very uncomfortable. Hoping I could make a polite escape, I looked back to the doorway through which I had entered the dining hall. A handsome young man holding a baby girl was blocking my emergency exit. He was watching me admire his work while the baby girl was just as content as could be. Visions of what a good father Dylan would make flashed before me. He was looking at me as if I was the only thing that mattered and my approval of his work was satisfying to him. Stronger yet was the contentment of the child in his arms and how natural he looked holding her. How I had hoped, at that moment, it was my future looking back at me.

"Follow me into the kitchen, and I'll walk you through our vision," Mr. Kampler said, interrupting my reverie. His wife, Gillian, joined us, linking her arm through Mr. Kampler's. She turned back and glared at me.

Did I just detect something?

Something was not sitting right. Mrs. Kampler was acting like she had just cut in on my dance. But, he was the one circling, making all of the advances, and I wanted no part of it, in case she had not noticed. How could I have been so naïve? That man was on the prowl, with Dylan and his wife right there, no less. My skin crawled.

"Dylan, would you show me the kitchen?" I asked, taking baby Kira from his arms, thinking she would provide the perfect shield from the likes of Mr. Kampler and the warning scowls of his wife. However, Kira was having none of it. She wanted to go right back to Dylan. With her arms outstretched in his direction, she started with a whimper that was quickly escalating. I handed her back immediately.

"Come on, stick with me. I'll show you everything," Dylan invited. *Thank God.*

DYLAN

I had had no idea that Rob and his family were going to stay for the weekend. He had neglected to communicate that one major revision in his plans, which also greatly modified the invitation he had extended to me, and I to Courtney, Derek, and Susan. Derek and Susan seemed to be adjusting just fine. Courtney was holding her own, and I was left holding the baby, literally.

With the cabinets delivered and our being there to install them, I kept hoping that everyone else would go home. However, that was just plain foolishness because it was closing in on midnight. Perhaps they would pack up and leave in the morning.

Now that "Uncle Dylan and Aunt Courtney" had finally arrived, the younger girls began dropping like flies. (Thank God, Court didn't seem to mind the children referring to her with such familiarity.) One by one they were being whisked off to their beds, and I began to wonder where the four of us were going to sleep. I had not seen the rest of the lodge. It was then that I wished I had snooped around when I had visited to measure the kitchen a year ago.

"Well, we didn't realize you were bringing guests, Dylan," Gillian groused, failing to conceal her agitation. "Derek and Susan, we will put you in the room at the top of the stairs. It has a king size bed and private bath, so you should be comfortable there."

"Now, Dylan, about you and Courtney . . . let's see . . ."

Their curious pubescent eighteen-year-old nephew, Joshua, became all ears. He wanted to hear if his aunt and uncle were going to tolerate or even play along with the more liberal views of my generation. Their ruling on our sleeping arrangements could have an impact on his highly anticipated future. A precedent was about to be set—or not. Little did he know that as of that date, Courtney and I

were still sitting the bench in separate dugouts, and the
game had been called on account of rain.

"I think we will have to put Aunt Courtney in with
Sienna," Gillian recommended. "I mean, you and Courtney
are just good friends, right?"

"Oh, yes, we're not like . . ."

Come on, Courtney . . . jump in here and save my ass!

Courtney remained silent.

"Yes, that will be fine, right Court?" I tried to redirect
Gillian's question.

"Of course!" Courtney responded happily. "As a matter
of fact, I'm very tired. I think I'll turn in now, if that's OK."

Joshua's face sank. Game over.

Courtney said goodnight to everyone and was on her
way upstairs with Sienna leading the way and talking a mile
a minute.

I think I just lost my "best friend" to a ten year old.

"Don't forget to show Aunt Courtney where the sheets,
pillows, and blankets are. And, for God's sake, don't keep
her up all night with your chattering!" Gillian yelled up
behind them.

That was the last time I saw Courtney until the next
morning. Oddly enough, and somewhat worrisome, she
seemed to be enjoying all of it.

COURTNEY

I woke up Saturday morning with the bright sun streaming through breezy pink sheers. The faint aroma of coffee was wafting through the air. The door blew open and there was Sienna holding a steamy mug just for me.

"Good morning, Aunt Courtney!" Sienna sounded so excited to see me awake. "Uncle Dylan said you drink strong coffee. How does he know that?"

"Oh, he's a good guesser, I suppose."

"Is he your boyfriend?"

"Uh, no."

"Don't you like him?"

"Oh, of course I do."

"Do you want to marry him?"

"Uh ... not really. He's like my brother."

"Oh, like I'm the big sister?"

"Exactly. I am like Uncle Dylan's big sister."

Great ...

"Does he have a girlfriend?"

"I don't know. Why don't you go and ask him?"

"No way. I'm not going to ask him. He's way too cute."

"That doesn't mean you can't ask him."

"Sure it does. He might think I like him."

"Oh, and do you? Do you want to marry him, Miss Sienna?"

"Eeeeewwwww ... nooooooo! He's a boy!"

Sienna told me about her friends at school. She told me that she could run faster than all the boys in her class. She said she's taller than her fourth grade teacher. She also mentioned that she wanted to be an artist one day.

"Oh! That's impressive. What do you like to draw?"

"Mostly people and animals."

"Oh, I'll bet there are plenty of subjects around here to draw."

In the morning light, I could see there was not another cabin or lodge in view from her window. The trees on the far ridge looked like broccoli. Shadows of clouds waltzed across their heads.

"What do you guys do up here?" I asked. Sitting up in bed, I sipped my coffee.

"Not much."

"Do you go hiking?"

"My dad won't let me hike the trail along the ridge unless he's with me, but he's always got this or that project to do. He says he'll take me after he's finished. But *after* never comes."

"What about your mother?"

"My mother? She always says she didn't bring the right shoes for hiking."

"Ohhh . . . I'll take you hiking, if that's all right with your parents."

"You would! Oh, yay! Let's go ask."

DYLAN

That night, I stayed in the one remaining empty guest room. As far as I could tell, that house had eight bedrooms and eight and a half baths. Once things settled down, it got very quiet. Still, I couldn't sleep. I was worried about Courtney and how the weekend was not living up to the billing I had given it. Talk about crash and burn. My fear was that Courtney would see it as bait and switch, or worse yet, that this was my idea of a weekend getaway or a good time. "How lame," she would probably think.

Maybe she is thoroughly repulsed by me, which would explain why she is spending all of her time with Sienna.

Saturday morning I got up with the sun. I was hoping that if I knocked out the kitchen early in the day, perhaps everyone would go home. On the other hand, it was a big job that could lead to future work and a good reference, so I wanted it to go well. The countertops were scheduled to be installed on Monday, so I had to get the cabinets in that weekend. It was time to worry less about Courtney and focus more on why I was called to be there in the first place.

While half the house was still sleeping, I began snapping lines and moving cabinets into place. After I had moved several, Sienna came bouncing into the kitchen.

"Hi, Uncle Dylan!"

"Hi, Sienna. What are you doing out of bed? Did Courtney's snoring keep you up last night?"

"No. And how do you know she snores?"

"Uh, I don't, actually. *Sadly, I don't.* Just a lucky guess."

"Well, you're wrong. She doesn't snore, but she's still asleep, and I got bored."

"Why don't you wake her up with a nice cup of coffee?"

"Do you think that would be OK?"

"Sure, go ahead. Tell her it's from Uncle Dylan."

"What do I put in it?"

"Nothing, she likes it strong and straight up, just like her ... Oh, never mind. Just tell her it's from me."

"OK." And off she went. The place was so big that I had no way of knowing if Sienna had safely landed that cup of coffee on the right runway, let alone the right airport. I guessed I would find out later.

It wasn't long before Derek came down, poured himself a cup, spread some cream cheese on a bagel, devoured it, and declared he was ready and raring to go.

"Let's get this done," he blurted out. Then he whispered, "I thought you said we would have this place to ourselves. This is like spending the weekend with The Brady Bunch and then some."

"Believe me, I had no idea. How's Susan doing?"

"Oh, she's fine. Sneaking me away from work for a weekend is a major victory for her, no matter the circumstances. She would be happy if the house was filled with chimpanzees."

We decided which wall would be best to start on and then began hanging the overhead cabinets. We put the hammers and drills to work while our conversation continued.

"Yeah, Derek, we've all noticed how much time you put into your work. In many ways, it's admirable how far you've brought your business in such a short period of time, but I'm sure there's a cost. How's Susan doing with all of that?"

I couldn't believe I had just butted my head into his business.

"I know. She's really paid the price. When she begged me to go on this trip, I really couldn't refuse. Little did she know that I had already intended to come up to help you, anyway."

"Hey, thanks! I appreciate it. This part is definitely not a one-man job. I hope you don't mind my asking—even though I think I know the answer: You jumped at the chance to come up here to help me, yet you have refused every invitation to lend a hand or even visit Ginny and Dex at the beach house."

"That's not true. I went down right after the fire. You have to remember, it's hard for me to get away. My business supports twelve other families, now. Competition is tough in advertising. I have to stay ahead of it."

"Unlike mine?"

"No. I know your business is competitive, too. But you own a niche, which, quite frankly, no one can duplicate. I mean, look at these cabinets. They're perfect for this place. No wonder Mr. Kampler waited years for you to come around and take the job. By the way, what took you so long?"

"I don't know."

"Well, I do. You've been spending all of your time in Lewes helping Dex and Ginny. See what I mean? Oh, and there's that little matter of Courtney, too. What's up with you two?"

"Nothing."

"Come on, Dylan. You didn't invite her to this mountain getaway for nothing."

"Seriously, Derek, don't make it sound so . . . whatever. I just like spending time with her."

"Yeah, just like Mr. Kampler liked staring, or more like leering, at her last night."

"Derek, you're treading on thin ice."

We finished hanging the first cabinet and stood back to look. I had to admit, the pine, while I was against it at first, fit beautifully in that huge rustic kitchen. We began prepping for the second section when we noticed Joshua was watching us and listening in on our conversation.

"Eaves dropping is impolite. But if you want in, you've gotta work," I bargained.

I had hoped he didn't just hear the words from Derek's mouth about his dad, and I couldn't believe that an invitation to join us had just come from mine. I probably made the offer thinking that with Joshua around, Derek would think twice about what he was going to say next.

The morning wore on and with Joshua's help, which was not much help at all, we finished hanging the wall cabinets around noon.

Courtney and Sienna breezed through around 10:30 and announced that they were going for a hike. They packed a few PBJs and a couple bottles of water. Sienna was carrying a large sketchpad and a tattered box of pastels. Courtney appeared excited about spending the morning with Sienna. Go figure.

"Are you sure you're OK with this?" I asked her as they were in the kitchen making their sandwiches on a makeshift table and Sienna was out of earshot.

"Oh, yes! It was my suggestion," Courtney explained.

With no effort at all, I was still losing to a ten year old.

Others were in and out as the morning wore on. Fortunately, most of the Kampler extended family stayed out of our way.

COURTNEY

Sienna was quiet around her family, but as soon as we were on the trail, she had a million questions for her new Aunt Courtney. She wanted to know where I lived. She asked about my mom and dad. She wanted to know if I had any friends. That was when the conversation between the two of us began to connect.

"Well, I have a few, like Dylan and his brothers."

"You mean Derek?"

"Yes, I guess you could call Derek a friend. And they have another brother, Dex. He and I are really good friends."

"Oh, so Dex is your boyfriend?"

"No, he's just a really good friend. You know, Sienna, you don't have to have a boyfriend all the time."

"I know. It's just that you're so pretty and all."

With the trail leading us up the mountain ridge behind the Kampler lodge, we were on a steep incline. As we walked, a light breeze blew through the tops of the trees, providing just the right amount of shade and cooling from the summer sun. Having hiked many times with my family, my eyes scanned back and forth, looking for indigenous flora and fauna. I had hiked all over Europe, yet never stepped foot on the mountains of Pennsylvania, until that day. It was the perfect family outing. Too bad Sienna's family had not taken advantage of their good fortune.

"How about you, Sienna. What do you and your friends like to do when you're not in school?"

"Oh, I don't know. Nothing, really."

"OK . . . Do you have sleepovers?"

"No."

"Do you ride bikes?"

"Not really."

"Sienna, what do you do on the weekend? Do you ever invite your friends over?"

"No. There's not a lot to do at my house."

"So, what do you do?"

"Draw, read books. Stuff like that."

She was a different child, of sorts. Yet, in many ways, she reminded me of me. I had no real close friends when I was her age. Even as an adult, I didn't have a group of friends that I hung around with, other than my sisters.

We walked silently for a while; following the trail down the other side of the ridge when I thought I heard water.

"Sienna, follow me."

We walked about fifty yards off the trail and found a peaceful mountain stream.

"This is the perfect place to stop."

We sat down beside the quiet, restorative water. Sienna laid her sketchpad across her knees, opened her box of worn pastels, and went to work. Leaning back against an old fallen tree, I watched her fingers dance across the textured paper until I eventually drifted off to sleep.

DYLAN

It was 2:00. The cabinets were in, and our work was done. Rob seemed exceptionally pleased as he cracked a few beers with us. Despite his help, Joshua was denied and had to settle for a Mountain Dew.

"Dylan, my boy, this was well worth the wait," Rob affirmed as we clinked the bottlenecks.

Susan had been reading a novel in the family room and came in as soon as she heard the beers open. She was duly impressed and gave Derek a big hug.

"You guys really did a nice job here!"

Derek sported a prideful grin that I had not witnessed since our father had passed away. Perhaps he had been in more pain than I had realized. He certainly had not been himself.

Hearing a small celebration taking place in the kitchen,

Gillian came out carrying her niece on her hip.

"Dylan, where is that girlfriend of yours? She and Sienna have been gone for hours now."

"Oh, well, I'm sure they're fine." Though, admittedly, having their absence brought to my attention was a bit unsettling. "I do remember Sienna taking a sketchpad, and Courtney had her camera, plus they packed a lunch before they left. It looked to me like they intended to be out for a couple of hours."

"Well, I think you should give her a call," Gillian demanded.

Against my better judgment, I met her request.

COURTNEY

Dylan was chasing me through the woods. I was running and laughing, hoping he would catch me. When I turned back, a large bear-like animal was chasing after him and was about to slash him to pieces. We were running past an electrified fence that emitted a humming pulsation. He must have touched it because he stopped short and his body gave a jolt. With the bear almost on top of him, I reached for his hand, and when our fingers touched, I startled and woke up.

My cell phone was vibrating in my pocket. I fumbled around and dug it out. I was out of breath and groggy.

"Oh, hey, how's it going back there?"

"We're done. Where are you? Are you OK? Sienna's mom is a bit frantic."

I sat up and looked around. Sienna was still sitting on the downed tree trunk with her sketchpad in her lap.

"We're fine. We took a break by a creek. We'll pack up and head back soon."

"How long will it take you to get back?"

"My guess is about an hour."

"Out that far, huh?"

"Maybe. It's quiet out here and I don't know if Sienna is finished with her sketch, yet."

"Sounds nice, I'll see you when you get back."

I wiped the sleep from my eyes and tried to center myself. My watch said it was 2:15. I stood and walked down the small incline to where Sienna was sitting next to the water.

"How's it coming along?" I asked her, indicating her drawing.

"Good."

"Can I see it?"

"Sure."

She turned her sketchpad toward me.

Her work was right out of a storybook. It depicted a princess sleeping under a knotty tree. The colors she used were true to nature. She didn't miss a single shadow or texture. The tree's bark was very rough and full of shaded knotty holes. The leaves, each and every one, were small and very detailed. She caught the sun streaming through the trees in the background without overshadowing the center focal point: the sleeping princess whose countenance was peaceful and dreamlike. Her skin was like porcelain. The sun illuminated her hair. A few white flowers tucked behind her ear spoke of her youth and innocence.

"It's you, Aunt Courtney!"

I didn't know what to say. Did she know how truly innocent, naïve, and inexperienced I really was? Was she that perceptive?

"It's beautiful, Sienna," I whispered in awe.

"You can have it."

"Really? I would like that very much."

We stayed a while longer and ate our sandwiches, packed up, and began the trek back to the lodge.

DYLAN

The weekend was a bust. We had finished the cabinets by 2:00 in the afternoon. Derek and Susan waited until Courtney and Sienna returned from their hike and then said they needed to head back to Valley Forge. Courtney and I had to leave Sunday morning. Courtney planned to drive back to Lewes once we reached my house in Unionville. And the Kamplers decided not to leave until the countertops were installed on Monday. Yep, the weekend was a complete bust.

For dinner, the Kamplers took us to a Rib and Steakhouse. It was small compensation for my staggering disappointment. Once back at the lodge, we all watched a movie in the theater room and shortly after, it was time for the children to head upstairs to bed. Little Kira had taken a liking to me and fell asleep on my shoulder during the movie. Cindy seemed delighted to have her hands free.

When it was time, Sienna asked Courtney to come upstairs and tuck her in. Courtney wished everyone a good night, as well.

"See you in the morning?" I asked, half as a sign-off at the end of a long day, and half as a request for reassurance. Courtney just winked. I had no idea what she was up to. I found out later.

I was one of the last to turn in. I could not have been asleep long when there was a tapping on my door. I pulled my jeans on and cracked the door open. As I had hoped, it was Courtney. We whispered.

"Do you want to come in?"

"No. Not really. That wouldn't be appropriate."

"Oh, and knocking on my door past midnight is?"

"I can leave."

"No, no. I was only kidding. What's up?"

"Can we talk?"

"Sure. Where?"

"Let's go outside."

We quietly made our way down the stairs and out the back door, making sure it would not lock behind us. Even though it was August, there was just a hint of fall in the air. Courtney had a blanket wrapped around her shoulders, pajama pants, and I believe a T-shirt under the blanket. I did manage to grab a sweatshirt before leaving my room.

Out back was a large brick patio. We sat down in the chairs that surrounded a table.

"Are you doing OK?" I felt the need to ask Courtney, once again feeling bad about the weekend that wasn't.

"Oh, I'm doing fine. How about you?"

"Well, with the job out of the way, I'd say I'm doing OK, too, but I'm sorry you got corralled by Sienna all day and again at dinner tonight. She's stuck on you like glue."

"Oh, it's really quite all right. She really is a nice girl. She reminds me of me, in many ways."

"Oh? How so?"

"She's smart . . ."

"And cute . . ." I added.

"Yes, she's cute. But she's also shy and doesn't have a lot of close friends her age."

"You were like that?"

"I still am. Outside of you, Dex, and my sisters, I really don't have any other friends that I pal around with."

"Well, for the record, I think you're a great friend." I gave her a little shove.

"Thanks. You're not so bad yourself."

A slight breeze out of the northwest complemented our silence as Courtney gazed up at the night sky and exhaled. I was getting up the nerve when a tree branch cracked, followed by an animal scream that sounded like someone was dying. It made both of us jump. It was coming from the woods just a few hundred yards from the patio. We both ran inside. Breathless, we tried to contain an eruption of fear and laughter. Courtney was very freaked out by it, and so was I. Having caught her breath, she was the first to speak.

"Thanks for bringing me up here this weekend, Dylan. It was nice to get away. I'd better head up to bed. I have a long drive tomorrow, and so do you."

She kissed me on the cheek, turned, and went up the steps.

That was it?

We left the next morning.

CHAPTER SEVEN

DEX

Well, I had asked for it. I asked Dylan what he thought I should do to win over Derek. Ginny and I had become something serious, and I wanted to straighten out my relationship with him, if only for Ginny's sake. Susan had made numerous visits since the fire. Sadly, she said Derek would no longer come. He had managed to avoid us each and every time we had invited them down. Ginny had even hinted at our driving up to visit with them, but Derek had always managed to come up with a reason for us not to make the trip. I was sure he would come down immediately after the fire, and he did, but never again since then. It must have really upset him.

Dylan suggested I invite Derek out on a fishing trip after things settled down. I thought his idea had potential, as long as he came along with us. Ginny liked the idea, too. However, when the day came, I had to admit that I was anxious about all of it.

When I had extended the invitation, I suggested that Dylan and Derek stay on the Right Tackle the night before our trip so we could get an early start the next morning, but Derek said he would not be able to fall asleep there. However, when they did arrive in town, we met on the boat to finalize our itinerary for the next day over a few beers. Then, Dylan and Derek left for a night's stay at Vesuvio's Motel, and I remained on the Right Tackle.

The alarm went off at 6:00 AM and already it was eighty degrees outside and the humidity made it feel like one hundred. I took a very quick shower and started to get dressed for a day on the water, when the phone rang. It was Dylan. It seemed he had come down with some sort of stomach bug. He said he had been vomiting most of the night and had a splitting headache. He was fine when they had left the boat, but half way through the night something violent had taken control of his gut. We couldn't think of anything he ate or drank that would have made him so ill. He thought he probably brought it with him from home.

Hopefully, it's nothing contagious.

"Sounds like we should cancel the trip," I suggested.

"I don't think so. Derek is up and getting ready to go."

"He still wants to go?"

"As a matter of fact, he was singing in the shower. I think it would be a big mistake to call off the trip."

"Dylan, you can't leave me to work this out on my own. Now, I think I'm going to be sick."

"You'll be fine. It might even be better this way. He won't have any other choice but to get along with you, and if nothing else, I think he will appreciate getting away from my spewing for awhile."

"Oh, man, are you still . . ."

"No, but he said he was tired of hearing me barf my brains out all night. He said he was in need of some fresh air."

"Nice."

"It'll be fine. In fact, maybe my not being there will help to speed things along."

"Oh, this is so not how I had hoped this day would go."

"Sorry."

"So, are you going to sleep it off all day?"

"Probably. Court has a few things to take care of at the office this morning, and then she said she would be over to see how I was doing."

"Oh, is this about you and Courtney having some alone time? Well, your timing is terrible."

"Dex, I was puking my brains out all last night. And anyway, we're not . . . you know . . . involved."

"Like fully involved."

"Fully involved is for infernos. Ours isn't even a slow burn. I don't think she thinks of me in that way."

"Dylan, are you blind? You must be seriously blind, and she must be in denial. Everyone can see it; everyone except for the two of you."

"Huh . . . Hey, Dex, I gotta go. Derek just finished reading the paper in the bathroom."

"Oh, thanks for that."

"Have a great trip. Hope everything works out today."

"Thanks, little brother. I'll see you later."

Did I just say that? "Little brother?"

I was so bummed that Dylan couldn't go along with us. It must have been my total disappointment that made me call him that. Though, he was a cool little brother.

DEREK

As soon as he had resigned himself to not going, Dylan called Courtney to whine in her ear. And, of course, she said she would stop by. Who are they kidding? At least it would keep the two of them occupied and out of my way. Mission thoroughly accomplished.

After I was dressed and ready to go, I asked Dylan one more time if he was going to be OK.

Of course, he was. I knew that.

So, it was time for me to go make nicey-nice with Dex. I couldn't think of a worse way—or a better way—to spend a day. It wouldn't take long, and when it was all over, it was going to be well worth my time. My stress level was going to be reduced exponentially by the end of the trip. I would persevere.

I arrived at the dock just after 7:30. In the main salon, as he called it . . . *la-dee-da* . . . Dex had coffee, bagels, and cream cheese out and ready. I had to give Dex credit; he did remember that an Everything Bagel with Philadelphia Cream Cheese was my favorite. Though, I was willing to bet that Ginny was the one who put it all together. That old man Charles was sitting at the table shooting the breeze and yucking it up when I climbed on board. Dex reintroduced us and then Charles promptly excused himself and left. Good.

From then on, it was so entertaining to watch Dex squirm as he tried to create small talk. He asked about Susan, although I was sure Ginny had filled him in on everything there was to know about my wife. He asked how the business was going. My one word answer, "Fine," brought his attempt to a halt. He tried bringing Susan back into our stalled conversation by saying what a great support she had been for Ginny through their latest ordeal.

Poor babies.

I nodded my head. He was not going to get a further comment from me.

Without a breath of air moving, that late August morning was working itself into a broiler. All of the windows and hatches on the Right Tackle were open and to no avail. As sweat began rolling down his temples, Dex suggested we head out, believing it would be cooler on the water. He began cleaning up breakfast, throwing the cream cheese into the fridge, bagging up the remaining bagels, and pouring the coffee into a thermos.

How I hate this boat.

Dex had me posted at the bowlines. I considered screwing it up, but Charles was next to us on his boat and it would have been too obvious, even to him. I didn't need any witnesses to my bad behavior. It wasn't like this was my first time on a boat, or manning the bowlines for that matter. Dex eased her out and soon we were in open water. Dex said I should join him on the fly bridge. I declined. No reason given, I just declined. His frustration was beginning to show.

The heat and humidity combined with the lack of the slightest breeze created a dense haze over the water. The surface was as smooth as glass causing the illusion of an endless sky. With no visible horizon, it was difficult to tell where the water ended and the sky began. The only thing to disturb the mirage was the wake left by the Right Tackle. Dex had the engines wide open. The breeze created by our speed provided some relief; however, it was going to be hotter than hell once we stopped. I wished he would blow an engine. It would help explain how she sank, but we needed to be farther out before that happened. Dex said we were headed out to the wrecks.

How beautifully prophetic!

We finally reached our destination, and as I thought, it was hotter than Hades when he cut the engines. I stripped down and dove in. Even the water was too warm. Remembering the jellyfish stings I had sustained when I was younger, I swam swiftly back to the platform. Back on board I doused the deck with water. It appeared Dex was not too keen on my little dip. I just wanted to make sure the water was OK before I sent him over for a swim of his own. Remaining hospitable, he cracked some beers and rigged the lines.

This is going to be a good day after all!

COURTNEY

Around noon I arrived at Vesuvio's. Dylan was sitting up and watching the Tour de France on TV. He had the shades drawn either to protect his eyes inside or keep the heat and humidity outside. He looked like he had had a rough night, indeed.

"How are you feeling?"

"I think I'm better, now. But I'm so tired and my heart is racing.... I think ... I'm just ... a little lightheaded."

I placed my hand on his forehead. It felt normal. I took his hand in mine and turned it over so I had access to his wrist and checked his pulse. He was right. His heart was racing, and fluttering.

"Dylan, something's not right. Let's take you up to Beebe Hospital."

He fought off my suggestion for another half hour before he surrendered to my pleading. We left for Beebe.

After a relatively quick examination, the doctor returned with another colleague and several theories. It was possible that Dylan had had a bad case of salmonella. However, that seemed unlikely; Dex and Derek had also consumed everything Dylan had ingested, and they were fine, and Dylan had not contracted salmonella weeks or months prior to that. So it was not a case of recurrence, either. (Apparently, salmonella can come back if it is not completely out of your system.) Also, salmonella did not explain all of his symptoms. Their next theory, which they also thought was highly unlikely, was that he had ingested a poison. Again, Dylan, Derek, and Dex had all eaten the same thing. The doctor ordered blood work and a urine sample, as well as an x-ray. He also speculated that Dylan could have had an allergic reaction to something he had eaten. However, they ruled that unlikely, too. Nothing they ate or drank was a common allergen. While not admitting him, the doctors decided to keep him a while longer for observation while they continued rehydrating him through an IV drip.

I called Ginny to let her know that I had taken Dylan to the hospital. She said she would call Dex to give them an update. She expected that when they heard that Dylan was in the ER, they might return sooner than later. She mentioned that Dex had not been thrilled when he found out that Dylan would not be making the trip that day.

Ginny called back several minutes later and said that Dex was not answering his phone. So she left a message for him and would try again later.

Around 2:00, the doctor revisited us asking more specific questions about what, where, when, and with whom Dylan had eaten in the last twenty-four to forty-eight hours. By 3:00 they had no need to keep him any longer. Nothing showed up on the x-ray; however, they said they would let us know of the lab results and suggested he see his family doctor when he returned home. They also said he should come directly back to the hospital if he started to run a fever, his heart began racing, or he began vomiting again. They reminded him to drink plenty of water all day to flush his system and stay hydrated.

I walked Dylan out to my car. He seemed unusually weak and needy. He allowed me to help him into his seat and up to the room when we arrived back at Vesuvio's. He requested a hot shower and a nap. Then he very quietly, almost embarrassingly, asked that I stay with him. He was either milking it, or fearfully not well.

While Dylan was in the shower, Ginny called. She was concerned because she still couldn't reach Dex, and the weather was turning for the worst. The weather forecast had called for possible storms in the afternoon. As we were talking on the phone, I heard the first rumble of thunder. I knocked on the bathroom door.

"Dylan, you'd better hurry up, it sounds like a storm's coming."

Then, I returned to Ginny's call.

"Ginny, I'm sure everything is going to be OK. Dex is one

of the best on the water. He's outrun and weathered many a nasty storm before this. They'll be fine."

"But it's been two hours and I still cannot reach him. I'm worried."

"When are you expecting them back?"

"Around 4:00, any time now."

"I'm sure they're OK. They're probably heading back and can't hear their cell phones over the engines. Hopefully, they've had a great day and aren't really concerned about anything. Call me when you hear from them."

As Ginny and I talked on the phone, Dylan came out of the shower and in one smooth move, removed his towel and slipped under the covers, immediately drifting off to sleep. After, my call with Ginny ended, I picked up the morning paper and read while Dylan slept.

I must have dozed off, as well. When I woke up, it was getting dark outside, even though it was only 5:00. Dylan was spooned up against my back. It occurred to me that we had never been that close for that amount of time. It was completely innocent, and I liked it. I didn't move for fear he would pull away and the moment would be lost. Dylan stirred at the next rumble of thunder. It shook the room. I rolled toward him, making sure his arm didn't leave my waist. I pulled the covers over top of me. The sheets were warm from his body heat. He slowly opened his eyes and seemed pleased with our physical closeness. He pulled me in tighter and our lips met. Our first kiss. Our first admission of what we had known all along. When I pulled away from him, I looked into his remarkably handsome face. His eyes remained closed as if he were lost in a dream. His arms were locked securely around me, yet loose enough that I could pull away from him at any time, if I wanted to. I chose to continue what he had started. My legs became wrapped around his. Our hands began to cautiously study the topography of the other. His slow patience was driving me to the point of no return.

"Court, I don't want to leave this bed, but what time were we supposed to be at Ginny's?"

Another rumble of thunder. It was much closer, this time.

"Ginny said she would call us when the guys got back."

"What time is it?"

"Around 5:00."

"And they're not back yet?"

"Not that I know of."

Dylan sat up. "Something's wrong."

My cell phone rang. Dylan began dressing.

"Courtney, how's Dylan?"

"He seems to be better. He's up and moving."

"Can I talk to him?"

"Sure."

DEX

The western sky had quickly turned dark; a deep bruising purple lined the horizon where the thick clouds touched the water's surface. The end of the water and the beginning of the sky were clearly delineated and it didn't look good. I set my fishing rod into its holder and went to the captain's station to listen to the weather radio. Derek was smugly sucking down another beer and had managed to cut off any conversation I had tried to initiate, except several times when I asked if he was ready to call it a day. We had caught a couple of good-sized blues, but he insisted we stay out longer. Against my better judgment, I decided to appease him. I should have known better, that pattern of his always had a way of leading us into trouble.

They were reporting storms bearing down on the Delmarva Peninsula with intense lightning and high winds. NOAA was advising small craft to seek shelter. I took a look at the radar scan. The storm was miles off, but moving directly toward us at a good clip. We would have to make a run for it. I started up the port engine.

"Hey Derek, it's time to hightail it out of here and head

for home," I yelled back, turning to make sure he had heard me.

He heard me all right, and instead of reeling in his line, he was wielding a gun, pointed right at me.

"Derek?"

He didn't respond.

"Derek, what are you doing?"

He waved the gun around. He had had a few beers too many, which made his behavior all that more erratic and frightening.

"I'm taking care of something that I should've taken care of a long time ago," he slurred, somehow managing to keep his rubbery sea legs under him.

He was glaring at me and there was nothing but a combination of hatred and exhilaration in his eyes as he once again tried to steady the gun in my direction.

The wind was picking up and blowing spray off the water's surface, creating a quickening of ripples that were turning dark and angry. The Right Tackle was shifting its direction with the wind change. As we stood there in our face-off, the water turned to a white-capped chop, swinging the Right Tackle broadside, and then stern to the wind. My only hope was to knock him off his feet. I rammed my elbow into the port throttle causing the boat to lunge forward, digging the stern down and her bow up. The single engine thrust swung her hard, knocking Derek off his feet and overboard. As the lightning shot overhead with earsplitting thunder, I felt a sharp burn in my left shoulder, dropping me to the deck.

DYLAN

It was like a dream. My long awaited fantasy was about to become reality. Then reality stepped up her game and showed her true self. Once again, it was not meant to be. As I was throwing on my clothes, I noticed how dark it was becoming outside. I opened the curtains and it was not much brighter out there than it was in the hotel room.

Courtney was now beside herself and handing me her cell phone. Ginny was on the other end and Court looked worried.

"Dylan, I have been trying to reach Dex for hours and he still doesn't answer," Ginny repeated in a near panic.

"They're probably at the dock, rushing to clean their catch before the storm hits. Tell you what; we're almost out the door. We'll stop by the dock and see what's going on. Why don't you call Susan and see if she can reach Derek. Better yet, don't do that. I don't need two panicked sisters-in-law on my hands."

Wait, is that right? I guess Ginny is still my sister-in-law? I don't know how that works. My head is spinning. It's all too much to worry about.

Awww, Court . . . it's just not our time.

Courtney and I got out the door and hopped into the truck. It was not until we were on top of the drawbridge, headed toward the beach and overlooking the canal that I realized several disturbing facts: the Right Tackle was not in her slip, the western sky was black, and we were going against a line of traffic. They had evacuated the public beach and everyone was leaving Cape Henlopen.

Courtney unleashed a barrage of questions: What if they had engine trouble? What if they got caught out in the storm? What kind of storms could the Right Tackle handle? How bad did I think the storm was going to get? How far away did I think they were?

We turned around and headed back over the drawbridge and straight to Sable's garage apartment where Dex and Ginny were staying. When we landed, I soon learned that against my better judgment, Ginny had called Susan.

SUSAN

"Hi, Ginny! How are the boys doing? Did they catch anything?"

"Well, that's why I'm calling. I can't reach Dex and I'm embarrassed to say that I don't have Derek's cell phone number. I was wondering if you would call him and see how they're doing."

"Did you call Dylan?"

"Yes, but Dylan didn't go out with them. He got sick last night and ended up in the hospital."

"What? I talked to Derek earlier. He called me from Dex's phone, for whatever reason, but he never mentioned Dylan wasn't with them. He said they were headed out and would call when they got back. That was it."

"Well, Courtney dragged Dylan to the hospital after the guys left, so he probably didn't know that part. He probably thought it was no big deal."

"I'm surprised Derek went out with Dex if Dylan wasn't there. I guess that's a good sign?"

"Yeah, Dex said Derek seemed eager to go, anyway. It surprised everyone. Go figure."

"Well, I'm sure they're OK. I'll give Derek a call and then I'll call you right back."

It was then that I wished I had gone along to Lewes. I had volunteered to watch my neighbor's two children while they moved her mother-in-law into their house. Something she was not thrilled about. Derek assured me that everyone would understand, especially because it was a guys' weekend kind of a thing, anyway.

His ringback played in my ear, and then I heard his ringtone coming from his office.

That's just great, he didn't take his cell phone with him.

That explains why he called earlier from Dex's phone.

I went into Derek's office, even though there was no need to verify what I had just heard.

I searched for his cell. It didn't appear to be on his desktop. I opened the drawer where he usually shoved everything. He called it his junk drawer. It was not in there, either. However, there was one thing that looked out of place. It was a lady's purse.

Why is there a lady's purse in his desk drawer, and how long has it been there?

I had to investigate further. My suspicions and disbelief were running a footrace in my head. Inside the purse, I found a wallet, a comb, lip balm, and a cell phone.

What the hell?

I was imagining the worst.

Where was he all those late nights? Is he seeing someone? Who is she?

My hands were shaking as I pulled out the wallet. Once I opened it and looked inside, there would be no turning back. I pulled out the driver's license.

Huh . . . I thought everything looked too familiar.

DEX

I blacked out for a second or two. As my vision returned, the world seemed a blur and I felt excruciating pain in my shoulder radiating down my arm and across my back.

Derek . . . where's Derek?

I had thrown Derek overboard and the boat, still in gear, was moving farther away from the spot where he had gone into the water. Lightning crashed overhead and the rain was coming down in sheets. I pulled myself up and brought the bow back into the wind. I staggered out to the open cockpit. The deck was wet and slippery. The rain and spray felt like a pressure washer shot straight into my face. The roll of the boat threw me again and a wave crashed over my body. I instinctively extended my left arm to grab the rail. An explosion of pain shot through my shoulder and chest. It was going to level me if the roll of the boat didn't do it first.

The pain was sucking the wind out of me. Out of breath and with water pouring down my face, and into my eyes and mouth, yelling for Derek was like shouting through a nightmare, trying to be heard from some other dimension. Barely a sound was coming forth even though I was putting so much force behind his name. All I could hear was the wind and thunder roaring all around me. I thought I heard him calling. It was difficult to tell where it was coming from, if it was real. He had to be close. Visibility must have been near zero. The waves were several feet high. I believed my only chance to spot him would be from up on the fly bridge.

SUSAN

I was furious now. I called Ginny back.

"Ginny, do you mind telling me what's going on?"

"I wish I could, but I honestly don't know. They should have been back by now, and we are in the middle of a bad storm."

"Ginny, why is your purse in Derek's office?"

"What . . . ? What are you talking about?"

"Your purse is in Derek's office, hidden in his desk. Your driver's license is right here. I'm holding it in my hand."

"Susan, are you sure?"

"Of course, I'm sure. It's all right here."

"Susan, I don't know what you're talking about, but I think the guys are in real trouble."

"Oh no, you tell me what your purse is doing in Derek's desk, in my house."

"What does it look like?"

"It looks like you're not being honest with me, that's what it looks like."

"Susan, get it together! Look, I need you to call Derek and find out where they are. This is urgent."

"Ginny, he doesn't have his cell phone with him. It's right here, with your purse, and you need to tell me what's going on. You all picked the one weekend I couldn't come down to do this, huh?"

"Now you're just being ridiculous," Ginny snapped.

Obviously, Ginny was not going to confess, and without giving it a second thought, I hung up on her.

I know I'm not being rational. Or am I? Maybe I've had my eyes shut this whole time. Has this been going on for some time now? Has she been playing me all along? Have they both been playing me? Who is this person that's supposed to be my best friend?

No, something is not right. Ginny clearly adores Dex. And

Derek, he clearly does not care for her, or does he?

I went back into Derek's office to see if I could piece things together.

DEX

I throttled back the port engine, started the starboard and threw it into reverse. It spun the Right Tackle's bow back into the wind once more. I climbed the ladder using my right arm, trying to keep my left arm tucked up against my chest; however, the seas were so heavy, I really needed both hands to climb and steady myself. The pain was blinding. My shoulder was on fire. I felt nauseous and about to pass out at any moment.

Once on the bridge, I could no longer hear his calls, but I did see what I thought to be Derek's head trying to stay above the onslaught of waves and spray. The bridge heaved wildly as she took a large roller broadside and came about. I grabbed the wheel to save myself from being thrown overboard and almost negated the heading I was after. Keeping my eyes on the spot where I thought I last saw Derek, I edged the Right Tackle forward against the wind. She had been blown quite a distance from Derek just in the short time it took me to scale the ladder. I knew I had to pass him in hopes that the wind would blow me back toward him. The timing would have to be perfect. I needed to be close enough to throw him the life ring.

The storm was now on top of us. The lightning was intense, the thunder deafening, and the wind was unrelenting. I was losing consciousness and was now aware of the blood flowing from my arm and being carried by the wash down to the deck of the bridge. The red stream disappeared with the spray being blown off its edge. With Derek's life at stake, I triggered the distress call.

GINNY

"I'm calling the Coast Guard."

"Don't you think that's a bit hasty?" Dylan countered. "Dex knows how to handle this weather. The Right Tackle can take it. She was built for this stuff."

My cell phone rang. It was Susan.

Good. Maybe she's come to her senses.

"Ginny, I don't know what's going on, but when I went looking through Derek's things to try to piece all of this together ... well ... his gun is gone. He never takes that thing out. Ever. I never knew why he had it in the first place. I'm not even sure he has a permit to carry it. Anyway, the point is: the gun's gone and at least one or more clips. And Ginny, there are blueprints here with your address and Dan's name on them. What the hell is going on?"

It was all coming together. The only possible way Derek could have possession of those blueprints and my purse would be if he had been in Lewes the night of the fire.

"Ginny, I can't bear to think this, but I'm scared of what Derek might be capable of when it comes to Dex ... and you."

"Susan, stay put. You know I love you, right? I gotta go."

That time I hung up on her and immediately called the Coast Guard. As I was describing the possible scenario, Dylan and Courtney listened in horror. Courtney took hold of Dylan's arm and whispered something into his ear about Charles.

The Coast Guard took the information. I did my best to give them a description of the boat and an estimation of where they might be. Not to my surprise, the gentleman on the phone knew Dex and the Right Tackle. He said they had not received any communication from the Right Tackle, so I should not panic. They would try to reach them via radio. If they didn't hear from them when the storm subsided, they would send out a cutter from the Indian River Station. "Let's hope we hear from them before dark."

As soon as I hung up, Dylan calmly said he was heading to the dock to look for Charles and see if he would take him out to search for the Right Tackle. He said Charles would most likely know where to find Dex. I begged to go along, but Dylan refused to take me. He said he needed me at the apartment to man the post.

He's right about that.

He quickly added that Courtney needed to stay with me to keep me company.

He meant to keep me from panicking, and he was right about that, too.

Dylan then took Courtney by the arms and gave her a kiss that lingered for more than just a "thanks-for-being-a-good-friend" kiss. It was more of a . . . well . . . you know, an intimate, soft, lingering "I'll miss you, be here when I get back" type kiss. He was out the door and down the steps. Courtney looked like she might cry as we sat down on the love seat. Silence filled that small space.

I needed to hear everything, every clap of thunder and every bang of the shutters. I needed to know I was hearing the same thing Dex was being exposed to in the midst of the storm. I wanted to be there with him. I plugged in my cell phone to make sure it stayed charged. That was when the power went out. The darkness was heavy and the silence raged as the storm took complete control of all things.

DYLAN

I drove back to the dock. The Right Tackle had not yet returned to her berth. Charles' boat, The Morning Starr, was open, but no one was on board. He had to be nearby. Against the wind and stinging rain, I ran up to Irish Eyes, and sure enough, there he was under roof, hanging around the cleaning stations, telling stories and riding out the storm with the other captains.

"Hey, aren't you Dex's brother? Where is that skunk?" He looked around me and down the dock hoping to see the Right Tackle at rest in her slip. He removed his drenched hat and pushed his wet hair back across the top of his head.

"Yeah . . . I'm Dylan." Due to my sprint down the dock, I was breathing a little heavier then.

"Nice to re-meet you Dylan. Why didn't I see you this morning? You missed the boat, man. Where's that brother of yours, anyway?"

"That's why I'm here." We were yelling to be heard over the wind, rain, and thunder.

I did my best to tell him something was wrong and alluded to our suspicion that Dex might be in more danger than just the storm.

"Well, let's go, then. I know he'd come looking for me."

Two of the other captains volunteered to go along with us.

Fear was running through my veins, and my hope was that we had seen the worst of the storm. I was afraid of going out into open water in the midst of the meteorological chaos, but I was more afraid of losing another family member. As we cruised through the inlet, we put on lifejackets. Lord knows the last time they had been worn.

Like a crew that had worked together for decades, the three captains had the Morning Starr in open water in no time. The wind and waves were bucking us as soon as we crossed beyond the breakwater. Visibility was zero. It was going to be an agonizing ride. Fortunately, Charles could navigate the Delaware Bay and the Atlantic Ocean with his eyes closed, and he knew all of Dex's favorite spots.

The Morning Starr was taking a pounding. The engines were screaming and spray was lashing over the gunnels and into her cockpit as we headed out beyond the sight of land. Everything was obscured by the height of the waves, the spray, and the rain.

Over the noise of the engines and pounding of the boat, the other two men introduced themselves to me as we stood across the back of the cabin holding on to the overhead handrails. They both knew Dex and expressed that they, too, were becoming concerned, adding that they were sure Dex was just out trying to create another storm adventure to trump any of theirs. I appreciated their attempts to add levity to the situation. As they were talking, they never took their eyes off the water. Fifteen minutes into the trip, the storm seemed to be beyond us. There was light on the horizon of the western sky. I prayed the storm was moving out. As the wind seemed to subside, our visibility improved steadily. How I had wished it would just stop. One of the captains grabbed a pair of binoculars and, despite the rolling of the boat, scanned the horizon. He and I cautiously climbed the steps to the fly bridge to get a longer view. Everything was wet and slick from the rain. Charles remained at the captain's station below and radioed the Coast Guard to see if they had received any communication from the Right Tackle. Indeed, our worst fears had been realized, the Coast Guard had received the distress call. My heart sank. They gave Charles the Right Tackle's coordinates and said they had a cutter on the way. I was now praying that the Right Tackle was not sitting on the bottom of the ocean. I needed to prepare myself for whatever lay in wait.

DEX

Derek was in sight. I put the engines in neutral and started down off the fly bridge. Falling on to the deck, I was in agony, fighting every useless screaming muscle to find my way to the life ring. Reaching it, I pulled myself up and saw Derek on the starboard side, drifting toward the stern. We had slipped farther past him than I had hoped, but close enough. I knew the first toss had to be a good one. I stood up, made sure the line was free and clear, and then heaved the ring in his direction. My momentum, plus a sudden lunge of the boat, propelled me back onto the deck of the cockpit. I fell into darkness.

When I came to, Derek was standing over me, drenched, shaking, and the look of the devil's terror was in his eyes. Blood from my shoulder, mixed with seawater was swashing across the deck. I didn't see the gun. I remember thinking I needed to find the gun, if only to keep it out of his hands. Derek grabbed my left arm and yanked me up.

"I'm going to sink you and this motherfucking boat."

I was blacking out as I tried to kick him away from me. I managed to take his feet out from under him. I remember seeing his blurred body coming at me again.

I hit the water.

DYLAN

With the storm past us, and contrary to the remaining high seas, visibility was improving with every passing minute. Lingering evidence of the storm's presence made it look like we were living in black and white. The sea spray and angry waves created a veil with caps of white. The stirred water was dark as coal. The sky was various hues of silver gray with random tendrils pointing down at the water like the demanding fingers of Satan, himself. The only hopeful hue to be found was the low orange-mustard sun peering out from the receding clouds on the western horizon.

One of the captains and I were on the fly bridge when he spotted the Right Tackle. She was still afloat. He held his binoculars to his eyes and tried to focus despite the rolling of the Morning Starr.

"They must have one helluva fish on 'cause there's a huge struggle on board."

Making adjustments, he kept his binoculars over his eyes while the rest of us looked on. Then he gasped.

"Charles, he's not struggling with a fish. It's Dex. It looks like he's taking a beating. Get the hell over there.... Dex is overboard.... He's in the water!"

Now, even I could see the boat with my naked eyes, but I could not see Dex.

"My God, the bastard is leaving without him. He's pulling away and leaving him in the water!"

"Don't lose sight of him," Charles yelled back from the captain's station.

We could all see the wake kick out as the Right Tackle throttled up and headed out to sea, leaving Dex behind to drown.

The Morning Starr was at full speed, but with Dex in the water, it felt like we were moving in slow motion. We just couldn't get there fast enough. Everything was fighting us. The second captain kept an eye on Dex as best he could while yelling directions down to Charles. Finally, I could see Dex as well. Even though he was a strong swimmer, it looked as though he was fighting a losing battle to keep his head up.

As soon as we were close enough, Dex began to go under. I was not sure he realized we were there. I removed my lifejacket and dove off the fly bridge. Charles was cursing as he threw a life ring in after me. Dex was below the surface and his thrashing had stopped. When I reached him, he was dead weight. It was a fight to haul him back up. Charles held out a long boat pole. With one arm under Dex and around his waist, I made several attempts to grab the outstretched pole with my free hand. Willing my self up, my body came out of the water high enough to grab on with one arm. I was holding on to Dex with the other. With both arms strained and my legs dead from kicking us to the surface, it was all I could do to keep both heads above water as we were pulled over to the side of the Morning Starr. The rough seas were making it nearly impossible to save us both.

Hang on, Dex. . . . How did the water we love come to hate us so much?

The two captains were on the platform. The severe rolling of the boat was making it dangerous to be anywhere near its thrashing hull. The men reached down, leaning dangerously over, and grabbed Dex, pulling him on board. They dragged his limp body over the transom and into the cockpit. Struggling to get us both back to the boat, I had taken in quite a bit of water myself. I hung on to the life ring, hoping strength would miraculously find its way back to me. That was when I felt a swift pull on the back of my shirt and under my arm as the two captains pulled me from the water. I was coughing and spitting when they dragged me into the cockpit. I waved them off, signaling them to take care of Dex. Charles was already performing CPR. Dex was not responding. One of the captains had the presence of mind to call the Coast Guard and give them our coordinates, as well as the heading of the Right Tackle. He also requested a medevac helicopter.

Dex's body lay still. He was not responding.

I could not take another loss. When I looked at Dex's limp muscle mass, I couldn't imagine Derek being able to do what he had done.

"Dex, don't you dare leave me!" I wailed. "Don't you do this . . . DEX!"

I was sick and regurgitated salt water. I tried in vain to reach for hope rather than the desperation that was fouling my stomach and had me pinned down to the deck. I could feel the angered panic that was growing like a cancer in my bones. I had to get up or it would consume me.

"DEX . . . !

I rose to my knees. Was it possible? Was life leaving his body? "NO . . . ! NO . . . ! DON'T GO!"

How would I tell Ginny . . . ? Susan . . . ?

Oh God, our dad would be devastated.

Charles kept working Dex's chest with intense determination, never missing a beat despite the pitch, and yaw of the Morning Starr. He was unaware of his moaning chant, "Come on, Dex. Come on, dammit . . ."

An eternity later, Dex began expelling and coughing seawater. His limbs were beginning to show signs of life. We had made it in time. When he opened his eyes, we could see the pain he was in as they rolled back into his head. He tried opening them again. There was a moment of relief when he realized who was hovering over him. I didn't know Charles all that well, but I could have kissed him right then and there.

"You've got a lot of nerve dragging me out into this storm," Charles scolded Dex, out of breath and exhausted. That was when Dex cracked a smile. It was about all we got out of him.

Breathing on his own, we could now examine the wound in Dex's shoulder. A gunshot. He was in and out of consciousness and may have lost a lot of blood. We could hear the helicopter approaching.

Thank God.

Dex was airlifted to Beebe Hospital.

All those years at the beach house, we had watched helicopters fly overhead as they circled to land on the rooftop of that hospital. I had never imagined in my wildest dreams that one day it would be for one of our own.

Once the helicopter was out of sight, I called Ginny and told her that Dex was on his way to Beebe, and that he was going to be all right. I told her there was an accident on board the Right Tackle and that he was airlifted, but he was going to be all right. I think I told her he was "going to be all right" after every sentence. She asked about Derek. I didn't want to lie to her; however, I couldn't tell her the truth over the phone.

"The Coast Guard is still with him." My answer being somewhere between the truth and a white lie.

Ginny sounded confused, and left immediately for the hospital.

Charles turned to me. "Well now, do we go after the Right Tackle?"

No one wanted to return without her. We owed it to Dex.

The water was still filled with haphazard rollers that had no rhyme or reason for their direction. It was like navigating chaos. Visibility had greatly improved and color was beginning to return to the seascape.

I had no idea how Charles knew what direction to take to track her down. Without sight of land, the only visual anchor we had was the western horizon, highlighted by the sun that was now below the back end of the storm. Trying to locate the Right Tackle was like trying to find a needle in a haystack. The ocean left no trail to follow. It covered the tracks of every deed, good or bad.

Riding through the churned up water, we were cold and wet. Exhaustion was setting in. Charles seemed superhuman to me then. The two captains, George and Nate, were concerned, yet at ease. Their ability to calmly work under stress must have been a product of the environment in which they made their living.

The sun was beginning to fall below the horizon. We had been out there for at least an hour after Dex had been airlifted and still no sight of the Right Tackle or the Coast Guard. Soon we would have to turn back. Charles radioed the Coast Guard once more. This time they told him they were able to catch up to the Right Tackle by following her distress signal. They boarded her, and had just taken Derek into custody. We learned later that Derek tried to outrun them, which was foolish. When they demanded that Derek stop several times, he chose to ignore them. They gave him three warnings and then shot across the bow to let him know they would do whatever it took. Derek, being unarmed, had no choice. They were returning him to Lewes where he would be turned over to the police and the boat would be impounded until an investigation had been completed.

During their search for evidence, they had found Derek's gun jammed under a stern locker. It was the piece of evidence that would seal Derek's fate.

The trip back was long and excruciating. My head was pounding like the rough water we had just fought. As the engines began to hum in calmer seas, I tried to piece together events that would give some logical explanation for what had happened. Every plausible explanation led back to a prior point in time in a string of events. It all seemed to go back to the reading of Dad's Last Will and Testament, and that was where the trail ended, or did it?

Why then, take this out on Dex? Perhaps it goes back to things we were never privy to.

The explanation may have been in the boathouse that fateful night. That may have been the night we had lost the Derek we all knew.

Courtney drove down to the dock to pick me up. Even before the lines were secured on the Morning Starr, Charles saw her waiting for me and told me to get going. I didn't know how to thank him and his friends enough, though I tried.

GINNY

I knew I was pushing the speed limit. I didn't care. In the hospital parking garage, I heard a helicopter approaching as I shut the door of the Jeep. That Jeep had become an old friend to me. I found myself giving its hood a pat as if to say, *"Here we go, it's you and me."*

Inside the hospital, I went to the desk of the Emergency Room and let them know that I was the girlfriend of the patient arriving by helicopter. I identified him by name and gave them mine. They kindly escorted me to a private waiting area and told me they would let me know as soon as possible when I would be able to see him. In the meantime, they needed to evaluate him first.

Where is everyone? Dylan is on the Morning Starr. Courtney is at the dock waiting for them to come in. Susan . . . Where is Susan?

I called Susan and got her voicemail.

Where is she?

Minutes felt like hours.

Why is this taking so long?

I began making a mental list of all the positive things I could think of:

Dex is strong.
He's smart.
He knows the water.
He has been through many storms.
I have been told that he has survived much worse.
The Right Tackle is a good boat.
She is well built.
She was built for this kind of weather.
The two of them are invincible.
"He's going to be all right."

That was when the police found me and introduced themselves.

"Ginny," the officer said, tipping his hat, "I don't know if you remember me, I'm Tom Pratt and this is Officer Jared Murray."

I did remember him. The sight of him was giving me the shakes. I felt myself losing control. Every time that man is involved, the news has been devastating. I rose out of my seat and gave him a shove. A big "put all of my weight into it" shove.

"Get out of here! Leave us alone! Get out!" I yelled in his face.

Officer Murray grabbed my arms and held me in his grip. I tried kicking him, but couldn't get any leverage.

"It's OK, Murray," I heard Officer Pratt say. "She has every right to be upset. All I've ever brought her is bad news."

Officer Murray let go of my arms, one at a time. I turned away from both of them, hoping they would disappear.

"Ginny, please have a seat. We need to ask you a few questions about the shooting."

"Shooting? What shooting?"

Oh, God . . . Derek had a gun.

I grabbed Officer Pratt's arm, not to shove or hurt him; I was pleading.

"Who was shot?"

"You don't know what happened? Ginny, everything is going to be OK. I am so sorry you are hearing this first from me. I wish, just once, we would meet under better circumstances."

I felt like I was going blind as the stress bore down on my eyes. I grabbed the back of a chair. I may have been losing my hearing, as well. A low hum filled my head. I was bracing myself for what was coming next. I just wanted it to all go away. I was shutting down. I didn't want to know. Officer Pratt helped me sit down. He pulled up a chair and sat across from me and spoke softly.

"Dex was shot in the shoulder. We have every reason to believe he's going to be OK."

The room froze over. It was cold . . . black . . . Pratt's voice had become a fog of muffled sounds locked in a black box. His face was a blur. I was taken back to when I was first told that Dan had died in the accident, the one where I was the driver. I felt like I was going insane. I reached up and grabbed his sleeve again.

"Ginny, he's going to be OK." His voice was a little stronger, more reassuring.

I sobbed. I needed to see Dex.

My heart was racing, and I was having trouble breathing.

It was then that Dan and Courtney walked into the room. Seeing the officers, they stopped and stood in the doorway, studying my face. I was so relieved to see them. I ran and jumped into Dan's arms. I didn't want to let him go. I knew if I did, the interrogation would begin again.

Please, make it go away.

"Dan, make them go away. . . . Please, make them go away. I need you to come home."

He put his hands on either side of my face, and looked

gently into my eyes.

"Ginny, it's me . . . Dylan."

He sat me down and took both of my hands into his.
Courtney left the room and brought back a nurse.

SUSAN

For the last two hours, I had been sitting on pins and
needles. Ginny and I were staying in touch about every
fifteen minutes or so. Then the calls stopped and I could no
longer reach her. I grabbed my purse, and started the drive
to Lewes. I was probably half way between Christiana and
Middletown when Dylan called. My first reaction was relief,
and then I remembered that he was not on board the
boat. Dylan asked if I was driving and then suggested I find
a safe place to pull over. Nothing felt safe. It all seemed to
confirm my worst fear. When he told me what had
happened and that Derek was in custody, I knew my life
was over. I didn't know what to do or where to go. I was
on the side of the road not knowing where I belonged or
where I had been the last five years of my marriage.
   Dylan must have read my mind. He said there were
people there that loved me. He said that if I felt I could
make the trip, he knew they would all be there waiting for
me.
   "Dylan, I am the last person you all need to see. I should
have known. I should have been able to do something. I
should have known Derek was . . ."
   "You're wrong, Susan. Had you not found Ginny's
missing purse and cell phone, no one would have pieced it
together. No alarms would have gone off had you not
realized Derek's gun was gone. Dex is going to be
fine. Thanks to you, we got there in time. He would not
have survived being left in the water much longer."

"I'm Derek's wife. Why didn't I see this coming sooner? How could I have missed it?"

Silence . . .

"Dylan, I pretty much accused Ginny of having an affair with my husband. You don't think that's possible, do you? Is that why he tried to kill Dex? Was he after Ginny, or the beach house? Or, was Ginny his ticket to the beach house?"

"Whoa, Susan, think of what you are saying. I don't have a clue what Derek was thinking. None of us do. But I do know that Ginny is madly in love with Dex. I do know that you are the best friend she's ever had."

"What have I done?"

"Susan, you are not responsible for any of this. The only one who appears to be responsible is Derek."

I was sobbing then, and the more I tried to hide it from Dylan, the harder it was to breathe. I was digging through my purse searching for a tissue. My eyes and my nose had become fountains.

"Susan, where are you?"

"I'm on the side of Route 1. I was coming up on Middletown, I think."

"OK, are you all right to drive the rest of the way to Lewes? Do you want me to come get you?"

"No, I'll be OK."

"If you're sure, I'll meet you here."

"Where?"

I could hear whispering in the background.

"Courtney suggests we meet at her place, and then we can figure out what to do from there."

"Oh God, Dylan, this is too much. I don't know if I want to see Derek. I don't know if Ginny, or Dex for that matter, will ever want to see me again. Courtney must think I'm an idiot."

"Susan, you are not an idiot, and no matter what Derek has done, you *are* family, and a friend, you're my sister-in-law. You need us and we need you. Now, if you are able to drive, get your ass down here. I will see you at Courtney's. We'll figure it out from there."

He was speaking forcefully now. He knew it was what I needed to hear. He was right about being family. I dried my eyes, blew my nose, took a deep breath, looked into the rearview mirror, and pulled back into traffic heading south.

DEX

When I woke up, Ginny was sitting next to me. Just the sight of her made me feel better, even though the drugs had numbed every nerve ending. She looked tired. I had no idea how much time had passed, or how long she had been there. There were no windows in the room, so I had no idea what time it was. I did feel the kiss she placed on my forehead. I did feel a tingle when her lips released a smile meant just for me.

My scope of vision began to widen when I heard Dylan's voice.

"Hey, how are you doing? We went through hell and some serious high water to get you!"

"He saved your life, Dex. Thank God, Dylan saved your life." Ginny was choking back tears.

I began to recall some of the events that put me there. I remembered Derek pointing a gun. I remembered throttling the Right Tackle around.

I bolted up. This time I felt a hot searing pain shoot from my shoulder blade all the way down my arm.

"Where's Derek? I threw him overboard."

"No, Dex, he apparently threw *you* overboard," Dylan stated emphatically.

Dylan obviously has Derek and me mixed up.

"No, I throttled the Right Tackle, and knocked him into the water. I tossed him a life ring, but I never got him back on board. Where is he? Did you find him? How did I get here?" My head was pounding. Dylan did his best to try to piece things together for me.

"First, Derek is alive and well. He's in police custody now. He threw you overboard. George saw him throw you in."

"George? George who?"

"One of Charles's captain friends."

"George Ramstock?"

"I don't know. He and Nate came along with Charles."

"Charles? How did Charles get mixed up in this?"

"Susan and Ginny pieced things together and realized that Derek had a loaded gun with him. We couldn't reach you and the storm was out of control. As soon as I found Charles, he and the other two didn't waste any time getting us out there to find you. That's when George, using binoculars, saw Derek throw you overboard. Don't you remember any of this?"

"No."

"Well, apparently you tried to tread water for a couple of minutes. You had gone under just when we reached you.

"Dylan pulled you out of the water," Ginny said, edging her way back into the storytelling and then hugged Dylan's arm in appreciation.

"Wow, that's some story. But honestly, I don't remember any of it. So, Derek is going to be OK?"

I later realized they had sugar coated their next answer. Derek was going away for a long time.

I was so grateful for Dylan's heroic dive into the storm to save me. I didn't know how grateful Derek was that I had apparently found him and threw him a life ring for a second chance.

COURTNEY

The next several days were all consuming. Susan came and stayed with me the first night. I took her to visit Derek shortly after her arrival, but he would not see her. His arraignment did not go well, either. He was assigned a public defender and was refused bail because he had tried to outrun the Coast Guard. He was rightfully viewed as a flight risk. Derek was sent to the Sussex County Prison until his hearing.

His arraignment was the first time Susan had seen him since he had left their home for the fishing trip with Dex. I sat next to Susan. Derek would not look her way or acknowledge her presence. It took all of five minutes and he was whisked away. Susan called out for him as he was handcuffed. He didn't even flinch at the sound of her voice. His priority was to get out of that courtroom. He was practically dragging the guards behind him because they were not moving fast enough.

"Courtney, something is very wrong with him," Susan whimpered.

I wanted to say, "Ya think?"

Derek's stability was in great doubt. That man was not even close to the man I had first met in my office, though overbearing at that time, too. The man I had met and thought I knew had checked out.

On the ride back to Lewes, Susan was quiet as she stared out the passenger window. I didn't try to strike up a conversation. I surmised she needed time to process what had happened and make plans for what was to come. I had my own thoughts to deal with.

When we arrived back at my house and walked through the door, Susan let her guard down. She was a mess. She was mad. She was worried. She was depressed, and she got sick.

I called the warden at the prison to let him know what I

could about Derek, his new inmate. The warden and my father had good history together. My observation was that Derek should be watched and could be suicidal. I gave the warden as much evidence as I could to suggest that Derek should be evaluated, immediately. He said he would take all of what I had shared into consideration. After I hung up the phone, I heard Susan vomiting again in the powder room. The poor thing, I never broke into the Carter family circle as much as I had wanted to; however, I wished I were close enough to offer her some sisterly comfort. Realizing I was not equipped, I called Ginny.

Ginny arrived within minutes. Susan was so blessed to have a friend like her. I was envious of their relationship. After letting Ginny in, I watched the two women bring comfort to one another. Ginny, without a word, rushed to Susan's side. Sitting on my sofa, in my house, they held each other and cried. Both were asking the other for forgiveness. Both shared how much they loved the other. Both reaffirmed that nothing would ever come between them. It was the first they had seen each other since their last phone conversation, trying to make sense of a found purse and missing gun. It was the first time they had spoken since learning the status of the men in their lives. One rejoicing inside that hers was still alive; the other not knowing if hers still existed.

GINNY

Susan thanked Courtney for all she had done to help her through the difficult days, stating it was time for her to get back to Valley Forge. She needed to meet with Derek's business managers and piece together what should happen with the company. I was sure they had already heard of Derek's incarceration and what he was being accused of. She packed up her things and said a teary goodbye. We promised to call each other at least once a day.

Dex would be released from the hospital in a matter of days. I spent each and every day in the hospital with him. We played cards. We read books. We watched TV. We napped. We took walks around his ward. I watched the nurses change his bandages. I watched him go through his physical therapy. I had gotten to know his doctor. Finally, several days later, he was released.

As soon as he was in the Jeep, Dex demanded that I take him straight to the Right Tackle. She was quietly resting in her slip. By looking at her, one would never know of the siege she had been under. The Morning Starr was out, which was kind of a shame. I think Dex was hoping Charles would be there. Charles had stopped by the hospital to visit, but you know how guys are: they don't talk much and he didn't stay long.

Dex's arm in a sling, we walked down the dock and onto the catwalk. I helped steady him as he climbed on board with the use of his one good arm. Her decks were clean. No sign of blood. No shell casings. No bullet holes. The life ring was dry and hanging in its bracket. He unlocked the cabin and we entered the main salon. Everything was neat as a pin. Then Dex said the funniest thing.

"I wonder what happened to the fish we caught?"

I stifled my laugh when I realized his eyes were watering. He bent over and braced himself on the table with his one good arm.

"Oh God, what happened here?"

He sat down so he could wipe his good arm across his eyes. He looked up at me. Anguish covered his handsome face. Grief was settling into his warm heart. Fatigue was overtaking what strength he had. Everything he had held at bay up to that point was now on a rampage and having their way. I sat down next to him and rubbed his back. I was at a loss for words. I had no answers for him.

"Ginny, I want to stay here. I don't want to stay in the apartment any longer. I want to be here."

"Are you sure?"

I had expected his reaction to be just the opposite. Up

to that moment, I was fearful he might sell the Right Tackle to rid himself of the memory, but I should have known better. Of the two of us, Dex was the one who took everything head on. What happened onboard was not going to bring him down.

"Would you like me to stay with you?"

"Please. I need you here."

"Tell you what. I'll go pack a few things and get Gilda. We'll stay here for a few nights and if this is what you truly want to do, I'll start to move our things back on board."

He leaned over and kissed me. A spark shot through me. We had not been alone in days. His kiss contained all the tenderness that I had missed. He wrapped his one good arm around me as I placed my hand on his face and slid the other down his chest.

"I love you, Dex. I was so scared. I never want to lose you."

"I love you, too, Ginny. I'm not going anywhere."

We kissed again. A kiss that went deeper.

"Dex, I need to go get Gilda and our things. Then I'll be right back. Will you be OK?"

"Sure, I think I'll check out a few more things on board and then I'm going to take a nap."

After I threw a few bags into the Jeep, I knocked on the Sables' door. I let Mrs. Sable know that Dex had elected to stay on the boat. Knowing that Dex was being released from the hospital that day, I didn't want her to worry if she didn't see us in the apartment. Mrs. Sable said she understood, but asked me to wait a minute before I left. In no time, she was back at the door with a large canvas duffle bag. She had made dinner and dessert for us. She didn't know if Dex was allowed to drink, but she threw in a bottle of wine and a few beers, just in case. She even threw in a doggie treat for Gilda.

I hugged her and thanked her.

"I wish I had a mother just like you. You're the best."

On the way back to the boat, Gilda rode in the back seat

wagging her tail. She knew exactly where we were going and she may have anticipated who was waiting for her. When I pulled up to the dock, she nearly jumped out of the Jeep before it came to a full stop. When I opened the door, she leaped out, ran down the catwalk, and jumped right into the cockpit of the Right Tackle. She turned and looked back at me, her tail wagging a mile a minute. As I boarded, my arms filled with the first load, she stood back up, waiting for me to open the cabin door. Remembering Dex's bandaged shoulder, I went in first to make sure the door to the master stateroom was closed so Gilda couldn't tackle him in his sleep. Leaving her out in the cockpit, she whined and whimpered as I went below. I peeked in, and Dex was indeed sound asleep. It was so good to have him out of that hospital room. I secured the door and went back up to empty the Jeep. Thoroughly confused, she watched me make several trips on and off the boat. After unloading and while Dex slept, I stayed with Gilda in the salon and called my dad.

We had spoken nearly every day. Dylan, my unsung hero, also thought enough to call my father right away before the story broke. It was a good call on his part. Unfortunately, the Carter brothers did make the national news. So, it was best that my parents heard about it from Dylan first.

Until Derek's arraignment was over, news vans lined Savannah Road in front of the hospital. Charles said that he was interviewed by a reporter from "ABC's World News Tonight." On the day she visited Dex in the hospital, Mrs. Pollock said that reporters were filing their reports in front of our new house, still under construction. Apparently, they had also learned that Derek would also be charged with arson. Once Derek's arraignment was over, things began to settle down.

We all knew it was the calm before the storm.

DEX

It was so good to be back on the Right Tackle. But, I had to retire from the fishing business, at least for a while. It seemed everyone wanted to take a trip on the boat with the captain that got shot up. It was bringing the crazies out of the woodwork. It made Ginny very nervous, to say the least. Plus, we had set up residence there for the time being. Pratt and the other Lewes officers were great at keeping gawkers away from the docks. Charles and the other captains were good at deflecting questions and the curious. We had to temporarily cover the Right Tackle's name on her transom. Ginny suggested that we consider changing her name. I told her it was bad luck to change a ship's name. She thought that was funny, thinking there was nothing worse that could happen to us.

With the pain and the haze of mind numbing drugs wearing off, I started into more rigorous physical therapy. The construction on the house continued in my absence, but I was so glad when I was cleared to return to work.

Ginny could be in her new home before Thanksgiving. The crew and I worked hard to make it happen. She stopped by every day with coffee, lunch, or some sweet treat she had baked or purchased for the guys and me. They had fallen in love with her, and rightfully so. They warned me that if I didn't marry her, they would, which just cracked me up because most of them *were* married. Gilda loped around the work site like she was in charge. She was a happy little building inspector.

Susan had come down a few more times to help Ginny pick out paint and furniture. With each trip, they brought back more color chips and fabric swatches. They had chosen colors that mirrored the beige of the sand, the green of the dune grass, and the blue of a pale summer sky. The trim would be slightly darker than the walls, yet within the same color family. All of the fabric for the furniture was light and summery. All of the floors, with the exception of the downstairs entrance, the kitchen, and baths, were hardwood. They were looking into area rugs, as well. Once they had it all figured out, they would place the orders.

Ginny had been very diligent in keeping her father informed of all the latest progress and developments. She had been skyping with him and emailing pictures. Her parents promised they would visit once she moved in.

I think my father and Dan would have been very pleased with how she had interpreted and captured their dreams. She added a few of her own touches, too. It would be stunning when completed.

Now there was one thing left to do, and I needed to get Courtney onboard to make it happen.

COURTNEY

Dex called and asked if we could meet privately. He spoke quietly and I detected a bit of anticipation in his voice. I must confess that every time he called, I still got a flutter of butterflies in the pit of my stomach.

Will I ever get over my crush on him?

Which was really stupid, because the one I really thought of every day was Dylan. I was an idiot when it came to men.

Dex and I agreed to meet at Jerry's Seafood on 2nd Street, at 7:00 PM. Jerry's was fairly new, however, we heard they had something called a Crab Bomb that was to die for.

I wore a deep V-neck sundress and sandals, hoping he would find the view delectable. There was a chill in the air, so I grabbed a matching shrug on my way out the door. Dex had walked up from the Right Tackle and was wearing his usual jeans and sweater. I don't believe there is another man sexier in jeans than Dex, with the exception of Dylan, of course.

We were seated at a nice corner table where we could watch all of the "comings and goings" on 2nd Street. We ordered drinks, Margaritas straight up, no salt, and then got down to the matter at hand. I felt like a schoolgirl sitting across from him. It was the first time he had asked me to dinner, and it didn't have anything to do with Ginny. My mind was racing with several different scenarios.

"So, to what do I owe the honor?" I asked as I spread my napkin over my crossed legs, looking right into his dreamy eyes.

"I need you to help me surprise Ginny."

"Ohhh . . ." The butterflies were fumigated just that quick. Gone.

Shit.

"So, what can I do?" I asked, trying not to look terribly disappointed, again.

"We'll be moving Ginny in this weekend. I'm assuming you'll be there with Dylan to help?"

"Oh, yes, he did mention it."

"Well, I need you to keep her occupied at Irish Eyes while her present is being delivered to the house. I will get her to the restaurant, but you have to keep her there."

"That shouldn't be too hard. She rarely goes anywhere without you." It probably sounded like a dig. Maybe it was.

"Well, the piano movers are going to call me when they get to the house and then I will have to leave.

"You're buying her another piano? Are you sure about this?"

"Yes, I'm using the cash Mr. Carter . . . er . . . Dad left me. It's what I want to do."

"You were still holding on to that money? For what?"

"I don't know. I thought he would want me to use it for . . . you know . . . a rainy day type thing."

"So this is your rainy day?" I asked, quite confused.

"No, just the opposite. This piano will chase away the rain from any day when she plays it."

"Shit, Dex, you must really love her."

"Court, I couldn't be happier, and if our relationship never takes another step forward, or if she throws me out tomorrow, I would still want her to have it."

So there it was, right in my face, again: Dex was head over heels in love with Ginny. He had never tried to hide it from me. In fact, Ginny was all he ever talked about when we were together. I had always chosen to ignore the obvious: It would never be me.

DYLAN

The time had come to move Ginny into her new home. I drove down Friday night and met Courtney, Ginny, and Dex at Irish Eyes. With the Certificate of Occupancy in their hands, they suggested we all spend the night camped out in the house. The bulk of the furniture would be delivered in the morning. The hot tub was installed on the top deck and was ready for its christening.

"Well, that's fine, but I didn't bring a bathing suit." I needed to make that fact known up front.

Before jumping up from the table to take a phone call, Dex said I could borrow one of his. Courtney said she would double back to her place and pick up some champagne and acrylic flutes she had on hand for such outdoor occasions. Ginny said she and Dex would stop by Lloyd's and pick up some cheese and crackers.

"Give me the keys and I'll go make myself at home," I wisely volunteered.

Dex had to leave just as our drinks had arrived. It had something to do with the hot tub installers leaving some tools in the house. Ginny volunteered to take care of it, but Courtney aggressively grabbed her arm.

"It's all right, sweetheart, it will just take a minute. I

know right where they left them. Be right back!" Dex instructed, and then he was off.

By the time Dex returned, his dinner was lukewarm and we were about ready to go. He asked for the check and a doggie bag. He sure was acting squirrely.

Dex picked up the tab and we all split off in our assigned directions.

I drove directly to the house. The outside lights were on, warmly inviting me in. Giving the impression that someone was home, the lights were left on inside, as well. Already it felt cozy. I slipped the new key that Ginny had given me into the lock and pushed the door open. I was immediately hit with the smells of fresh paint and hewn wood. It was very pleasing to my senses. I took my shoes off and left them by the back door. The entrance down stairs had a tiled floor that led to the oak staircase. I was glad to get off the cold floor and on to the carpet stair runner as I made my way up. The second floor windows were left open in several of the bedrooms; probably to help the paint fumes dissipate. In the bedrooms on the bayside, the sheers were gracefully dancing in the breeze coming off of the water. Up on the top floor, a wall of sliding glass doors provided a lookout over the water. The glass didn't reflect the light from inside, so despite all of the lights being on, the view was as if I were standing on the deck with nothing between the water and me. I also remembered Ginny saying the glass composition blocked people from being able to look in at night, while we could still see out. In the middle of the glass wall of sliders was a fireplace. I could only imagine how beautiful it would be when lit on a cold snowy night. I felt a familiar calm pour over me. I thought I heard my dad say something, but it was only the sound of the still house settling.

There was only one piece of furniture in the entire place, as far as I could tell. It was a magnificent baby grand piano. I remembered Dex saying how well Ginny could play. I remembered that she had one in the old house for a matter of hours. I approached it carefully. Something about its predecessor led me to believe this one could be very fragile and disappear at any time, too.

"Bosendorfer ..."

I continued over to the window and looked out across the water. Dad was right. His house—his piece of heaven—was left in the right hands. His dreams had come true. Though unfurnished and virtually empty, the house was full of anticipation. There was healthy electricity moving through the air. They had never left us. They were right there, waiting for all of us to come home.

Now available:

"BAY AVENUE II: The Courtship"

BAY AVENUE II: The Courtship finds an attractive Lewes, Delaware attorney learning to love and be loved in spite of her own destructive insecurities. Often the "outsider-looking-in," she painfully learns to overcome life's scars.

"BAY AVENUE III: Pratt-ically Speaking"

BAY AVENUE III: Pratt-ically Speaking, the finale of the series, finds three young couples struggling to survive the choices they have made and the hands they have been dealt. Life is not fair. Love can be complicated. Not all endings are happily ever after, or are they?

If you have enjoyed the "BAY AVENUE" series, consider reading other novels written by Jill Hicks.

"The Long Climb Back"

The Long Climb Back is a story about an adventurous young woman who strikes out on her own after an over-the-top marriage proposal from a winery heir. Her travels introduce her to two engaging brothers. Will she be able to return to her fiancé with her mind, body, and soul intact?

"Adrift"

Adrift follows the journey of Carly Young Mariner, a devoted wife, mother, and second grade teacher, who walks in on an encounter that upends her ordinary life. Over time—but not out of time—she distances herself from her family and everything that has given her a sense of purpose. With the hope of finding contentment and a place to contemplate her options, Carly escapes to the Outer Banks of North Carolina. Shortly after her arrival, a minor accident transforms her and those around her.

424

"Sundial"

During an extended visit to her hometown, located at the head of the Chesapeake Bay, Faith Livingston has the opportunity to resolve her greatest "what if." When presented with a do-over involving those who still hold her heart, should she take it? How much of her present life is she willing to risk? Is it possible to reconcile one's future path with an unforgettable past?

ACKNOWLEDGEMENTS

First, I wish to thank Harris and Evelyn Hicks, God rest their souls, who wisely purchased their Lewes family beach house in 1963 for $3,500! It has blessed the generations.

A loving "thank you" to my mother and father, Jean and Randall Yarnall, who taught their six children the "rules of the road," while spending our summers on the Chesapeake aboard their beloved "Jeanie." My father has since passed away and there is not a day that goes by that I do not think of him and miss his gentle spirit. He gave his heart and time so generously to his family and friends.

I need to thank my husband, Bill Hicks, who listened tirelessly as we explored plot options. (I am forever thinking aloud.) He was my chief editor on this project, helping me with sentence structure and grammar. He also surprised me with a beautiful and perfect cover design. He is the best! Love you!

I also need to thank my sister Jane Niven and her husband Mike, a.k.a. Monkey Mike, who took the time to read the book in its entirety, sending me corrections they found along the way. Great job, guys! It was their encouragement, along with Bill's, that gave me permission to consider publication.

My endless gratitude I give to a man who has coached me on my latest editions and continually inspires me to be a better writer. Ralph Painter, a long time friend of the Hicks family, worked as a typesetter through high school and college. He is an avid reader and a wealth of information. I could spend hours—and have done so— eagerly listening to Ralph as he eloquently explains uses of grammar and best practices in writing. Ralph, your kindness and patience overwhelm me. Thank you.

ABOUT THE AUTHOR

Jill Hicks was born and raised in West Chester, Pennsylvania, and currently resides in Lewes, Delaware, with her husband, Bill. Together, they have two daughters. Tragically, they lost their first born, Jamie, in an automobile accident when she was just twenty. Jamie is survived by her younger sister, Jessie, and her half-sister, Jenn.

Jill is very close to her extended family. She draws on her personal experiences and the stories of others to express the joys and sorrows of life and love.

Jill is a graduate of Penn State University with a degree in Music Education. In her spare time she loves to read, play piano, ride her bike, sail, and spend quality beach time with her husband, family, and friends.

Ironically, Jill loathed reading until just several years ago. Suddenly, poring through twenty to thirty books a summer, she ran out of beach books to read and decided to write her own, ergo her first novel, "BAY AVENUE I: The Inheritance."